BLOOD & SUGAR

LAURA SHEPHERD-ROBINSON was born
in Bristol in 1976. She has a BSc in Politics from the
University of Bristol and an MSc in Political Theory from
the London School of Economics. Laura worked in politics
for nearly twenty years before re-entering normal life to
complete an MA in Creative Writing at City University.
She lives in London with her husband, Adrian.
This is her first novel.

Laura
Shepherd–Robinson

BLOOD
&
SUGAR

MANTLE

First published 2019 by Mantle
an imprint of Pan Macmillan
20 New Wharf Road, London N1 9RR
Associated companies throughout the world
www.panmacmillan.com

ISBN 978-1-5098-8078-2

3 5 7 9 8 6 4 2

A CIP catalogue record for this book is available from the British Library.

Endpaper map courtesy Warwick Leadlay Gallery

Typeset in 12.5/16 pt Adobe Caslon Pro by Jouve (UK), Milton Keynes
Printed and bound by CPI Group (UK) Ltd, Croydon, CR0 4YY

Visit www.panmacmillan.com to read more about all our books
and to buy them. You will also find features, author interviews and
news of any author events, and you can sign up for e-newsletters
so that you're always first to hear about our new releases.

For Adrian

Cast of Characters

London in 1781 is a ravenous behemoth, swallowing forest and field, outlying villages, entire towns. The city is the centre of a fledgling empire, the capital of a country at war. Political and commercial deals are struck in her elegant drawing rooms, washed down by bowls of sweetened tea: the product of Britain's mercantile power.

Five miles to the east, on the banks of the River Thames, lies Deptford: gateway port to distant oceans and untold riches. A town where fortunes in sugar and slaves are made and lost, thieves and prostitutes roam the streets by night, and sailors lose themselves in drink, trying to forget the things they did and saw upon the Middle Passage.

Here are some of the people to be found there ...

IN LONDON

Captain Henry Corsham (Harry) – *a war hero with political ambitions.*
Caroline Corsham (Caro) – *Harry's wife, a society beauty.*
Gabriel Corsham – *Harry and Caro's infant son.*
Thaddeus Archer (Tad) – *a barrister and campaigner for the abolition of slavery. Harry's oldest friend.*
Amelia Bradstreet – *Tad's sister, a widow with a scandalous past.*

Cast of Characters

Moses Graham – *a former slave. A gentleman painter of watercolours. Also an author and campaigner against the slave trade. Friend to Thaddeus Archer.*

Ephraim Proudlock – *a former slave. Assistant to Moses Graham in matters of art and abolition. Also a friend to Thaddeus Archer.*

Caesar John – *a former slave turned villain.*

Jupiter – *a former slave. A member of Caesar John's gang.*

Nicholas Cavill-Lawrence – *Under-Secretary of State for War. Harry's patron.*

Napier Smith – *owner of sugar plantations. Chairman of the West India lobby. Probably the richest man in the kingdom. Not yet twenty-five.*

Pomfret – *Harry's butler, a former navy man.*

Sam – *Harry's coachman.*

Bronze – *a former slave. Tapwoman at the Yorkshire Stingo tavern.*

In Deptford

Lucius Stokes – *a slave merchant. Mayor of Deptford.*

Scipio – *a former slave. Secretary to Lucius Stokes.*

Cinnamon – *a beautiful mulatto slave girl owned by Lucius Stokes.*

Peregrine Child – *the Deptford magistrate.*

John Monday – *a slave merchant with a religious calling.*

Eleanor Monday – *his wife, mother of two children.*

Evan Vaughan – *a slave ship captain.*

James Brabazon – *a slave ship surgeon.*

Frank Drake – *a slave ship officer.*

Daniel Waterman – *a slave ship cabin boy.*

Nathaniel Grimshaw – *a young nightwatchman, soon to take his late father's place as a slave ship officer.*

Cast of Characters

Marilyn Grimshaw – *Nathaniel's mother, a grieving widow. Landlady of the Noah's Ark tavern.*

Jamaica Mary – *a former slave turned prostitute.*

Alice – *a prostitute.*

Abraham – *footman to Lucius Stokes. A slave.*

Isaac Fairweather – *a sailor. Friend of Frank Drake.*

Rosy and her husband – *owners of the coaching inn at Deptford Broadway.*

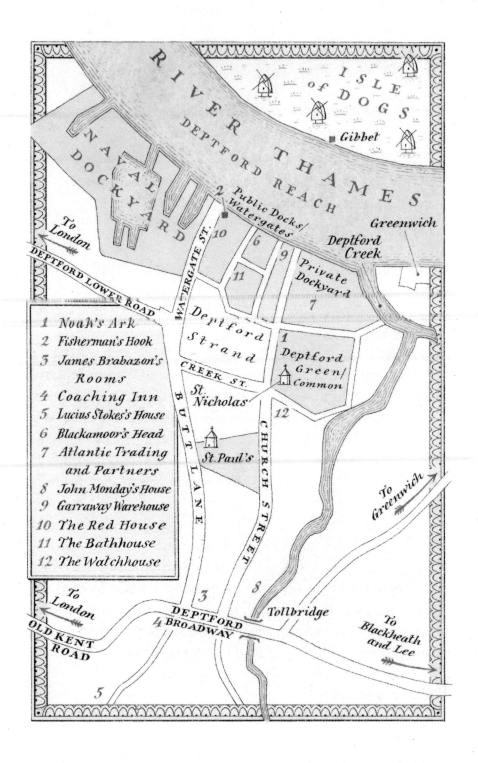

RIVER THAMES

DEPTFORD REACH

ISLE of DOGS

Gibbet

NAVAL DOCKYARD

To London

DEPTFORD LOWER ROAD

2 Public Docks/ Watergates

WATERGATE ST.

10

6

9

11

Greenwich

Deptford Creek

Private Dockyard

7

Deptford Strand

CREEK ST.

St. Nicholas

BUTT LANE

St. Paul's

1 Deptford Green/ Common

12

CHURCH STREET

To Greenwich

1 Noah's Ark
2 Fisherman's Hook
3 James Brabazon's Rooms
4 Coaching Inn
5 Lucius Stokes's House
6 Blackamoor's Head
7 Atlantic Trading and Partners
8 John Monday's House
9 Garraway Warehouse
10 The Red House
11 The Bathhouse
12 The Watchhouse

To London

OLD KENT ROAD

3

4

DEPTFORD BROADWAY

8

Tollbridge

To Blackheath and Lee

5

PROLOGUE

Deptford Dock, June 1781

The fog hung thick and low over the Thames. It rolled in off the water and along the quays, filling the squalid courts and dockside alleys of lower Deptford. The local name for a fog like this was the Devil's Breath. It stank of the river's foul miasma.

Now and then the fog lifted, and Nathaniel Grimshaw caught a glimpse of the Guineamen anchored out on Deptford Reach: spectral lines of mast and rigging against the dawn sky. His greatcoat was heavy with damp and his horsehair wig smelled of wet animal. He had been pacing in that spot for nearly half an hour. Each time he pivoted, Jago growled. The dog's black fur stood up in spikes and his eyes shone like tiny yellow fog-lamps in the gloom.

Nathaniel could hear the fishermen talking, and he could taste their tobacco on the wind. He wanted a pipe himself, but he wasn't sure he could hold it down. He didn't know how they could stand there, in such close proximity. A figure loomed out of the mist, and Jago growled again, though he quietened when he recognized the stocky, square frame of the Deptford magistrate, Peregrine Child. A pair of bleary eyes peered at Nathaniel between the wet folds of the magistrate's long wig of office. 'Where is it, lad?'

Nathaniel led him through the fog to the wall that divided

the Public Dock from the Navy Yard. The fishermen parted to let them through, each man turning to observe Child's reaction.

On the quayside stood a ten-foot pole topped by a riveted iron hook, where the fishermen liked to hang their largest catches. Lately it had displayed a shark that had washed up here last month. Now the shark was gone and in its place hung a man. He was naked, turning on a rope in the wind, secured under the arms, with his hands tied behind him. Nathaniel didn't like blood and there was a lot of it – dried on the dead man's chest and back, smeared across his thighs, in his ears, in his nose, in his mouth. He had seen murdered men before – washed up on the mudflats, or dumped in the dockside alleys where he worked as a nightwatchman. None of them had prepared him for this. This one was more than a corpse. He was a spectacle, like the boneless man at the Greenwich Fair.

Steeling himself, he studied the man again. He was about thirty years of age, very thin, with long black hair. His eyes wide open, staring accusingly. His lips were pulled back in a frozen rictus, white skin stretched taut over angled cheekbones. Beneath the first mouth was a second: a gaping, scarlet maw where the throat had been slashed.

Child stepped forward, his face inches from the body. 'Jesu.'

He was staring at a spot just above the dead man's left nipple. The lines seared into the pale, hairless skin were smooth and deep. The flesh around them was puckered and blistered. From where he stood, Nathaniel could just make out the design: a crescent moon on its side surmounted by a crown.

'It's a slave brand,' he said. 'Someone's marked him like a Negro.'

'I know what it is.' Child stepped back, still staring at the body.

Jago's growling rose in pitch, and Nathaniel made soothing noises, though his heart was in full sympathy with his dog.

'You recognize him, don't you, sir? It's that gentleman, Thomas Valentine. You met him, didn't you, sir, before?'

'I met him.' Child's abrupt tone discouraged further discussion upon this point.

Nathaniel studied the magistrate surreptitiously, trying to understand his mood, trying to work out if he himself was under suspicion. But Child seemed to have forgotten that he was even there. He mouthed something beneath his breath that Nathaniel didn't catch, only a waft of sour brandy fumes on the chill dawn air.

'Cut him down,' Child said at last. 'Not a word to anyone. Understand?'

Nathaniel dragged an old shipping crate over to the hook, and clambered onto it. The dead man's eyes gazed unseeing at the still, brown river. Out on the Reach, the Guineamen creaked, and the fishermen muttered sullen, riverine prayers. On every side of them, the Devil's Breath coiled and smoked.

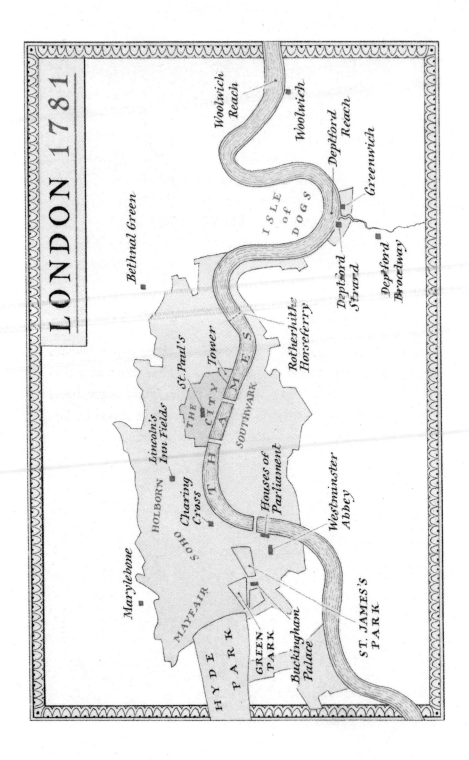

PART ONE

21–24 JUNE 1781

That thing is said to be free (*liber*) which exists solely from the necessity of its own nature, and is determined to action by itself alone. A thing is said to be necessary (*necessarius*) or rather, constrained (*coactus*), if it is determined by another thing to act in a definite and determinate way.

I. Of God, Ethics, Baruch Spinoza

CHAPTER ONE

THE WORST SURPRISES are those we think we see coming.

Amelia Bradstreet called at my London townhouse at a little after nine in the evening on the 21st day of June 1781. I was playing with Gabriel at the time, lining up rows of lead soldiers on the Turkey rug in my bookroom, so that he could knock them down with a stick. My infant son's delight in this simple activity was matched only by my own, yet the rap at the front door extinguished all such pleasure in a moment. A week ago, at around this hour of the evening, a young gentleman had called at the house without invitation, and I feared that this same troublesome individual had now returned. Yet when my butler knocked and entered, he swiftly disabused me of that notion.

'There is a lady to see you, Captain Corsham.' Pomfret handed me the card on his tray.

'Mrs Bradstreet,' I read.

'She says that you knew her once as Amelia Archer.'

I stared at him in surprise. Tad's sister. It must have been over ten years since I'd seen her last. Dimly I recalled a thin, bookish, birdlike girl, with her brother's large grey eyes and pale skin. I'd been in America when she'd left England and had consequently missed much of the scandal that had attended her departure. She had returned last year after the death of her husband, and Caro had been adamant that we should not receive her. As far as I was aware, nobody did.

I hesitated, pondering her motives. Had Tad sent her here? What could she want?

'She came in a hired carriage, sir. No servant to speak of. Shall I tell her that you are indisposed?'

Pomfret, like my wife, was a stickler for the proprieties. Not the fact of the thing, but the look of the thing. Some call it hypocrisy, others society. For my part, I had seen men entangled in their own entrails upon the battlefields of the American rebellion, and the crimes of the drawing room seemed small by comparison. Nor was I minded, at that moment, to please my wife. Call it my own act of rebellion, if you will.

'Show her into the drawing room, would you, Pomfret, please?'

I dispatched Gabriel into the care of his nursemaid, and went to the console mirror in the hall to retie my cravat and straighten my periwig. Then I walked into the drawing room, where Amelia Bradstreet was waiting.

She did not look like a widow, was my first thought. She was standing in the centre of the room, gazing about – at the furniture and the silver and the portrait of Caro by Thomas Gainsborough over the fire. My eyes were drawn at once to her gown, which was close-fitting with bared shoulders, the silk a rich and vibrant shade of indigo. She had matched it with a Kashmir shawl embroidered with golden flowers, and an amethyst necklace.

She turned, and we appraised one another. I recalled that Amelia was three years younger than Tad and I, which would make her twenty-seven years old.

'Captain Corsham,' she said faintly, holding out her hand for me to kiss. 'How long it has been since those happy days down in Devon. I hope you can forgive my intrusion at this late hour.'

Her eyes were silver in the candlelight, her hair a dark, lustrous brown. She had curled and pinned it high, and I admired the curve of her throat and the rich glow of the amethysts against her skin. Her features were all angles: high cheekbones, a pointed chin, a sharp little nose. When she spoke, I caught a glimpse of tiny white teeth.

I caught other things too. Agitation, in her movements and the way she spoke. Poverty, in her cheap perfume – a sickly wash of jasmine – and the shabby slippers I spied beneath the hoops of her skirts. Finally, I sensed resilience in her gaze and in her bearing.

'It is no intrusion,' I said. 'Won't you sit down, Mrs Bradstreet? Some Madeira perhaps?'

While we waited for the wine, she examined Gainsborough's portrait. 'Caroline is not at home?'

'At Carlisle House.' I smiled to reassure her. 'Taking on all comers at the faro table.'

Her relief was palpable and she sank onto the sofa, her fingers tugging at the sleeves of her dress. The footman knocked and entered, bearing the Madeira, and I noticed his eyes slide over Mrs Bradstreet as he served her, alive with carnal interest and contempt.

'You carry off the redcoat,' she said, as the door closed behind him. 'Not all men do.'

'It isn't vanity.' I felt an unaccountable need to explain myself. 'The War Office likes us to wear it.'

'You have earned the right to wear it, have you not?' She regarded me solemnly. 'I read about you in the newspapers. Captain Henry Corsham, scourge of the American rebels. They say even the King knows your name.'

'They exaggerate,' I said, and there was an awkward pause, while I tried again to divine why she had come. To borrow money, perhaps? To lay claim to a connection on the grounds of our long acquaintance? Or did Tad hope to mend the rupture in our friendship? The thought made my scalp crawl as if with lice, and in my mind I juggled words of polite refusal.

Amelia leaned forward, her eyebrows knotted. 'I hope I do not embarrass you and Caroline by coming here tonight, but I'm afraid my business was far too pressing for a letter.'

I frowned. 'Mrs Bradstreet, forgive me for asking, but are you in some kind of trouble?'

'Not I, but I fear that Tad might be.'

'I see.' I tried to mask my anxiety with irritation. 'Is he in a debtors' prison? Is it money that you need?'

She blanched a little at my tone. 'He is missing. He called at my cottage nearly a week ago now, on his way out of the city on business. He said that he would call again on his return to London, but he never came. I have tried at his rooms, but he's not there. The porter hasn't seen him since he left town. Neither has anyone else.'

'When were you expecting him?'

'This Thursday past.'

'That's only four days,' I pointed out. 'Tad never was the most reliable fellow.'

She touched her necklace and the stones flashed in the candlelight. 'Tad told me he was on his way to Deptford,' she said quietly. 'Deptford is a slaving town, is it not?'

Tad and slavery. I remembered our pamphlets and our essays and our speeches. The unfashionable cause of abolition had once fired our youthful souls. We had nearly been sent down from Oxford because of it. Since my return from the war, I had turned my mind to more orthodox political matters, but Tad had only grown angrier and more determined over the years.

I spoke gently to assuage her fears – and my own. 'I am sure there is no cause for undue concern. They might not like abolitionists in Deptford, but the worst they'd do is run him out of town.'

She was silent a moment. 'I am worried for him. It isn't just Deptford. Tad was mixed up in something dangerous. He told me that he had made some powerful enemies.'

'He was always prone to grandiose language. And he used to see enemies everywhere.'

'That doesn't mean they didn't exist. He was afraid. I could see it.' Her voice caught. 'He said that people had been following him and that someone in Deptford had tried to kill him. I told him to go to the authorities, but he said the authorities were in league with the slavers.'

You know what he's like, I told myself. He's probably locked in some Deptford sponging house after running up debts, or hiding from his creditors in London. Yet a little knot of fear flagellated these more cynical thoughts. What if someone really had tried to kill him? What if that person had tried again, and this time succeeded?

'Did he say anything else about these powerful enemies?'

'He said he'd lit a fire under the slave traders. He said he was going to burn their house to the ground.'

'I presume he meant it metaphorically?' With Tad you could never quite tell.

'I think so. He said that after he had finished with them, the slave trade would never recover.'

I didn't smile, though in other circumstances I might have done. It was the kind of thing we used to say when we were students together at Oxford. 'We'll end child labour. End bearbaiting. End slavery.' Childish dreams, as impossible as they were laudable.

Amelia was waiting for my reaction, and when none came, she pressed on: 'I told him that was ridiculous. The trade in

Africans is worth many millions of pounds. It spans three continents. How could one man hope to end all that?'

'What did he say?'

'Only that he was going to Deptford to collect something that his enemies would want, something he could use against the slavers. If anything happened to him while he was there, then I should go to Harry Corsham. He said that you would know what to do.'

I stared at her. 'He said that? I haven't seen him in over three years.'

'I think you are the only person he truly trusts.' She held my gaze with those grey eyes that were so like Tad's. 'I do not pretend to understand what happened between you and my brother, Captain Corsham, but there was a time when he was your dearest friend in all the world. Will you go to Deptford and see if you can find him?'

Still I hesitated. I had no wish to see Tad again and open up old wounds. Yet how could I not?

'Of course I will go. First thing tomorrow morning. In the meantime, do try not to worry.'

Her eyes were bright with emotion, but I did not want her gratitude. I only needed to know that Tad was safe. For that brief moment, when I'd imagined his death, I'd felt cold as marble in a crypt. It was as if a shadow had passed across my soul.

CHAPTER TWO

I SLEPT FITFULLY, and woke before six. For over an hour I lay there, thinking about Amelia's visit. Many times I told myself that my fears of the night before were unfounded. By the time I was washed and dressed, I had managed to convince myself that I would find Tad in Deptford, doggedly trying to change the world, blithely unconcerned at all the trouble he had caused.

Caro's bedroom door was closed. I'd heard her come in last night, sometime after three, and I decided not to wake her. I went downstairs, where I asked Pomfret to have Sam ready the carriage. In my bookroom, I scribbled a quick note to Nicholas Cavill-Lawrence, the Under-Secretary of State for War, explaining that I had been called away from London on urgent business. Since I had been invalided home from America, I had been attached to the War Office, and was shortly due to enter Parliament myself. I made a difference there, I felt, though increasingly I found all the factions and the committees and the administrative labyrinth rather wearisome. I told myself that a day away from the intrigues of Whitehall would do me good.

I gave my note to one of the footmen to deliver, and then took breakfast with Gabriel in the nursery. We made castles out of kedgeree, which we stormed with soldiers made from toast. My son's laughter had the power to drive all anxiety from my thoughts, and I left the house with my spirits much restored.

Sam took the road south out of the city, over London

Bridge. The streets jostled with carts and carriages and gigs; the drivers smoking or swearing or flicking their whips to startle the horses of rival carters. We made slow progress, held up by barrowmen and farmers driving their flocks of sheep and cows to the Smithfield market. On the outskirts of Southwark, scaffolding covered the buildings, and labourers swarmed over them like ants. London was gobbling up the countryside in all directions, but at last we left the traffic and the bustle behind us. The wheels gave a long low note of protest against the turnpike as the horses picked up speed, and I settled to the swaying rhythm of the carriage.

I had never visited Deptford before, though I was familiar with Greenwich, which lay only a little way along the river. Yet I knew from my work at the War Office that the town comprised two separate settlements, joined by a road which cut through open field. Deptford Broadway was where the town's merchant class lived, near to the toll-bridge where the Old Kent Road crossed Deptford Creek. Deptford Strand lay nearly a mile to the north, on the banks of the River Thames, and comprised the Public and Private Docks, the Navy Yard, and workers' housing.

Perhaps an hour after our departure from my house in Mayfair, we rattled into Deptford Broadway. I glimpsed large stone houses and a street of elegant shops with curved windows. Gentlemen and ladies with parasols promenaded in the sun, followed by little black pageboys and towering African footmen. My intention was to find the town magistrate, who would be the best-placed person to know if a gentleman from out of town had fallen ill, or suffered an injury here in Deptford. I had Sam stop at the coaching inn, where I learned that the man I sought was named Peregrine Child. At this hour, I was informed, he would be down in Deptford Strand, taking stock of all the crimes that had been committed in that place overnight.

Soon the gentility of the Broadway was but a distant memory, and we were jolting along the rough dirt road towards the Thames. The carriage steadily filled with noxious air: pitch and sulphur, brick kiln and tannery, the stench of the slaughter-house, sewage from the river. My apprehension at seeing Tad again had grown with every mile we'd travelled from London. Now it was sitting like a stone in my gullet. Why the devil had he told Amelia to seek me out? I had seen him only once since I had returned from America, over three years ago, and the memory of that meeting grated often upon my conscience. I regretted the hurt I had caused him, but I had no wish to revisit my decision. Our shared past was a dark and dangerous place.

We clattered into Deptford Strand a few minutes later, pass-ing dingy brick houses and a large flint church. My bad leg was stiff after the journey and I was eager to walk it off. I rapped on the roof, and we halted next to a wide field of mud, which appeared to pass as the town green. This dismal patch of ground was surrounded by crooked rows of houses and shops, and a number of stalls perched on the mud were selling fish. Sam climbed down from his box, and fitted the steps for me to descend.

'Have a drink in one of the taverns,' I told him, 'but make sure that you are back here by midday.'

There were a great many taverns for Sam to choose from. Men were already staggering along the street, though it was not yet eleven o'clock. Many wore sailors' slops and had the wide-hipped gait men acquire after years at sea. A cacophony of whores were soliciting for custom, and I proved a magnet for their attentions as I walked in the direction of the river.

'Feel its olive skin.' One ageing Delilah touched my face. 'Soft brown eyes like my daughter's. Oh, I'll take you to Para-dise, my handsome soldier.'

Looking around myself at the rag shops and the pawn-brokers and the gaunt, grubby prostitutes, I struggled to imagine a more distant destination. I disentangled myself from her embrace, gave her a penny, and asked her for directions to the Deptford watchhouse.

'You looking for Perry Child?' she asked, showing me a mouthful of blackened teeth. 'He'll be having his breakfast. Try the Noah's Ark.'

This establishment proved to be an old half-timbered inn on the north-west corner of the Green, the upper storeys leaning so far over the cobbles, I was half afraid the entire edifice would come crashing down on top of me. The road carried on to the river, and I paused to admire the vast brown sweep of Deptford Reach. The docks jostled with vessels of every conceivable size, a forest of masts pricking the cloudless sky.

Perhaps a dozen men sat drinking in the taproom, and they turned to stare as I walked in. The place smelled of fried fish; the conversation punctuated by the rattle of dice. A young man in a horsehair wig was cleaning tankards behind the bar, and I asked him to point out Peregrine Child. He directed me to one of the wooden booths in the tavern's dining room, where a man of middling years was eating alone.

'Mr Child?' The man looked up from his fish pie. 'Captain Henry Corsham.' I bowed and he gave me a curt nod. 'Forgive me for interrupting your breakfast, but I require a few minutes of your time.'

Child ran a sceptical eye over my uniform: from my black bicorne hat to my leather boots, by way of my scarlet coat, buff breeches and silk stockings. 'What's it regarding?' he asked through a mouthful of pie. His accent was local, devoid of gentlemanly inflection, and he didn't try to hide it.

'A friend of mine is missing. He was last believed to be in Deptford. I would like your assistance in locating him.'

Child wore a shabby blue coat, and his cravat was stained with grease. He was about forty-five, I guessed, though his double chin and the full dress wig made it hard to be certain. His eyes were swift and button-black, his mouth was small and cynical, and his bulbous nose was a filigree of broken veins. A bottle of red wine, almost empty, stood beside his elbow.

He stifled a sigh, and gestured me to the seat opposite. 'What's your friend's name?'

'Thaddeus Archer, though most people call him Tad. He is thirty years old and he travelled here from London.'

'A gentleman?'

'A barrister. Lincoln's Inn.'

'Lawyers. My father used to say they were put on this earth to make excise men look good. I've never heard of your friend, Captain, I'm sorry to say.'

'Mr Archer should have returned home five days ago now,' I persisted, 'but no one has seen him since he left London. His sister is concerned for his—' I broke off as he started to shovel more pie into his face. 'Perhaps I could wait for you to finish your breakfast, sir, and then accompany you back to the watch-house? That way you could make notes.'

Child tapped his skull with the tines of his fork. 'It lodges here, I assure you, sir. Lawyer. Archer. Sister. Do go on.'

I found Child's manners to be as coarse as his costume, but I restrained my impatience. 'As I was saying, Mr Archer's sister is concerned for his welfare.'

Child took a long pull on his wine. 'Look, I would like to help you, sir, but we have many visitors here in Deptford. They come and they go, and accidents happen. Men get drunk and fall in the river, or someone helps them fall. The Reach gives them up eventually, though there's often not much left of them when it does. If that's the way your friend's gone, it could be weeks until we find him.'

It was plain that Mr Child had taken a dislike to me, probably based on my appearance and my class. Perhaps he also disliked me as a military man. I knew there were tensions between the town and the Navy Yard. It was time to dispense with good manners.

'A gentleman has disappeared in your town and on your watch, sir. I have no desire to make trouble for you in Whitehall but, believe me, I will if you won't help me.'

At last Child looked up from his breakfast. 'Whitehall, is it, sir?'

'I am attached to the War Office.' I handed him my card. 'Now which is it to be, sir, friend or foe?'

Child moistened his lips with his wine-stained tongue and regarded my card with a baleful stare. 'Was your friend here on business, do you know? A lot of London lawyers have dealings with the merchants and the wholesalers in Deptford Strand.'

'I don't think his visit was connected to his legal affairs at all. Mr Archer had political interests too, the radical kind. One of his principal passions was the abolition of slavery.'

I anticipated further hostility on the part of Mr Child – I could well imagine his opinion of abolitionists. Yet when he spoke, it was with urgency rather than malevolence.

'Describe him, will you, Captain, please?'

His bearing had stiffened and his eyes burned into me like coals. I was alarmed by the change in him, and a sensation of foreboding crept over my skin.

'He is about five feet seven inches tall. Very thin, rather pale. Long black hair. People will remember him – they always do. He dresses like a lawyer, but he talks like a priest.'

'An apt description,' Child said heavily.

'Apt?' I frowned. 'I thought you said you didn't know him?'

'*Mutato nomine de te fabula narrator.* Change but the name and the tale is told of you.' Child pushed his plate away and wiped his mouth with his napkin. 'Captain Corsham, you'd better come with me.'

CHAPTER THREE

IT WAS THE size and shape of a man, and covered by a sheet. Tad's size. Tad's shape. Acid flooded my mouth. Peregrine Child was talking, but I barely heard him.

'Our corpse here called himself Thomas Valentine, and this wasn't the first time he'd stayed in town. We found him four days ago, down at the dock. I have been making inquiries with the London magistrates, trying to locate his kin. If Valentine was an assumed name, that would explain my lack of success.'

We were back in Deptford Broadway, in the apartment of a surgeon named James Brabazon, on the first floor of the town's apothecary shop. The room was fitted out with shelves of glass bottles and jars, and wooden racks of saws, knives and scissors. A dreadful smell hung in the air, not quite of putrefaction, but a powerful stench of overripe game that mingled with the surgeon's cologne. I noted all these facts peripherally, for I only had eyes for the thing upon the table.

'As I said,' Child went on, 'the description fits, but maybe you'd prefer to send for someone else? A servant who knew him, perhaps? The body is not a wreath of roses.'

I raised my head. 'And I am not a flower girl. Please proceed.'

Child gestured to Brabazon, who pulled aside the sheet.

My world swam. I stood motionless, absorbing the shock. I had been expecting it, but still it hit me like a team of oxen.

Tad's fine-boned features were swollen, but still painfully recognizable. My eyes travelled over the gaping chasm in his neck, the countless cuts and abrasions that covered his body. The injuries seemed unreal, like a painting of a tortured saint.

I stared at him dumbly, wanting to shake life back into his body. I wanted to drop to my knees and pray to a God I was no longer sure existed. My ears buzzed, as they sometimes did at times of stress, damaged by proximity to the artillery cannon at Bunker Hill.

'It's him,' I heard myself say. 'That's Thaddeus Archer.'

Brabazon offered me a sympathetic smile. He had a gaunt, narrow face and wore his own dark brown hair long, tied back with a ribbon. His eyes were quite startling: one blue in colour, one brown. Each stared back at me, brimming with concern.

'Had you known him long, Captain Corsham?' he asked in a soft Scottish brogue.

'For over ten years. We were up at Oxford together.' The words came distantly and didn't sound like my own.

'He died when the throat was cut,' Brabazon said. 'At the end, at least, it was mercifully quick.'

'Brabazon believes he died not long before we found him,' Child said. 'Sometime during the early hours of June eighteenth.'

'The timing of rigor mortis suggests it.' Brabazon peered at me. 'Captain, would you like to sit down?'

In my worst imaginings last night, I had contemplated his death – but never this butchery, this savagery. 'Dear God, but he was tortured.' I stared at a grotesque mark upon his chest. The flesh had been burned and some sort of design seared into it: a crescent moon turned on its side, so that the horns pointed south, surmounted by a band with points, like a crown. 'What devilry is that?'

'Whoever killed him saw fit to brand him like a Negro,' Brabazon said. 'It is extraordinary. I've never seen anything like it.'

'Turn him over,' Child said.

I swallowed as I took in the raw mess of Tad's back. 'This was done with a whip,' Brabazon said. 'I'd guess fifty lashes. He was probably tied to a post for it. You can see the rope abrasions here – around his wrists and ankles.'

'Show him the hands,' Child said.

I'd already noticed them. How could I not? Each was grotesquely swollen, the knuckles puffed and purple. Some of the fingers stuck out at odd angles.

'I fear a thumbscrew was used on him,' Brabazon said.

'A thumbscrew?' I stared at him, appalled. 'Where would a man obtain such a thing in this day and age?'

'Oh, they are in regular use aboard the slaving ships. It's not a pleasant aspect of the trade, I grant you, but sometimes their application proves necessary. If a cargo of Negroes are suspected of plotting a rebellion, for instance, the thumbscrew can force their plans out of them. I take a voyage as a slave ship surgeon every other year, and I have applied the device myself. Mr Archer's injuries are entirely consistent.'

Dear God, these people. This town.

'As I said, this wasn't the first time that the man we knew as Valentine came to Deptford,' Child said. 'I had dealings with him myself. He'd been harassing one of the slave merchants here in the Broadway, and stirring things up with the local Negroes. I advised him to get out of town and not come back.' He moved to stand over the corpse, pointing at Tad's injuries as he spoke. 'The whip. The brand. The thumbscrew. Slaving punishments. Your friend came here looking for trouble and he found it.'

Brabazon rolled Tad onto his back and stepped away. I knew

this scene would be etched upon my memory forever. 'Do you have the man who did this in custody?'

'Not at present,' Child said.

'What are you doing to find him?'

'What I usually do when I have a corpse and no witnesses. Issue a reward and see if anyone comes to claim it.'

'In London many magistrates also investigate crimes.'

Child regarded me evenly. 'This isn't London.'

My gaze kept returning to the mark on Tad's chest, imagining the smell as the hot iron burned his skin, his screams. 'If the killer is familiar with slaving punishments, doesn't it stand to reason that he is a slaving man?'

'Doubtless he is, but half the men in town have worked the Guineamen at one time or another. That's near three thousand suspects. I asked around the slaving taverns, but I didn't find any answers. Nor did I expect to. Slaving men look after their own.'

'What about the brand? The design is quite distinctive, wouldn't you say?'

Brabazon had his back to us, tidying away some apparatus. Now he turned. 'Oh, there are countless old slave brands to be found around Deptford, sir. I wouldn't set too much store by it.'

'The way I see it,' Child said, 'your friend picked an argument over slavery with the wrong man. He was followed to some quiet place where the killer overpowered him. The villain had his sport –' Child grasped his index finger and made a violent, wrenching motion – 'and once he got bored, he cut Mr Archer's throat.'

'You cannot think he was tortured to death merely over a political disagreement?'

'What else could it be?'

A curious stillness had descended over the room. Both men turned, waiting for my answer.

'Mr Archer told his sister that people had been following him. He said that someone in Deptford had tried to kill him. Perhaps that's why he used a false name – because he feared for his life?'

'Did he say anything else about this person who tried to kill him?'

'Only that his enemies were powerful. Slave merchants, I think. Archer was mixed up in some sort of scheme to bring an end to the African trade.' It sounded so foolish, and yet I couldn't escape the evidence of my eyes. Tad had said that people wanted him dead, and now he was.

Child raised his eyebrows. 'End slavery, sir? How exactly did he propose to do that?'

I frowned, trying to remember what Amelia had told me. I needed to talk to her again. 'He said he was coming here to collect something that his enemies would want.'

Again I sensed their interest. 'What sort of something?' Child said.

'I don't know.'

'I found nothing out of the ordinary in his room at the Noah's Ark.'

'Where are his things? I'd like to examine them myself.'

Child hesitated. 'They're at the mayor's house.'

'Why would the mayor have them?'

'A gentleman was murdered in his town. Mr Stokes takes an interest.'

'Then I'll need to see Mr Stokes.'

'If you think it necessary. I don't hold with conspiracies myself. Ockham's Razor is my watchword. *Lex Parsimoniae.* Give me two explanations, one simple, one complicated, and I'll take the straightforward answer every time.' Child gestured at the corpse. 'Cover him up, will you, Brabazon? We're done.'

My eyes pricking, I stared into the bright shaft of sunlight that penetrated through the open window. I was no longer in that room, no longer in the presence of the ravaged corpse upon the table. I was walking along the banks of the Cherwell on a bright September morning twelve years earlier. I turned a bend in the river and there he was.

We had never spoken before, though I had often seen him around Wadham College, where he was already accounted quite the eccentric. A small, slight young man, I guessed he weighed significantly less than the large sack he was struggling to lift. He was dressed all in black, and he wore no hat or wig. Later I discovered that he'd mislaid the former in a gin shop, and that he never wore wigs because he considered them undemocratic. His hair was tied back into a queue, one black forelock tumbling over an eye. Prominent cheekbones, pale skin, a wide mouth and large grey eyes. Less a student of law than a romantic poet come to duel.

He thrust his arms into the sack, bringing out handfuls of white powder, which he cast into the water like a farmer from a parable. This action he repeated several times, and I divined that he was trying to lighten the sack so that he could lift it. I stood watching, shielding my eyes against the glare of the sun on the water, until he happened to glance up and notice me.

'West Indian sugar,' he cried, by way of explanation. 'They ground the loaves for the month yesterday. I stole it from the college kitchens last night – for it is polluted with the blood of African slaves.'

'Then the river is the best place for it.' I grinned, and he grinned back.

'I've been looking for you,' I said, as he cast more sugar into the water. 'Those things you said about slavery in the refectory last night. I agreed with every word. The trade in Africans is an abomination, a canker on the body politic.'

His expression grew more sombre. 'That slave merchant on the dean's table left without making a donation. I fear the provost means to send me down.'

My voice rose, as my courage mounted. 'I'll stand with you, if you like, against the dean and the provost. They can't send us both down just for having an opinion.'

He paused to catch his breath, looking me up and down, and his face lit up again with that broad smile. 'It seems the Lord has sent me a Heracles to help me lift this sack. Don't just stand there staring, sir. Come and help.'

That was the beginning. Just as this was the end.

Chapter Four

Brabazon walked us down the stairs to the street. My chest hurt, as it hadn't since the day my mother died. I wanted the years back. All that time in America, when I'd put an ocean between us. The London years, when we'd lived so near, yet strangers.

Brabazon drew back the bolts and opened the door to let us out, but pulled back with an exclamation of annoyance.

'Forgive me, gentlemen, there is a dead bird outside my door. Take care to step over it.'

We did as he advised, and I saw that the bird was a white dove, its wings outstretched as if in posthumous flight. The belly had been slit open, and the innards were spread around the carcass, almost in a circle. Even to my distracted eye, the bird did not look as if it had been placed there by some furred or feathered predator, but rather by human hand.

Child and Brabazon exchanged a glance, and they looked up and down the street. A boy was herding geese along with a stick. Three young ladies were giggling over a bonnet outside a shop window. A pair of black footmen walked past, deep in conversation. Brabazon kicked the bird aside and called for his manservant to come and clean it up. He apologized again, we exchanged bows, and made our departure.

My carriage was idling outside the coaching inn, where Sam had doubtless slaked his thirst once more. Child gave him directions to the mayor's house and we climbed inside. I watched from the carriage window, as the world without Tad passed by.

*

The mayor lived on the outskirts of Deptford Broadway, in a white, Italianate villa surrounded by lush gardens. A white-haired African porter opened the gates for us, and the horses crunched up the drive to a turning circle with a fountain in front of the house.

A black manservant in footman's livery met us at the door. A tall, thickset fellow with protruding eyes and a squashed nose, he seemed to know Child well. After a short wait in an anteroom, we were shown into a spacious parlour with large glazed doors opening onto the gardens. Chinoiserie cabinets displayed collections of ivory and jade, and yet it was the elaborate plasterwork that held my attention. Instead of the usual key motif or acanthus leaves, the cornicing was embellished with the sculpted heads of submissive Africans.

Child made the introductions. The mayor, Lucius Stokes, was a man of my father's generation, and in many respects he resembled him, too. Tall, with a strong chin and patrician good looks, his black velvet coat was embroidered with silver thread, and his indigo cravat carelessly knotted. He wore his own hair short and powdered, with side-whiskers over the ears – a young man's fashion. Unlike Father, whose trembling handshake had betrayed his dissolution, Stokes had a firm grip and a politician's smile. Sitting on the sofa by his side was a very beautiful mulatto woman.

'Tea, gentlemen? See to it, Abraham.'

I bowed to the woman, unsure of her position in the household. Her glossy black hair was piled and pinned in imitation of an English lady. She was dressed like one too, in a close-fitted gown of canary-yellow silk, cut low in the bodice. My bow elicited a faint smile from Mayor Stokes.

'Captain Corsham is here about Valentine's murder,' Child said.

I sensed movement across the parlour, and for the first time I noticed another African, sitting writing at a secretary desk in a corner of the room. He was dressed as a gentleman, wearing a periwig. I judged him to be about my own age. His quill had frozen on the page, and he was gazing at me with a peculiar intensity.

Child explained to Stokes that the man who had come to Deptford calling himself Valentine had been identified as a London barrister named Thaddeus Archer. 'Captain Corsham was a friend of his.' He handed Stokes my card.

'A distressing business.' Stokes gave a regretful smile. A gentle aroma of civet scent and Virginia tobacco surrounded him. 'Some said when Valentine first came here, that I should have had him run out of town. Perhaps, all things considered, that might have been best. Yet I pride myself that Deptford is a liberal, tolerant place. Every man has a right to speak his mind here, even an abolitionist.'

'Evidently not everyone felt the same way,' I said.

'Indeed, and I regret it most profoundly. Yet your friend – Mr Archer, was it? – bears some responsibility for what occurred. Just as a wise man does not walk into a bear's cave and poke him with a stick, nor does he stride into a slaving town crying liberty. Mr Child did try to warn him, the first time he encountered trouble here. Had he listened, he might be alive today.'

'What trouble was this?'

I sensed Child's reluctance to speak of the incident. 'About a month or so back, Archer had a fracas with a slave ship sailor down at the dock.'

'This could be the attempt on his life that he spoke about.'

Child waved a dismissive hand. 'A bout of fisticuffs, that's all.'

'Is this sailor a suspect?'

'He had an alibi. A good one. I checked.'

The woman rose from the sofa and crossed the room to look out at the garden. Every man present, even the black gentleman at the desk, turned to follow her progress. She was much younger than I had first realized, perhaps sixteen years old. Her skin was the colour of honey, her features a glorious marriage of the European and the black. When she moved, it was like watching sunlight glide across the parquet floor.

Abraham, the thickset footman, returned with the tea tray, and I smiled my thanks as he poured me a bowl. His eyes met mine, blank and hostile. I couldn't bring myself to add sugar – the memory of Tad on the river lay too nearly upon me – and the bitterness of the leaves was a fitting companion for the grief and the guilt confounding my thoughts.

'Mr Stokes, perhaps we might talk about Mr Child's investigation.' Or lack of it, I thought grimly. 'I cannot help thinking that a more active inquiry, one less reliant upon rewards for information, would be more likely to apprehend the killer.'

'Mr Child does not have the resources available to magistrates of the London bench,' Stokes said firmly. 'I am quite sure he is doing his best under the circumstances.'

'He needs to do more. This is no ordinary murder, sir. The torture. The brand. Archer told his sister that he had made powerful enemies in your town. I think he meant slave merchants. He was frightened for his safety, and I imagine that was why he used an assumed name. This was not some argument over abolition gone too far.'

'Captain Corsham has a theory about the murder,' Child said. 'He believes Archer was killed because he'd found the means to end slavery.'

'Does he, by Jove?'

'I am aware that it sounds foolish,' I said, 'but that's what he told his sister. However unlikely, if this scheme is what brought him here to town, then it is surely pertinent. Archer said he was coming here to collect something that his enemies would want. If we can find out what it was, then it might shed some light upon his murder.'

'End slavery,' Stokes mused. 'I'm struggling to think. A genie's lamp? A magic wand? Forgive my bluntness, sir, but you'd need to work a spell upon the English people if you ever hoped to end slavery. They like cheap sugar in their tea and cheap tobacco in their pipes. No amount of handwringing will ever change that.'

'I've told Captain Corsham that we found nothing out of the ordinary in Archer's room at the inn, yet he feels the need to examine his effects for himself.' Child gave Stokes a pointed glance.

'I'd like to take his things with me.' I didn't want to examine them here under Child's beady eye. 'Mr Archer's sister will want to have them. I am on my way there now to break the news.'

'I don't see why not. By rights they belong to his kin. Mr Child?'

The magistrate shrugged.

Stokes turned to the African at the desk. 'Scipio, there is a black valise in the closet of my bedroom. Go and get it.'

Why were Tad's things even here in the first place? I recalled that he had told Amelia that the Deptford authorities were in league with the slavers. I thought it likely that Mayor Stokes was a slave trader himself. As for Mr Child, I had met Covent

Garden cardsharps I trusted better. There had to be more to
Tad's murder than these men claimed.

'Are there many slave merchants living here in Deptford?' I
asked, while we waited for Scipio to return.

'Several dozen,' Stokes said. 'This town was built upon the
African trade. This country too, in many respects. I tried to help
Mr Archer understand this, but he had a child's way of looking
at the world. He refused to acknowledge our contribution to the
nation's finances, or the history of slavery in Africa itself, or the
civilizing effect European slavery has on the blacks themselves.
He had a lot to say about profiting from human misery, but had
he troubled to take a proper look around this town, he would
have discovered the profits of slavery for himself. Philanthropic
enterprise, schools for the poor, donations to the church.'

So Stokes had met Tad too. 'What is the name of the slave
merchant Archer stood accused of harassing?'

Child frowned. 'I don't see the relevance, sir.'

'Isn't it possible he was one of the enemies Archer mentioned?'

'There is no evidence of wrongdoing on the merchant's part.
On the contrary, Archer made several unwanted visits to his
home and pestered his wife and servants in the street. The merchant was the victim of the piece, not Mr Archer.'

'The merchant is not the one on Brabazon's table. Why did
Archer single out this particular man for special attention? We
must understand his purpose in coming here to Deptford.'

The girl had walked back across the room to retake her seat
next to Stokes on the sofa. This time we'd been too busy looking
at one another to look at her. Now she leaned forward in a waft
of rose perfume.

'He came here to see his dark angel,' she said.

Her accent was faint, her English precise. Stokes glanced at

her, and then struck her very hard across the face. She fell side-
ways onto the sofa with a faint cry.

I was already halfway out of my chair, ready to intervene, but
the girl caught my eye, and gave a swift shake of her head. Not
wanting to make things worse for her, I kept my seat.

Scipio came through the door with the bag in his hand, and
seemed to take in the situation at a glance. He shot his master
a malevolent look.

Child stared out of the window. Abraham took up the
teapot and refilled his master's bowl. I studied the mark Stokes's
hand had left on the girl's skin and fought the urge to take him
by the lapels and throw him through one of his glazed garden
doors.

'There now.' Stokes massaged his hand. 'All your bowing and
scraping has made my pretty nigger forget her place.' He smiled
to rob his words of offence.

I had no desire to share such a joke with him. 'A gentleman
does not strike a lady, sir.'

'Miss Cinnamon is my property,' Stokes said mildly. 'I can
see you own no Africans yourself. They need a firm hand, especially when one dresses them up like this. Now is there anything
else that I can help you with, Captain Corsham?'

I could see there was little more to be gained here. For all
his urbane manners, Stokes was as obdurate as the magistrate,
Child. The girl was holding her face, gazing blankly at the floor.
As I took the bag from Scipio, I shot her a last look of concern.
He came here to see his dark angel. I only wished that I could ask
her what she'd meant.

CHAPTER FIVE

AMELIA BRADSTREET LIVED only five miles from Deptford, but north of the river. It consequently took us over two hours to drive there, crossing the Thames by means of the horseferry at Rotherhithe. The hamlet of Bethnal Green was a jumble of dilapidated houses and pig farms, surrounded by moorland and beanfields. A lunatic asylum loomed, grey and forbidding, over the green. Unkind voices – Caro's friends in the Mayfair salons – said that Amelia Bradstreet must fit in rather well.

I followed the directions she had given me, discovering that her cottage lay a few streets back from the green. It had a sagging, thatched roof covered in bird droppings and appeared to have been built on the garden of a much larger house. A sow was suckling her piglets in an adjoining vegetable patch, and the air was rich with the yeasty tang of a brewery.

An elderly Indian maidservant answered my knock. She gazed at me blankly while I explained my business, but Amelia called indistinctly from some other part of the house and the maid stood back to let me enter. She showed me into a tiny parlour where Amelia, pale and pensive, came forward to greet me.

She saw I was alone and her expression fell. 'I so hoped you would find him.'

I struggled to find the right words – could there be any right words? 'Please, Mrs Bradstreet, won't you sit down?'

She read my expression. 'He's dead, isn't he?'

I made a hopeless gesture. 'I'm so sorry.'

I was ready to catch her if she swooned, but she only sat down on the sofa and raised a hand to her temple. I admired her fortitude. She had lost three children in the cholera epidemic that had also claimed her husband. Now she had no one.

I drew up one of the battered armchairs. The room was cramped and cold, with whitewashed walls. The furniture was old and riddled with worm. A faded carpet of Indian design covered the bare boards, and a few pieces of painted oriental porcelain were the only ornaments of note.

Amelia listened without interruption as I told her about my time in Deptford. I sought to spare her many of the details. The thumbscrew. The lashes. The brand. I wished I had the power to erase them from my own memory. I kept thinking of Tad, lying there on Brabazon's table. At times it overwhelmed my resolve.

'So his enemies killed him,' she said. 'Just as he feared they would.'

'I think that's what we must presume. Can you recall anything else Tad said about them? Or that first attempt on his life?'

'I have been trying to remember. He talked very fast – the way he always did when he was excited – and some of it seemed so far-fetched. He mentioned enemies in Deptford, but he also talked about a cabal of wealthy slave traders. They controlled Parliament, he said, and their power ran deeper in this country than most people would ever know.'

'The West India lobby.' During our time at Oxford we had often described them in such terms.

'You have heard of them then? I wasn't sure if they really existed.'

'They are a group of the wealthiest plantation owners and slave merchants who act in concert to protect their interests.

Like the East India Company. Or the wool merchants. Their trade might be unsavoury, but there's nothing sinister about them.'

'Are you sure? If Tad really thought he could end slavery, then wouldn't they have a motive for wanting him dead?'

'But how on earth did he expect to do that? You said it yourself, slavery is a vast commercial enterprise. Many of the richest men in the kingdom invest in slaving voyages, and ordinary people like the cheap commodities it allows them to buy. The trade can't just disappear overnight.'

'Tad seemed to think it could – or at least that he could deliver it a mortal blow. Did you tell the magistrate he'd gone to Deptford to collect something?'

'He didn't seem interested. Or rather he pretended not to be. Neither he nor the mayor would answer my questions. It made me wonder if they're protecting someone in the town. Tad had rancorous dealings with one of the local slave merchants and he was attacked by a slave ship sailor at the dock.'

'Have you looked to see if the thing he went to collect is in his bag?'

I hadn't been able to bring myself to examine it in the carriage. The realization that Tad was dead kept hitting me again and again. Each time was worse than the time before.

'I think it unlikely. Mayor Stokes and the magistrate, Child, were quite content for me to take it.'

We laid Tad's possessions out on Amelia's tea table. A dirty shirt and stockings, a half-empty bottle of gin, a volume of the writings of the radical thinker Thomas Paine, a bundle of abolitionist pamphlets, Tad's mahogany writing box, a ring of keys. Amelia opened the writing box and we spent a few minutes looking through the letters inside. They were mainly bills and angry missives from creditors, along with a few items of legal correspondence. As Child had said, nothing seemed relevant to his murder.

Amelia picked up one of the pamphlets.

'*F is for freedom*,' she read,

> '*In England all men shall be*
> *Released from chains of bondage*
> *In equal liberty.*'

An engraving beneath the verse depicted a muscular African breaking the shackles that bound him. Below, in bold black capitals, was a proclamation: SLAVES OF ENGLAND, FREEDOM IS YOURS TO WREST. THE CHILDREN OF LIBERTY WILL PROTECT YOU.

'Tad fought for the rights of slaves in the London courts,' she said. 'Many dozens of them are free because of him.'

'Mr Child said he had been stirring up trouble with the slaves in Deptford. Did Tad ever mention these people in the pamphlet, the Children of Liberty?'

'Not that I recall. Might they know more about his scheme to end slavery?'

'It's possible, though I don't know how we'd find them.'

She stared at the pamphlet disconsolately. 'I am so fixed upon my own struggles I confess I barely give the plight of Africans a thought. Tad had his troubles too, yet he cared only for the enslaved, the dispossessed.'

'He saw the world as a sculptor sees a block of stone. Not how it is. How it could be.'

'You cared too, as I recall? About slavery, I mean. Most young men don't.'

I gazed at the engraving, remembering. 'When I was a child, my mother had a black pageboy named Ben. We played together often – when Father wasn't there to see it. I had been raised to believe that Africans were inferior as a race, but I discovered that Ben saw and felt and thought much the same as I. Once I knew it, slavery just seemed wrong to me.'

'Where is Ben now? Still a slave?'

'Father sold him after Mother died. I was nine years old, Ben only a little older. I begged Father not to do it, but his debts were mounting, and Ben was worth thirty guineas. I remember watching as the carriage drove away, knowing I'd never see him again. His new owner took him to the Caribbean to work on a plantation.'

'Do you still believe in abolition?'

I hesitated. In Whitehall, West Indian revenues were spoken of in hallowed tones. A young placeman countenancing abolition could wish farewell to his political prospects. In time, when I had more influence, I hoped to own my true convictions. For the moment, I judged it prudent to hold my tongue. Yet here, with Amelia, I felt compelled to speak the truth.

'I think slavery the most abhorrent design ever conceived by man. How we can call ourselves a Christian nation, I don't know. But abolition will never happen. Not in my lifetime anyway. The trade's too lucrative. And people just don't care enough about Africans on the other side of the world.'

She smiled. 'Tad would have said you needed faith.'

Her words made me think of Miss Cinnamon's curious statement. 'Someone at the mayor's house told me that Tad went to Deptford to see his dark angel. Does that mean anything to you?'

'A woman, do you mean?'

'Perhaps.'

'Tad had women, I do know that.' A wash of colour flooded her cheeks. 'A lot of women, by all accounts, though not the sort you'd introduce to your sister. Maybe this woman – his dark angel – will know what Tad was doing in Deptford?'

My attention had wandered, disjointed thoughts racing through my mind. All the events of the day. All the unanswered questions. He'd told Amelia to go to me if anything happened to him. He'd said Harry Corsham would know what to do. Except I didn't.

I picked up the ring of keys. 'These must be Tad's. I think I should take a look inside his rooms and see if anything there will tell us more.'

Amelia gave me a wan smile. 'Thank you, Captain Corsham.'

She had found a leather pouch in one of the side pockets of the valise, and she opened it and shook it over her palm. A small package of red waxed paper fell out. She unwrapped the paper, which was inked with oriental characters. Inside was a brown lump about the size of a damson. Amelia sniffed it and passed it to me without comment. The lump was malleable between my fingers, like glazier's putty. It held an aroma of fresh-mown hay.

'It's opium,' I said. 'Men like to eat the smoke of it. It fills their heads with wild dreams and delusions.'

'I know what it is. I lived in India, remember.'

'Did you ever see Tad smoke it? It was not a vice he had before I went to America.'

'Never.' She dropped the opium onto the table, and studied me intently. 'Why did you go to America? One minute you were here, and the next gone without a word. You and Tad argued, I do know that. Was that why you left?'

'Is that what he said?'

'He said it was over a girl. That you loved the same woman. Is that true?'

For a moment I couldn't speak, as the events of the day hit

me once again. Tad was dead and things could never be put right.

'It was a long time ago,' I said.

Still she wouldn't let the matter drop. 'Just know that he loved you – whatever wrong you might have done him, or the reverse. He was never the same after you left. He missed you, Captain Corsham.'

Each word was a stiletto thrust into my conscience. I bowed my head, trying not to listen.

'So many of my memories of him are memories of you. The pair of you down from Oxford. Days on the river. Papa and his dogs. You were as much an Archer as any of us who bore the name. Mama wept when you left. She loved you like a son. But then you would hardly be one of us, would you, if you had not disappointed her?' She smiled at me sadly. 'And now you and I are the only ones left.'

CHAPTER SIX

WE REACHED THE limits of London at a little after eight o'clock. The great dome of St Paul's was gilded by the evening sun, the City bustling with clerks and stockjobbers heading home or in search of their dinner. As we wended our way west to Soho, the streets grew livelier, spilling with gentleman revellers and their whores. I watched distractedly, absorbed by memories of Tad. London looked the same and yet everything was different.

We pulled up outside Carlisle House, and I jumped down from the carriage, without waiting for Sam to fit the steps. The doormen knew me and waved me through, to cries of protest from those queuing to get inside. I hurried through a series of gilded anterooms into the ballroom.

Light and music and colours whirled past me: satin gowns, embroidered waistcoats, silk fans. I searched the room for my wife, dazzled by the play of light upon crystal and mirror. I couldn't see her in the ballroom and I hurried on. Over the Chinese Bridge, through the courtyard garden, into the Star Room where faro and hazard were played. The newspapers likened Carlisle House to the Fall of Rome. Caro called it Eden without the innocence. Tad, who had objected more to the people than to the pleasure, had called it the tenth circle of hell.

Tonight it felt like it. My uniform was suffocating and my cravat felt like a noose, though the players at the gaming tables seemed oblivious to the heat. I passed men I knew and they wished me luck in the by-election. They weren't to know that nothing was further from my mind. I thought only of Tad. Tad and Caro. There she was.

She was laughing, one hand raised to her piled chestnut hair, adorned tonight with a spray of ostrich feathers. In the candle-light her features held a misleading fragility: delicate bones, the softest mouth. She was wearing a *robe en chemise* of oyster satin, the bodice gathered with turquoise ribbons. Her diamond brace-lets cast rainbows as she shook the dice.

The gentlemen surrounding her wore white dress suits and attentive smiles. I looked for the young viscount who had called at the house last week, but I couldn't see him. Perhaps he had been banished from her circle. To turn up at her house, drunk, trying to provoke her husband into a duel, was surely in breach of whatever rules she made them play by. Not the fact of the thing, but the look of the thing. Even love was con-strained by the iron laws of Caro's drawing room.

I pushed my way through to her side, and drew her away from the group. 'Ho there, Corsham,' someone called after us. 'Bring her back soon, old man. She's luck.'

I pulled her into one of the little alcoves garlanded with leaves that were supposed to resemble lovers' bowers in a pleas-ure garden. 'Harry?' she said. 'Whatever is the matter?'

'Thaddeus Archer is dead.'

She stared at me. 'Good Lord. How very shocking.'

'He was murdered.' My voice broke. 'They tortured him first and then they cut his throat.'

I had spared Amelia Bradstreet those details, but Caro was her father's daughter. She had the old bastard's mettle and fixity of purpose. Her only reaction was a slight intake of breath.

'I've been in Deptford. That's where his body was found.'

'Deptford?' She said it as though it were China or Hades. 'Whatever was he doing there?'

'Some scheme to do with slavery. Amelia and I are trying to find out.'

She frowned at the name. 'Surely that is down to the Deptford authorities?'

'The authorities can't be trusted. Tad told Amelia as much, and today I saw what they were like myself. I'm on my way to his rooms now. I hope to find something there. I didn't want you to worry.'

I was aware that I was babbling. My face wore a sheen of sweat, and I could feel a pulse beating in my neck. Caro was looking at me as one might regard a patient at the Bedlam Hospital, concerned and cautious all at once.

'I cannot think it right to get involved.'

'Tad told Amelia to come to me if anything happened to him. Nothing about this feels right, Caro. He said there was a conspiracy against him, slave merchants and politicians. He said they wanted him dead.'

'All the more reason to leave it well alone.' She lowered her voice. 'You are about to enter Parliament, Harry. If there ever was a time to be caught up in a sensational murder, this isn't it. Just think of the constituency. Some of the freeholders are slave merchants themselves.'

'The freeholders will vote the way the ministry bribes them to vote. Cavill-Lawrence assures me that I needn't worry on that score.'

'Even so. Why take the chance?' Again I saw the late Charles Craven in his daughter's eyes, the banker's mind swift to calculate risk and reward.

'Because he asked for me. Because Amelia has no one else.'

She tipped her head on one side to look at me, a Whitechapel prize-fighter's jut of the jaw. 'If Amelia's friends have deserted her, then whose fault is that?'

My leg ached after the exertion of the day. Tiredness seemed to penetrate the marrow of my bones. 'It was years ago, and Lord knows she has paid for her mistake. Was it really such a crime to fall in love?'

'The crime wasn't the falling in love. The crime was to elope to Calcutta with another woman's husband. Leonora Bradstreet was crushed by what they did. They humiliated her, and she died of a broken heart.' Caro frowned. 'Did you give her any money?'

'A little. Just to cover the costs of the funeral. Look, never mind Amelia. This isn't about her.'

'Then what is it about? You have hardly seen Thaddeus since Oxford.'

I grappled for an explanation she'd understand. 'He was a friend when I needed one most. After Father died. Other than Mother and Ben he was the first person who ever gave a damn.' My eyes swept over the familiar faces around the gaming tables, men I also called 'friends'. A word that could encompass nothing and everything.

'If you find what you're looking for at his rooms? What then?'

'I will take the evidence to the Deptford magistrate, and hope it compels him to act.'

'And if it doesn't?'

'Then I will spend a few days in Deptford asking around. If I can discover who murdered Tad, then I can bring a private prosecution against them. I can use my influence to have the case moved from Deptford to London.'

The measure of Caro's opposition could be judged by the length of her silence. In the one that followed, an army might have laid siege to Troy.

'Harry, this is madness. A scandal could ruin everything. You must see that.'

By everything she meant the by-election and the ministerial offices that would surely follow. In time, a peerage and a seat at the Cabinet table. Perhaps – though we rarely spoke of it, even between ourselves – occupancy of a certain house in Downing Street. It all seemed so inconsequential to me now.

'I will be discreet, I promise. But I must do this.'

We looked at one another, each willing the other to understand. Eventually Caro lowered her eyes. 'Then there is nothing more to say.'

I watched as she walked back to her admirers, smiling, as if nothing was amiss. Someone handed her the dice, she kissed them, and everyone laughed.

The newspapers called us a gilded couple and predicted great things for us. To the world, we presented a federal front. As Homer says, we confounded our enemies and delighted our friends. It was to my eternal regret that we so rarely delighted each other.

CHAPTER SEVEN

LINCOLN'S INN HAD always reminded me of an Oxford college. The imposing brick gatehouse on Chancery Lane, the chapel, the dining hall, the students of law and the barristers in black silk robes. I hurried through the darkened courts and alleys, moonlight silvering stray coils of river fog. Snatches of evensong drifted from the chapel.

I had only visited Tad here once before – on the last occasion I'd seen him alive, just after my return from the American war. Our meeting kept returning to me in flashes. I kept seeing his bleak, ashen face. More awful even than the face on Brabazon's table.

I turned into New Square, gravel crunching underfoot. Red-brick houses loomed tall and still in the mist. I was so distracted by my thoughts that I wasn't looking where I was going, and collided with someone on the steps of Tad's building.

'Watch yourself, damn loitersack,' he said.

The speaker was a young African, rather short in stature, muscles bulging beneath his moss-green coat. A red, three-cornered hat was pulled down low over his face and as he turned, I saw one side of it was a twisted mess of hideous scars. The disfigurement compounded the feeling of menace his expression provoked.

Muttering apologies, I spun away from him into the lobby of Tad's building. I'd come armed with money for bribes, but the porter was asleep in his booth. A tortoiseshell cat on his counter watched me as I crept up the stairs.

On the landing, I struggled to remember the way to Tad's rooms. The building was a maze of corridors lined with doors to sets of barrister's chambers, the walls hung with portraits of long-dead lawyers in lacy jabots. Eventually, after a few wrong turns, I found Tad's door and fitted his key into the lock with unsteady fingers.

The sitting room was large and cold. A window had been left open and moonlight lay in pale rectangles on the ceiling. I froze in the half-light, as I saw a man walking towards me. For an instant I thought that it was Tad. He veered away from me to grab two large leather bags on the floor by the window. I stared, confused, as he swung his legs over the sill, and disappeared.

Spurred to life, I ran to the window, expecting to see him lying broken on the cobbles below. But he had landed eight feet down, upon a cast-iron porch over the Carey Street entrance to Tad's building. He threw his bags onto the street, and jumped down after them. I shouted and he glanced up at me. I glimpsed a blurred white face. Then he snatched up his bags, and ran off in the direction of Chancery Lane.

I wanted to go after him, and in another lifetime I would have done. Yet the drop to the porch and then to the street, was precisely the manner of activity the surgeons had warned me against. I couldn't risk another fracture, and so I stood there helplessly, watching him disappear into the night.

Struggling to make sense of what I'd just seen, I stumbled to the mantelpiece, groping around until I found a lamp. I lit it with a tinder from my pocket, and it cast a sallow glow around the room. The sitting room appeared much as it had the last time I'd been here. Everything a little shabby, few items of value that hadn't been pawned, books of philosophy and law, and not much else. Had I disturbed a burglar? If so, then he must have been disappointed. Tad had lived frugally, one of the poorest gentlemen I knew.

Yet as I inspected the room more closely, a new theory formed. The last time I'd been here, the cabinet by the door had bulged with legal documents and correspondence. Now every pigeonhole was empty. Similarly, the wall above Tad's desk was bare, when before it had been covered with paper. Charts and tables. Maps of Africa and the Caribbean. A diagram of a slave ship, black bodies packed in like herrings in a barrel.

Everything was gone. I stared at the pinpricks in the plaster, the pins scattered over the desk. The place had been searched. All Tad's documents had been taken.

I thought about the man who'd jumped from the window. He hadn't been panicked by my appearance. Quite the reverse. His self-possession suggested someone used to breaking and entering. Could it have been Tad's killer? Or someone else who had an interest in his papers? I thought of my conversation with Amelia, Tad's fears about the West India lobby. Then I chastised myself for my own foolishness. I was starting to think like Tad. The lobby didn't go around stealing lawyers' papers.

And yet someone had.

Why now, tonight, when Tad had already been dead several days? I wondered if that man, or whoever had sent him, hadn't known Tad's real name until now? Which meant they must have learned it today, after my visit to Deptford. Which meant either the mayor, Lucius Stokes, or the magistrate, Peregrine Child, must have told them.

I walked into the bedroom. Tad's bed was unmade, but that was normal enough. His clothes were folded in his armoire, and the drawers of his bedside table were closed. It was hard to tell if the room had been searched or not, and yet if I had disturbed the intruder before he'd got this far, then it was possible that something might remain here that could help explain Tad's murder.

I looked in the drawers of the bedside table first, but found nothing of any note. I searched the pockets of his clothes, and discovered only coins and dog-eared pamphlets. I even felt beneath his mattress. Nothing.

Everywhere I looked conjured visions of Tad. A cravat tossed on the floor, a claret-encrusted wineglass by the bed, a jar of dead violets on the windowsill. My eye came to rest on the painting of Tad's mother that had once hung in the set of rooms we'd shared at Wadham College. Carried on the surge of emotion it elicited came a memory of Oxford. I could hear Tad's voice as though it was earlier that day.

'Mama keeps all my secrets. She never breathes a word, though she knows I'll burn in hell.'

My breathing quickened. *Harry Corsham will know what to do.*

I took the portrait down from the wall. Examining the back of it, I realized I needed a knife, and returned next door.

Tad's desk drawers contained a jumble of sealing wax, pawn-broker's tickets, packets of ink powder and broken pens. Something metallic caught my eye amidst the clutter, and I rooted around for the source. Not a knife but a flattened rectangle of beaten silver. It was about the size of a large snuff box and I guessed it was a ticket to provide admittance to some place of fashionable resort. It held my attention because it was plainly worth something and Tad hadn't pawned it. The number fifty-one was stamped on one side in Roman numerals, surrounded by engraved flowers that might have been lilies. I put it in my pocket, thinking that Amelia could sell it.

Triumphantly, I retrieved an old quill knife from the back

of a drawer, and returned to the bedroom with it in hand. I levered the blade into the gap between the frame and the back of the picture, and it didn't take me long to work it free. In the old days, Tad had kept his radical pamphlets and private papers here. Now the cavity contained only a few scraps of paper. I held them up to the light, and a chill broke over me.

STOP ASKIN QUESTSHUNS. STOP POKIN YUR NOSE INTO OTHER MENS BIZNESS. SHOW YUR SHITTEN FACE AGIN IN DEPTFORD AND YUR DED

I AM WOTCHIN YOU. LEEV TOWN BEFOR I GUT YOU SHITTEN FUCKSTER

The third was the most succinct of all.

GET OWT OF DEPTFORD OR ILE KILL YOU NEGRO LUVVER

Outside on the street some men were arguing. Something about an idiot and a horse. My ears were buzzing again and I struggled to think. *Why didn't you come to me, Tad? If you were in trouble, being threatened – why didn't you come to me?*

At the back of the cavity was a folded wad of old paper, which I had at first taken to be packing to hold the letters in position. Carefully, I unfolded the brittle, stained pages on the bed. They appeared to have been torn from a book, each sheet inscribed with columns of numbers. Next to each number was inked a human skull. Dozens of them. Hundreds. A trickle of icy sweat ran along my ribs. The skulls seemed to march across the page like fat black beetles.

CHAPTER EIGHT

WHEN I ARRIVED home, I went upstairs to the nursery, where I watched Gabriel sleeping. Studying the curve of his lashes against his cheek, Caro's dark hair and my olive skin, I was gripped by a terrible fear that something would happen to him whilst I was in Deptford. It was irrational, but when I went downstairs, I told Gabriel's nursemaid that one of the footmen must always accompany them on their excursions to the park. Consoled by this precaution, I asked Pomfret to have Gaston grill me a bone for my supper. Despite everything else that had happened that day, when I went into the drawing room, I found myself thinking about my conversation with Caro.

The Caro in Gainsborough's portrait had the same oval face as my wife, the same dark blue eyes, and her expression held an exhilaration that enhanced her beauty. Once she had looked at me like that. Yet somehow, very swiftly, everything had gone wrong. I had spent many hours trying to understand it.

If ever I broached the subject, I received unsatisfactory answers. If I persisted, I ended up wishing I had not. The last time we had talked, she had looked at me calmly. 'Please explain in what duties as a wife I am remiss.'

I had said something about love, and as she turned away, I thought I glimpsed a flash of pain upon her face.

Yet when she turned back, her eyes were clear. 'We are not

lovers in a novel, Harry. I have given you an heir and a fortune. Your interests are my interests. Is that not enough?'

The young viscount who'd come to the house last week was neither the first, nor would be the last. I resented it, but I would not lock her up. To become a tyrant like my father, despised by his wife and son, was the one thing I could imagine that would be worse.

Thus our discontent festered, her unhappiness midwife to mine. Sometimes I caught her looking at me oddly, and I feared she could read my private thoughts. Sometimes I wondered if she hoped that I would die.

I didn't know how to mend it. I didn't know if I wanted to try. All I knew was that for me, there could only be Caro.

*

A little later, I went to my bookroom, where I took up inkpot and quill. From memory, I made a drawing of the slave brand. A crescent moon turned on its side, so that the horns pointed south, surmounted by a band with points, like a crown.

'Is it not grotesque?' Tad had said to me once. 'A human being stamped with his owner's mark, like a label sewn into a coat?'

Whose mark is this? I stared down at the picture I had made.

On the desk I laid out the things I'd found that day: the abolitionist pamphlet, the opium, the threatening letters, the wad of old paper with the skulls, the silver ticket. Then I thought about the man I'd seen in Tad's rooms: his blurred white face. Try as I might, I could recall nothing else about him.

> *STOP ASKIN QUESTSHUNS. STOP POKIN*
> *YUR NOSE INTO OTHER MENS BIZNESS.*
> *SHOW YUR SHITTEN FACE AGIN IN*
> *DEPTFORD AND YUR DED*

The script was crude, an uneducated hand. Or an educated hand pretending to be uneducated. The author clearly came from Deptford, and the letters suggested Tad had been conducting some sort of inquiry there. Maybe the wad of old paper was also connected to that inquiry? I took a magnifying glass from my desk to make a closer study.

The list of numbers next to the skulls ranged from one to three hundred and sixteen. It made no more sense to me now than it had done in Tad's chambers. Some of the numbers had Christian crosses drawn next to them instead of skulls. I counted ten in total. It perplexed me.

On one page I made out a date: 12 Dec 1778 – just over two and a half years earlier. I pored over the rest of the pages, making out more dates in the margins, interspersed between the skulls: 14, 16, 17, 19 December. Five dates, seven days apart. There were other numbers too, which made no sense to me at first. Finally, I made out a single, faded sentence: *Latter part of the day very hot weather and calm . . .* The rest of the sentence was rendered illegible by water damage.

Pomfret had been a navy quartermaster during the Austrian wars, and when he brought me my grilled bone, I asked him to take a look. 'Could these numbers be geographical bearings, do you think?'

Pomfret examined them, one hand clasped to his long chin,

so that he resembled a thoughtful puppet. 'They could be, sir. It looks to me like the journal of a ship's master.'

'Do you know what these crosses and skulls mean?'

'The master draws a cross when a crew member dies at sea. I've never seen skulls before. And why so many? Were they transporting animals, perhaps?'

I gazed at the long lines of skulls, my flesh prickling. 'I rather think that it was slaves.'

'Poor devils.' Pomfret shook his head. 'Not a profitable voyage. What the deuce happened?'

'I don't know,' I said. 'Something bad.'

Chapter Nine

WE BURIED THADDEUS Archer two days later.

The church at Bethnal Green smelled of wax and dying flowers and mouldering leather. The vicar's prayers were long and my bad leg cramped in the pew. I sat next to Amelia. Against her black cambric gown, her complexion held a marble pallor. Her grey eyes glistened, though neither of us wept. I recognized some of our fellow mourners: Lincoln's Inn lawyers; Oxford men and their wives. They must have read the notice Amelia had placed in yesterday's newspapers. A number of old women were sitting together, and I guessed they were part of the local congregation.

Only one mourner stood out: a lady, sitting alone, without even a servant. She wore a black lace veil pulled forward, obscuring her face. Her hair was also black, twisted into a simple knot secured with ivory pins. As the vicar said the final prayers, she rose from her pew and I saw that she was unusually small in stature. From the hands that clutched her Bible, I guessed that she was young. Afterwards I looked for her outside, but I couldn't see her.

I escorted Amelia to the graveside. A featherman with his staff led the way, followed by the pallbearers with the coffin, and half a dozen professional mourners. As we rounded the corner of the church, Amelia gripped my arm a little tighter.

'Captain Corsham, do look.'

Gathered around the hole that had been dug to receive Tad's earthly remains were about two dozen Africans. The colour of their skin ran from tawny beige to darkest ebon; their clothes vivid shades of yellow, scarlet and turquoise. The women wore caraco jackets and the men had feathers in their hats. Some carried trumpets or clarinets. A very fat African dressed as a gentleman made a gesture in the air, and the musicians struck up Pope's funeral hymn. The remaining Africans broke into song.

> *'Hark! they whisper; angels say,*
> *Sister spirit, come away!*
> *What is this absorbs me quite –*
> *Steals my senses, shuts my sight,*
> *Drowns my spirit, draws my breath?*
> *Tell me, my soul, can this be death?'*

The vicar was speaking rather heatedly to the featherman, and the pair of them approached Amelia. 'I am so sorry, Mrs Bradstreet,' the vicar said. 'I will have the verger disperse them in just a moment.'

'No,' she said. 'I believe they must have known my brother. Pray let them finish.'

We stood watching while the Oxford men and the other mourners shifted around us. Tears rolled down the Africans' faces as they sang. After a time, I realized that the fat gentleman had stopped singing. He was staring at another black man standing some way off from the rest, behind the low wall that bordered the churchyard. This second man was also watching the funeral, a red hat held against his breast. This time I made out the scars on his face very clearly. It was the same African I'd bumped into two nights ago at Lincoln's Inn.

He and Tad must have known one another, and I wondered if he was connected to the Children of Liberty. I kept glancing at him as the coffin was lowered, and the vicar read more prayers. A pair of gravediggers stepped forward to shovel earth onto the coffin. The first clods struck the lid, and the Africans broke into song once more. I stood watching as Tad was claimed by the hard, baked ground. Amelia swayed on my arm, and when it was over she let out a little sigh.

Afterwards I thanked the vicar and the featherman. They were stony-faced because of the Africans, and quickly left. One of the mourners came to speak to Amelia and I excused myself. I wanted to talk to the young black man with the scars. As I crossed the graveyard towards him, he saw me coming and walked away. By the time I reached the churchyard wall, he was halfway along the street, heading in the direction of the green. I climbed over the wall and hastened after him. He glanced over his shoulder, and quickened his pace. I increased my own, though my infirmity held me back. He turned onto the green, and by the time I reached the spot, he'd vanished into the swirl of shoppers and farmers going about their business. I scanned the crowd, but I had no further sight of him. Disappointed, I walked back towards the church.

When I returned, Amelia was talking to the fat African gentleman. 'Allow me to name Mr Moses Graham,' she said. 'Captain Corsham was one of my brother's oldest friends. Mr Graham is a painter of watercolours – and when his work permits, he campaigns for the abolition of slavery. That's how he knew Tad.'

We bowed. Moses Graham's round, meaty face was elongated at the mouth, with a flat nose, and bushy white eyebrows. His coat and waistcoat were scarlet velvet, trimmed with gold braid; his wig large, heavy and old-fashioned.

Next to him stood a tall, skinny African in a blue martial jacket. 'Ephraim Proudlock,' Graham introduced him. 'My assistant in matters of art and abolition.' His voice was rich, the English inflected only by a slight lisp.

Proudlock bowed. His hair was plaited into many tiny braids, tied back in a queue with a yellow ribbon.

'Mr Graham was just telling me that he has written a book about his experiences,' Amelia said. 'He hopes his account will change people's minds about slavery.'

'I should be glad to read it,' I said. 'Were you a slave yourself, sir?'

'Indeed, I was.' Graham indicated the other Africans with a sweep of his pale palm. 'Many of the men and women here owe their freedom to Mr Archer. They have come to give thanks to the Lord in his memory.'

I knew Tad had often represented black clients. Nine years ago, a slave named James Somerset had sued his owner in the London courts, and the Lord Chief Justice had reluctantly ruled slavery to be incompatible with Magna Carta. The case had set a precedent, and some claimed slavery was now illegal on English soil. In truth it wasn't as simple as that – the law was a muddle – but slaves could resort to the courts to prevent their removal by force to the Caribbean. As a consequence, most blacks in England were now paid servants. Only in the slave-trading ports – Bristol, Liverpool, Deptford – did Englishmen still own slaves in significant numbers. People said the Africans in such places often didn't understand that the law could help them, nor that lawyers like Tad would represent them pro bono. Little wonder they were confused. English liberties might have prevailed upon English shores, but Magna Carta made no prescription against hypocrisy. The judge's ruling did not apply to our Caribbean colonies, where the plantations were dependent upon slave labour.

'Mr Graham, do you know of an abolitionist society named the Children of Liberty?' I asked.

'I have heard of them, though I wish that I had not. They do more harm than good to the cause of abolition.'

His reply confused me. 'Don't they help runaway slaves?'

'They do, but their methods are often confrontational, sometimes violent. Last year they helped a slave escape from a house in Blackheath, and a footman who tried to stop them was beaten badly. Mr Archer was one of the lawyers they used to represent the slaves they assisted.'

'Do you know where I might find them?'

'I regret that I cannot help you. They operate in secrecy, you see. Their activities have made them many enemies amongst the slavers, and they fear reprisals. For these reasons, I would advise against seeking them out.'

Despite Moses Graham's warning, I decided that when I returned to London I would try to find them. 'That man in the red hat with the scars. I saw you looking at him just now. Who is he?'

He hesitated. 'His name is Caesar John. Another African who gives my race a bad name.'

'Is he an abolitionist?'

'He is a villain,' Proudlock broke in, his accent much thicker than Graham's. 'You have doubtless read newspaper reports which claim that London is awash with free blacks lying in wait to rob your house or cut your throat? Such stories are founded upon prejudice, and yet we have our rogues and ne'er-do-wells just as your race does. This Caesar John is one such man.'

'What was he doing here? Was he a friend of Mr Archer's?'

'I wondered that myself,' Graham said. 'He is a dangerous man. I counsel you to stay away from him, sir.'

'How about Tad's dark angel?' Amelia said. 'Have you ever heard of her?'

Proudlock looked up sharply. He had a smattering of freckles across his broad nose, and they stood out against his russet skin. Graham shot him a warning glance.

'Tad's dark angel,' Amelia repeated, also observing this reaction. 'We know that's why he went to Deptford. Captain Corsham believes that if we can find out more about what he was doing there it will lead us to his murderer.'

'We know nothing about that, madam.' Graham pulled his watch from his waistcoat pocket. 'Please forgive us, but we are late for an appointment. Once again, I am so sorry for your loss.' He bobbed a hasty bow and they moved away.

'Wait.' I started after them. 'If Mr Archer was your friend, then please tell us what you know. It is imperative.'

Graham swivelled round and his voice dropped to an urgent whisper. 'You place black lives in danger merely by asking about her, sir. I beg you never to speak of her again.' He gave me one last look of entreaty, and then he and Proudlock hurried away across the grass.

'Well,' Amelia said, as we watched them go, 'there walks a man frightened half to death.'

'Two men,' I said. 'Whatever they are afraid of, it cannot just be a Deptford danger. They feel unsafe even here.' I resolved that when I returned to London I would seek out Moses Graham again.

'If one's enemy is powerful,' Amelia said, 'I suppose he can reach one anywhere.'

It was a sobering thought. We stood for a few last moments at the graveside, and I bowed my head, remembering the Africans' song. It seemed a more fitting tribute to Tad than any of the vicar's pious prayers.

The world recedes; it disappears.
Heaven opens on my eyes, my ears,
With sounds seraphic ring.
Lend, lend your winds! I mount! I fly!
O Grave! Where is thy victory?
O Death! Where is thy sting?

*

My parting from Amelia Bradstreet demands a mention.

'I don't like to think of you going back to that dreadful place,' she said, as we stood at the churchyard door. 'It may be dangerous.'

I pulled aside my coat to show her my sword and flintlock pistol. She did not look overly reassured.

We were standing in the shadows of the belfry. Amelia gazed after the retreating line of the mourners' carriages.

'Most of them could hardly bring themselves to speak to me.'

'For the women it is a point of principle,' I said. 'As for the men, I suppose they are afraid of insinuation if they are kind.'

'You have been kind, and you do not seem afraid.'

I did not wish to give her false hope that we could maintain an acquaintance once our inquiry into Tad's murder was concluded. It would only make things worse with Caro.

'Tad was my oldest friend. I could hardly do otherwise.'

She lowered her gaze. 'Yes, of course.'

I regretted the words almost as soon as they were spoken. 'Forgive me, Mrs Bradstreet, I did not mean—'

'Yes, you did.' She stared at the thin golden band on her finger. 'It was wrong what we did to poor Leonora Bradstreet, I do know that. Yet I would do it all again in a heartbeat. To have loved like that just once – without a thought for the

consequence – I am not ashamed of it. Can you possibly understand?'

'Love? Yes, I understand it.'

'Respectable love, you mean, the sanctioned kind.' She raised
her chin to look at me, and I saw pride and anger written there.
'I can withstand their censure, their gossip, even your pity,
Captain Corsham. It's the loneliness I find I cannot endure.'

PART TWO

24–26 JUNE 1781

In the mind there is no absolute, or free, will. The mind is determined to this or that volition by a cause, which is likewise determined by another cause, and this again by another, and so ad infinitum.

II. Of the Soul, *Ethics*, Baruch Spinoza

CHAPTER TEN

I COLLECTED MY horse, Zephyrus, from outside the church, and took the road south out of Bethnal Green, heading for the river. We crossed the Thames as I had done previously, at Rotherhithe. I soothed Zephyrus with soft words as the horse-ferry navigated the treacherous currents, breathing in the pungent scents of the carters and oyster-women around us. Once deposited on the south bank, we took the road east at a canter.

As I rode, I thought about the master's journal and the skulls. Was it possible that more than three hundred slaves had died aboard a single vessel? And if so, *how* had they died? I knew that disease sometimes ravaged slave ships, but this would have been a veritable plague. It couldn't have been a wreck or a fire, as the dates suggested the deaths had occurred over several days. I had read appalling reports about slave ship sailors who brutalized Africans in their care, yet surely no captain would ever countenance the destruction of such a large portion of his ship's cargo?

Between these thoughts, I dwelt much upon Amelia Bradstreet. I felt badly for the way I'd spoken to her and wished very much that I could take it back. I decided to call on her when I returned from Deptford, that I might explain.

The road dipped south, following the great curve of Deptford Reach. Soon I encountered queues of carts and cavalrymen waiting to enter the Navy Yard. This vast compound was a small town in itself, protected from thieves and radical elements by ten-foot walls. Beyond the Yard, ramshackle houses lined the road into Deptford Strand and I breathed the appalling stench of the town once more.

I found the Deptford watchhouse easily enough. A squat building with a conical roof, it looked better suited to serve the law enforcement needs of a small village, rather than a town of Deptford's size and reputation. I tethered Zephryrus to a post outside the door.

Peregrine Child was inside, playing cards with an old man with a ginger beard. Three bottles of wine, two of them empty, stood on the table. 'Captain Corsham,' Child greeted me – a little warily, I felt. 'Back again.'

He made no move to get up and the old man, whom I took to be a constable, followed his example, offering me only a toothless grin.

'Good afternoon, Mr Child. I have brought you evidence pertaining to Mr Archer's murder.' I handed him the threatening letters. 'It is unclear whether this correspondence was sent to him here in Deptford or in London, but the Deptford connection is plain enough. I found them at Archer's chambers, where I encountered an intruder searching the place. I told you there was more to this murder than first appeared.'

Child grunted. 'Word often gets around when a person dies. Petty villains rob the dead man's house while it's lying empty.'

'Petty villains don't take legal documents. Nearly all Archer's papers were stolen. If I hadn't disturbed the intruder, he might have got these too.'

Child gave the letters a cursory examination, and then handed them back. 'What of it? I told you that your friend upset people here.'

'These letters prove that Archer was asking questions in this town – it was that which angered the author, not simply his views on slavery.' I had decided to make no mention of the pages from the master's journal until I knew more about them myself. 'At the very least these letters suggest he knew his killer.'

'Whoever wrote these letters didn't like Archer very much, but it doesn't follow that the author then killed him.'

'It is surely worthy of further investigation?'

Child smiled blandly. 'Last time you were convinced a slave merchant killed your friend. This doesn't look much like the hand of a merchant to me. Or do I take it you have abandoned that particular theory?'

'Slave merchants employ uneducated men. Or the merchant might have disguised his hand.' I bit back my frustration, adopting a more even tone. 'Have you made any progress at all since I was last in town?'

'I'm afraid my reward remains unclaimed. It's as I told you: slaving men look after their own.'

'How about that slave girl, Miss Cinnamon? She said Archer had come to Deptford to see his dark angel. What did she mean?'

'I have no idea.'

'You didn't ask her?'

Child folded his arms, his expression combative. 'On the night Archer was killed, there were three more murders in Deptford Strand: two knife fights in the taverns and a strangled whore. There were countless brothel brawls, a theft of gunpowder from the Navy Yard, and many more thefts from the warehouses down at the dock. I'd like to say that was unusual, but I'd be lying. I have my hands full, sir. I can afford to give no corpse special treatment.'

'I can see how busy you are.' I gave the bottles on the table a pointed glance. 'With that in mind, I have decided to look into the murder myself.'

Child's face betrayed no surprise, only a hint of calculation. 'That is your prerogative, of course. Yet I counsel caution, sir. I am sure you are a fine hand with your sabre and your pistol, but Deptford is not a battlefield – at least, not one like you've ever encountered before. There is little enough honour among gentlemen to be found in these streets, and the only distinction your redcoat will bring you here is a sign on your back saying that you're ripe for robbing.'

'Thank you for the warning, but I'm afraid my heart is set on it. Now I would like to see the place where you found the body, Mr Child. Will you show me?'

I anticipated another refusal, but Child only shrugged. 'Go on then. I have some business down at the dock anyway.'

Perhaps he wanted to keep an eye on me. He was welcome to do so if he wished. But given the evasions and the obstinacy that were my experience of Peregrine Child to date, I was equally inclined to keep an eye on him.

Chapter Eleven

The dockside streets echoed to the sound of hammers and saws. The stench grew stronger as we neared the river. Peregrine Child glanced scornfully at my limp, and rather than check his gait so that we walked at the same pace, kept striding ahead and then waiting ostentatiously for me to catch up. We passed roping yards and coal stores, warehouses and shipping offices. On every corner, gangs of men were standing around in the sun, looking for work.

'Slaving ships are a favourite target of the French, damn their eyes,' Child said. 'If they can't capture them, they sink them. The town lost a lot of men last year. Investment isn't what it used to be and fewer voyages means less work. Not just aboard the Guineamen, but in the shipyards, the victuallers, everywhere.'

'Tell me about the man who assaulted Archer.'

'Assault's a strong word for it. Your friend was handing out his pamphlets in one of the quayside taverns. Slavery is a sin, and a lot of other words to that effect. With the mood here in town, it's not surprising there was trouble. I had a similar scene last year with a Quaker gentleman who gave a sermon on the evils of the African trade in the middle of the High Street. The fishwives pelted him with oyster shells and he came crying to the watchhouse.' He grinned at the memory.

'We were talking about Mr Archer, sir.'

'So we were.' Child spat onto the cobbles. 'What can I say?

Archer interrupted a game of dice with his speechifying and a fight broke out. He was half the size of his opponent, and he ended up with a bloody nose. I broke things up, and told him to get out of town. I hoped he'd listen.'

We emerged from between the buildings and I was momentarily silenced by the impressive sprawl of the docks. Several hundred vessels rose and fell with the tide, tugging at their moorings, flags snapping in the breeze. A gang of stevedores were heaving shipping crates up the quayside, unloading one of the Guineamen out on the Reach. Barges floated around the larger vessel like nursing whale calves.

'Did you arrest the man who attacked him?'

'If I arrested every man who got into a fight down here, they'd have to level the church to make room for the prison. Besides, Archer gave as good as he got. Bit the other fellow on the hand. It looked nasty.'

The stevedores had noticed the magistrate and they struck up a dirty song. Child raised his hand to acknowledge the compliment and they laughed.

'What was his name? This sailor?'

'The man has an alibi. He wasn't trying to kill anyone, just teach your friend a lesson. I've ruled him out. That's all you need to know.'

I was intrigued by his refusal to name Tad's assailant. If the man was as innocent as Child claimed, then why did he feel the need for circumspection?

'Does this man have any connection to the slave merchant Archer was harassing? The one you also refuse to name?'

Child gave me a look. 'Only that they both endured Archer's provocations.'

The hammering and sawing grew in intensity as we approached the Navy Yard. Men shouted and whistles blew.

Occasionally great plumes of steam shot fifty feet into the air. I knew they were getting ready to send more troops to the American colonies. My patron, Nicholas Cavill-Lawrence, said the war would be won by Christmas, but then he'd said that last year and the year before that.

Child stopped at the base of a metal hook upon a pole. 'Here's where we found him. Archer's hands were tied, and he was naked. His clothes haven't turned up. Either the killer sold them or they're at the bottom of the Thames.'

I gazed at the hook, the bleakness of this corner of the dock. 'Why put him up there? Because the killer was proud of what he'd done? Or as a warning to others?'

'The latter, I'd say. Abolitionists not welcome here.'

'Especially ones who think they know how to end slavery.'

'If you say so. We haven't found the murder weapon either. Brabazon, the surgeon whom you met the other day, thinks something larger than a pocket knife was used.'

'A hunting knife?'

'More like a bayonet. There was no sawing, just one clean cut.'

I could hardly bear to think of it, and yet I must. 'How about the slave brand? Have you identified the merchant who uses it?'

'What good would that do?'

I restrained my impatience. 'The killer might have crewed one of the merchant's ships?'

'Why would the killer brand him with a symbol that could identify him? That makes no sense.'

It was a fair point, but not one I was willing to concede without closer inquiry. 'Who found him?'

'A lad named Nathaniel Grimshaw. He works as a night-watchman in those warehouses over there. Young Nate went out for a pipe of tobacco around four, and found your friend swinging here. Archer had been staying at his mother's inn – the Noah's Ark, where we met before. The lad recognized him right away, and roused the watch constable, who fetched me from my bed.'

'Do you have any idea what time he was put here?'

'Nate says he passed by earlier, about one, and Archer wasn't here then.'

'So between one and four?'

'After two is more likely. This stretch of the dock sees a lot of traffic from the riverside taverns before then. The killer would have been taking quite a risk.'

'The torture would have taken some time. At least an hour.'

'I'd say more,' Child said, his face unsmiling.

I took another look around, at the warehouses and the taverns and the proximity of the Navy Yard with its guards. 'He can't have been tortured here. The killer would have needed somewhere quiet. One of the warehouses, perhaps?'

'A lot of them are lying empty. A score of Deptford merchants have gone out of business in the past few years.'

I sensed a slight unbending in his manner, and I wondered if Child was more troubled by the murder than he appeared. Magistrates in provincial towns were appointed by the wealthiest citizens. Here, I presumed, that meant slave money. Perhaps Child was concerned for his position? Or afraid where an investigation might lead?

'He'd need to be tall and physically strong to get him up there.'

'Unless he had help.'

'Do you think that's possible?'

Child's face seemed to close in on itself, adopting its old belligerent lines. 'Anything is possible.'

'And you have no other suspects?'

Child gazed at the barren marshland on the Isle of Dogs across the water. A gibbet stood there and the corpses of three hanged men – mutineers or pirates – rotted slowly in the afternoon sun.

'Nobody's talking. Nobody wanted him here in the first place. If anybody does know who did it, then I'm the last person they would tell. They'd probably be down the nearest tavern, buying the killer a drink.'

'So you think anyone could have done it, except the one man whom we know attacked Archer before.' It was horseshit. He hadn't even tried.

'That's about the size of it. *Caveat viator.*'

Let the traveller beware. I was getting a little tired of the magistrate's cod Latin.

'You think he got what he deserved?' I asked sharply.

'Nobody deserves that. But slaving men are a breed apart. It's the trade that does it to them. Deadens the goodness in the soul. Pick a fight with men like that –' Child gestured at the hook – 'you come off worse.'

CHAPTER TWELVE

CHILD WENT OFF to attend to his business, and I wandered the streets of the dockside quarter alone. The wholesalers here all catered to the shipping trade: sailcloth merchants, victualling yards, ironmongeries. It was the last of these that interested me.

I went from shop to shop — there were nearly a dozen iron-mongeries in Deptford, I was told – and in each I showed the drawing of the slave brand. I sweetened my questions with a little silver, but each time they were met with blank looks. Until the seventh place I tried.

The ironmonger had a mane of greying hair and a large mole on his nose. He peered at my drawing. 'That's one of mine. You want one like it?'

'Maybe. Can you tell me about it?'

Samples of his wares hung around the walls of the shop: lengths of chain in different thicknesses – sold by the mile; collars, manacles, fetters. A sign above the collars read: 'Every size from four years up.'

I thought of a collar encircling the neck of Ben, my child-hood friend. Then I thought of Gabriel, not much younger than the boys for whom the tiniest collars were intended. I breathed deeply to dispel the fury these images provoked.

The ironmonger scratched his stomach through his leather apron. 'It could have looked better, if you want to know the truth. Iron is all well and good for initials, but for a picture it should be gold.' He pressed a knuckle into the back of his hand and made a hissing noise. 'Gives a crisper edge. Customer didn't want to go the extra mile.'

'Can you give me his name?' I held up a silver crown. 'If he's brought any slaves back here to Deptford, he might let me take a look. I'd prefer to see it in the flesh, as it were.'

The ironmonger smiled at my little sally, eying the coin. If he didn't believe my story, then he didn't care. He took a book down from the shelf behind his counter, and spent a little while turning the pages.

'Here.' He turned his book round so I could see. The page had a sketch of the same design as my drawing: a crescent moon surmounted by a crown. Next to it was a record of the order, together with the name of the merchant who'd commissioned the brand: *John Monday Esq. Atlantic Trading and Partners.* I made a note of the address, a warehouse in the Private Dock, and my coin disappeared into the ironmonger's pocket.

Flushed with triumph, I made my way out of his shop. Next to the door stood a tailor's dummy, painted chocolate-brown. The face had grotesquely exaggerated African features. Fitted to its mouth was an odd metal contraption.

'What on earth is that?' I asked.

'Behold the speculum oris.' The ironmonger came out from behind his counter, and turned a screw on the side of the device. Slowly the dummy's hinged jaw inched open. 'Some slaves get a touch maudlin upon the Middle Passage and refuse to eat. The oris allows them to be fed against their will.'

'Ingenious,' I murmured, bile rising in my throat.

It was too late to go to the Private Dock now, and I needed to find lodgings before dark. I decided to try the Noah's Ark, where Tad had stayed. After collecting Zephyrus from the watchhouse, I made my way there.

The landlady, Mrs Grimshaw, welcomed me in the taproom. A tall woman in widow's weeds, with red-brown hair, she had a trace of Irish in her accent. She ran a practised eye over my uniform, and I felt as if I was being priced by the yard.

'I can offer you the Barbados room, sir. It is our finest, with a lovely prospect over the river.'

She named a princely sum and we haggled, eventually agreeing terms. I entrusted Zephyrus to the care of her stable boy, and then Mrs Grimshaw showed me upstairs to my room. It was small and square, crammed with old, oaken furniture. On one wall was a picture of the harbour in Bridgetown, Barbados. The 'lovely prospect over the river' proved to be a vista of the inn's stable-yard and a slaughterhouse in an unloved corner of the Private Dock. Beyond the warehouses and other buildings, I could just make out the quays, and a row of the giant Guineamen anchored out on the water.

'Is this where he stayed?' I asked. 'The man who was murdered?'

Her face fell. 'You heard about that? This is our finest room, so naturally a gentleman would stay here. I can give you another room, if you wish?'

I looked around at the place where Tad had spent his last night on earth. 'This will do very well.'

She smiled and handed me the key.

'Did you have much to do with him? The dead man?'

'Only at breakfast and dinner. My boy, Nate, spoke to him more. Said he seemed a good and honest gentleman for all his odd opinions. He'd stayed with us twice before, but mostly he kept to himself. If only he'd gone back to London as he'd planned.'

'Do you know why he changed his mind?'

'Only that he decided to stay another night at the last minute. Poor devil.'

That fitted with what Amelia had told me. She had been expecting Tad to call on the night of the seventeenth. I wondered what had made him change his plans.

'It was my Nate who found the body,' Mrs Grimshaw went on. 'I don't care what people say. It was a terrible thing to happen.'

I agreed it was.

'If you want any errands running, sir, or letters delivering while you are here, then my Nate is your man. His room is over the stable, or you can find him about the inn during the day.'

She offered me refreshment, and I asked for a plate of fried anchovies. She went downstairs to see to it, while I unpacked my bags, and formulated a plan for my time in Deptford. I was unwilling to accept Child's assertion that the slave ship sailor who attacked Tad at the dock was blameless in the matter of his death. People must have heard about the incident, and I decided to ask around the dockside taverns to see if I could find out his name.

Tomorrow I would go to the Private Dock to find the merchant who'd commissioned the slave brand, Mr Monday. It might also be a good place to ask around about the dead slaves in the master's journal. Surely if the ship had sailed from Deptford, someone would remember such a voyage? I was still baffled as to how and why those slaves had died.

I also wanted to talk to Nathaniel Grimshaw, my landlady's son – he had found the body, and he might know if Tad had ever had a visit from a woman here at the inn. *He came here to see his dark angel.* I remembered Cinnamon's words, and Moses Graham's reaction to them, thinking of the lady in the black lace veil at Tad's funeral. Could that have been her? Tad's dark angel?

There was the opium to look into, and then there was the silver ticket I'd found in Tad's rooms. My original intention had been to give it to Amelia to sell, but I'd since had second thoughts. Season tickets in silver, brass and gold were often issued by places of fashionable resort: pleasure gardens, theatres and assembly halls. Caro and I, for instance, had a gold ticket for Carlisle House. Yet Tad had hated the recreations of the *bon ton* with unbridled passion.

Such tickets were also used in exclusive brothels and gambling houses, but the Tad I remembered would never have had the means, nor the inclination, to squander his money in such a fashion. For him to have outlaid what I imagined was a considerable sum, this ticket must have been important to him – and nothing mattered to Tad more than the causes he served. Perhaps the ticket was connected to his inquiry and provided admittance to some place of recreation here in Deptford? The town certainly had no shortage of brothels and other houses of debauch.

Finally, there was Tad's interactions with the slaves of Deptford Broadway. In particular, I desired to speak to Miss Cinnamon again, anxious to learn what she knew about Tad's business here in Deptford. Yet I'd have to get past her owner, the mayor, Lucius Stokes first. I wondered what his reaction would be when he discovered I was back in town. Would it trouble him? I rather hoped it would.

Chapter Thirteen

I WENT DOWNSTAIRS to the dining room, which was busy with patrons taking supper. Mrs Grimshaw had kept a table aside for me, and as she was showing me to it, I heard a voice calling my name. It was the surgeon, James Brabazon, who was dining alone in one of the booths.

'A pleasure to see you again, Captain Corsham.' He smiled at me over his plate of battered fish and boiled greens. 'Are you taking supper? Would you care to join me?'

I said I would, thinking he would be a useful person to talk to about the town and its inhabitants. I also had some questions for him about the nature of Tad's injuries.

I took the seat opposite him in the booth, wincing a little at the cramp in my leg as I slid in.

'Does it trouble you?' Brabazon asked. 'I noticed your limp the other day.'

'Only a little. It's always stiff after a journey.'

'How did it happen, if you don't mind my asking?'

'My horse was shot from under me at Saratoga. The poor creature landed on top of me and broke the leg in two places. I was lucky not to lose it.'

'I am glad that you were in good care. Too many surgeons are too quick to resort to the knife, though broken legs always present a challenge. I am presently treating a patient with such an injury myself, a young man with whom I once sailed. Things were looking hopeful for a time, but an infection has set in. I am praying for a miracle, but I fear it will have to come off.'

His long face in the candlelight looked suitably grave. He had thick, slanted eyebrows, hollow, slightly pox-scarred cheeks, and a cleft chin. His tailoring was dark and soberly cut, with a starched white stock at the throat. With his unpowdered hair and clipped Scottish tones, I was reminded of a puritan from the last century, one of those old lawyers in the portraits at Lincoln's Inn. His eyes were no less startling upon a second inspection: one a rich brown, flecked with amber and gold, the other the pale blue of a northern loch.

'It is called heteroglaucous,' he said, noticing my interest. 'A rare but harmless abnormality.'

'Forgive me, I did not mean to stare.'

He smiled to signal he had taken no offence. 'If I am an oddity, then I am in good company. Plutarch says Alexander the Great had eyes of different colours, and the first Emperor Anastasius was known as Dicorus for the same reason.' He nodded at my leg, which I'd stretched out beyond the confines of the table. 'I have a tincture of laudanum which might help with the stiffness. If you come to my rooms at the Broadway, I should be glad to prescribe it.'

I thanked him. 'Do you make the laudanum yourself?'

'I do.' He looked surprised by the question.

'I ask because I wondered if there was anywhere a man might purchase opium in town?'

'There is a den down in the Lascar quarter. Near the Upper Watergate. People call it the Red House. If you intend on going there for recreational purposes, then I feel duty bound to try to dissuade you. The poppy drug is a cruel mistress. She makes slaves of her suitors. A sea captain I know was consumed by the stuff.'

'I have no wish to try it myself. It's possible Mr Archer was a customer.'

'You surprise me. Normally I can tell when I meet a man if he is an opium eater. I recognized none of the signs.' He examined me curiously. 'Is it Archer's murder that brings you back to town?'

'Yes, there remain many unanswered questions. I did not realize that you had met him when he was alive?'

'We dined together once, and spent an enjoyable evening arguing about slavery. I knew him then as Valentine, of course. Deptford is not overburdened with cultured company, and I tend to seek out interesting visitors to town. I met him again when I treated him. He'd had a spot of trouble down at the dock.'

'This would be the fight Child told me about?'

'He mentioned it, did he?' Brabazon looked faintly surprised. 'Poor Mr Archer was quite a mess. I patched him up.'

'I had not realized he was badly hurt.'

'A couple of cracked ribs and some bruising. His assailant wore a fistful of rings and they'd made a mess of his face. Had Mr Child not stepped in when he did, it could have been worse. I advised bedrest, and Archer duly returned to London. I was surprised when he came back. Your friend was nothing if not headstrong, Captain Corsham.'

Anger coursed through me. A bloody nose, Child had said. Damned liar. I was convinced this was the attempt on his life that Tad had told Amelia about.

'Do you know the name of the man who attacked him?'

Brabazon took a sip of wine and refilled his glass before answering. 'I don't believe I ever learned his name.'

Mrs Grimshaw approached our table, and placed a platter of anchovies in front of me, as well as a bowl of bread and a glass of yellow wine. Brabazon took advantage of the interruption to change the subject.

'How long were you in America?'

'Six years, until Saratoga. I left Oxford to enlist.'

'What made you sign up?'

I smiled. 'The usual. A woman.'

Brabazon gave a grimace of understanding. 'Your story mirrors my own tale, as it happens. I was training to be a physician in Glasgow, until I fell under Eve's spell. I lost my head and dropped out of my studies. In my case, the refuge was slaving.'

'You've never thought about completing your degree? There is a lot of call for Scottish physicians in London society these days.'

'The money in slaving is better. I hope soon to acquire a vessel of my own.' Brabazon raised his glass.

I had little desire to toast his good fortune, but I was not there for my own pleasure. I murmured the usual platitudes and drank the vinegary wine.

'I have been thinking about Mr Archer's injuries,' I said. 'The tortures he endured. Mr Child presumes they were inflicted to punish him for his views on slavery, but I wonder if he is correct. The whip, I accept, is commonly used to punish slaves, but isn't the brand simply a mark of ownership?'

'I believe it is occasionally used as a punishment too. On the plantations, rather than the slave ships.'

'How about the thumbscrew? Have you ever applied it as a punishment?'

He looked offended. 'Only ever for information – and only then when lives were at stake. I am not a monster, sir.'

'I only wonder if the thumbscrew was used on Archer for its traditional purpose?'

'To force information out of him? What might the killer have wanted to know?'

I judged there was no harm in telling him about the letters. 'Someone was sending Archer letters demanding that he stop asking questions in Deptford. Perhaps the murderer wanted to find out how much he'd learned?'

'That he was asking questions, I can attest. He paid sailors money to tell him about the conditions aboard the Guineamen. What he wanted most of all was stories about the mistreatment of slaves. He spoke to some of the Negroes up in the Broadway too. It caused quite a stir.'

I thought of the master's journal and the skulls. Had Tad's questions related to one particular ship and one particular voyage? Was that why the sailor had taken such exception?

'Can you remember anything else Archer said about his business here in town? Did he have dealings with any women, do you know?'

Brabazon was stripping the flesh from the bones of his fish with surgical precision. 'I don't recall him mentioning a woman. We talked mainly in the abstract – about philosophical matters. Aquinas on slavery, that sort of thing.'

'Did you come to any conclusions?'

'Only that old Aquinas liked to have his cake and eat it.' He smiled. 'How does Mr Child feel about you being back in town?'

'Not overjoyed. What he lacked in encouragement, he made up for in blunt advice.'

'I can imagine.' Brabazon's lips twitched. 'Child might be forthright in his opinions, but he keeps the more villainous elements of the town in check. The merchants like him because he has greatly reduced thievery at the docks.'

'He certainly seems to have the blessing of the mayor.'

'He wouldn't last long in Deptford if he did not. Lucius Stokes owns half the town.'

'Is he popular? Stokes, that is?'

'I would say rather that he is respected. People say he has close connections in Whitehall and with the West India lobby. The new West India dock will be a test of his powers in that regard. There is strong competition from Wapping, but Stokes is confident that he can convince the ministry to build the dock right here in Deptford.' He raised his eyebrows. 'As for Mr Child, he has to tread a careful line between the Broadway merchants and the men of the Strand – and between the town and the Navy Yard. Every time something goes missing from the Yard, the Admiralty are quick to point the finger at Deptford.'

'Being magistrate here sounds a thankless task.'

Brabazon gave an odd little smile. 'It has its compensations, I am sure.'

I would have liked to ask more, but the dining room door swung open and a young man in a horsehair wig strode into the room. He had a thin, handsome face and soft green eyes that were bright with agitation. I recognized him as the lad who had shown me to Child's table the other day. He gave me a distracted nod and addressed the surgeon. 'He is asking for you, sir. Will you come?'

Brabazon was already rising from his chair. 'My patient,' he explained. 'The boy with the broken leg. Mrs Grimshaw and her son are looking after him. I am sorry to break up our conversation, Captain. Perhaps we can resume it another time?'

I said I would be glad to, we bowed, and they departed. As I finished my dinner, I reflected upon our conversation. Had it not been for my purpose and his slaving, I'd have enjoyed

Brabazon's affable, intelligent company. Yet I had detected reticence when I'd asked him about Tad's assailant at the dock.

A surgeon who applied thumbscrews. It was a perfect Deptford paradox. And a salutary reminder: trust no one.

Chapter Fourteen

THE DOCKSIDE SLUMS were a disconcerting prospect after dark. A maze of narrow alleys leached down to the river, jostling with brothels and ginshops and tumbledown lodgings. Attic storeys pressed in overhead, blocking out the night sky, echoing to the sounds of Deptford life. Men talking and laughing in voices ragged with drink. Lovers pitching battle, or making congress without a care. Somewhere up above an Irishman sang of home, and a woman screamed at the Papist bastard to be quiet.

As Child had warned, my uniform soon attracted the attention of some of the town's rougher elements. Syphilitic whores tried to waylay me, while other eyes watched me from the shadows. I was followed for a time by a pair of heavy-footed rogues, until I paused to give them an eyeful of my sword and pistol. They slunk away, but I remained vigilant of every rustle and flitting shadow in the darkness.

I was looking for a tavern where slaving men might drink, and I found one near the quays which looked a suitable proposition. It was named the Blackamoor's Head, and the inn sign depicted an African boy with a slave-collar around his neck.

In the taproom, I was greeted by an eye-watering blast of sweat and cheap West Indian tobacco. The place was packed with hard-faced, hard-drinking men and their whores. Their voices held the dialect distinctive to Lewisham and Deptford: a rough blend of the Cockaigne of East London and the broad Kentish dialect. Occasionally I heard other languages too: Dutch and Portuguese, perhaps Russian. I could see no one who matched the few descriptive details of Tad's assailant that I had gleaned from Child and Brabazon.

I elbowed my way through to the bar. 'We've rum and we've beer, friend,' the tapman greeted me. 'Which will kill you first?'

His wiry, ill-fitting wig had raised a rash of pimples across his forehead. A navy service medal was pinned to his yellow waistcoat. I asked for a beer and he filled a greasy-looking pot with a thick, yeasty mixture from his jug.

'You looking for company, friend? The fragrant kind?'

'A game of dice, actually.'

He eyed me like a fattened calf. 'Dice we can do. I know some coves who'll give you a game.'

'Oh, I already know the man I want to play with. A friend told me he ran the best game in town. He gave me a description, but I've had no luck finding him yet.'

'Perhaps I might know him? Give me a try.'

'He's a slave ship sailor, a big man, wears a fistful of rings. The other month when my friend was in town, he had a nasty bite on his hand.'

The tapman scratched the coarse tuft of hair at the neck of his shirt, and I was convinced I saw a louse scuttle across it. 'You sure you don't want to play with these coves of mine?'

'I only ever play by recommendation. When I'm betting with gold, I never want to risk cogged dice. No offence to your friends.'

'None taken.' I could tell the tapman liked the sound of my gold, and I presumed that like most tavern keepers he would expect a cut of any game. Still, he hesitated.

I opened my purse to pay for my drink, making sure he got

a good look at the gold it contained. It proved sufficient enticement.

'The man you're looking for – he sounds a lot like Frank Drake.'

I smiled. 'There's a name it would be hard to forget.'

'He claims he's a descendant, though it's probably horseshit. Drake was bitten by some vermin down here a month or so back. When I say vermin, I mean the human kind. He's the man you're looking for, I'm sure.'

'Do you know where I might find him?'

The tapman came out from behind his bar and walked to one of the tables, where a trio of men sat smoking long, Dutch-handled pipes. He whispered a few words to them and with a glance at me, they vacated the table. The tapman patted it and smiled.

'You just sit right here, friend. I'll fetch Drake.'

*

I knew it was Drake the moment he walked into the tavern. He had the height and solidity of a wall, and a path opened up before him as he swaggered through the crowded taproom. Once he must have been remarkably handsome, but his broad, brick face was bloated from too much ale and he was starting to lose his long flaxen hair. His turquoise coat was embroidered with gold thread, and his boots looked like Italian leather. Each ham fist glittered with a row of rings.

The tapman indicated me with a nod, and Drake approached my table, flashing white teeth.

'Frank Drake.' He held out his hand. 'I'll singe any beards you ask, only don't come looking to me for a game of bowls.'

It had the ring of a line he'd used many times before. I smiled dutifully. 'Just dice, Mr Drake.'

His accent was local, and his handshake firm to the point of discomfort. I'd wondered if he would inquire further into my mythical friend with whom he'd once diced, and I had a few vague replies prepared. In the event, I didn't need them, for Drake seemed anxious to get down to the business of emptying my purse.

He'd brought a couple of other players with him, presumably men he'd been dicing with in whatever tavern the tapman had dragged him from. One was lean and dark with a crude tattoo of a naked woman on his bulging forearm. Like Drake, he wore his own hair long. I presumed there was little call for wigs aboard a Guineaman. The other was a fat fellow in merchant's garb with a florid complexion and a cavalier's blonde moustache. His accent was Flemish and largely impenetrable.

We played hazard, my father's game, and I used him for inspiration, adopting the role of a gentleman who thought he played dice rather better than he did. At first they let me win. Almost every time I called the main, my throw was good and soon I had accumulated a little stack of half-guineas in front of me. The tapman was a frequent visitor to our table, his rum and ale flowing freely.

I told them I was in town on business, and everyone toasted the health of my investments. Drake, I learned, was awaiting his next slaving voyage, but his ship had been delayed in port. Isaac, the man with the tattoo, had lately returned from a stint aboard a man-o'-war in the North Atlantic, harassing French ships under Letters of Marque. The Dutchman told me he had been in port only two days, and I guessed they were playing him for a chub as much as I. Drake held court as we played, making jokes about his bad luck, and sharing his opinions on a variety of topics, from women to horseracing to the perfidy of the Navy

Yard, who had impressed a dozen drunkards in one of the taverns last night.

'Poor bastards will wake up with a sore head to find they're scudding across the Solent. I'm a patriot, Captain, but that ain't right.'

We had been playing for about an hour, and the dice had started to turn against me. To mix a metaphor, it was time to shake the tree, before I lost my shirt.

'Did you hear about that dead abolitionist they found down at the dock?' I said. 'Someone hung him up and cut his throat.'

'We heard.' Isaac grinned. 'Tortured him too. Must have died howling.'

I drank deeply from my pot to disguise my anger. 'I can't abide abolitionists,' I said, once I'd recovered my equanimity. 'Might as well hand over the keys of the Bank of England to the French. As for whoever killed him, now there's a man I'd like to buy a drink.'

'Aye,' Isaac said. 'Wouldn't we all.'

'I heard it wasn't the first time they'd crossed swords,' I went on blithely. 'They say the killer had a run-in with the dead man down here at the dock a month or so back. Our fellow would have ended it then and there, but there were too many witnesses around. So he came back later to finish the job he'd started.'

Drake had cast the dice, but he didn't watch them fall. He was looking at me and the bonhomie had drained from his bright blue eyes. 'I'd check your facts before you start spreading rumours, Captain. The fellow at the dock wasn't the man who killed him.'

'Are you certain?' I said, as though oblivious to his change of mood. 'The man who told me seemed very sure.'

'Aye, I'm certain. I was there.'

Isaac grinned and mimed a boxer's punches into the air. Then he raised his pot to drink Drake's health.

'That was you?' I cried, all astonishment.

'Aye, and I know I didn't kill him, because at the time he met his maker, I was at the bathhouse. Cock-deep in nigger cunny from dusk 'til dawn.' He gave me a hard stare. 'So watch what you say.'

'My mistake,' I said cheerfully. 'What started things between you, anyway?'

'He asked too many questions. Now cast the damned dice.'

Asking questions. The same charge levelled at Tad by the author of the anonymous letters.

We played a little more, and some of our old cheerfulness returned. The dice were plainly cogged, and they fell in such a way as to entice the Dutchman into making several large and risky bets. Soon he was down a good ten guineas. I played more cautiously, much to the frustration of Isaac and Drake.

'Of course,' I said, a little later, 'we all know why that abolitionist really came to town.'

'Handing out pamphlets,' Isaac said. 'The sort you use to wipe your arse.'

'I heard there was more to it. He was here because of the slaves who died on board that ship.'

A silence descended, broken only by the Dutchman muttering about his luck.

'What slaves?' Drake's tone was underscored with menace.

'Over three hundred of them. It must have been quite a voyage, wouldn't you say? Does anybody know the full story? How did they die?'

Drake's fist crashed onto the table, making the dice and the Dutchman jump. 'What the devil?'

'Come on, Drake.' Isaac gave my stack of gold a pointed

glance. 'He's only repeating what he heard. He means no harm.' He smiled at me reassuringly.

'Certainly I meant no offence,' I said. 'They were only slaves, right? No one will miss them.'

'Only the cotton fields.' Isaac placed his index finger on the edge of his pot, gave it a flick with his other hand, and the finger plopped into his ale. He repeated this curious gesture several times, and I was given to understand that it was another of his mimes.

'Thirsty work, eh, Drake?' He winked.

'Shut your mouth. Both of you.' Drake scraped back his chair. 'This game's over.'

Isaac didn't like that. They'd hardly begun to recoup the money they'd let me win. 'Christ, Drake. It's not even eleven o'clock.'

'I said it's over.' Drake swept his money into his palm, and strode from the tavern. Isaac followed, frowning. I exchanged a bemused glance with the Dutchman and pocketed my winnings. The tapman looked dismayed and offered to find me more players. I declined, and once I'd finished my pot, I too left the tavern.

Drake hadn't liked me talking about his fight with Tad, but he'd liked me talking about the dead slaves even less. I suspected he had been one of the sailors on board that ship. Tad must have questioned Drake about it, and Drake had beaten him senseless. I believed him more than capable of torture and murder. I would pay a visit to the bathhouse tomorrow night, to see if his alibi withstood scrutiny as Child claimed.

Yet Drake, a slave ship sailor, would hardly count as a powerful enemy. If he had murdered Tad, perhaps he had been acting upon instruction? Were the deaths of those slaves somehow behind Tad's conviction that he could end slavery? Everything he'd said to Amelia suggested this was much more than a local Deptford quarrel.

As the noise of the taproom receded, I was conscious of the quiet of the dockside alleys. The air still held the warmth of the day, and the smells were no less pungent for the dark. The cobbles were slippery with seaweed and rats scuttled in the shadows. I heard a noise behind me – a scrape of boot against stone? – and I turned, drawing my pistol.

'Who's there?' I waited, head cocked, aware that Drake and Isaac might consider me unfinished business. I heard nothing more, and after a moment I walked on, thinking about the curious mime Isaac had performed. His finger dropping into the ale again and again. Could the crew have drowned the slaves? Drake's reaction suggested foul play, and yet I struggled to find any plausible reason why the crew would destroy their own cargo.

I was still puzzling this mystery, when two dark figures stepped out at the end of the alley to block my path. One lean and lithe. One built like a wall. Knives flashing in their hands. Isaac and Drake.

Drake saw my flintlock pistol, and gave a warning shout. Isaac either misunderstood, or thought he could reach me before I could get off a shot. If the latter, he was wrong. As he came at me, I brought my pistol up and fired. A burst of white light, the sear of burned powder, and a crack resonated through the alleys. Isaac clutched his chest, and gave an astonished laugh. Then he dropped to the ground.

Seeing I had no time to reload, Drake charged me like a bull. We went down, and I landed awkwardly, my bad leg folded beneath me. The pain brought flashes to my eyes. Nevertheless, I managed to get in a couple of good blows to Drake's skull – until he put his knife against my throat.

He dragged me up, taking my sword from its scabbard, and throwing it down the alley, along with my pistol. 'Who sent you here?' Drake breathed the sickly odour of rum into my face. 'What do you know about that voyage? Damn you, speak.'

I knew he was going to kill me, whatever I said. I'd seen that cold, determined look in men's eyes before. I tensed myself to make a move: a knee to the groin, a grab for the knife-hand. If he didn't slice my jugular vein first.

'Speak, soldier boy, or I'll cut your pretty face. Who sent you here asking about that ship?'

A new voice spoke out of the darkness: 'There'll be no cutting tonight.'

Drake whirled round. Peregrine Child stood behind him, his staff of office in one hand, a pistol in the other. 'You heard what I said, Frank. Put your knitting needle away before someone gets hurt.'

Drake scowled. 'This ain't your business, Perry.'

'I say it is. Now do as I say. We're good friends, you and I. Let's keep it that way.'

'He killed Isaac.'

I looked down at the man I'd shot. A black stain was spreading across his shirtfront.

'It was self-defence,' I said. 'These men attacked me.'

'It seems to me,' Child said, 'that you're all square now. No need for any more quarrelling. Or for this business to end up in my courtroom. Am I right?'

I could have insisted Child arrest Drake, but I didn't have much confidence in Deptford justice. Isaac's death also complicated matters. I had no wish to see my name in the newspapers accused of shooting a man dead, however mitigating the circumstances.

'You'll hear no argument from me,' I said.

I could see Drake didn't like it, but he returned his knife to his pocket and stepped away.

'Good,' Child said. 'Think you can take old Isaac out for a swim, Frank, while I walk Captain Corsham back to his lodgings?'

Drake gave me a look, pregnant with promise. 'I can do that.'

'With a bit of luck the tide will take him down to Greenwich. Let Isaac be their problem, eh, not ours?'

Drake grunted unhappily, and crouched down next to Isaac. He started going through his friend's purse and clothes, pocketing whatever he found. Child looked away, whistling a tune. I groped around in the dark until I found my sword and pistol. Then Child and I walked up towards the Green.

'Were you following me, Mr Child?' I asked.

'I told you to watch your step in these alleys, Captain Corsham. No more games of dice, that's my advice.'

'They attacked me because I asked Drake about Archer's murder. If he is the best example of an innocent party that Deptford has to offer, I'd hate to meet one of your guilty men.'

'I told you, Drake's alibi is sound.'

'You also told me he merely gave Archer a bloody nose. That was a pack of lies as well.'

We walked the rest of the way in uncompanionable silence. When we reached the Noah's Ark, Child put his staff across the door to arrest my progress.

'Go home,' he said. 'There's no profit for you here. Don't think I'll always be around to play your wet nurse.'

'If you'd only do your job, I'd happily go.'

He muttered an oath beneath his breath – I only caught the words 'London' and 'fuckster'. 'On your own head be it,' he said, as he walked away.

Chapter Fifteen

Drums rolled and muskets crackled. A thousand scarlet coats filled the field of my vision. Officers shouted panicked orders, my own voice among them, until a great roar of artillery cannon drowned out all other sound. An explosion of earth and smoke and blood sucked everything else away. Blood mingled with saltpetre in my mouth.

I glimpsed stumbling figures in the acrid haze around me. I ordered them back into formation, but they kept walking, blood running from their ears. The cannons roared again and startled me awake.

My heart was pounding, my bedclothes soaked. I could still hear the crackle of muskets, until I realized it was the clatter of hooves on the cobbles outside. I remembered, in an awful, piercing moment of clarity, that I was in Deptford and Tad was dead.

I went to the washstand and splashed water on my face. My leg was a torment after my encounter with Drake in the alleys last night, and I limped to the window, gazing out over the stable-yard towards the quays. I had such dreams less often these days, but they still had the power to chill my soul to ice. My thoughts turned to the poor boys who would soon be boarding the merchantmen moored in the Navy Yard dock. I gave little thought to Isaac, the man I had killed last night.

Better men than he had died at my hands on the battlefield – and with less justification.

The stable boy was shovelling straw in the yard below, and a large black dog lay sleeping in the sun. A gentleman in a black coat walked across the yard, and I recognized James Brabazon, presumably back to see his patient. The surgeon climbed the steps at the side of the stable, which led up to a living loft above it. His knock was answered by the same young man who'd approached our table last night. I presumed this was Nathaniel Grimshaw, my landlady's son. He and the surgeon went inside, and Nathaniel reappeared a few moments later. He ran downstairs, pausing in the yard to pet the dog, and went into the stables. I dressed swiftly and went down to find him.

The stable-yard was ringed with outbuildings and smelled of manure. A stone passage – wide enough for a carriage to pass through – gave access directly onto the Green. The black dog raised its head to watch me as I passed. I found Nathaniel in Zephyrus's stall, brushing down his silver flanks. I gauged the lad at about seventeen years old. He was in his shirtsleeves, well built and muscular for his age. Zephyrus gave a whinny of recognition when he saw me, and Nathaniel glanced up and smiled.

'Nathaniel Grimshaw? Captain Corsham. I'm staying at the inn.'

He bowed. 'My mother told me. Are you in town on business, sir?'

'In a manner of speaking. I was a friend of the man you found murdered at the dock. I am trying to find out more about what happened to him.'

He regarded me warily with his soft green eyes. 'Mr Valentine was a friend of yours, sir?'

'Mr Archer was his real name. Yes, he was.'

'He told me his name was Valentine.' He seemed resentful.

'I think he had good reason for wanting to keep his real name a secret. Do you mind if I ask you some questions about his time in Deptford?'

'I already told Mr Child everything I know.'

'I'd like to hear it from you. I'll give you a shilling for your time.'

That got his attention. 'I'll talk to you, sir. Got nothing to hide.'

'Mr Child tells me that it was you who found his body?'

'That's right.' He kept the brush moving as he talked. 'I keep watch most nights over some warehouses at the Public Dock, patrol them every two hours between midnight and six. I was having a pipe after my four o'clock round when I saw him hanging there.'

'You didn't see anyone else?'

'It was quiet. Some fishermen came later, but whoever killed him was long gone.'

'It must have been quite an ordeal.'

'I've seen worse.' His voice was strained, and I could tell it was false bravado. 'A lot of people in town think he had it coming.'

'Do you?'

'Don't know. No. Not really.'

'Your mother said he had stayed at the inn before?'

'Three times including the last. The first was about eight weeks ago. The second four or five weeks after that. He stayed for a few days each time. Except the last – that was only two nights.' Nathaniel draped a blanket over Zephyrus and filled a trough with oats from a sack.

'Do you remember when he was hurt? He had cracked ribs and a cut face.'

'Aye, sir, that was the second time. Mr Child brought him back here and sent me to fetch Mr Brabazon.'

'He was attacked down at the dock by a sailor named Frank Drake.'

The wariness returned. 'I don't know nothing about that, sir.'

'Do you know Drake?'

His eyes slid away. 'A little. He was a friend of my da's. They crewed together.' The boy frowned. 'I just remembered something. Mr Archer asked me a lot of questions once. Wanted to know if I'd seen who'd left a letter for him here.'

I noted the swift change of subject – I guessed Drake had that effect on people – but I decided to go along with it anyway.

'Did you see who left this letter?'

'No. Nor did ma.'

'When was this? Which time?'

He thought for a moment. 'The second again – before he got hurt.'

I wondered if it was one of the threatening letters – and if Drake had been its author.

'Did Archer have any visitors? Can you remember where he went or who he saw?'

'He was out a lot of the time. I don't remember any visitors, except for Mr Brabazon and Mr Child.'

'No women?' I said, thinking again of Tad's dark angel, and the lady in the black lace veil at his funeral.

He gave me a curious glance. 'No, sir. Once I saw him heading off east, Greenwich way. People say he was causing trouble with the Negroes in the Broadway, but I never saw it myself.'

'Your mother said you run errands for people staying here at the inn. Did you run any for him?'

'Got him a hot pie once. A bottle of gin.' He smiled, his cheeks dimpling. 'Anything you need, sir, you just come and find me. Either here, or after dark at the Garraway warehouse on the Public Dock.'

'I may well do that. Right now, it's the Private Dock I need to get to. Can you show me the way? There's another shilling in it for you if you can.'

I knew the way to the dock – you could hardly miss it – but Nathaniel was loosening up a little, and I was keen to cultivate our acquaintance. Living at the inn, he must hear a lot.

His face brightened. 'Just give me a moment, sir.'

I waited while he closed up the stable and put on a blue coat with brass buttons. 'Come on, Jago,' he called. The dog came running as we walked out onto the Green.

A man with a yellow parrot on his arm was standing outside the Noah's Ark, taking coins from passers-by to make it talk. 'God save the King,' it squawked. 'George Washington is a whoreson.'

'I'd like a bird that talks,' Nathaniel said. 'I wonder where it's from?'

'The Americas, I should think. Perhaps Brazil.'

'Da went to Brazil once. He fell in with some Portuguese who were an officer short in Elmina. In Rio they passed off a cargo of black gristle as prime African rump. Da's share was nearly two hundred pounds.'

'An enterprising man,' I said, in as neutral a tone as I could muster.

'Aye, sir, he was.' Nathaniel's voice caught on the words. I remembered Mrs Grimshaw's widow's weeds, and guessed his father had died recently.

We were walking the same way I'd walked with Child the day before, following the high wall of the Private Dock. Weary fishermen and whores were trudging home after their night's catch, while coal-heavers and stevedores were just embarking upon the day's business. On the other side of the street, the taverns were already busy, and I wondered if they ever closed their doors.

'Were you present when Mr Child cleared Archer's room after the murder?'

'I let them in, but Mr Child asked me to wait outside.'

'Child wasn't alone?'

'He had Mayor Stokes's Negro with him. The one who dresses like a swell.'

'His secretary, Scipio?'

'That's him.'

'When was this?'

'The morning we found your friend. I took the body up to Brabazon's on a cart I borrowed. When I came back to the Ark, Mr Child and the Negro was already there.'

Stokes and Child had moved fast, I thought, for two men who were so ambivalent about finding the killer. I wondered if they'd been looking for something in particular? The same thing as the man who'd searched Tad's rooms? The thing Tad came to Deptford to collect?

Jago was sniffing around a chicken bone, and Nathaniel called him to heel. 'Were you in America, Captain Corsham?'

'For a time, until I broke my leg.'

'My friend Danny's got a broken leg. Brabazon says he might lose it.'

'He told me. At least your friend is in good hands.'

'Aye, sir, the best.' There was an edge to his voice that surprised me. He kicked a stone and it spun along the street. 'I'm going to be seeing the world myself, sir, before too long. Slaving, not soldiering. Got a place on my da's old ship. An officer's post.'

I detected no great enthusiasm in his tone. Little wonder. I'd read that one in three slave ship sailors died at sea. It saddened me to think of this impressionable young man dragged down by slavery, becoming a brute like Frank Drake. 'Child tells me jobs in the trade are hard to come by.'

'Not if you know the right people,' he said, with a bit more swagger.

We walked a little further, him chattering away, and I steered the conversation back to our previous topic. I was wondering if Scipio would be willing to talk to me. I had discerned no great affection for his master on his part.

'Tell me, is Scipio a slave?'

'No, he's free. There's not many free Negroes in Deptford. They're too afraid someone will slip a draught in their drink, and they'll wake up in a slave-hold Atlantic-bound.'

'Is Scipio not afraid?'

'He works for the mayor. No one will touch him.' Nathaniel frowned. 'My da always said a nigger had no more business learning to read than old Jago here, but Mr Valentine – sorry, Mr Archer – he said blacks were as fitted to learn as you or I.'

He was looking at me to see what I thought. 'Mr Archer wasn't wrong. I met a black gentleman only yesterday who had written a book.'

He grinned. 'Da would spin in his grave.'

We had reached the gates of the Private Dock, and Nathaniel gestured to the guards. 'They'll touch you for some silver, sir, but don't be bilked. No more than a shilling. Even that's highway robbery.'

I tossed him the coins I'd promised him, and he caught them deftly.

'Remember, come find me at the inn, sir, if there's anything else you need. Or come by the warehouse later after dark. It can be lonely work, keeping watch all night long. I like the company.'

Pleased to have made an ally in Deptford, I said I might. He offered me a military salute and walked off whistling.

Chapter Sixteen

The Private Dockyard contained perhaps a hundred warehouses, as well as wet and dry docks, slipways and repair yards. The roads between the warehouses were strangely quiet, and before too long I discovered the reason for it. I rounded a corner, following the gate guard's directions, and saw a large crowd of working men gathered outside one of the warehouses, their attention fixed upon some spectacle. From the feverish expressions on their faces, and the flinching and wincing, I guessed it was a cockfight or a boxing match. I pushed my way through the crowd to discover that I was wrong.

A half-naked man was pinned down over a barrel by two stevedores, his back a criss-cross of bloody stripes. A fourth man in his shirtsleeves stood behind them, holding a bullwhip. He flicked it into the air, and the crack as he brought it down reverberated around the wooden warehouses. A sickly miasma of blood rose into the air, and his victim spasmed and groaned.

I asked the man nearest me what the fellow had done to merit such a punishment.

'Who knows?' The man's jaw worked a wad of tobacco. 'Blasphemed while he laboured. Diced on the Sabbath. Don't take much to make you a sinner in John Monday's eyes.'

Monday was the merchant I sought, and I studied the man holding the whip with interest. He was about fifty years of age, I judged, tall and broad as a barn door. His shirt was plastered with sweat to his muscular torso. He wore no wig and his shaven head, baked a dark mahogany by years of exposure to foreign suns, shone with perspiration like a conker. He raised his arm, and the lash came down again.

'Mercy,' cried the man over the barrel.

I could see no mercy in Monday's deep-set eyes. The flogging seemed to last an age. Finally, he stood back panting, and threw the whip to one of the men who'd held his victim down. 'Get him cleaned up.'

The crowd murmured their disappointment at the curtailment of the spectacle and began to drift away. Some of them filed into the warehouse behind us. Monday took a towel from the top of a shipping crate and dried his hands.

'Mr Monday?' I stepped forward.

He appraised me a moment, giving me the opportunity to look more fully upon his face. His brown skin was riven with cracks and crevices, like an old piece of wood much scoured by the elements. The two deepest lines framed an aquiline nose and nearly touched the corners of his taut, unsmiling mouth.

'You have the advantage of me, sir.' His voice held enough of the local dialect to suggest he was not a gentleman born.

I handed him my card, introduced myself and bowed. Monday only waited for me to state my business.

'I'm looking for a suitable venture in which to place an inheritance. Someone said you might be looking for investors.'

I had decided to conceal my true purpose, not least because Tad's connection to Monday and his company was so unclear. Despite Child's belief that the killer wouldn't implicate himself by using his master's brand, I thought it possible that the man I sought was a member of Monday's crew. Perhaps Frank Drake, perhaps another man. In London a gentleman might expect a merchant to assist him if one of his workers was suspected of a crime, but as Child was fond of reminding me, this wasn't London. It had also occurred to me that Monday might be the slave merchant Tad stood accused of harassing. It was even possible he was involved in Tad's murder himself.

Monday examined my card. 'War Office, eh? Serve any time in the Colonies?'

'Several years, until I was injured at Saratoga.'

'Then I'm glad to know you, Captain. War can be a wretched business, but a necessary one too. Much like slavery. How much are you looking to invest?'

I plucked a substantial figure from the air. 'A thousand pounds.'

Monday threw the towel onto the shipping crate and retrieved a mustard-yellow coat and a silver periwig lying next to it. He put them on and extended a hand for me to shake.

'I'm currently putting together a syndicate for my next voyage. Seven hundred would be enough to buy you in. I can tell you more about it, if you'd care to come inside.'

I glanced at the barrel as we passed, brown with the flogged man's blood. Monday seemed to sense my disapproval. 'Our ways might seem a little coarse to you, Captain, but the man socked a pouch of tobacco from one of my crates. I won't have anyone stealing from me or my investors.'

Inside the warehouse it was cool and dark. Men clambered over stacks of shipping crates, or heaved them along the aisles. Others were attaching ropes and lifting them by means of hoists and pulleys into the eaves. The only light came from a row of small windows near the roof. Dust motes danced in the sunbeams like Danaë's golden rain.

'How much do you know about the Atlantic Trade, Captain Corsham?'

'Only a little.' Not quite true, but I wanted to find out more about his business.

Monday led me down one of the aisles, calling to a man to fetch him a crowbar. I watched as he levered a crate open. Inside were bulging canvas sacks and Monday slit one open with a knife from his belt. He gestured me forward to inspect the contents. Glass beads. Thousands of them. At his invitation, I lifted a handful, letting the tiny coloured spheres slip through my fingers.

'The Negro princes like them,' Monday explained. 'Five hundred beads buys one African prisoner. They like rum and tobacco too. Also guns. Give them guns and the slave tribes can capture more prisoners from rival tribes. Those tribes in turn, seeking to defend themselves, come looking to us for guns of their own. The only currency we accept is slaves, which is how we have spread the trade up and down the Guinea coast. It holds a pleasing symmetry, don't you think?'

I could think of other words for it, most of them unrepeatable, but I murmured a few polite sentiments nonetheless.

'The next stage of the voyage is the Middle Passage across the Atlantic.' We moved deeper into the warehouse. 'Are you a religious man, sir?'

'I try to be.'

'Then be content that this investment is the Lord's work. The blacks lead an immoral existence in Africa. They practise polygamy, in thrall to pagan gods. They have never known the solace of the Testament.'

'You give them that solace?'

'It is a privilege of my position. I have my captains hold prayers on deck after the Negroes have taken their exercise. They read to them from scripture and then they sing a psalm. Sometimes it takes a little while to warm them up, but they embrace the Lord eventually. Picture a sea of black faces, out there on the ocean, their eyes uplifted to the heavens. It is quite a sight.'

I had already heard quite enough of The Gospel According to John Monday. 'In which parts of the Caribbean do you sell your slaves?'

'We usually aim for Jamaica, sometimes the Windward Isles, sometimes Bermuda. There we exchange the slaves for goods destined for the European markets.'

He ordered more crates opened and showed me samples of the various commodities to be found inside. 'Bermudan tobacco. Jamaican coffee beans. Barbadian sugar – white gold. If you come up to my office, I can show you the expected returns.'

I followed him up a flight of wooden stairs to a little room that overlooked the warehouse floor. It was furnished with a desk, a stove, a cabinet for files and two chairs. A large crucifix hung on the wall, next to a map of the Atlantic Ocean. Monday paused to plot the stages of the voyage on this map, drawing a triangle with his finger. 'From Deptford to the slave coasts, the Middle Passage across the Atlantic, then home with a hold full of profit.'

He retrieved some papers from the cabinet, and took them to his desk to show me.

'Seven hundred pounds will buy you a ten per cent stake in my next voyage. The profit is hard to predict with any certainty, but my investors usually see returns of between twenty and twenty-five per cent, sometimes much more.'

It was a very good rate of return – much better than that offered by any of my genuine investments. 'Are the profits divided equally between the syndicate?'

'Each of the seven members will see ten per cent. I take twenty, the captain five. The surgeon takes three per cent and the remaining two is divided between the other officers. Because they take a share of the profit, they have a greater interest in the success of the voyage.'

'How many ships do you own?'

'Five Guineamen, each commissioned for the African trade. Ordinary merchant vessels never compare. My ships are fitted out with racks to hold the slaves, which means we can fill the hold to maximum capacity. The racks are removable, so that when we reach the Caribbean, the hold can be filled as normal.'

Even thinking about it made my skin crawl. 'How many slaves do you intend to buy?'

'*The Phoenix* holds four hundred and fifty, give or take. Some merchants pack them in wherever they will fit, but it's a false economy. Too many die on board, and some get damaged. It's also miserable for the blacks and I won't tolerate cruelty on my vessels. I don't skimp on food either. The blacks are given fresh meat, as well as vegetables every day. It means my costs are higher than some of my competitors, but most slave merchants lose seven per cent of their cargo, some as much as fifteen. I lose between three and five.' He showed me another table of figures. 'I get better prices for them too. Do you have a dog? You know how the meat brings out the shine in the fur? Same principle.'

I thought of the skulls in the master's journal. 'You say you lose three to five per cent of your slaves. Never more?'

A spark of emotion seemed to light his muddy brown eyes. Then he turned back to his figures and I wondered if I'd imagined it. 'Slavery is a risky business, sir, which is why the profits are so high. I can't control the weather, any more than I can account for the French. Then there's insurrection – the Negro is a dangerous beast, never more so than when he's caged. Yet my insurance covers most eventualities. I've never lost money for an investor yet. Perhaps you'd like to come and see my ships?'

The road that led down to the dock was busy with carts pulled by teams of oxen and shire horses. One was stationary on the verge and customs men were making an inspection.

Before us stretched Deptford Reach, wide and brown and jostling with wherries, hoys, barges, merchantmen, pleasure craft, sculls and dredgers. A team of men were hauling a frigate down a slipway to the wet dock, under the watchful eye of an engineer. We passed close to the mast pond, where Baltic timbers were pickling in seawater, and little oakum boys danced with death by leaping across them. In the dry docks more ships were undergoing repairs, crawling with carpenters and pitch-men. Looming over them all, the Indiamen and the Guineamen, anchored out on the water in stately rows, seemed like the vessels of a race of giants. In the distance, on one of the quays, a small crowd of well-dressed gentlemen were looking out at the river.

Monday followed my gaze. 'Our mayor, Mr Stokes, is showing a delegation from Parliament around town. We hope they will decide to build the new West India dock right here in Deptford.'

'I hope the murder doesn't put them off,' I said.

Monday's head whipped round. 'The murder?'

'That dead abolitionist they found at the dock a week ago. It was the talk of the taverns last night.'

He frowned. 'Such a crime should not be sport for uncouth men in their cups.'

'You don't think he deserved it? That seems to be the consensus here in town.'

His lips pressed fleetingly together. 'No man deserves to die that way. He was mistaken in his views, but he was a man of God. That was my impression, at least.'

'You met him?'

'Yes, I did.'

I waited for him to go on, but he gestured with his arm at a row of Guineamen moored in the dock. 'Those end two are mine. That one there is *The Phoenix*. You see the sun on her hull? That's copper sheeting. It protects the wood from worm.'

I wasn't looking at *The Phoenix*. Neither was I listening anymore. I was gazing at the other ship Monday had indicated. The vessel had three masts with furled sails and a bowspit to the rear. Her figurehead was a woman, and her carved, wooden face possessed a severe, restless beauty. She was painted black and her wings were tipped with silver. When the ship was riding the waves, it must look as if she was flying.

There she was. I had found her. Tad's dark angel.

Chapter Seventeen

I left John Monday with the promise that I would give his venture due consideration. He gave me his address in Deptford Broadway, and said I might call upon him if I had any further questions. No doubt I would. We bowed, and I made my way back along the dock towards the gate.

As I walked, I drew connections in my mind, just as Monday had plotted the stages of the slave voyage on his map. From the slave brand to *Atlantic Trading and Partners* to *The Dark Angel* to the master's journal and its skulls. Everything pointed to *The Dark Angel* as the vessel in question. How had those slaves died? Why did Tad think he could end slavery? How had his visits here made him powerful enemies?

Absorbed in these thoughts, I almost walked right past them. They were standing in one of the alleys that ran between the warehouses. Cinnamon and Scipio, heads bent together, talking urgently.

Cinnamon wore a stiff-bodied gown of ivory lace with a wide neckline and bared shoulders. Her glossy black ringlets were piled beneath an oval bonnet, and she held a fringed parasol in one gloved hand. She had a look of entreaty upon her face, and Scipio shook his head. He said something I didn't catch, and the girl's arm swept the air.

I walked towards them. Both looked up, and fell silent.

'Miss Cinnamon, Scipio. I am very glad to see you once again.'

Scipio returned my bow. His blue-black skin made a striking contrast to his snow-white periwig. He held a long roll of paper in his hand – I guessed a map or architectural plans. Cinnamon watched me with dark, wary eyes.

'I'd like to speak to you about *The Dark Angel*,' I addressed her. 'I need to know how and why those slaves were killed.'

Scipio moved between us. 'Return to the carriage at once, Miss Cinnamon.'

I tried to catch her eye over his shoulder, but she lowered her gaze and walked off down the alley.

Scipio's expression was thunderous, and for a moment I thought he was going to strike me. He loomed over me by several inches, and I took an instinctive step back. His frown dissolved. 'Forgive my rudeness, Captain Corsham. If Mr Stokes suspects she spoke to you, he would beat her. I would most likely get the blame, and he wouldn't hesitate to dock my wages.'

'Mr Stokes won't hear it from me,' I said.

'He would find out anyway. He has eyes and ears everywhere.'

You should know, I thought, studying him curiously. Aside from the colour of his skin, Scipio appeared every inch the poorer sort of English gentleman. His tailoring was passably fine: a dove-grey coat, linen stockings and polished shoes with brass buckles – everything starched and brushed and spruced and worn very well. High cheekbones, a long nose, and plump, intelligent eyes lent him a patrician air.

'I also have a question for you, Scipio. When you went with Mr Child to clear Archer's room at the inn, did you find anything other than the black valise?'

'You mean did we find the thing Mr Archer told his sister that he came here to collect? No, we did not.'

I produced a half-guinea from my pocket. 'You are sure?'

'Quite sure.' He eyed my coin with disdain. 'As for your bribe, I have been bought for English gold three times in my life. That was quite enough.'

I returned the coin to my pocket, feeling faintly ashamed. 'Then talk to me because you want to. Archer was killed because he came here to help your people.'

'Which people are those? You cannot mean slaves, for I am now a free man. Do you mean secretaries, perhaps? Or the Yoruba, the tribe into which I was born? Or the citizens of Deptford, where I make my home? I know you cannot mean the Negroes of the Kingdom of Dahomey, who took me from my village and sold me to the white man.'

He was trying to tell me that he was a book of many pages and I had chosen only to see the cover. 'I am sorry if I offended you. That was not my intention.'

He smiled. 'I am only teasing you, Captain Corsham. I am sorry about your friend. But I am in a difficult position. Mr Stokes wouldn't like me talking to you.'

'What does Archer's murder have to do with the mayor?'

His smile broadened. 'You are not listening, sir.'

Yet he wanted to help me. I could feel it. 'Is there anything at all you can tell me? About *The Dark Angel*? Or about the slaves Archer spoke to in Deptford Broadway?'

He sighed. 'Archer should have left the poor devils alone, the trouble it caused them.'

'What do you mean?'

He hesitated, and whatever moral question he was wrestling with, eventually decided to speak. 'Archer explained the law to them – that they could be free if they escaped to London. He told them to go to the Yorkshire Stingo in Marylebone, and people there would help them. Some of the slaves were caught talking to him and punished severely.'

'What is the Yorkshire Stingo?'

'An alehouse where Africans go to drink – I visit it myself sometimes when I'm in the city. Only one of the Deptford slaves was brave enough to risk the journey. A maidservant named Abigail. She is now in a slave-hold bound for the Guinea coast.'

'I don't understand.'

'Her owner tracked her down on the London road with dogs, and brought her back to Deptford. She was bundled aboard a Guineaman the following morning. She'll be sold in the Caribbean – if she lasts the voyage. So you see, Captain Corsham, Archer's inquiries did not only endanger himself. If you insist on pursuing this course, then I ask that you have a care for others. Miss Cinnamon in particular. Mr Stokes is a jealous master.'

'Of course I will,' I said, taking from my pocket one of the pamphlets I'd found in Tad's valise. 'Have you ever heard of these people, the Children of Liberty?'

He glanced at the pamphlet. 'No, but if they help escaped slaves, then maybe someone at the Yorkshire Stingo can tell you where to find them?'

I nodded. 'I will go there once I've exhausted my inquiries here.'

'You might find that happens sooner than you think. Deptford gives up its secrets grudgingly, like the mudflats of the Thames. It can be as treacherous too, as your friend found out to his cost. I would advise you to go home, except I don't think you'd listen.' He held up his roll of paper. 'Now I must leave you. Mr Stokes is waiting.'

We bowed, and I watched him walk off down the quay,

wondering what else he might be able to tell me if he was so minded. Why would a free African choose to work for a slave merchant, a man he plainly despised? I could only presume he didn't have much choice.

I walked back in the direction of the gate. Cormorants were spearing for fish on the river, making white streaks against the ochre water. I rounded the customs house wall, and glimpsed a woman in the distance, standing on the edge of the dock. Even fifty yards away, I recognized Cinnamon's slender figure and ivory dress. Somehow I knew that she was waiting there for me.

As I drew nearer, I saw that she was gazing at the ship in the dock, at the winged woman, the dark angel.

'I need to know about the ship,' I said, as our shadows merged together. 'I need to know how the slaves died and their significance to Mr Archer.'

She glanced at me. 'They did not die. They were murdered.'

I studied her profile, the slight upturn of her nose; her sooty black lashes against her honeyed skin. 'How were they murdered?'

She turned to the river. 'Why do you come here?'

'To find the man who killed my friend.'

'What about the dead slaves? Do they not also merit justice?'

'If they were murdered, then of course. Rest assured my views on slavery are as one with Mr Archer's.'

'Mr Archer was a liar and a fraud.'

I stared at her in surprise. 'Why do you say that?'

The breeze stirred her ringlets. 'I will tell you everything, but you must help me first.'

'How can I help you?'

'I want my freedom.'

I spread my hands. 'That is hardly in my gift.'

'If you bought me from Mr Stokes, then you could free me.'

I almost smiled, imagining Caro's reaction were I to bring home a beautiful African slave girl. Even if I freed her right away, there would still be a record of the sale – and given Cinnamon's looks, aspersions would inevitably be cast. It was precisely the sort of scandal I needed to avoid.

'I could give you money,' I suggested. 'If you made your way to London, you could get an injunction so that Mr Stokes would have no claim on you. I could help arrange a lawyer.'

'Mr Stokes has me searched every day, sometimes twice. He would find the money even if I hid it – and besides, there is no one in Deptford whom I trust to take me to London. If I walked, they'd only track me down.'

I could drive Cinnamon there myself, I reflected, yet the risks were just as high. Even if we made it to London without being caught, I'd face censure if my part in her escape were discovered. The West India lobby were a powerful force in Parliament, and stealing the slave girl of one of its prominent members – which was surely the way they'd see it – would draw their enmity. Nor would it be looked on favourably by my masters at the War Office. Yet I was anxious to learn what she knew, and I kept remembering how Stokes had struck her. It made my blood boil still.

She turned to walk away. 'Wait,' I said. 'I do want to help you – for your own sake, as well as mine. Let me think about it, please. I'm sure there is a way. In the meantime, will you at least tell me how the slaves were killed?'

She gave me a long look. 'They were drowned.'

'All three hundred?' I remembered Isaac's mime in the tavern. What had he said? *Thirsty work.*

My incredulity seemed to anger her, for her voice thickened. 'The crew brought the slaves up on deck. One by one they unshackled them from their chains and pulled them, struggling, to the side of the ship. It took two crewmen to kill each male slave. Many fought back, but it was no good. They were thrown over the side, into the water to drown.'

I remembered my voyage to America, the vast vista of unbroken ocean. I imagined clinging to the side, as men forced me over it. The drop to the water below. Resurfacing, salt burning the lungs and the eyes, looking on helplessly as the ship sailed away.

Cinnamon was watching for the effect of her words upon me. 'The women were weaker. It took only one crewman. The children they left to the cabin boy.'

I stared at her aghast. 'They threw children to their deaths?'

'Six little boys. Also three girls, the youngest not yet five years old. As the cabin boy carried them to the side, they screamed for their mothers. Yet their mothers were in chains and could not help them.'

I could hardly comprehend it. 'Why?'

Her eyes burned into mine with a hot, dark fury. 'The same reason they do everything. For profit.'

Chapter Eighteen

Cinnamon would tell me nothing more, though I begged her.

'My freedom first,' was all that she would say.

We parted on the dockside and, at her instruction, I waited several minutes before following the path she'd taken to the gate, lest anyone report our interaction to her master. I was as confused as I was enlightened by what she'd told me. It made no sense that a slaving crew would destroy a cargo from which they stood to profit – especially as Cinnamon had suggested that profit was their motive. I needed to hear more – and I was also moved by the girl's plight – yet to involve myself in her quest for freedom seemed such a reckless proposition. The more I thought about it, the more misgivings I had. A solution eluded me, and resolving to find one, I returned to the Blackamoor's Head in search of other answers.

The tavern's taproom was already raucous, a lad of about twelve standing on a table swigging rum from a bottle, cheered on by the press of sailors around him. I found a vacant table, and it wasn't long before some of the customers tried to draw me into conversation, encouraged by my willingness to buy them drinks. In such a fashion, I learned the name of *The Dark Angel*'s captain.

'The man you're looking for is Evan Vaughan. Ship's been under his command for near ten years.' The old seadog who told me this had a briar pipe wedged between a set of false teeth fashioned from ivory, his gnarled face garlanded with smoke.

'Vaughan's been sick,' a man at the next table put in, clearly hoping for a share of my generosity. He had a moulting black beard and a missing arm. 'I heard Monday's sent for another captain, a Liverpool man. Should be arriving in town next week.'

I remembered Drake saying that his ship had been delayed in port. 'She'll be sailing then?'

'Aye,' the seadog said, 'provided Monday can get a full complement of crew.'

If Drake was involved in Tad's murder, that meant I didn't have much time. 'Why wouldn't Monday be able to crew her? I thought jobs in slaving were scarce.'

He grinned. 'Some say the ship sails under a bad star.'

'She should have embarked weeks ago,' Blackbeard pitched in. 'But his sailors wouldn't serve on her. Some found posts on different vessels, others took the King's shilling. Monday's upped his wages, but he's still struggling to find takers.'

'Lot of ghosts aboard that Guineaman,' the seadog observed.

The boy had finished his bottle, and he hurled it against the wall. He was carried aloft around the tavern on the shoulders of two older sailors, looking distinctly queasy.

'Do you mean the drowned slaves? Why were they killed? I can't see how it would profit the crew to destroy their own cargo.'

The two men locked eyes. 'Don't know nothing about that.'

'You must have heard something?'

The seadog shrugged. 'They had a bad voyage. It happens.'

I asked a few more questions about the dead slaves, but they would say little more. From the looks that passed between them, I wondered if they thought they'd already said too much.

'Do you know where I might find Captain Vaughan?'

'He lodges at the coaching inn up Broadway.'

I'd seen the effect Frank Drake's name had on people, and I decided against asking about him directly. Yet I remembered Nathaniel saying that Drake used to crew with his father. 'Did a man named Grimshaw ever sail *The Dark Angel*?'

'Amos Grimshaw? Aye. He was Vaughan's first officer. Until the ague carried him off this winter past. I hear the family are struggling now. Crying shame.'

I smiled. I'm on to you, Frank Drake. I doubted it was coincidence that Tad had lodged at the home of one of *The Dark Angel*'s officers. This ship seemed central to everything he had been doing in Deptford. Had Nathaniel been entirely honest with me? I didn't think so.

*

Jago was sleeping in the Noah's Ark's yard. Flies buzzed over the manure. I looked for Nathaniel in the stable, and when I couldn't find him, climbed the steps to the living loft above it.

I had to knock twice before he answered, wearing only a pair of breeches, rubbing the sleep from his bleary eyes.

'Captain Corsham.' He gave me another of his military salutes. 'Forgive me, I often catch a rest during the afternoon.'

I returned his smile. 'I'm sorry to wake you. Might I speak with you a moment?'

'Of course, sir. Come inside.'

The loft was long and hot and dark, though I imagined it would be freezing in winter. It was furnished simply: a chest of drawers, a rocking chair and a bed in which a young man lay sleeping. A mattress took up the floor next to the bed, presumably where Nathaniel slept. The place smelled of sickness and chamberpot.

'How is your friend?'

The young man on the bed had a thin grey face and lank yellow hair. His chin held a furze of golden stubble.

'Brabazon has given him laudanum for the pain. He says there is still no improvement. If there is none by Sunday, then Danny's leg will have to come off.'

'I'm sorry. Have you been friends long?'

'Since school. Our fathers crewed together. It seemed natural to fall in together ourselves. I thought it was the worst thing that could happen when Danny went slaving. Now I'm to go myself, and he won't be there. He'll never sail again, Brabazon says.'

'Where is his father now?'

'Died four years before my own da. Lost overboard. His ma's gone too.'

'Then he is fortunate to have a friend like you. The surgeon's bills alone must be costing you a fortune.'

'We can't take credit for that. The merchant who owns Danny's ship is paying Brabazon's bills.'

'That's good of him.'

'I suppose.'

His tone made me curious, and I remembered the way he had spoken about Brabazon that morning. I placed a comforting hand on his shoulder and he seemed to collect himself. 'Forgive me, sir. You don't want to hear about our troubles. What can I do for you?'

'Mr Archer came to Deptford because of *The Dark Angel*, your father's ship. He must have asked you about her. Why didn't you tell me?'

His soft gaze flitted around the room. 'It slipped my mind.'

'I don't believe that.'

He looked down at Danny and sighed. 'People round here,

they didn't like that Archer was asking about the ship. They wouldn't like me talking about her neither.'

'People like Frank Drake?'

He muttered something beneath his breath.

'What was that?'

The words burst out of him. 'Look, I want to help you, sir. I didn't like what happened to your friend. But I don't want no trouble from Drake, nor anyone else.'

'You need to trust me, Nathaniel. When I find out who murdered Archer, everyone who helped protect the killer will be in a deal of trouble.'

'I'm not protecting anyone.'

I wondered if that was true. 'I won't tell anyone we have spoken, but I need to know what happened on board that ship.'

'I don't know anything about that damn ship, do you hear? Only that they drowned a lot of slaves. I don't know why. I don't know nothing. Da never talked about his slaving. The first I heard about it was when Archer came that first time, asking all his questions.'

'Questions about the dead slaves? About the crew?'

'Both.' His eyes met mine. 'Do you think one of them killed him?'

'Do you?'

He had made no move to put on his shirt, and I noticed again how muscular he was. He wore some sort of ivory charm on a strip of leather around his neck.

'I don't know. They all seemed afraid.'

'Afraid of what?'

'Your friend, Mr Archer, I think. Danny said even old Mr Monday looked like the devil had walked across his grave. Danny did too, come to think of it.'

'What does this have to do with Danny?'

'That was his ship – *The Dark Angel*. He was on that voyage.'

I stared at the lad on the bed. He looked about sixteen years old. 'It was nearly three years ago. He must have been little more than a boy.'

'Cabin boys start as young as twelve. That was Danny's first voyage. When he came back he looked like a ghost. I knew something bad had happened.'

I thought about what Cinnamon had told me. This boy, all but a child himself, throwing infant Africans to their deaths.

'When did his accident occur?' Before or after Tad's murder was the pertinent point.

'Three weeks ago. He slipped on the waterstairs. Landed with his leg bent the wrong way.'

Three weeks would place it well before Tad's murder. 'Can he walk?'

Nathaniel gave me a look of disbelief. 'He can't even make water by himself, sir.'

'That's quite an injury from a tumble down some stairs.'

He looked away. 'It was a long way to fall.'

'Has he talked since it happened?'

'Yes, sir. This is just the laudanum.'

A new thought occurred to me then, one that made a few more things fall into place.

'Brabazon said he'd sailed with Danny. Was he the surgeon on board *The Dark Angel*?'

'Yes, sir. Our good Mr Brabazon.' Again I heard the hostility in his tone.

Was that why Child had taken Tad's body to Brabazon's surgery? I recalled that it had been Brabazon who'd originally steered me away from the slave brand. Yet he must have recognized it – he'd surely applied it himself, countless times. As to his dinner with Tad, I was willing to bet that they'd talked about a damn sight more than Thomas Aquinas.

'Did a man named Isaac crew with your father?' I described the man I'd killed last night.

'Isaac Fairweather? He works the privateers. Not been slaving since before the war.'

Then Isaac's friendship with Drake had cost him dear.

'Do you know the names of any other men who crewed *The Dark Angel* on that voyage? Anyone who has been in town these past few weeks?'

'Only the officers are left in Deptford now, aside from Danny. The men didn't want to crew her. They've left town.'

'Because the ship sails under a bad star?'

Nathaniel touched the charm around his neck. 'Not just that. Captain Vaughan's been sick, and the voyage was delayed. Him and Mr Monday are close, see, or he'd have been replaced weeks ago. Danny only stayed on in Deptford because he wanted to sail with me.'

'How many officers are there, aside from the captain and the surgeon?'

'Three. But Drake is the only one who sailed her back then. Da's dead, and the old second officer threw himself overboard a year after the slaves were drowned. Slaving affects some men that way.'

I was making headway, and yet there was still much that I didn't understand. Why were the slaves drowned? How had Tad presented a threat to the officers? The slaves had been killed at sea, where they would be accounted property. It wasn't as though anyone could be prosecuted for murder. And how did any of it threaten the existence of slavery itself?

'Your father never mentioned anything about that voyage?'

'Like I said, he rarely talked about his slaving. I knew it was bad, though. Da had a lot of nightmares, just like you.'

He flushed under the sudden sharpness of my gaze. 'I heard you this morning, sir. Didn't mean to, but I did. I always check in on Ma after I come back from a shift at the dock. Her room's next to yours.'

I didn't like the thought of him listening to me talking in my sleep, yet he looked so stricken I felt obliged to explain. 'War leaves its legacy too. Sometimes when we choose not to think about things, those thoughts force their way out of us through our dreams.'

He nodded, as if he understood. 'Da called it the black serpent. He said it wrapped its coils so tight around you, sometimes nothing but the bad could come out.'

I wondered if they had bad dreams too, those men who had sailed *The Dark Angel*. Captain Vaughan I was yet to meet. Frank Drake, who'd attacked me last night. And James Brabazon, who'd told me a pack of lies from start to finish.

Then there was John Monday, *The Dark Angel*'s owner. He'd spoken of Tad with compassion and he claimed to be a man of God, but I was learning that religion took strange forms in Deptford. I remembered the way he'd wielded the whip outside his warehouse. It wasn't hard to imagine him hanging a man up and cutting his throat.

I imagined this puzzle as a painting, stained over the years with layers of soot. I knew I was seeing only a small part of it. None of these men, even Monday, would count as powerful enemies by Tad's standards. This had to be more than slaving men killing to protect themselves. Yet I had rubbed a small portion of the blackness away to reveal the colours beneath.

Four names, no motive, but the beginnings of a trail. Every instinct told me that it would soon lead to Tad's murderer.

Chapter Nineteen

✳

The Deptford bathhouse lay at the heart of the warren of alleys near the slaving taverns.

An ogre of a doorman was stationed outside, flanked by flaming torches. He examined me with gimlet eyes over a broken nose, then nodded me through. In the dimly lit lobby, the proprietor came forward to meet me. He had a rat-like countenance and snuff stains on his busy fingers.

'Greetings, sir. Welcome to the Temple of the Naiads. I have baths of scented water that will ease every ache and torment. I have girls to sate every appetite. Name your flavour.'

'Black,' I said, remembering Drake's alibi and his uncouth description of the girl he claimed to have tumbled that night.

'Negress cunny? You are a man of strong tastes, sir. I applaud it. Jamaica Mary is the girl for you. She's one of the prettiest nymphs I have. Nay, I do her a disservice. Less a nymph than a Nubian goddess, sent down from the very heavens for your delight.'

I forestalled any more of his patter. 'Is she the only African you have?'

'Divine, ebon, and sadly unique. If it's two girls you are after, I have a meek little Malay who could join you?'

'Mary will do fine.'

I paid him and was shown into an anteroom, where sailors and other rough men were drinking wine, dandling half-naked girls upon their laps. After a short wait, the proprietor returned, and I followed him along a passage to a small steamy room lit by candles. A stone bath, about six feet by four, was sunk into the floor, and a mattress piled with soiled linen occupied one corner. A naked black woman was lying in the bath, and she eyed me without much interest. The proprietor wished me eternal happiness and withdrew.

Jamaica Mary might once have been pretty – it was hard to tell in that light – but she was fast approaching forty and the demands of her profession had taken their toll. Her skin was the colour and texture of old shoe leather, and her hair was coarse and curly. She gave me a perfunctory smile of invitation, and I saw that she was missing several teeth.

'Why don't you come in, sir? The water's hot.' The words rolled from her lips in a West Indian drawl, with a slight edge of Deptford on the vowels.

'I only wish to talk to you.'

'You want Mary to tell you tales from the bathhouse, sir? Some men like a story to get them primed.'

'I have a particular story in mind. A particular night and a particular customer.'

'Give you a good report, did he? Mary sends them all away happy.' She ran her hands over her small brown breasts. 'Tell Mary his name, sir, and she'll see if she can remember. Sometimes all these nights drift into one.'

'His name is Frank Drake. The night I have in mind is Thursday last. You'll remember it well enough, I'm sure. The next morning they found a murdered man on a hook down at the dock.'

She sat up to examine me, the water rolling off her nipples. She had a small heart-shaped face tapering to a point at the chin, and slanted yellow cat-like eyes. 'You're not one of Perry Child's men. Mary don't have to talk to you.'

'I may not be a constable, but I am a man of means. I will reward you well if you tell me the truth. Shall we say three shillings?'

Her eyes narrowed. 'Five.'

'Three. But only if you tell me the truth.'

She pouted. 'You want to know what Mary and Mr Drake was doing that night?'

'Spare me the details. I only want to know if you were with him.'

'All night long,' she said, without hesitation. 'He came in around eight. Went home a happy man the morning after. God's honest truth.'

She had the sort of face that would make you think she was lying if she told you the sea was blue. I wondered if she was frightened of Drake, or had some other interest in protecting him. Perhaps I just didn't want to accept the truth.

'Well? Where's Mary's reward?'

'I have a few more questions for you first.' It occurred to me that Mary must know many of the men in Deptford, and that I might as well make use of her time now I had paid for it.

'Ask what you like.' She lay back, watching me. The candle-light made patterns on the perfumed water. 'Long as Mary gets what she was promised.'

'Do gentlemen from the Broadway ever come down here?'

'Sure they come. Can't keep away.'

'A gentleman surgeon named James Brabazon? Does he come?'

'That grim old sawbones?' She pulled a face. 'Not here.'

'You don't like him?'

'Mister Fred sent Mary to see him once, after she got poxed.

He looked at her like something you'd kick off the quayside. He got no taste for African cunny, that's for sure.'

'Do you know what his tastes are? Where he goes to sate his pleasure?' I was thinking of the silver ticket I'd found in Tad's rooms.

'There's brothels aplenty in Deptford. They're welcome to him.'

I fished in my pocket for the ticket. 'Did you ever hear of any brothel where you might need a ticket like this?'

She squinted at it, then shook her head. 'There's no call for silver tickets down here in the Strand. All you need is brass in your pocket and wood between your legs.'

'How about in the Broadway?'

'Mary wouldn't know. They don't let her ply her trade up there.'

'Do you know a lad named Danny? He is younger than Drake, but they sailed together.'

'The Waterman boy? Drake and Amos Grimshaw brought him here a few times. Mary heard he took a tumble down some steps.' She made a snapping sound with her tongue. 'Luck's a bitch, soldier, especially when she's given a helping hand.'

'What do you mean by that?'

'Just talk, that's all.'

'What kind of talk?'

'Danny Waterman had light fingers. Helped himself to someone else's property. That someone taught him a lesson he wouldn't forget.'

I recalled that Nathaniel had been evasive upon the topic earlier. Could Waterman's 'accident' have something to do with Tad's murder? They had happened only a week or so apart.

'Did Amos Grimshaw come here often?'

'Aye, he was a lusty one, old Amos. They say the pimps cried into their tankards the day he died.'

'How about John Monday, the slave merchant? Does he ever come down here?'

She cackled. 'Bible John? He wouldn't know what to do with Mary's cunny if she stuck it in front of his face. They should have called him Sunday. Ain't that the truth?' She squinted at me. 'You done talking yet, mister? Mary's feeling lonely all by herself.' She let her legs fall open and made a crude gesture with her hands. She seemed to consider me a professional challenge.

'I'm married,' I said. 'Do you know a sea captain named Evan Vaughan?'

'Married?' She smiled contemptuously. 'Half the men in Deptford are married, sugar. Don't stop them coming here. You should see what their wives get up to when they're halfway across the world. What's your wife doing when your back is turned?'

'Just answer the question, Mary. Do you know Evan Vaughan?'

Her smile faded. 'He comes in from time to time.'

'Was Vaughan here that night with Drake? When the man was killed at the dock?'

'He hasn't been here in over a month. There was some trouble.'

'What kind of trouble?'

She brought her hands together, making a circle with her fingers. 'He tried to strangle one of the other whores.'

'Do you know why?'

She shrugged, as if it happened every day. Perhaps it did.

'What's the whore's name?'

She pulled a bored face. 'Alice.'

'What does Vaughan look like? Is he a big man?'

'Big enough. Tall, muscular, but slim in the waist. He cuts a fine figure – and he knows it.'

'How about his face?' I wanted to know him if I saw him.

'Brown as a gypsy. Long curly black hair. An old scar.'

'Did you ever hear of Vaughan having trouble with anyone else besides the whore?'

Her eyes flickered, and I sensed she didn't like the question. 'Mary's bored of talking now. Where's her three shillings?'

'I said I'd give you the money if you told me the truth. I think you're lying about Frank Drake and I want to know if you ever heard of Vaughan having trouble with anyone else. The man who was killed at the dock, for instance.'

'Mary never told a lie in her young life. You ask Perry Child.'

I smiled at the implausibility of this statement, whilst noting her apparent familiarity with the magistrate. 'These particular lies could get you into a lot of trouble, Mary. I bet Drake didn't think to tell you that. If he murdered that man, then you could hang for an accessory.'

Her lips parted, and I thought she was going to speak. Instead she screamed. I stared at her in bewilderment, as she leaped from the water and threw herself to the floor. A moment later the door burst open, and the proprietor and his doorman rushed in. Mary clutched her face. 'He hit Mary, Mister Fred. Threatened to cut her open with his nasty sword.'

I protested my innocence, but at a signal from his master, the doorman grabbed me by the arm and the back of the neck. I could have reached for my pistol, but I had no desire to kill anyone else. Nor did I wish to be arrested for a brawl in a bawdy house. I allowed the man to force me from the room and march me back down the passage to the lobby. He kicked the door open and jostled me down the steps to the street. To my chagrin, I slipped on the slimy cobbles and fell on my backside.

'Go fuck somewhere else, soldier boy,' the proprietor said. 'Don't even think about coming back.'

The indignity stung, and in the morning I'd have another bruise to add to my Deptford collection. The door to the bath-house banged shut and I picked myself up. I trudged back towards the dock, cursing Mary's name.

I was convinced she had been lying about Drake, but unless I could prove that lie, what good would it do? I kept thinking of Peregrine Child in the alleys last night, when he'd prevented my murder at Drake's hands. *We're good friends, you and I. Let's keep it that way.*

Frank Drake, Peregrine Child and Jamaica Mary. They formed a little knot that needed unpicking. As I walked, I pondered which was the loosest thread.

CHAPTER TWENTY

IT WAS NOT yet eleven, and I decided to go in search of the opium house Brabazon had told me about. From one house of debauch to another. This was Deptford after all.

The quality of the dwellings deteriorated as I neared the Upper Watergate, the faces darkening from white to brown. The East India Company employed many Lascar and Malay sailors to crew their giant Indiamen, and the foreigners seemed to have made these squalid streets their temporary home. Bunches of dried herbs and roots hung in lodging house windows, and scents of incense and spices drifted on the breeze. It did little to mask the deeper stench of offal, tar and sewage. Lascar sailors watched me from windows and doorways, and I saw trepidation in their eyes. I guessed that most of the white men who ventured down here after dark came looking for trouble.

I passed a few ramshackle stalls selling brass lamps and legs of mutton. A Lascar in a robe embroidered with stars offered to tell my fortune. I asked him the way to the Red House, and for a farthing he showed me.

The house was older than its neighbours and only the door was painted red. When I knocked, I heard footsteps, and a panel in the door slid back. A pair of glittering black eyes filled the hole.

'Poppy drug?' I said, and I heard the sound of several bolts being drawn back.

The eyes belonged to a woman, a round Malay dressed in black. As she ushered me into the hall, the smell hit me: heavy, sweet and inviting. The woman led me through a fringed curtain into a long dark chamber. Little red coronas of light glowed in the shadows, now bright, now dim, now bright again. As my eyes grew accustomed to the darkness, I made out men lying on straw pallets around the perimeter of the room, each curled round a long wooden pipe. Recalling Brabazon's analogy, it brought to mind Tad's diagram of the slave ship.

An old Malay, I guessed the woman's husband, was sitting at a table, serving a customer. The woman gestured to me to wait until he had finished. The Malay took a tube of cloth from a black, japanned box and unrolled it on the table in front of him. Inside was a long piece of the poppy drug, and he cut a segment from it with his knife. He wrapped it in red wax paper, just like the wrapping around the opium Amelia and I had found in Tad's valise. The customer paid, and I stepped forward to take his place.

I showed Tad's opium to the Malay. 'Do you know if this was bought here?'

'How I know?' Annoyance flashed across his wrinkled walnut of a face. 'You want buy poppy or not?'

'You can keep it if you talk to me.'

Mollified, he examined the opium. 'Could be mine. Could not be mine.'

I described Tad to him: his long black hair, his size, his pale skin. By the time I had finished, he was nodding furiously.

'Was he alone?'

'Yes, alone.'

'Did he smoke any of it here?'

'Take away for dream at home.' He grinned suddenly, showing me all three teeth in his head.

'How much did you sell him?'

He pointed at the opium, and spread his fingers.

'More than this?'

'Again as much.'

'Can you remember when he came here? A week ago? Longer?'

'One week.' His fingers wobbled, which I took to mean 'more or less'. Just before Tad was killed.

The man held up two fingers. 'Two time.'

'He came here twice? When was the first?'

A shrug. 'Two month maybe.'

Which must have been the first time Tad had come to Deptford. Two visits to buy opium. Yet he'd shown no signs of addiction, and Amelia had never seen him smoke it. Nor had I found any trace of opium use at Tad's rooms.

I handed the Malay the pouch, and he bowed with his palms together. That was the conclusion of our business.

As I was leaving the smoking room I stepped back to avoid a customer coming through the curtain. He walked past without seeing me, but I saw him. Tall and broad, wearing a periwig. A grim face much scoured by the weather. John Monday, *The Dark Angel*'s owner, was here buying opium.

Outside, I lingered in an alley with a view of the opium house. After a few minutes Monday emerged and walked in the direction of the quays. I let him open up a suitable distance between us and then I followed him. He walked swiftly and with my infirmity I found it hard to match his stride. The alleys twisted and turned, and I kept losing sight of him. By the time I reached the river he had disappeared entirely. The ships were ghostly in the mist, the docks deathly quiet. I walked along the harbourside, hoping to catch sight of him.

I heard voices up ahead, and drew back into the shadows,

moving cautiously in the direction of the sound. Warehouses and shipping offices faced the Public Dock, with cobbled yards out front for loading carts. In one of these recessed yards, two men stood talking. Their faces were obscured by shadow, but one of them had Monday's height and build, and wore a periwig. Their voices were low and their movements furtive. I saw a flash of silver as money changed hands.

The second man unlocked the warehouse door and the pair walked inside. For a moment I saw their faces clearly in the moonlight. The gentleman was not John Monday, though he did have the look of a merchant. His clothes were fine, and he had a plump, pasty face. He took a long look around the dock, before ducking inside. The second man was younger and wore a horsehair wig: Nathaniel Grimshaw.

I presumed that I was witnessing a criminal act. Perhaps thievery, perhaps smuggling, perhaps something else. It intrigued me, and I lodged the encounter in the back of my mind. It might be a useful lever to exert pressure upon Nathaniel should I need it. Yet John Monday's presence in the opium house was surely of greater significance. I walked on.

I progressed a hundred yards down the quays, but I had no further sight of him. A light rain had begun to fall, stippling the surface of the ink-black Thames. Coils of cloud wound round the moon like opium smoke. I studied the buildings around me, wondering where Monday had gone. Few of the windows had any lights. The dock seemed deserted. I gazed out over the water, listening to the creak of ships on the tide. Somewhere a bell rang, warning of fog. The wind came from the north, over the river, over the slave ships. It filled my nostrils and it held the scent of death.

*

I walked back to the Noah's Ark without further incident. The taproom was lively, filled with officers from the Navy Yard singing a cheerful ditty about slaughtering the French. I went upstairs to my room.

On the floor inside my door, I discovered a letter. The missive was addressed to me by name alone, and no insignia adorned the black wax seal.

I walked to the window, and threw it open. Over the rooftops I could see the fog-lamps of the Guineamen out on the water. I slit the seal with my thumbnail, trying to pick out *The Dark Angel* by counting the lights.

One of the lights was moving, travelling along the deck of a ship. I couldn't be sure it was *The Dark Angel*, but it might have been. A watchman? There was no way to tell. But why would anything of value be stored on those ships, when they lay in the Private Dock with its warehouses and guards?

The light disappeared, but I kept watching, and soon I saw it again. I followed its progress, until again it disappeared. This time it didn't come back. I stared into the darkness, then unfolded the letter in my hand.

> *GET OWT OF DEPTFORD BEFOR IT IS TO LATE. REEMEMBER WOT I DID TO YUR SHITTEN FREND.*

The message was written in the same ill-formed script as those I'd found in Tad's rooms. In the lamplight, the words flickered and writhed like serpents.

Chapter Twenty-One

Mrs Grimshaw served me breakfast in the dining room. Her face was flushed from the steam of the kitchen and strands of copper hair escaped her black cotton cap.

'Might I speak with you a moment, madam?'

She gave me a sharp look. 'If you're going to ask me about those dead slaves, then you might as well save yourself the trouble. My Nate told me why you are here. I know nothing about that blessed boat.'

'Forgive me, Mrs Grimshaw. I should have been honest with you from the start.'

'Yes, you should,' she said, slightly mollified. 'I'll tell you what I told your friend Mr Valentine or Mr Archer or whatever he was called. My Amos left all his slaving down at the dock. "When I walk through this door, Marilyn," he'd say, "I'm a taverner, nothing more."' She gazed at me hotly. 'I know nothing about it, God's truth.'

'Actually, I wanted to ask you about a letter pushed under my door last night.'

She frowned. 'If it was pushed under your door, sir, then it wasn't me who put it there.'

'You are certain?'

'I always put my guests' letters right in their hands. Saves the chance of anything going astray.'

'Did anyone go upstairs during the day other than your guests?'

'Only my Nate and the serving girl. Oh, and Mr Child. He fixed a broken window casement for me on the upstairs landing.'

'Do magistrates usually undertake carpentry work in Deptford?'

'That was Mr Child's trade, sir, before he became a magistrate. He's never been one to put on any airs. He and my Amos went back years.'

'And you saw nobody else go upstairs?'

'No, sir, but the inn was busy last night. I can't say for certain.'

The letter had unsettled me, coming so close upon the heels of Frank Drake's attack in the alleys. Either the killer was behind the letters and watching me, or someone wanted me to think he was. I wondered fleetingly if Child had put the letter there himself. He was certainly eager enough for me to leave town. Yet anonymous missives didn't quite seem his forthright style. Perhaps Nathaniel had seen someone. I would ask him.

*

The air was fresher after last night's rain, and the beans in the market gardens that flanked the road between the Strand and the Broadway seemed to throb against the blue sky and the dusty ground. Sparrowhawks circled overhead, swooping for their breakfast. I passed farmers, and a milkmaid leading a cow. Buildings intermittently lined the road: sundry houses, a laundry, a tavern. Many more were in a state of construction, claiming the fields to the east for the town. I passed a bright white church, around which fine houses were being built. Beyond them I could see gravel pits and mill-wheels along the pewter line of Deptford Creek. Perhaps one day, I thought, the two Deptfords would meet and merge, doubtless to the displeasure of the Broadway's refined inhabitants.

Such concerns still seemed a long way off. Entering the Broadway after the vicissitudes of the Strand was like stepping into another world. The shops on the High Street were temples to genteel consumption: London fashions, Canary wines, Venetian glassware. Ladies sheltered beneath parasols trading gossip and advice about servants. Gentlemen stood in little clusters talking matters mercantile. The rich fabrics they wore and the glossiness of their horses bore further testament to the town's commercial power. Even in these straitened times, money plainly flowed into Deptford Broadway, much of it carried on a tide of African sweat.

I had decided to pay another visit to *The Dark Angel*'s owner, John Monday. Nathaniel Grimshaw and Peregrine Child knew my true purpose for being in town, and Frank Drake had a good enough idea. It was surely only a matter of time before somebody told Monday – if they hadn't already. If he did still believe that I was a potential investor in his business, then it was an advantage I must press home before it was too late.

Monday lived in a terrace of large brick mansion houses overlooking Deptford Creek. Elaborately carved lintels over the front doors incorporated the emblems of their owners' trade: here a leaf of tobacco, here a glossy nutmeg, here a grinning African holding up his chains. Monday's house was one of the largest in the street.

A plump black maidservant answered my knock. I asked to see Monday, offering her my card. Seemingly reassured by my uniform, she invited me inside.

'Will you wait here, sir, while I speak to my master?'

The hall smelled of beeswax and the lilies sitting in a vase on the marble-topped console. Fine paintings of biblical scenes hung on the walls. I heard a sound of running feet and two children, a boy and a girl, burst into the hall. Neither of them noticed me, and the girl advanced upon the boy, trapping him against the side of the staircase. He was about ten years old, dressed in the pink waistcoat and breeches of a gentleman's son. I stared at his face in surprise. His skin was only slightly darker than mine, but in the shape of his lips and nose, and his curly black hair, I discerned a trace of African blood. The girl was younger and wore a pudding cap. Her colouring was fair, not like the boy's at all.

'Give it to me,' the girl said.

He shook his head violently.

Whatever it was, she tried to take it, but he pushed her away.

'Blueskin.' She said it softly. 'Picked any cotton today, boy? Dirty blackbird.'

The boy lashed out, striking her with his fist, and she burst into loud, heaving sobs. Almost immediately, a nursemaid appeared from one of the adjacent rooms. In a rustle of starched skirts, she seized the boy by the arm, dragging him off, spanking him as they went. 'Little savage. What have I told you about hurting your sister?'

The girl smiled through her tears, and followed them into the room from which the nursemaid had emerged. The door closed upon the boy's muffled cries.

Upstairs, I heard a fleeting clamour of raised voices and then silence. I shivered. My disquiet was not just a product of the encounter between the children – though the girl's pleasure in her torment of the boy had been unsettling. It sounds melodramatic to say so, but in that place I felt a malevolent presence. Something in the air and the stillness reminded me of my childhood home. I knew an unhappy house when I stood in one, and I did so now.

A door opened above and the maid descended the stairs. 'My master asks if you will wait for him in his study. He will only be a few minutes.'

She opened a door off the hall and stood back to allow me to enter. She offered me refreshment, but I declined. 'Please ring the bell if there is anything you need.'

She left, pulling the door ajar behind her. Such opportunities we are rarely gifted. I moved fast.

Between the long windows overlooking the street was a mahogany desk. I went to it and opened a drawer at random. It contained a neat array of writing implements: quills, ink, seals, tapers, sand. I tried another drawer and found an account book, which I opened. Household expenditure, mainly payments to merchants in Deptford Broadway. Monday's accounts looked healthy, decidedly so.

I put the book back and tried the other drawers. Two were locked and the others held little of consequence. Monday probably kept his business papers in that cabinet in his warehouse office. I replaced everything in the desk and surveyed the rest of the room.

For all Monday's religion, there was little evidence of monastic forbearance. His inkwells were silver, a pair of crystal decanters held port and sherry wines, and the carpet was a fine Persian weave. The mantelpiece was elaborately carved, fashioned from black marble. Sitting upon it was an ornate silver casket. I lifted the lid and saw that the interior was lined with sandalwood, divided into three long compartments. Two of the compartments held knives, their handles finely worked in silver. The third was empty.

I tested the blade of one of the knives against my thumb. Very sharp.

'They were a gift from a prince of the Aro Confederacy,' said a voice behind me. 'I have been trading with his family for over twenty years.'

I turned and saw Monday in the doorway. He had moved silently for such a big man.

I put the knife back and closed the lid. 'Forgive my curiosity, Mr Monday.'

He gestured to signal its inconsequence and we bowed. 'Such gifts establish trust, upon which a good slaving venture rests. The Aro Negroes know I will never try to cheat them. In turn, I know they will never try to sell me an inferior product disguised as something better.'

'That happens?'

'Never underestimate the Negro's capacity for trickery. The uninitiated men of my trade are sold slaves painted with nut juice to disguise their injuries, or plugged with oakum to hide the symptoms of dysentery.'

My expression must have offered some clue to my disgust, for he hastily drew back a chair and indicated that we should sit. Given the impact of the war on Deptford's trade, he was plainly eager to close the deal on an attractive investment.

'I hope you have given my proposal sufficient thought. I could have my lawyer draw up a contract of investment this afternoon.'

I studied his weathered face, wondering what he was doing in the opium house last night. I wanted to ask him, but I did not wish to arouse his suspicions. To use an expression appropriate to Deptford, I had other fish to fry.

'I regret to say that I do have one concern, Mr Monday. I have heard a disquieting rumour about your business.'

He frowned. 'What have you heard?'

'That one of your ships made a voyage on which the greater part of the cargo was lost. Three hundred slaves thrown overboard by the crew. You told me that you only lose three to five per cent of your cargo, but this must have been more like sixty-five per cent. I must say, the prospect of my money lying at the bottom of the Atlantic Ocean does not enthral me.'

He nodded. 'A tragic incident, and one I regret profoundly. Yet the slaves were insured. None of my investors lost a penny. The voyage even made a small profit.'

'I struggle to understand it. Why were so many slaves killed?'

'It was unavoidable. Yet I have taken measures to ensure it could never happen again. You have my word.'

'In these circumstances, sir, I require more than your word. I desire an explanation.'

He frowned. 'Very well. Though it is not a cheerful tale.'

Monday interlaced his fingers on the desk, and stared at them as he spoke. He seemed ill at ease, and I knew we would not be having this conversation had he not believed a large investment was at stake. 'To understand it, you need to know a little about the early part of the voyage. *The Dark Angel* – that's the name of the vessel in question – sailed from Deptford in the spring of '78. She reached Africa without incident and was plying for slaves along the Bight of Bonny, when the captain, a gentleman named Evan Vaughan, had what appeared at the time to be a piece of luck. He went ashore to meet the commissioner of one of the slave forts, and was offered a captured French Guineaman for sale. All my captains carry letters of credit backed by my investors in case of opportunities such as this. Vaughan jumped at the chance. He appointed his second officer to captain the captured vessel, and divided his crew between the two ships. To make up the shortfall, he took on Dutch sailors he found drifting around the slave forts. The two ships plied the Guinea coast for a little over four months, while Vaughan bought slaves. The *Duc d'Orleans* sailed first. She is now named *The Phoenix*, the ship I showed you yesterday in the dock. *The Dark Angel* weighed anchor two weeks later, bound for Kingston, Jamaica, with four hundred and sixty Africans on board.'

Monday passed a hand across his chin. 'I cannot fault Vaughan's actions in any regard. He is one of my most experienced captains and he acted quite properly. Yet the Dutch sailors proved difficult to master and that diverted his attention. Otherwise, I am certain that the leak would have been discovered sooner.'

'The leak?'

'In one of the water tanks. They found it four weeks into the Middle Passage. By the time it was discovered, the tanks were running so low on water that a stark fact could not be avoided. There was not enough water left for the remainder of the voyage.'

I frowned. 'You're saying the slaves died of thirst? I understood they went into the water alive, not dead.'

'My officers were faced with an unenviable dilemma. If they continued to provide water to all the slaves, then the water would run out, and all would die. Calculations were made and the officers realized that only around one hundred and fifty slaves could be saved. They brought the Negroes up on deck, and assessed their condition. The strongest hundred and fifty were separated from the rest. The weakest were then thrown overboard, as you have heard.' He shook his head. 'Those poor men, having to make such a wretched choice. I feel for them.'

Thirsty work. Again I imagined the long drop to the water, the currents dragging wasted limbs below the surface. The children. I felt hot, sickened – also confused.

'They might have met another ship,' I objected. 'Surely another vessel would have spared them water? Or it might have rained? By their actions, the officers guaranteed that the slaves would die.'

'They also guaranteed that the remaining slaves would survive. As an investor, I'm sure you appreciate that. It is possible that a fortuitous event, such as you describe, could have saved the cargo in its entirety. Yet they would have been taking quite a risk. My insurance only covers the initial purchase cost of the slaves, not their price at market. By ensuring that a portion of the cargo remained alive and fit and healthy, the officers made certain that a significant profit was still made. The deaths I regret enormously – a tragic product of unique circumstance – but I console myself with the thought that they went to their graves good Christian souls. Their lives were foreshortened, but they were spared the Devil's fire.'

Some might view the events Monday described as an unfortunate commercial mistake. I considered it a terrible crime. Hundreds of men, women and children, who should not have been on that damn ship in the first place, consigned to oblivion because Englishmen didn't want to risk their profit. I knew Tad must have shared my fury – he would have wanted these men to face justice. Such a crime demanded retribution.

As I contemplated the massacre, the sounds of a commotion reached us. We both turned as the door flew open, and the mayor, Lucius Stokes, strode into the room. Behind him, I glimpsed the bulging eyes of Abraham, his black footman, and the anxious face of Monday's maidservant.

'Forgive me, Mr Monday. My business will not wait.'

'Mr Stokes.' Monday rose from his chair. 'I regret to say that I cannot receive you right now. I am in the middle of a meeting with an investor.'

'That is why I have come.' Stokes gave me a hard stare. 'I fear you have been imposed upon, sir. This gentleman is no investor. He is a friend of that murdered abolitionist. Child tells me Captain Corsham has been making inquiries into the murder around town. I would have come before, but I was busy with the delegation.'

Again the mayor reminded me of my father, this time less for his patrician looks, more for his hectoring tone and threatening eye. As Monday listened, a succession of emotions trailed across his face. I identified confusion, anger certainly, perhaps even fear.

'Is this true?' he asked.

'It is,' I replied.

The muscles of his cheek contracted. 'Then I must ask you to leave. Your conduct is not that of a gentleman.'

'I would not have misled you had I not thought it necessary. Mr Archer came to Deptford because of the slaves murdered on your ship. I believe he was killed to prevent his inquiry into that crime.'

'What crime?' Stokes exclaimed. 'A man can no more murder his slave, than he can his dog or his chair. If the crew of that ship had cut the throats of every Negro aboard in cold blood, it would not be accounted a murder by any English court. My ships have sailed the Middle Passage for over thirty years, sir. I assure you I am familiar with the law.'

'Mr Stokes is right.' Monday had quickly recovered his composure. 'I fear you have been labouring under a misapprehension, sir. Neither myself, nor my crew, had anything to fear from Archer's inquiry. I told him so myself, to no avail. Even after he upset my wife and servants, I still treated him with courtesy.'

On the point of law, I knew they were correct. Yet something wasn't right with their story.

'Then why was Archer receiving threatening letters? Why

did I receive one myself last night? Why did his killer burn your company's brand into his chest? Why have I been attacked on the streets of Deptford by one of your officers?'

I noticed Stokes shoot Monday a curious glance. Neither man had any answers for me. 'I will not be deterred, gentlemen. I will find Archer's killer, and I will see him hang.'

'You should know,' Stokes said, 'that I have written today to the War Office, complaining about your conduct in the strongest terms. I have also written to Napier Smith, the Chairman of the West India lobby.'

My heart sank at the thought of having to explain myself to my patron, Nicholas Cavill-Lawrence. As Under-Secretary of State for War, he would surely read Stokes's letter, and would doubtless share Caro's opinion of my actions. He would also be anxious about upsetting the West India lobby. I did not subscribe to Tad's conspiratorial theories about the lobby, but their influence I didn't doubt. They gave substantial donations to the governing party, and had the power to halt a young parliamentarian's rise before it had even begun. I was still mulling this disastrous turn of events when the silence was broken by a woman's cry of distress.

Monday ran from the room. Stokes and I followed, and we caught up with him outside his front door. A lady was standing on the street, gazing at the front steps. Scattered over them were a great many animal bones, the stairs resembling the shelves of an ossuary. On the top step lay the corpse of a rooster. The bird's entrails were spread around its body like the dead dove I had seen on Brabazon's doorstep.

Stokes's footman, Abraham, was beside the woman, and seemed to be trying to calm her down. Monday glared at him. 'You, boy. Are you responsible for this?'

The footman swivelled round. 'No, sir.'

'Sir, please,' the woman said, stammering slightly. 'It could not have been Abraham. He came out of the house just now, when he heard me scream. The bones were already here.'

'Of course it wasn't Abraham.' Stokes kicked the bird and it sailed into the street. 'I'll have another word with Child. We'll catch them soon enough.' He descended the steps and bowed to the lady. 'Dear Mrs Monday. Pray don't distress yourself.'

The lady seemed much shaken by the incident, her fingers twisting the handles of her basket. She was much younger than her husband, no more than thirty, short in stature, with a pleasing figure that even her high-necked green gown could not disguise. Her black hair was scraped back in a simple knot, secured by ivory pins. A long straight nose was her dominant feature, below a pair of darting blue-green eyes. Her high forehead wore a shine of perspiration. Monday placed his hands upon her shoulders.

'There now, Eleanor. I have told you that these devilish tricks have no power to harm you.' He stroked her face, and I thought I saw her flinch.

She took a deep breath. 'Forgive me, gentlemen. I did not mean to startle anyone.' Like Monday, her voice held a Deptford edge.

I bowed. 'Madam.'

She started to speak, but her husband spoke over her: 'Captain Corsham was just leaving. He and I have no more business to discuss.'

He placed a hand in the small of her back and steered her towards the house. Lucius Stokes and his footman followed them inside. Doubtless they intended to talk about me. I stole a final glance at Mrs Monday as she passed through her front door. Her black hair, her small stature, the ivory pins in her hair. There was little doubt in my mind. She was the woman in the black lace veil who had sat alone in the congregation at Tad's funeral.

Chapter Twenty-Two

Why had Eleanor Monday, wife of *The Dark Angel*'s owner, attended Tad's funeral? Was she simply a Christian woman, appalled by the manner of his death? Or were her motives more complicated? She certainly hadn't wanted to be identified. I needed to speak to her, but I could hardly knock on her door when Monday and Stokes were inside. Frustrated, I walked back towards the High Street.

Mayor Stokes's letters to the War Office and the West India lobby had changed everything. My inquiry now had the potential to turn into the scandal Caro feared. I decided I had better return to London to explain myself. If I left Deptford this afternoon, that would leave me enough time to call in upon Amelia Bradstreet and still be home before nightfall. Then I could speak to Cavill-Lawrence first thing tomorrow morning, hopefully before he'd read Mayor Stokes's letter. That plan still left me a little time in Deptford and I was determined to put it to good use.

A man was selling fried whitebait to shoppers on the High Street, and another was giving donkey rides to children. Outside the coaching inn, gentlemen were drinking in the sun, well-dressed whores soliciting discreetly for their business. The merchants of the Strand might move to the Broadway when they made their money, but they plainly didn't leave all their old habits behind them.

The landlord had an amiable face the colour of ham, and wore a brown powdered wig. I asked for Captain Vaughan, but he shook his head.

'I haven't seen him in six weeks. I think he's gone out of town.'

'But he does lodge here?'

'For the moment. He's late with his rent.'

'Do you know where he's gone?'

'To ground, I imagine. Probably running from a jealous husband.' He looked me up and down. 'Not you, is it?'

'Not guilty.' I held up my hands and he grinned. 'A common problem with Vaughan, is it, cuckolded husbands?'

'Man's an old dog. I told him if he ever laid a finger on Rosy, I'd cut it off. He'd be lucky if I stopped at the finger.'

I smiled. 'That sounds like Evan Vaughan.'

'Friend of yours, is he?'

'We go back years. I heard he'd been sick. It concerned me.'

A fair, buxom woman with brawny arms came into the bar from the room behind. 'What's this?'

'Fellow here is a friend of Evan Vaughan. Wants to know about his illness.'

She tapped her skull. 'Cavorting with the fairies half the time.'

'He's been acting strange for a year or two now, if you want to know the truth,' her husband said. 'Lately it got worse.'

'Did a gentleman ever come here to talk to Vaughan?' I described Tad.

'Aye, I remember him. Scrawny fellow. Came a couple of months back. They went upstairs to the captain's room. Talked for a time.'

'That was the night Vaughan smashed up his furniture,' his

wife reminded him. 'We nearly fetched Perry Child. Couldn't calm him down.'

'He paid for the damage, but he frightened Rosy half to death. I wasn't happy.'

'How long was this before he left town?'

They looked at one another. 'Two weeks or so? The scrawny fellow came back looking for him a couple of times.'

I wondered where Vaughan was now, and if he'd been running from more than a jealous husband.

'Don't forget the other goings-on,' the landlady put in. 'That unsettled Vaughan too.' She made a sign with her fingers, the sort country folk make to ward off the evil eye. 'Two horrible black chickens left on the doorstep. Bones too, and strange signs chalked on the tavern walls. Vaughan took it badly. It stopped when he left town. I think those birds were meant for him.'

I digested this news, wondering if I should discount Vaughan from my inquiry. He had left Deptford long before Tad was murdered, and yet I could not preclude the possibility that he had returned. He and Tad must have talked about *The Dark Angel* and it had certainly sparked a reaction. The description of Vaughan's behaviour matched Jamaica Mary's account of his assault on the whore at the bathhouse. Perhaps he'd murdered Tad in a fit of frenzy? Yet the slave brand, the torture, and the placing of the body at the dock suggested forethought.

The story about the dead birds also intrigued me. A dove on Brabazon's doorstep. A rooster on John Monday's. Black chickens for Vaughan. Were these strange offerings connected to the dead slaves? Was someone trying to send the crew a message? If so, then I did not think it was kindly meant. Dead birds and bones. It felt like a curse.

*

James Brabazon. I had thought about him often since I had discovered he was *The Dark Angel*'s surgeon. I remembered our dinner at the Noah's Ark with little affection. Before I left Deptford I wanted to confront him with his lies.

I knocked at his door, but received no reply. So I stuck my head into the shop and asked the apothecary if he knew where I might find his tenant.

'He's in the city on business,' the man said. 'I'm not expecting him back for a couple of days.'

I chafed at the news. Everywhere I encountered obstacles to my progress. I was more convinced than ever that Tad had been killed to prevent his inquiry into the massacre on board *The Dark Angel*, though how that inquiry threatened the ship's officers was still a mystery. Nor did I understand how it related to his scheme to end slavery. Nor his powerful enemies. I was missing something important, perhaps several things.

John Monday would tell me nothing more, now he knew my proposed investment was a sham. James Brabazon and Evan Vaughan were out of town. Frank Drake had an alibi I was unable to disprove. Peregrine Child and Scipio had their own motives for refusing to help me. Daniel Waterman, the cabin boy with the broken leg, was sedated by laudanum and couldn't talk even had he wished to. Other than Nathaniel Grimshaw, only Cinnamon was willing to speak to me, and then at a price.

I walked back to the Noah's Ark, where I found Nathaniel in the taproom. I packed my bags and then settled my account with him. He looked disappointed to learn I was returning to London. At least someone in Deptford was sorry to see me go.

'I will be back in a few days,' I said, and he brightened.

I told him about the letter I'd received. 'Mr Archer received similar letters, I think from the same author. I suspect one of them was the letter he asked you about. Did you see anyone go upstairs when you were here yesterday?'

He shook his head. 'I was in and out, but Mr Child was here all afternoon. You could ask him?'

'Your mother told me. I will.' Not that I expected much help from that quarter.

I wondered about the transaction I'd witnessed between Nathaniel and the well-dressed stranger at the warehouse last night. I decided not to ask him about it. It was unlikely to have any connection to my inquiry, and I wanted to keep him as an ally. I hoped it wasn't anything too dangerous. I knew what it was like to lose a father and be thrust into penury. Father's creditors had circled like buzzards after his death, and had it not been for the pity of a distant cousin, I would have been left penniless. Perhaps I could help Nathaniel and myself at the same time? I took the silver ticket from my pocket. 'Have you ever seen anything like this before?'

'Can't say I have, sir. Looks expensive.'

'Can you ask around the brothels and the gaming houses in the Broadway and the Strand? See if any of them uses a ticket like this?'

He made a grab for it – a little too swiftly, I felt – and I moved it out of his reach. 'Just remember what it looks like. I'll keep hold of it for now. But if you find the right place, then after I've been there, I'll let you keep it.'

He gave me a smile that made his dimples dance. 'You can count on me, Captain Corsham.'

'One last thing. Did you ever have a problem with someone leaving dead birds here at the Ark?'

His smile vanished. 'Not just birds, sir. Someone left a cat's head in the yard once, and before that it was three dead rats, crawling with maggots. It's slave religion, sir. Black magic.'

'When did it start?'

'Just after your friend came to town that first time. People say he told the story of the drowned slaves to the Negroes up in the Broadway and it riled them.'

'Does anyone have any idea who is behind it?'

'I caught a glimpse of them once, when I was coming back from my shift at the warehouses – saw two Negroes running away. Footmen from their build. That was the time we found the cat's head in the yard.'

'Has anyone else had trouble aside from Monday and the officers?'

'Everyone who crewed *The Dark Angel* when the slaves were drowned. That's why the men refused to serve on her. It fuelled the rumour that the ship was cursed.'

'Why didn't you mention it when we talked before?'

Again that wary look entered his eyes. 'Ma don't want anyone to know. Thinks it will frighten our guests away. That's not why you're leaving, is it, sir?'

'It will take more than a few dead birds to scare me. When was the last time anything was left here at the inn?'

He thought for a moment. 'The night before I found Archer dead. A doll made of twigs was nailed to the stable door. You could tell it was supposed to be a blackamoor by the hair. If you don't mind, sir, don't mention this to Ma. It scares her witless. After the doll, she got all manner of ideas in her head. Pestered Mr Child for days. I don't want to start her off again, if I can help it.'

'What kind of ideas?'

He rolled his eyes. 'We'd had a spot of trouble at the inn earlier that day. Ma caught that Negress whore from the bath-house skulking around.'

'Jamaica Mary?'

'Aye, that's her. She was probably looking for something to steal. I boxed her ears and threw her out. Then later that evening, Ma saw Mr Stokes's free Negro in the yard. He was only looking for Brabazon, but Ma got it into her head that he and the whore were responsible for the doll.'

Scipio certainly struck me as an unlikely practitioner of witchcraft. 'Did Mr Child question him?'

'Aye, sir, but like I said, he was just looking for Brabazon. He's the one Negro in Deptford with prospects. Why would he be in alliance with a penny-fuck whore? Why would he risk his position with Mr Stokes for a bit of foolery? Mr Child thought the same, but there's no reasoning with Ma where Negroes are concerned. She thinks they're all out to murder us in our beds.'

'It doesn't frighten you? Witchcraft and curses, I mean.'

He touched the ivory charm around his neck. 'Got one of these, haven't I? It's a nigger finger bone – gives protection from their magic. You want me to get you one? I can buy them down at the dock for half a crown.'

Swiftly, I held up a hand. 'Thank you, there's no need.'

'Just that silver ticket then. I'll get right on it, sir. If it's come from a place in Deptford, then I'll find it.'

As I rode out of town, I carried the sulphurous smell of the place with me. It pervaded the clothes and the skin and the hair. Three hundred drowned slaves. 'Nigger finger bones'. In my absence, I reflected, it would be no great loss if someone put a tinder to this place and burned it to the ground.

Chapter Twenty-Three

At Rotherhithe there were problems with the horseferry and a crowd of oyster women were screaming at the poor ferryman. In the end, tiring of the delay, I rode on into London, crossing the Thames at London Bridge. I doubled back on myself, heading east out of the city again to see Amelia. It added nearly two hours to my journey, but I was determined to make the trip. Even amidst all my other concerns, I was still painfully aware how I had left things between Amelia and I.

The sun was low in the sky by the time I rode into Bethnal Green. The sow in the neighbour's garden eyed me from her bath of mud. The door to Amelia's cottage stood ajar, and I pushed it open, calling her name. I stopped. Shards of broken china crunched beneath my boots. Something was wrong.

Drawing my pistol, I opened the parlour door. A scene of disorder greeted me. Every sofa cushion had been slashed open, feathers floating through the air. The tea table was on its side, and a broken lamp lay beside it. I moved further into the room, and almost stumbled over a woman lying on the floor.

'Amelia!' I cried.

I crouched down and rolled her over, immediately realizing my mistake. It was Amelia's Indian maidservant. The poor woman's head lolled back grotesquely, where the throat had been cut. My hands sticky with gore, I stared appalled.

Somewhere up above a floorboard creaked and I raised my

eyes to the ceiling. Another creak – my senses alert, I tracked the sound. Someone was trying to move silently in the room above. Amelia or the killer? I couldn't be sure.

My pistol primed, I returned to the hall, listening intently. Whoever was up there must have heard me calling Amelia's name. If it was her, then why hadn't she replied or come down? I walked slowly up the stairs. Two doors opened off the landing, both of them closed. I examined the one that led into the room over the parlour. Sweat snaked across my back. I reached for the handle.

The person behind it must have been listening out for me, for the door swung open suddenly, knocking me backwards. My pistol fell from my hand and clattered along the floor. A hooded figure dressed in black leaped over me and made for the stairs. With no time to recover my pistol, I went after him. He was already halfway down the stairs, and notwithstanding the advice of my surgeons I vaulted over the bannister to cut off his escape to the front door. A jolt of lightning split my leg as I landed.

Seeing that his route was blocked, the man turned, seeking another exit. I ran after him as quickly as my injured leg would permit, catching him up in a small kitchen to the rear of the house. A door led out to a vegetable garden, and my quarry was kicking it hard. I almost had him, but the door splintered, and he barged through it.

He reached the garden wall in seconds, and took a leap to grab the top of it. I was slower, but I managed to seize hold of his boot. He kicked out with his other foot, striking me in the face. I stumbled backwards and he pulled himself up and over the wall. I climbed after him, but by the time I reached the top he was sprinting away down an alley on the other side.

Amelia. The thought forestalled any idea of going after him. I jumped down and hurried back through the garden, dimly aware of a neighbour peering at me from an upstairs window. I took the stairs as fast as I could, and burst into the room. My breath came in painful gulps as I took in the scene. A cast-iron bathtub stood on the floor, at the foot of a half-tester bed. Amelia was kneeling in front of it, fully clothed, her hands tied behind her. Her face was in the water. I could see bruising at the back of her neck, where he'd held her under. Prayers tumbled from my lips, as I pulled her out.

Her face was white, her lips purple. Her eyes rolled back into her skull, the whites crackled with blood like a pottery glaze. Dear God.

I had once, in America, seen a man revive his son, after the lad was trapped under ice in a lake. He had forced the water from the boy's lungs by applying pressure to the abdomen. Desperately, I tried to remember how it was done. I interlaced my fingers and pressed down upon her stomach. I did it again, harder, willing life back into her body.

My arms ached with exertion and tears rolled down my face. The seconds turned into minutes that felt like hours. I don't know how long I laboured like this, but her limbs remained limp. I knew she was dead long before I accepted the fact. Eventually, I pulled her head into my lap, overwhelmed with despair. How could I have failed to foresee that Amelia was in danger?

I gazed at her face, remembering the awkward, birdlike girl I'd ignored in Devon and the lonely woman who had asked for my friendship. I wept for her and for Tad, sitting there on the floor in that cold, miserable room with the light fading around us. I did not even move when I heard voices and the pounding of feet upon the stairs. Three stout men clattered into the room and one produced a pistol.

'Blackguard, you are under arrest for murder.'

PART THREE

26–29 JUNE 1781

If we imagine that a thing which is wont to affect us with an emotion of pain, has something similar to another thing which is wont to affect us with an equally great emotion of pleasure, we shall hate it and love it at the same time.

III. Of the Affections or Passions,
Ethics, Baruch Spinoza

CHAPTER TWENTY-FOUR

THE CONSTABLES DRAGGED me from the cottage, the neighbours peering at me from windows and doorways. One of them must have summoned help, after hearing the commotion. I was manhandled along the street to the Bethnal Green watchhouse, where I was shoved into a cell. One of the constables set about chaining me to the wall, while the others stood over me as though I was a dangerous animal.

'I didn't kill her.' I had already told them this many times. 'My name is Captain Henry Corsham. Please send for my lawyer.'

The man chaining me to the wall gave me a slap. 'You'll hang while your lawyer watches, murdering bastard.'

One of his friends drove his stick into my belly as a parting shot, and the door crashed shut behind them. I was left to moulder overnight with the rats and the stink and my own despair.

Why hadn't I seen Amelia's murder coming? Why, when I knew that Tad's rooms had been searched, hadn't I anticipated that the killer would take an interest in his only living relative? It never occurred to me that the murders were unrelated. I didn't believe in coincidences like that. What was the killer looking for? The thing Tad went to Deptford to collect? Had he forced her head under the water to make her tell him where it was?

I held my skull in my chained hands as I contemplated her

last moments. To be tortured for information you didn't possess was every soldier's secret terror. Amelia's life had been hard, but none of it would have prepared her for her death.

My leg throbbed unbearably and I hardly slept. When I did, I dreamed of Tad and black winged women. When I woke I thought of Amelia's cold damp face and the man who'd killed her. I had few recollections of him, save a sense of size and swiftness and a faint smell of sweat. I kept seeing his pink hand grabbing the bannister pole.

By the time the first misty fingers of dawn penetrated the bars of my cell, I was no nearer any answers. One of the constables unlocked the door and placed a bowl of slops in front of me. I asked again for my lawyer, but he ignored me.

A few hours later, the local magistrate came to see me. He had a thin grey face scattered with warts, and seemed genuinely horrified by the murders of Amelia and her maid.

I protested my innocence, which bored him. Then I tried bribery, which angered him. Finally, with little option left, I invoked the name of my patron, Nicholas Cavill-Lawrence. The magistrate gazed at me with scepticism, but I must have planted enough seeds of doubt in his mind, for eventually he hurried off to dispatch a message to Whitehall.

I felt little relief. By now Cavill-Lawrence would have received Lucius Stokes's letter. He would know about my inquiry into Tad's murder. Now I stood accused of a sensational murder myself.

I passed many more hours in that cell. The day lengthened and it grew dark outside. Where was Cavill-Lawrence? Why didn't he come? Was he angry, leaving me to stew? Perhaps, having read Stokes's letter, he had washed his hands of me altogether? I contemplated every possibility over those long, anxious hours, including a dismal death at the end of a hangman's rope. Finally, I heard the rattle of a key in the lock. A lantern dazzled me, and I turned away.

'That's him,' I heard Cavill-Lawrence say. 'That's Henry Corsham.'

Distaste coloured his tone and I realized how I must look. My wig was crawling with lice and my coat was stiff and black with the maid's blood.

Cavill-Lawrence's voice rose with characteristic impatience. 'Get those chains off him, sir, before I have your job. The man's a war hero.'

My shackles were duly unlocked and my money and weapons returned to me. Cavill-Lawrence instructed the magistrate to have my horse and bags returned to my house in Mayfair. Then he had the constables line up outside the watchhouse to offer me their sullen apologies. A short time later I was ensconced in Cavill-Lawrence's large black carriage, the lights of Bethnal Green retreating into the distance behind us. My legs felt brittle as twigs and the stink rising off me was pungent. I hadn't touched the filth the constables had called food and I was dizzy with hunger.

I glanced at Cavill-Lawrence, trying to gauge how angry he was. 'Forgive me if I have caused you any embarrassment, sir. The magistrate wouldn't listen to my explanations.'

'Forget Mrs Bradstreet's murder,' he said tersely. 'You should be more concerned about Lucius Stokes's letter. The West India lobby are in high dudgeon about it all. Stokes says you were prowling around Deptford asking questions about *The Dark Angel* – what were you thinking?'

'A friend of mine was murdered, Mrs Bradstreet's brother. I think they were both killed because of a massacre that happened on board that ship.'

'Do you think I don't know this?' Cavill-Lawrence shook his

head. 'Dear God, Harry, but you should have come to me. I'd have told you not to tangle in this wretched business.'

Our faces were orange in the dim glow of the carriage lamps. Cavill-Lawrence was approaching fifty, but you might have guessed sixty. His stomach strained against his velvet waistcoat and his jowls spilled over the top of his cravat. Heavy pouches beneath his eyes seemed weighed down by the responsibilities of the offices of state he held: Under-Secretary of State for War, trusted member of His Majesty's Privy Council. It didn't altogether surprise me that he seemed to have already known about Tad and the ship. Caro said he held more secrets than an Ottoman dungeon.

'Napier Smith is most displeased about your role in all of this. He thinks you are an enemy of the slave trade and he suspects you of much more. I have tried to convince him that your worst crime is naivety. That had better be true.'

I stared at him in alarm. Napier Smith, the Chairman of the West India lobby.

'I only wanted to find the man who killed my friend, sir. I am sorry that you were dragged into all of this.'

His gaze was unforgiving. 'Caro is like a daughter to me. Her father was one of my oldest friends, but I'll not make an enemy of Napier Smith for you or any other man.'

The carriage swung off the highway onto one of the country roads running north of the city. Cavill-Lawrence answered my look of inquiry with another hard stare.

'He wants to see you tonight. I imagine he has a lot of questions. So do I.'

I bowed my head. The prospect of meeting Smith when I was so disordered in thought and appearance filled me with trepidation. My mistakes were compounding, everything falling apart.

Yet I was still capable of rational thought and I strung a few together now. Lucius Stokes was a tadpole compared to Napier Smith, and yet Smith had involved himself personally in this matter. Now he wanted to see me at eleven o'clock at night. This couldn't simply be because I'd trampled on Stokes's patch. I'd always suspected that the Deptford mayor had some secret agenda where Tad's murder was concerned. Perhaps that agenda was shared by the West India lobby?

We drove at speed through the outlying villages and hamlets. Trees pressed in on either side. Sometimes I glimpsed the startled eyes of a rabbit or a deer in the hedgerows.

Tad's words kept coming back to me: *They are a cabal of wealthy slave merchants. Their power runs deeper than most people in this country will ever know.* He had told Amelia that the West India lobby was part of the conspiracy ranged against him. A week ago I had dismissed it. Now I wasn't so sure.

Yet Lucius Stokes's complaint was that I had been asking questions about *The Dark Angel* – not Tad's murder. The ship must be important to them – but why? Africans died at the hands of slave traders every day, though never in such large numbers, or where profit underpinned those murders so starkly. Was that it? Was it the scale of the deaths that was significant?

I remembered my horror when I'd first learned of the massacre. My reaction wasn't much mirrored in Deptford, but in London it would be a different story. Out in the countryside too. I thought of the Wiltshire village where I'd grown up. People there had simple ideas about right and wrong. I knew instinctively that if someone told them about *The Dark Angel* they would not like it.

I nurtured this thought as we drove. Cavill-Lawrence sat very still, saying nothing. His eyes were half closed and if I hadn't known him better, I'd have said he was asleep.

I had assumed Stokes was protecting the murderer, and maybe he was, but what if that wasn't his primary motivation? What if the West India lobby were concerned with a bigger secret: the story of the massacre itself? I knocked this notion around in my mind, trying to see it from all vantages, determined to understand the chain of cause and effect. By the time we turned off the main road, onto a private drive somewhere north of Hampstead, I believed that I had it all worked out.

Chapter Twenty-Five

THE MANSION GLEAMED like marble in the moonlight. I kept catching glimpses of it through the elm trees that lined the drive. I knew its name: Fairmount. I had read countless reports in the newspapers about the cost of its construction and the ceilings it had taken a team of Italian masters a year to paint. Built to dominate, rather than inspire, Fairmount's critics bemoaned the vulgarity of new money. Caro, who came from new money herself, said that by vulgarity they meant power.

We rounded a bend and the house loomed before us. We passed through an ornate set of gates into a gravel forecourt, and liveried footmen descended on us from all sides. They ushered us into a high-domed hall, where Cavill-Lawrence was relieved of his hat and gloves. I'd lost mine back in Bethnal Green and the footmen did a passable job of pretending not to notice my disordered appearance. We were escorted along a colonnade lined with statues of Greek gods into a library painted with classical scenes. The master of the house was waiting there to receive us.

I had seen Napier Smith around Whitehall, though we'd never been introduced. He had inherited his father's old seat in Parliament, along with a hundred thousand acres of sugar plantations in the Caribbean. Unmistakably tall and thin, tonight he wore a pea-green coat with diamond buttons, and a powdered periwig. Cavill-Lawrence made the introductions and I apologized for my dishevelment. Smith appraised me coolly. 'I care nothing for that.'

In direct contrast to Cavill-Lawrence's heavy wearing of his years, Smith's hairless skin and high-pitched voice made him seem younger even than his tender age of twenty-four. He had a long white face, a largish nose, and a wide, unsmiling mouth. The volume in his hand was Machiavelli's *Il Principe*. I wondered if he was really reading it or if it was a prop. Legend had it that old Jasper Smith, the father, had once bankrupted a man because the poor fellow's racehorse had seen off his own at Ascot. People joked uneasily that the son lacked the old man's compassion.

Smith gestured us to an arrangement of chairs beneath a large Italian painting. He made no offer of refreshment, though I could have sorely used some wine.

'I have received a report from Lucius Stokes about your activities in Deptford, Captain Corsham. To say they disturbed me would be an understatement. Yet Mr Cavill-Lawrence has always been a friend to the West India lobby, and he believes that your intent may not have been malign.' His eyes roamed my face. 'We shall see.'

It was unbearably hot in that room. A huge fire blazed, though it was not long past midsummer. Amelia's cold face kept edging into my thoughts. Tad's ravaged body on Brabazon's table. Just get through this, I told myself. Say whatever you need to say. Then you can think.

'I understand you were a friend of the late Mr Thaddeus Archer,' Smith said. 'When did you first hear of his murder?'

'About a week ago,' I said. 'Mrs Bradstreet, Archer's sister, told me he was missing. I discovered he was dead when I went to Deptford the following morning.'

'How many times did you see Mrs Bradstreet subsequently?'

'Twice. Once when I returned from Deptford. Then again at Archer's funeral. Last night would have been the third.'

He questioned me like this for upwards of two hours. I answered him truthfully – I didn't see that I had very much choice. I told him nearly everything. About *The Dark Angel* and her crew, about Drake's attempt on my life, about the things I had found in Tad's rooms. I left out only my conversations with Cinnamon, Scipio and the Africans at Tad's funeral. I didn't want to get anyone else into trouble.

Smith seemed particularly interested in my views on slavery, and I assured him my opinions were perfectly orthodox.

'You don't believe in abolition?'

Under the circumstances, I could hardly afford to be equivocal. 'No, sir.'

'Lucius Stokes believes you do.'

'He is wrong, sir.'

'Did you ever come across any documents relating to the ship?' Cavill-Lawrence asked. 'At Archer's rooms or anywhere else?'

'Documents, sir?' My ears pricked up.

'Legal papers? Contracts? Anything of that sort? We know Archer took possession of them shortly before he died.'

'Only the pages from the master's journal I told you about.' From Cavill-Lawrence's face I could see this wasn't what he was after. 'Perhaps they were stolen by the man who searched Archer's rooms?'

'The man you saw at Archer's rooms was working for me,' Cavill-Lawrence said. 'We took Archer's papers to stop them falling into the wrong hands. Yet certain documents we sought were not among them.'

'I see.' What did this mean? I couldn't think. 'Archer told his sister he was going to Deptford to collect something important. Perhaps it was these papers?'

Cavill-Lawrence glanced at Smith. 'Do you think it possible?'

Smith thought for a moment. 'If they were still in Deptford, then Lucius Stokes would have surely found them. The killer can't have them, for why else would he have tortured Mrs Bradstreet?'

Cavill-Lawrence closed his eyes. 'Those papers were precious to Archer. If he'd taken possession of them that last time in Deptford, then why didn't he simply return to London? Why risk being caught with them? They were stolen property after all. And why wait around to be murdered?'

Smith toyed with a jewelled snuffbox in his hand. 'Archer might have been talking about anything. My guess is that he received the papers from the thief in London, and then gave them to someone he trusted for safekeeping. We know he had help.' His cold, blue eyes returned to my face. 'Did he give them to you?'

'On my word as a gentleman, I never saw them.'

'In my experience gentlemen lie just as well as other men.'

'I'm not lying, sir.'

I was taking a careful mental note of everything they said. What thief? What papers? And what was Cavill-Lawrence's part in all of this? It felt like more than a simple political favour to the West India lobby.

His gaze wasn't much warmer than Smith's, and I realized that he didn't believe me either. 'You are a pragmatic man. I cannot see you as a secret radical. Loyalty would more likely be your weakness. Perhaps Archer asked you to look after these papers and a promise was made? Now you feel beholden.'

'No, sir. That did not happen.'

'Perhaps you think Archer's motives were honourable? Nothing could be further from the truth. He was a secretive, dangerous man, obsessed with *The Dark Angel*. Ultimately she proved his undoing.'

'I know he felt very strongly about what happened to those slaves.' I was hoping to draw them out on the subject of the ship. As long as they thought I might have these papers, I could keep them talking.

'You think this was all about the dead slaves? You couldn't be more wrong. Archer knew a good opportunity when he spied one. He planned to prosecute those sailors for his own political ends.'

That much I had worked out in the carriage, but one part still eluded me and I gave voice to my objection now. 'Those slaves were accounted property. They couldn't be murdered under English law. So how could Archer prosecute the crew?'

Cavill-Lawrence made an ambiguous gesture with his thumbs, and Smith spoke sharply: 'We are concerned here not with the how, but with the why. Suffice to say that Archer found a way. He was a devious, clever man and he knew a lot of devious, clever lawyer's tricks.'

I chose not to press the point. Smith was still watching me like a Spanish inquisitor, and I didn't want to let them see the extent of my interest.

'We don't think Archer came across *The Dark Angel* entirely by chance,' Cavill-Lawrence said. 'We think he'd been looking for something like this for a long time. To him, you see, this was so much more than one rogue voyage. So much more than three hundred slaves drowned at sea. The crew were largely irrelevant, a means to an end. For all Archer's indignation, so were the slaves.'

This part, at least, I believed I understood. 'The ship was a symbol. The worst example of the slave trade he could find.'

'Precisely,' Smith said. 'It wasn't representative at all. Yet when did the facts ever count in the court of public opinion? Put those men on trial, force them to defend themselves, and standing alongside them in the dock you'd have the entire institution of slavery itself.'

Cavill-Lawrence's signet ring winked in the candlelight. 'We are a nation of hypocrites,' he said quietly. 'That's the simple truth. People don't inquire too closely into how their sugar gets into their tea, because they don't want to know. Put it in a courtroom, put it on the front page of a newspaper, and it's hard to ignore. Win or lose, you force men to stand up in court, on oath, saying things we'd rather not hear said.'

Again Smith took up the thread: 'The housewives hold the purse-strings and those sailors dropped children into the sea. It doesn't take a clever lawyer to work out what comes next. Petitions and pamphlets, people disavowing West Indian sugar. It was a gift to the abolitionists and Archer knew it. Where it would have gone from there, God only knows.'

Tad thought he'd known. He had told Amelia that he believed he could end slavery. Originally, I had believed it another of his exaggerations. It still seemed a leap to suppose it could have such powerful ramifications. Yet looking at the tense, troubled faces of the men sitting before me now, I realized that they believed it too.

Tad's murder had solved one problem for them, but it had presented them with another. If one of the ship's officers had killed him to prevent the prosecution, then any trial of his killer would inevitably touch upon motive. The story of *The Dark Angel* aired in a public courtroom, precisely the outcome the West India lobby wished to avoid.

Presumably Lucius Stokes had ordered Peregrine Child not to exert himself over Tad's murder. He'd had Tad's room at the Noah's Ark searched, trying to find these missing papers. They'd swept everything under the rug – until I'd come along and swept everything back out.

'We are a nation at war,' Cavill-Lawrence said, 'and one of our foremost industries is under concerted attack. Archer was not an agent for the French or the Americans, but he might as well have been. His confederates may seek to pick up where he left off. If he gave you those papers, then it is imperative that you tell us now.'

Were the Children of Liberty Tad's confederates? Or Moses Graham and Ephraim Proudlock, who had looked so frightened at Tad's funeral?

'Tell him the rest,' Smith said, mistaking my silence for complicity. 'Archer's debauchery. His vile habits. Let him truly understand the man he called a friend.'

I gazed at his young, arrogant face and my flesh prickled with unease. 'If you mean that Archer consorted with prostitutes, then that was well known. Lincoln's Inn almost evicted him from his chambers over the scandal.'

Smith's eyes shone with malice. 'I wasn't talking about his whores.'

'Mr Smith had a man look into Archer's habits,' Cavill-Lawrence said. 'He managed to track down one of those jezebels from Lincoln's Inn. What she told him is curious, to say the least. Archer invited her to his rooms, that part is true enough. Yet when she got there, he didn't bed her. He didn't even try. They simply conversed for an hour, he paid her, and then she left.'

My ears were buzzing again. I chose my words very carefully.

'You're saying he manufactured the scandal himself? Why would he do that?'

'To conceal a different stripe of debauchery altogether,' Smith said. 'Archer was a molly. A sodomite. A buggeranto. Whichever word you use to describe his perversions, it's all the same.'

The buzzing grew louder. 'I don't believe it.'

'He imposed upon you,' Cavill-Lawrence said. 'He deceived his friends. You must ask yourself whether any promises made to such a man should be respected.'

'I never made any promises.' Blood had rushed to my face. 'I never saw your damn papers.'

Ultimately, I think it was my discomfort that convinced them. They mistook it for disgust, for anger, for embarrassment. All the things they supposed a man would naturally feel, if he'd just found out his oldest friend was a secret sodomite.

Cavill-Lawrence arched an eyebrow. 'Then where the devil are they?' he muttered. 'Corsham doesn't have them. Archer didn't have them at his rooms in London or in Deptford. Mrs Bradstreet didn't have them. Nor, we presume, does the killer. Is it possible Archer gave them to some sodomite friend he trusted?'

'His encounters at the molly-brothels seem to have been of the fleeting variety.' Smith gave a sardonic smile. 'Yet my man is looking into his past. If he ever had an attachment of greater significance, the molly will be found.'

A tingle of fear skittered down my spine, an old, unloved acquaintance. Smith turned to me, his eyes devoid of emotion. 'Return to Deptford again and I will hear of it. Make any more inquiries into Archer's murder and I'll hear of that too. Involve yourself in my business again and I will take your life apart piece by piece.'

I bowed my head. 'I understand, sir.'

Again I was treated to Cavill-Lawrence's hard stare. 'Captain Corsham is an ambitious man. Of course he won't involve himself again. Not now he understands the consequences for the kingdom – and for himself.' His lip curled with distaste. 'As for Mr Archer, corrupt in mind, corrupt in body. If he wasn't already dead, I'd have him hanged for a sodomite.'

Chapter Twenty-Six

WHEN I GOT home, I went to my bedroom and locked the door. It still lay upon me. Fear's cold shadow. A face from an old memory, an echo of a voice once heard.

I knew what I should do. Forget Tad. Forget Amelia. Forget I ever heard of *The Dark Angel*. Do and say all the things I had been doing and saying for the past few years, until Amelia Bradstreet had knocked upon my door.

Had they believed me? Napier Smith and Cavill-Lawrence? Had I betrayed myself in gesture or in word? Done anything to give them cause to suspect I'd already known about Tad's secret desires?

It was all flooding back over me. Oxford. His earnest face. So much engraved on my memory, no matter how hard I tried to forget.

I stared at my reflection in my dressing table mirror, and it was as if I gazed into all my past selves. The man I was before Tad. The man I was with him. The man I was with Caro. The man I was now.

Memories came thick and fast, and I struggled to catch hold of them. That day with Tad on the river. Days together in taverns and teagardens. Nights talking and laughing in our rooms. The day I left for America. The day I first killed a man. The day my father opened his jugular vein with his own quill knife.

Something else was building inside me besides the fear. I had been conscious of it before, but I felt it stronger now. It was as if a tide had been rising ever since I'd learned that Tad was dead, perhaps for many years before that. I felt the pressure inside my chest, inside my stomach, inside my head. I gasped for breath and a lurching sob came out.

'I'm sorry,' I said. 'Oh God, Tad, I'm so sorry.'

It was the living Tad who answered. 'Prince Hal,' he said. 'I heard a rumour you were back. It's good to see you.'

We were in his rooms at Lincoln's Inn, over three years earlier. It was the last time I'd seen him alive – six years since we'd last met, since I'd run away to America without a word. Six years since the fear had last crawled inside of me.

We had faced one another in his sitting room. The lamps were dim and the fire low. I saw things I recognized: his writing box, the Turkey rug. The place smelled of him: a faint musk of wine and scent and tobacco. His face was cast in shadow. One cheekbone shone like a sliver of ivory. God, how I'd missed him.

'No more letters, Tad. It needs to stop.'

My voice was constricted, my tension mirrored in his rigid body. I'd meant to work up to it, to talk to him first as old friends do. But I couldn't do it.

I saw something go out in his eyes. Some faint gleam of hope, perhaps. 'That's why you've come?'

'Those letters could ruin us both. If they fell into the wrong hands – people would misunderstand.'

His hands trembled and his voice caught. 'They are only the truth, Hal. How I think, how I feel. Would you take that from me too?'

'Just because a man feels something, it doesn't mean that it is right.' I drew a deep breath. 'I'm getting married. That's the other thing I came to tell you.'

Silence. Then his voice came quietly from the shadows. 'Do I know her?'

'Caroline Craven. You probably remember her brothers.'

'I remember all the Cravens. Caroline was a friend of my sister.' Another silence. 'It is a good match.'

Don't let him cling to that. 'It isn't the money, you understand. We are in love.'

He came forward into the light and I saw his face properly for the first time. The shadows beneath his wet eyes looked like bruises.

'An ocean,' he said. 'A marriage. Why not just build a wall?'

Why would he never understand – even though it had cost us both so much? 'I'm not like you, Tad. You're wrong. You just can't see it.'

I took the bundle of letters from inside my coat. Some he'd written at Oxford, some in the years that followed. Each blotched with tears, written in drink-soaked moments of despair.

He gazed at them, and then at me. 'If they are so dangerous, then why did you keep them all these years?'

I had no answer for him. Nor any answers for myself. I only knew that it needed to stop. For his sake, for mine, for Caro's. 'I'm going to burn them, and you're going to watch me do it.'

It was a way of making him understand. Cruel, but necessary – the hardest thing I'd ever done before or since. I stoked the fire, unable to look upon his face. Then I untied the ribbon and dropped his letters into the flames. We stood and watched as the pages blackened and curled.

'There you are, Hal,' he said, at last, in a quiet, fractured voice. 'Now I might never have existed. I'm just a ghost in a story you once told of yourself.'

I cried silently, there in my bedroom, great sobs that wracked my body. Whatever had been rising in me since Tad's death, the banks had burst. It washed everything else away, even the creature that was fear. I knew only the loss of him. The loss of myself.

As I wept, I tallied the debits: America, the letters, my absence from his side when he'd walked into danger. I thought of Amelia too. Our conversation at the church. The last words she'd heard me say were that I didn't wish to know her. I gazed at the man in the mirror in his tattered uniform. I remembered those battlefields in America where I'd wanted to die.

Press on with my inquiry and I risked everything. My seat in Parliament, my reputation, Caro and Gabriel. Do nothing and I might as well be dead. The realization calmed me. I had to go forward, because I could not go back. If it seems like the height of madness, then perhaps it was – but you did not know Thaddeus Archer and you never will.

I thought of the murderer then, a hood where his face should be. I thought of Tad on the Cherwell, smiling, sugar flowing through his fingers. I chose to see it in Deptford terms, not as love or honour, but as a transaction. I owed, and that debt would be paid in full.

Chapter Twenty-Seven

Sleep brought me respite from my memories, if only for a while. I woke much later than usual and by the time I had washed the stink of the cell from my aching body, I could hear that Caro was up and about. I went downstairs to the dining room, where I found her breakfasting with Gabriel. She wore a silk dressing-gown and her hair hung in loose curls. Gabriel had a rim of chocolate around his mouth, and she was reading aloud to him from the newspaper, putting on funny voices to make him laugh. It was the scene I had always imagined: my contented house.

Except none of it was real. My marriage was a blighted moor. All we had was Gabriel and a shared interest in my political prospects. Those prospects would be worth nothing without the support of Cavill-Lawrence. He controlled the ministry's borough-mongers and the electoral purse-strings. One word from him and my seat in Parliament would vanish like a pricked bubble. Under such circumstances, would Gabriel be enough? Divorce was unthinkable, but separation was a different question. Caro's inheritance was tied up in trust, which gave her options. I couldn't bear the thought of parting with Gabriel. And yet how could I take my son from his mother?

Caro noticed me standing in the doorway. 'Pomfret told me you were back.' She registered my expression. 'Has something happened?'

I nodded and she rose from the table. We slipped into the hall, where we spoke softly so that Gabriel couldn't hear.

'Amelia is dead, murdered by the same man who killed Tad.' Briefly I recounted the story. Her face paled.

'You might have been killed. I can hardly comprehend it. And arrested, Harry! Are you certain no word of it will get out?'

I wondered if it was my death or the prospect of a scandal that so alarmed her. I searched her sea-blue eyes for a clue. Sometimes I believed the depths they contained were impossibly vast. Other times I thought them implausibly shallow. Today I found I had no opinion at all.

'Is that all you have to say? Nothing about Amelia?'

She frowned. 'Don't imply that I don't care. You have no right.'

'I'm only asking what you think. It isn't a crime, Caro. Perhaps you believe she brought it upon herself?' I wasn't angry, only tired now of all the lies and hypocrisy.

Two spots of colour had risen on her cheeks, and when she spoke her tone was crisp. 'If you want to know what I think, then I shall tell you. Thaddeus and Amelia were cut from the same cloth. They fought against everything people know and believe to be true. Thaddeus and slavery. Amelia's elopement. They thought they could refashion the world to suit their own private desires. Yet you cannot break the rules without consequence, Harry. Rightly so.'

'She was a lonely, unhappy woman. She only wanted to find the man who killed her brother.'

'No, she wanted *you* to find him. She didn't care who else got hurt. The Archers never did.'

Perhaps we might have said more, words we would have been unable to take back. Yet Gabriel must have heard some part of our argument, for he burst into tears and she ran to him. I pulled my watch from my waistcoat pocket, the numbers blurring before my eyes. 'Please excuse me. I must get to White-hall.'

*

I spent the late morning and early part of the afternoon at my desk in the War Office, working through a pile of dispatches that had accumulated in my absence. My clerks were diligent and I fear I tried their patience sorely. All I could think about were the mysteries I'd left behind in Deptford. As soon as I could, I manufactured an excuse to leave my desk. In the lobby I walked past Cavill-Lawrence, deep in conversation with one of our generals. His eyes followed me out the door.

I still didn't fully understand his involvement in this busi-ness. The ministry had sound fiscal motives to protect the slave trade from its detractors, and it was also in their political inter-est to placate the West India lobby. Yet when Cavill-Lawrence had questioned me, I had sensed a deeper concern. I felt he hadn't merely been trying to reassure Napier Smith and the West India lobby of my lack of complicity – he had been trying to reassure himself.

It was yet another mystery, and I was convinced that some of the answers might lie here in London. Last night Cavill-Lawrence had said that Tad hadn't acted alone. Tonight I intended to go to the tavern Scipio had told me about to look for the Children of Liberty. Tomorrow I would try to find Moses Graham, the fat gentleman from Tad's funeral. It had been obvious that he and his skinny assistant, Proudlock, had been hiding something.

First I wanted to look for *The Dark Angel* here in Whitehall. I was acutely aware that any search of the ministry's archives would carry me into dangerous territory. I did not take Napier

Smith's threats lightly and I had few illusions about Cavill-Lawrence. If he felt I'd betrayed his trust, then he'd throw me to the wolves. Yet since last night, I viewed the world through a different prism. It wasn't that I didn't care about the consequences. It made me sick just to think of them. Yet Tad had walked willingly into danger and if I was to settle my account with him, then I must be prepared to do so too.

I stepped out onto Whitehall. The street was a sea of government clerks, hurrying between government offices, their wigs a froth of grey scurf on a black, silk tide. To my right, the spires of the Palace of Westminster stood stark against the sun-bleached sky. I walked in the opposite direction, towards Charing Cross.

During times of war, many merchants lodged records of their trading voyages with the Admiralty. Should a ship be sunk by the Americans or the French, the owner might have a claim to reparations once the war was won. Lodging a record precluded any dispute over ownership or the value of a cargo. It was possible that John Monday had done so for *The Dark Angel*.

I showed my credentials to the guards at the Admiralty gatehouse, and was admitted into the courtyard. Naval officers in blue uniforms strutted like peacocks between the pale stone buildings. I had been here many times before on War Office business, and no one batted an eyelid as I entered the principal building and went upstairs. The Admiralty reading room was long, light and airy, hung with paintings of ships and navy Sea Lords. Lawyers from the Admiralty courts sat at long tables, poring over precedents and statutes.

I knew the clerk on the desk, a man named Moseley. We exchanged a few words about the latest news from America. Then I asked him if the Admiralty held any records on *The Dark Angel*. He was gone an unusually long time, and when he returned, he looked a little troubled.

'We have no records on her, sir. Not here.'

'Are you saying there are records somewhere else?'

'I cannot answer that, sir.'

'What do you mean you cannot answer that?'

He examined me with what I fancied to be a trace of suspicion. 'Any queries relating to this ship are to be referred to Under-Secretary Cavill-Lawrence. Would you like me to put your request in writing, sir?'

That could only mean that the documents had been designated a secret of state.

'No,' I said swiftly. 'I will take it up with him myself.'

'Very good, sir.' Moseley's eyes were definitely distrustful. I wondered who he'd been speaking to during his absence.

'Can you search for another vessel? The *Duc d'Orléans*? The owner is the same man as before, John Monday of *Atlantic Trading and Partners*. Her name is now *The Phoenix*, but I'm interested in her first voyage after she was bought by Monday – before the name was changed.'

This time the clerk was gone only a few minutes and when he returned, he had a file in his hand. 'You need to sign the docket, sir. And again when you return it.'

I did as he requested, and withdrew to one of the library tables. A cavalry exercise was taking place on the parade ground outside, and the thump of hooves and barked commands drifted up to me through the open window.

It took me nearly half an hour to go through it all. The file contained a copy of the certificate of sale, as well as a bundle of correspondence between the Admiralty and various interested parties. Letters from John Monday, from Captain Vaughan, from the naval officer who had captured and sold him the vessel, and from the acting-commissioner of the slave fort at Cape Coast who had witnessed the sale. The letters only mentioned *The Dark Angel* in passing and told me nothing of significance.

The final letter was from Monday's insurer, a gentleman named Hector Sebright of Lloyd's Coffeehouse, Pope's Head Alley. It confirmed that the vessel and its cargo had been insured with him for the sum of eight thousand pounds. According to the letter, the ship's manifest and a list of the investors were attached. I turned the document over, but I couldn't see them. I went back through the file, looking for these documents. They weren't there.

Had they been mislaid? Perhaps. Yet another possibility occurred to me too. Monday had said that Vaughan had bought the *Duc d'Orleans* using letters of credit backed by his investors – the same syndicate which had financed *The Dark Angel*. Had Cavill-Lawrence removed the names of these gentlemen from the public record, just as he'd removed all trace of *The Dark Angel*?

I returned the file to Moseley and the fussy fellow handed me his docket to sign. As I did so, an entry on it caught my eye. The file had been withdrawn as recently as yesterday and I knew the name of the man who'd signed for it very well. I stared at his signature, wondering whether I needed to re-examine any of my suspicions in the light of it. Deptford's magistrate, Peregrine Child, had come here looking into the *Duc d'Orleans*. I wondered if he had taken the same path through the files as I had – if the genesis of his search had been *The Dark Angel*? Almost certainly.

Pondering this discovery, I left the reading room. At the door I glanced back. The clerk was still watching me, his face sharp and thoughtful. I departed by the rear entrance, onto the Horseguards Parade Ground, where formations of cavalry wheeled and turned. As I walked towards Buckingham House, the shouts of the cavalry officers ringing in my ears, I couldn't shake the feeling that I was being watched.

*

I spent several more hours searching for *The Dark Angel* in the archives of the Southern Department and the Court of the King's Bench. Either nothing had ever been there, or Cavill-Lawrence had been thorough.

My last port of call was the Cockpit, a rambling, red-brick building on Whitehall, where Tudor courtiers had once watched their King play tennis. These days it housed the Board of Trade and the Privy Council, with bedrooms for clerks squeezed into the airless attics. It had occurred to me that the arrival of *The Dark Angel* in Jamaica, missing two-thirds of her cargo, would have been quite an event. It was possible that the governor of the island had mentioned it in his dispatches.

I showed my credential to the Board of Trade's archive clerk and asked him for all correspondence from the Governor of Jamaica during the months of December 1778 and January 1779. He returned with three packets of documents and I signed the corresponding docket, uneasy that I was leaving a trail of my inquiries across Whitehall. I took the documents to one of the cubicles designated as reading rooms.

The first dispatch contained only the usual diplomatic business that a governor of an English crown colony has with his masters back home: summaries of meetings with local dignitaries and planters, reports on the condition of fortifications, and the inevitable pleas for better naval defence and extensions to crown grants. I read it through, and then put it to one side.

The second dispatch seemed little different to the first, and yet as I scanned the pages, a name leaped out at me. *The Dark Angel.* Here she was at last. My heart beat a little faster. Cavill-

Lawrence had been diligent, but even he was capable of making a mistake.

I turn now, your Lordship, to an odd piece of business that has lately been the talk of all Kingston. A slaving vessel, by name *The Dark Angel*, lately docked in port, the larger part of the cargo having been destroyed by the crewmen during the voyage. I happened to be down at the dock on business when the surviving blacks were led off the ship, blinking in the sunlight, looking as if they had been carried to hell and back.

Anxious to understand what had occurred, I had the captain brought to me, along with the ship's surgeon. The pair claimed the vessel had run out of water and the slaves were drowned to preserve the health of the crew and remaining Negroes. Yet the captain's account was rambling and confused, and my overall impression was that the pair were hiding something. The captain, a swarthy character named Vaughan, is said to be an opium-eater and perhaps his habit played a part in what transpired. If the captain fears for his professional reputation, that might explain his reticence.

The surviving slaves have now been sold – all save one, the personal concubine of the captain – and the usual purchases of sugar and tobacco been made. The ship is due to weigh anchor for Deptford tomorrow morning. Though I pray nightly that Providence delivers our merchant shipping safely to these shores, I do not mind saying that I will be glad to see her go.

In such sentiment, I fear I am not alone. Even here in Jamaica, the slaves' demise in such a fashion was greeted with some distaste. I do not doubt that the reaction at home would be infinitely more censorious. I therefore ask that all efforts be made to suppress reporting of this matter, should it reach the ear of our journalist friends in Grub Street. Our plantation owners are beleaguered enough as it is. They need no more burdens with which to contend at this difficult time.

My fingers tingled with the sensation a new discovery begets. The news that Captain Vaughan smoked opium was surely pertinent to my inquiry, but more significant still, I felt, was the revelation that he had brought a woman slave, a survivor, back to Deptford. Vaughan's landlord at the coaching inn had made no mention of a slave girl and I wondered if he'd subsequently sold her. If so, I could hazard a guess at the name of the buyer.

I remembered Cinnamon's expression as she'd described the murder of those children, her voice shaking with the passions her tale inspired. Was it the anger of one who'd undergone that hellish voyage and lived to tell the tale?

CHAPTER TWENTY-EIGHT

THE SHADOWS WERE lengthening by the time I reached the parish of Marylebone on the north-west fringes of the city. I remembered when there had been little but fields between here and Oxford Street, but the city had been steadily encroaching northwards, and now threatened to swallow up Marylebone entirely. I was greeted in the village by the thwack of cricket balls on the green and laughter from the many skittle-grounds and taverns.

The Yorkshire Stingo was distinguishable from the other taverns only by its patrons. An overgrown garden was packed with drinking blacks, many wearing footmen's livery, evidently enjoying their evening off. Other Africans wore ragged versions of my own uniform, or the shabby coats universal to working men.

Inside the taproom, a band were playing a jig and couples were dancing. Most were black, but a few white patrons bounced African whores upon their laps. The black tapwoman smiled at me.

'You looking for a friend, soldier? A drop of dark honey to sweeten your ale?'

She was a pretty girl with a freckled nose, a flash of gold tooth, and plump brown breasts spilling out of her stays.

'I'm looking for the Children of Liberty. Someone said you might know where I could find them.'

The gold tooth disappeared, along with her smile, and she snatched up a cloth. 'Can't help you there, soldier. Mind out now.' I drew back as she swept her cloth along the bar.

I guessed they had to be wary about spies and informers. 'Thaddeus Archer was a friend of mine,' I persisted. 'If you could just pass on that message.'

'I told you, soldier, you're in the wrong place.'

Looking at her expression, I decided against offering a bribe, and retreated with my pot to a nearby table. She gave me a cold stare, and leaving her potboy to mind the bar, walked to a curtain in the wall that presumably led to one of the back rooms. Standing in front of it was a huge African built like a boxer. He stepped aside to let her through.

She emerged a few moments later, and I felt her gaze on me again. Who had she been speaking to back there?

For the next hour, I sat and watched the drinkers, looking out for anyone who displayed overt signs of abolitionist allegiance. Most of the patrons were engaged in the usual tavern pursuits, and the only political activity I witnessed was a shabby African handing out pamphlets. I held out my hand for one. It advertised an abolitionist meeting in Bishopsgate later in the week. I saw with interest that Moses Graham, the fat African gentleman I'd met at Tad's funeral, was listed as one of the speakers.

I called the pamphleteer back. 'Do you know where I might find the Children of Liberty?'

He shot a sidelong glance at the tapwoman, who shook her head.

'I don't know them, boss. I'm sorry.' The man scurried off.

It was obvious that the tavern held a connection to the group, and I refused to be discouraged. I noticed an African in footman's livery approach the huge man by the curtain. The pair spoke briefly and the latter stood aside to allow the former through.

Curious, I walked over and attempted to follow the footman. The big African moved to block my path. 'This room's private.'

'Someone just went through.'

'He had an appointment.'

'Can I get an appointment?'

'No.'

Trying to barge past him would have been an act of suicide. I was debating my next move, when I spotted a face in the crowd I recognized. Scipio was sitting alone in a corner of the tap-room, next to a boisterous party of blacks racing snails. He'd said that he sometimes drank here when he was in London.

I walked over to join him. 'Good evening, Scipio. How propitious that we should meet here, so far from Deptford.'

He rose and we bowed. 'Mayor Stokes has business in London. He did not need me tonight, and so I have a rare evening in the city to myself.'

'Does his business concern his new dock?'

'Everything does, these days. The West India lobby are meeting tonight to decide if they will support our Deptford plans.'

'How do you rate your chances?'

'We have a strong argument, but the Wapping merchants will counter our proposal. Given the divided opinions of its membership, I anticipate the lobby will stand neuter. Then the decision will be down to a Parliamentary Committee.'

'In which case you might have your new dock sometime next century.'

He smiled. 'Have you come here looking for the Children of Liberty?'

'Yes. You should know that the murderer struck again two

nights ago.' My smile faded. I was still much shaken by the memory. 'This time he killed two women.'

He stared at me. 'Which women?'

'Archer's sister and her maid. They were murdered at her home in Bethnal Green.'

Scipio sat down, visibly shocked. 'You are convinced it was the same man?'

'It would seem an unlikely coincidence. Archer's sister was also tortured before she died.'

He drew a deep breath. 'I can hardly credit that someone would do such a thing.'

I wondered if I could turn his evident horror to my advantage. I drew up a chair, and he made no objection when I sat down, seemingly lost in a reverie inspired by my news.

'The killer is a monster,' I said. 'He must be stopped. I beg you to tell me anything you know.'

He blinked, seeming to collect himself. 'I am sorry for your friend and his sister, truly I am. But I can say nothing that might jeopardize my position. Posts for educated Africans are scarce, and for all his faults, Mr Stokes appreciates my abilities.'

Yet I could sense the conflict within him. Perhaps I could ease him in gently. 'Then let us speak of something else. When I was with Stokes the other day, some dead birds were left on John Monday's doorstep.'

'I heard.'

'And you know this isn't the first time this has happened. I hear Mrs Grimshaw saw you in her yard on one such occasion?'

I thought it unlikely that the birds had a direct connection to Tad's murder. Yet it was part of the puzzle, and I wanted to understand it.

'One of Mr Stokes's servants had cut his hand badly that night, and needed a surgeon. I tried at Brabazon's rooms, but he wasn't there. His landlord told me that he might be at the Noah's Ark treating a patient in the stable-loft.'

'Did you find him?'

'No, in the end I went to another surgeon.'

'Did you see anyone else at the Noah's Ark while you were there?'

'Only Mrs Grimshaw's son. We had an exchange of words. He was in the stable and I startled him, I think. Mrs Grimshaw is a woman consumed by fear and prejudice. I'm afraid she has raised her son the same way. He had many offensive things to say about my race.'

I wondered if there was a side to Nathaniel I had not yet seen. 'Can you tell me about it? The dead birds, I mean?'

He smiled. 'It is called obeah, African folk magic. Just as you have your wise women who bury apples under trees at midnight, we have obeah men and women with spells and potions and charms to make you fall in love or kill your rival.'

'Is it commonly practised among Africans over here?'

'Hardly at all. I know little of it myself. Some of those who were brought here from the Caribbean still cling to the old rituals, but even over there it is being slowly suppressed. In Dominica, where I was a slave, the obeah men were punished harshly. The planters thought it was a cover for insurrection. It probably was.'

'Then you don't believe it has any power?'

'It has the power to frighten credulous men, which should not be underestimated. But it flies in the face of reason to suppose that it can curse or kill.'

'Thank heavens for rational minds. There seem to be few enough of those in Deptford. Where did you obtain your education?'

'In Dominica. My second owner was a good deal kinder

than my first. He saw that I had an inquiring mind and taught me to read and write. In time he made me his secretary and gave me the run of his library. He was originally from Deptford, and when he returned to England in ill health, he took me with him. When he died, I attained my freedom in his will.'

Out of the corner of my eye, I was still watching the curtain, and I noticed another black footman go through it.

'Do you know what goes on back there?'

He followed my gaze. 'I have no idea. A brothel? Or more gambling perhaps?' He shot a look of disapproval at the snail-racers on the next table.

'How did Cinnamon come to be owned by Stokes?'

'Her father was a white man, a commissioner of a slave fort on the African coast. Her mother was a girl from the local village. She was raised in some comfort, within the commissioner's quarters, but after he died, she and her mother were sold by his fellow officers. Cinnamon was brought to England as a child, where she was trained to be a lady's maid to a Bristol sugar merchant's wife. Her master sold her to Stokes a year ago.'

If that was true, then Cinnamon could not be the slave who had returned to Deptford on board *The Dark Angel*. Was Scipio lying? To obfuscate my inquiry on behalf of his master? If not Cinnamon, then who?

'Mr Stokes does not keep her as a lady's maid,' I observed.

'No,' Scipio said heavily. 'But do not make the mistake of thinking her duties any less onerous.'

One of the snail-racers, unsteady on his feet, chose that moment to cannon into our table. He attempted to right himself and stumbled back into his own table, scattering coins and snails everywhere. His friends roared their amusement and one poured a jug of wine over his head.

Scipio's jaw tightened. 'No wonder Africans are looked

down upon if such men serve as models. They have their freedom and look what they do with it. They make no attempt to better themselves.'

'Plenty of white men squander their time drinking and gambling in taverns,' I observed.

'Your race has that luxury. Mine does not. If we are ever to abolish slavery, then free blacks must lead by example – in our conduct and our learning. We must be the living proof that our race are not animals, to be kept in chains. I look at men like that and I despair.'

His anger saddened me, and I realized I had little conception of the barriers he must face. I had heard of English Jews who, driven by the prejudice of their Christian neighbours, had shaved their beards and shunned their religion, so that they might pass as Christians themselves. No such course was open to a black man, and in many respects I was glad of it. Why should a man have to hide his true self away? Only by accepting our differences would we find a better way to live. Only by confronting bigotry would we slay the monster of division. Yet none of this would help Scipio, who seemed to carry the weight of English intolerance upon his shoulders. Africans escape one set of chains, I thought bleakly, and we simply fashion more for them. If there was such a thing as a savage race, then I was its sole representative at this table.

I was about to return to the topic of Cinnamon, when I noticed a familiar figure walk into the tavern. Moses Graham's ample girth and huge wig provoked ridicule from the patrons standing nearest the door. He didn't look as if he cared. His eyes searched the taproom with a distracted, anxious air. He saw me and froze.

'Excuse me,' I murmured to Scipio. 'There is someone I must speak to.'

As I rose, Graham turned and hurried out of the tavern as swiftly as his legs would carry him. The taproom had filled up with drinkers from the garden and it took me a little while to fight my way through the press to the door. I stepped outside and saw Graham hurrying away down the darkened High Street. Cursing the limitations of my infirmity, I hastened after him.

The street was busy with revellers and a camp of gypsies on the common were dancing around their fire. Some of them tried to waylay me, pushing their heather and lucky charms into my face. I shouted after Graham, but he didn't turn back.

He was nearing the end of the village, where the houses thinned and then petered out entirely. The road continued on into London, a sulphurous glow across a strip of darkened field. I called his name again. This time he turned, and then broke into a waddling run, abandoning the road and taking to the fields.

I cursed again, not understanding his fear. 'I only want to talk to you,' I called.

The moon rolled behind a cloud and I lost sight of him. Houses in varying stages of construction covered the ground between here and the city, muddy spaces marked out between the buildings for grand avenues and squares. The place resembled a city devastated by war.

The moon emerged again and I caught a glimpse of Graham, hurrying across a patch of ground between the grey walls of two half-built houses. I glanced around, uneasy. I had left my sword and pistol at home – as I always did when working in Whitehall – and these fields were notorious for thieves. Yet Moses Graham's panic drew me on. Now, as at Tad's funeral, he was behaving like a man with much to hide.

Chapter Twenty-Nine

THE GROUND WAS treacherous with hidden obstacles: bricks, tangles of scrub, broken tiles. Moonlight bathed the half-formed avenues and crescents, shafts of it piercing the empty windows of the tooth-like houses.

'Mr Graham?' I called. 'You have nothing to fear.'

I could hear only a faint hum of music and laughter, drifting from one of the London stewpots. Now and then a carriage or a cart rumbled past on the London–Marylebone road. I reached the spot where I'd last seen Moses Graham, flitting between a pair of half-built mansions.

I heard a faint rattle of stones, and swivelled round. It seemed to have come from one of the larger houses, a future home for a marquess or a duke. I walked towards it, casting a wary glance around, and climbed the steps. Inside it was dark as a tomb. I struggled to dispel the ominous feelings this place provoked.

'Mr Graham? I won't make trouble for you, I promise.'

Silence. I crept further into the house, straining to see. I made out the sweep of a grand staircase and a half-laid marble floor. Scaffolding towers and carpenter's benches rose amid the chaos. I could hear a faint rustling towards the rear of the entrance hall and I approached the spot swiftly. I rounded one of the scaffolding towers, and something shot across the floor, a vibrant streak of colour in the darkness. An unearthly scream pierced the night air. A fox.

As the echo died away, I heard another sound: a faint crackle, repeated at intervals, as if someone was trying to move silently across the debris-strewn floor. Tracking the sound to its source, I peered into one of the darkened rooms that led off the hall.

'Mr Graham?'

I edged further into the room and heard a patter of footsteps. Instinctively, I stepped back, just as something heavy swept the air in front of my face. The blow caught me on the arm, but it was a feeble strike. I grabbed my assailant's stick before he could hit me again, and pivoted him around to put him up against the wall. It was not a difficult endeavour. My assailant was large and soft and weak. Moses Graham.

His eyes were wild in the moonlight and his wig had fallen off in our struggle. 'Please don't hurt me, sir,' he cried. 'I never intended you harm.'

'You swung a stick at my head.'

'I only wanted to knock you down, so that I might escape.'

'Why? I don't understand why you ran from me.'

'Didn't you hear me at Archer's funeral? I am in danger. So is Mr Proudlock. If our enemy knows that you and I have spoken, then you will be in danger too.'

I remembered Ephraim Proudlock from the funeral, Moses Graham's skinny assistant in matters of art and abolition. I doubted their fear was connected to the painting of watercolours.

'This is about *The Dark Angel*, isn't it? Please tell me what you know. If the knowledge places me in danger, then I'll take that chance.'

His eyes were flitting around in the darkness. His voice rose in agitation. 'We thought that too at the beginning. But we didn't know how far they'd go.'

'You and Thaddeus Archer?'

'And Mr Proudlock. The three of us who discovered *The Dark Angel*.' He peered at me, biting his lip. 'Have you seen him? Mr Proudlock?'

'You don't know where he is?'

'He went missing two days ago. I was looking for him at the Stingo. Proudlock thought he was being followed, just as Mr Archer did. Sometimes I feel it too.'

So did I. 'Someone tortured and killed Archer's sister and her maid two nights ago.'

'Oh, the poor woman.' Graham sank his face into his hands.

'There's still so much I don't understand,' I said. 'How do the Children of Liberty fit into all this?'

'They don't. I told you before, I have nothing to do with those people.'

'Could Archer have involved them without consulting you? He had some of their pamphlets with him in Deptford.'

'Why would they want to be involved? There is no profit for them in dead slaves, only the living.' Graham's voice was underscored with a contempt I didn't understand.

'What profit? I thought they helped slaves escape their masters?'

He shook his head. 'They are bad people. Just know that.'

Perhaps Tad had needed bad people. Stronger allies than a gentleman painter of watercolours and his skinny assistant.

I studied his anguished face, his bald head, his crumpled clothes. 'I need you to trust me, Mr Graham. Together we can stop the killer.'

'He is protected. Haven't you learned that yet?'

Protected by the West India lobby. The Deptford authorities. Men like Nicholas Cavill-Lawrence.

'They protect him because they are afraid. We can take comfort in that. Now, please, Thaddeus Archer planned to prosecute *The Dark Angel*'s crew, that much I understand. And yet the slaves were property. No charge of murder could ever be brought. So how did he intend to bring the case to court?'

'You just said it, didn't you? The slaves were property. That was the key to it all. Everything hinges upon it. The crime, the prosecution, the murder—'

He broke off as light flooded the room. Not the bright white light of the moon, but the yellow light of a lantern. Someone had entered the building. We could hear him moving about in the hall.

'It is Archer's murderer,' Graham whispered. 'He has found us.'

I put a finger to my lips and peered into the hall. I could see the lantern, making slow curves through the air as the man who held it walked around the room. I couldn't make out his face, but I had an impression of size and strength. Was it a night-watchman looking for trespassers? Could Scipio have followed me here from the Stingo? Or was it the killer, as Moses Graham supposed?

Part of me ached to find out, but I was unarmed, with only Graham for assistance. Steering him by the shoulder, we crept away from the hall, towards the rear of the house, into a vast chamber that ran the entire width of the mansion. Plainly intended for summer balls, many doorways opened onto an outdoor terrace.

I could hear the man with the lantern behind us. He was still moving around, going from room to room. We hurried across the ballroom onto the terrace. It looked out over a long, muddy strip of garden with high walls on either side. I might have scaled them, but Graham hadn't a chance. I had to hope there was a door at the end of the garden.

The terrace steps had not yet been built, and it was a drop of six feet to the ground. I lowered myself down, and Graham dropped heavily into the mud beside me. I peered over the top of the terrace, and saw that the light was now in the ballroom. Had he seen us? I didn't know – but he was coming this way.

Graham was almost insensible with panic. I pulled him, unresisting, into the shadow of the garden wall. We froze as footsteps approached. The man stood at the edge of the terrace, his lantern sweeping the ground in front of it. He turned this way and that, cocking his head to listen. Frank Drake? Or John Monday? It was impossible to look more closely without revealing myself.

Each second felt like eternity. Graham wouldn't stop shaking and I feared that at any moment, his panic would overwhelm him and he'd do something to give us away. The lantern stopped moving and the figure leaned forward. If he jumped down into the garden, he would surely see us. Sweat poured off me. My muscles twitched. Graham mouthed a prayer.

The figure turned, and walked back into the house.

Graham gave me a shaky smile. We waited a few moments longer, and then crept down the garden, keeping to the shadows. Relief coursed through me when I saw an open doorway in the rear wall.

Beyond it a muddy square of ground held the foundations of more buildings. A mews yard, I guessed, with a coach-house and stables. More half-built houses backed onto it, with a passage running between them. We hurried down it, emerging onto open ground once more. Ahead was the Marylebone Road, and to our right lay London. Yet the danger wasn't over yet. The killer was still out here. We needed to reach the city as quickly as possible.

A carriage was rattling along the road and we ran to cut it off. I feared the driver hadn't seen us, but at the last moment he pulled on the reins. With a great squeal of horse and axle, the carriage lurched to a stop.

Graham tugged my arm. 'Look.'

He was gazing back towards the houses. The dark figure stood there, holding up his lantern. I couldn't make out his face in the glare. Then he extinguished his light, merging with the darkness around him.

The coachman was an elderly African with a white beard and an old patched coat. An ancient-looking blunderbuss rested in his lap.

'My friend and I have been attacked,' I said, stretching the truth a little, though Graham in his wigless, dishevelled state could easily pass for a victim of crime. 'Please will you give us a ride into town?'

The old fellow pointed his blunderbuss at me, and I held up my hands, thinking he had mistaken us for highway robbers. One of the carriage doors opened, and Graham stared into the vehicle, his lips parted in horror. I moved to see what he was looking at, just as someone came up behind me. I turned, and was struck on the head very hard. My brain seemed to bounce inside my skull and I dropped to my knees, aware only of a powerful sense of confusion.

I cried out to Graham to run, but my words came out mangled. Rough hands lifted me under the arms and bundled me into the carriage. More hands were waiting there to drag me inside. I kicked out and someone hit me again. Doors slammed and the coach moved off. A bag was put over my head, but I was already sliding down into darkness.

Chapter Thirty

I don't know how long I lay unconscious. I awoke on the floor of the carriage, my head aching intolerably, my ears still buzzing from the blow I had sustained. My hands were tied behind me and the bag was still over my head. Around me I could hear the familiar sounds of the city by night: the rumble of produce carts, revellers shouting, the cries of a nightsoil man. From the smell, I guessed we were somewhere near the river. I sensed several people were in the carriage with me, but none of them spoke. I lay there trying to work out who had taken me. Was Moses Graham beside me? Or had they left him out there on the roadside with the killer?

The noise gradually receded, until I could hear only the clop of hooves and smell sharper industrial odours: the tang of a vinegar yard, and a stench of rotting flesh and urine that could only come from a tannery. I guessed we were somewhere in the industrial quarter, west of the Borough.

The carriage halted, rocking as the driver climbed down from the box. Someone opened the door, and cooler air washed over my body. I was hauled out and briefly felt cobbles beneath my feet, before I was pushed into a building. I heard a clattering of chains and bolts as the door was secured behind me. More steps forward, and I felt the warmth of a fire. Hands lowered me into a chair and the sack was removed.

Everything swam before my eyes, faces gradually forming in

the blur: four young, black, angry, male faces. One of them I recognized: the huge African who had been guarding the curtain in the Yorkshire Stingo. Moses Graham sat next to me, bound just as I was. He flinched from his captors and they laughed.

Three more black men and two black women sat on the floor against the wall. Their clothes were shabby and they gazed at me with wide, frightened eyes. I knew instinctively that they were runaway slaves. Sitting in a wingchair next to the fire was an African in a red hat. One side of his face was horribly scarred. He held a glass of wine in one hand, and a pistol in the other. Caesar John.

'The fat one was with him when we caught up with him,' one of the young blacks said. 'They'd gone off road for some reason, but we made another pass and then we found them. We took the fat one too in case he peached on us.'

They must have been watching me in the tavern. 'You are the Children of Liberty,' I said.

When nobody denied it, I turned to Moses Graham. 'You said Caesar John had nothing to do with them. You said he was a villain.'

Graham looked even more pitiful than he had in Marylebone. His coat was torn and covered in mud, and he had a bruise on his cheek. Yet as he gazed at Caesar John, he mustered a measure of dignity. 'He *is* a villain. A wretched parasite who preys upon the weak and the vulnerable. I lied only to protect you, Captain Corsham. You should have listened.'

Caesar John glared at him. 'I've saved more slaves than your books and speeches ever have.' His accent was as thick and local as London clay.

'If by saved you mean drawn into a life of criminality from which you profit, then you indeed have that distinction,'

Graham said. 'But do not think for a moment that there is any honour in it, sir.'

'If we take, it's because we were taken from. Now watch your mouth, Negro. Before I cut out your fucking tongue.'

My thoughts were sluggish. 'Where are we?' The place was furnished like a sitting room in a cheap boarding house, except all the windows were fitted with iron bars. 'Why have you brought us here?'

'This is an old sponging house.' Caesar John had an ivory toothpick wedged between his teeth and it waggled as he talked. 'It's not Buckingham House, but I find it fit for purpose. We don't keep debtors here, but runaway slaves. You are here because I want some fucking answers.' He gestured to his men. 'Bring them through.'

Our arms still tied behind us, we were marched through the hall, into another room. The other men withdrew and Caesar John closed the door behind them. I didn't understand his anger, but I was afraid of it.

We appeared to be in some sort of storeroom. Handsome pieces of furniture were piled against the walls. Stacked around them were paintings in gilt frames, silver candelabra, clocks, jewellery boxes, vases, silk drapes, piles of fine clothes and wigs, even a bag of golf clubs. If Caesar John was involved in criminal enterprise, then my best guess was housebreaking. I remembered those footmen going through the curtain in the Yorkshire Stingo. Most free blacks worked as servants, and the slaves he'd freed could doubtless pass on much useful intelligence about their employers' homes.

Caesar John picked up a lamp and walked to a table at the far end of the room. It was fashioned from richly carved mahogany and a dozen people might have dined around it. A naked

African was lying on it, and I stared at him in horror. Moses Graham gave a howl of despair.

Caesar John gestured to the corpse. 'You know him?'

Moses Graham only moaned.

'His name is Ephraim Proudlock.' My throat was dry. 'He was Mr Graham's assistant.'

'Poor boy. What has he done to you?' Moses Graham cried.

Proudlock's body was covered in cuts and contusions, the blood a darker brown against his russet skin. Like Tad, his throat had been cut. Like Tad, a thumbscrew had been used on him, the fingers grotesquely ill-aligned. Like Tad, Monday's mark had been seared into his chest: a crescent moon surmounted by a crown. Worse than any of this was the sight between his legs: a horrible mess of blood-matted hair and mutilated flesh. The poor man had been castrated. I prayed that it had happened after he'd died – even as I knew that it had not.

'A week ago, one of my men, Jupiter, was found like this,' Caesar John said. 'He'd been flogged like this poor devil here and someone had mangled his fucking hands. That same fucking slave brand. Whoever killed him prised out one of his fucking eyeballs.'

'Did Jupiter know Thaddeus Archer?' I said. 'Did he ever mention a ship called *The Dark Angel*?'

He silenced me with a glare. 'I have business rivals and I thought one of them might be responsible. They denied it, so I let Jupiter's wife go to the magistrate. He didn't give a flying fuck about a dead Negro, so I paid a thief-taker to make inquiries. Last night he heard a rumour that another mutilated black had been found out at Spitalfields. So I went down there and claimed this poor bastard here. Then I read in the newspaper that Thaddeus Archer had been tortured too, which got me to thinking. Archer was one of the lawyers we used for our runaways. I wondered if there was a connection between his death and Jupiter's, so I questioned my men. I discovered that in recent weeks, Archer had paid Jupiter to do a job for him.'

'What kind of job?'

He studied me for a moment with his sharp brown eyes. 'He wanted someone followed, a Deptford sailor.'

'Do you know his name?'

'No, only that Archer paid Jupiter well. Then you come to my tavern, saying you know Archer. I want to know who killed Jupiter and why.'

That's why we were here. He was angry about the murder of his man. I sympathized, but that anger made him dangerous.

'I think the murderer is one of the officers of a slave ship named *The Dark Angel*. I don't know which of them it is, but I'm trying to find out.'

'What beef did he have with Archer? With Jupiter? With this poor fuckster here?'

Briefly, I summarized my investigation to date: the massacre on the ship, the suspects, and my different avenues of inquiry. Caesar John listened, his jaw set.

'Archer wanted to bring the ship's officers to trial, but I don't understand how.' I looked at Graham, who had fallen silent. A tear rolled down his cheek. 'Perhaps Mr Graham can tell us more. In any event, someone wanted Archer dead. I think he was tortured to find out who else was involved in his inquiry. He must have given them Jupiter and Proudlock's names.'

Graham's head snapped up. 'Thaddeus Archer would never betray his friends.'

'You didn't see what was done to him,' I said quietly.

Caesar John studied the corpse. 'Why cut off his cods? Why take Jupiter's eye?'

'They are slaving punishments.' Graham's voice was thick

with anger. 'If a slave is making trouble at sea or on the plantations, sometimes they make an example of him to discourage the others. Some part of him is mutilated, an eye or an ear. Sometimes his penis. Anything except a hand or a foot – that would render him incapable of work.'

'I imagine he wanted to know if Proudlock had told anyone else about Archer's inquiry. As a slaving man, these methods of torture would be a natural choice.' For a moment fear washed over me, as I remembered that dark figure in Marylebone. I knew about *The Dark Angel*, and he knew that I knew.

Caesar John pointed his pistol at Moses Graham. 'What do you know? Speak.'

I turned to him too, eager to hear the rest of the story he had begun to tell me in Marylebone.

'Well? Speak, you fat fuckster.'

'Very well – just don't point that thing at me.' Graham spoke in a quiet, halting voice. 'It was poor Mr Proudlock who heard the tale first. It had travelled here from Jamaica, circulating in whispers in the black taverns and the coffeehouses. A story of a Guineaman, a vessel of lost souls, three hundred slaves thrown overboard to drown. Later, we learned the ship's name, *The Dark Angel.*'

Caesar John gestured impatiently with his pistol, and Graham spoke more hastily, his words tripping and falling over one another.

'Mr Archer saw its power from the start. To us, it was just another terrible act of cruelty, but he saw it differently, through English eyes. He believed it had the power to change the way people thought and felt about slavery. Perhaps he was right. I don't know. He became obsessed with the ship. Proudlock too. I helped, though I confess it made me nervous. Too many people had too much to lose. I was worried what they would do when they found out.'

His eyes strayed to Proudlock. 'We never believed the official story, you see. Not all of it. A leak was discovered too late and the ship was running out of water – that part I do not contest. But the rest of it was a dreadful lie. The truth, we believed, was infinitely worse.'

My body tensed, knowing I was about to learn something significant.

'A slave voyage is a finely balanced undertaking. It rests upon the principles of mathematics. Air, food, hold space, water. There is a formula for each.'

I recalled John Monday, rattling off his figures in his warehouse. The costs of keeping men alive and subdued.

'The clue is that the slaves were killed in batches. Five massacres over the course of seven days. They knew how much water they had, so why not kill them all at once? Why waste water on slaves you knew would have to die?'

Our faces must have looked blank, for Graham smiled thinly. 'Have either of you gentlemen ever heard of refuse slaves?'

He placed the emphasis in the word *refuse* firmly upon the first syllable: waste, litter, junk. We shook our heads.

'When slaves arrive in a Caribbean port – let us say Kingston, Jamaica – they are marched off the boat in chains, then herded into a corral about the size of a cricket pitch. They are confused and frightened and their relief at being upon dry land once more is tempered by the sight of the buyers. The auctioneer rings a bell and the planters rush in, each determined to grab the best slaves first. Africans are fought over, wrenched from the hands of rival buyers. The refuse slaves are the ones left at the end. The lame, the sick, the dying. The ones no one wants.'

'What happens to them?' I asked.

'Usually the captain cuts his losses and offers the slaves for sale as a batch. He takes the best price that he can get, usually significantly less than he paid for them.'

'People buy dying slaves?'

'Some die, some survive. They call it the African lottery. The buyer hopes enough slaves survive to make the purchase a good bargain. Every Guineaman has a few refuse slaves, more if the journey was arduous or stricken with disease. Odd then, that *The Dark Angel* had none at all. All the surviving slaves were sold for full price at market.'

'The crew have attested they killed the weakest slaves first.' I was struggling to grasp his point. 'That is surely not surprising?'

'Only if you believe their story. As I say, we never did. I believe that with careful rationing of the water, most of those slaves would have made it to Jamaica alive.'

Nausea rose in my gullet, as I started to see it. 'If they had survived,' I said slowly, 'then they would have been sick, wasted with thirst. Refuse slaves. The voyage stood to make an enormous loss. And all the ship's officers would have lost their part of the profit.'

'Quite. Yet the slaves were insured at their purchase price. They were worth more to the officers dead than alive.'

I could see that Caesar John understood it too. His expression didn't change, but his free hand clenched into a fist.

'Five times the slaves were brought up on deck. Five times the surgeon assessed them. He and the captain made their calculations. They determined which slaves had gone past the point of profit and those slaves were killed.'

I understood now why Tad had been so convinced that this story would change the way people felt about slavery. I saw the rest of it too – how he planned to bring the case to court, and ensure the massacre was written about in every newspaper. He couldn't bring a charge of murder against the crew, because the slaves were property and so couldn't be murdered under English law. So he conceived a different way to prosecute them – to quote Napier Smith, a devious, clever lawyer's trick – one that would only work *because* the slaves were property.

'When the insurance claim was made,' I said, 'the officers would have had to provide a notarized account of the voyage. Their lie would be on record and underpin the claim. If you could prove that lie, then you'd have grounds on which to prosecute – only the charge would not be murder, it would be fraud.'

Graham's expression was sombre. 'It is ironic, is it not? You can kill three hundred black slaves at sea and your courts account it nothing at all. Yet steal from a white man and the chances are you'd hang for it.'

It was as clear a motivation for murder as I had ever heard.

CHAPTER THIRTY-ONE

PALLID DAWN LIGHT was squeezing through the cracks in the shutters. I tried to ignore my pounding headache and the exhaustion crowding my thoughts, listening intently as Moses Graham pressed on with his story.

'Of course,' he said, 'to convict the officers upon a charge of fraud, first we had to prove their story a lie. To do so we needed a witness, someone prepared to testify in court as to what really happened upon that voyage. At first Archer had high hopes for the ship's captain, a man named Evan Vaughan. Archer said he seemed remorseful. But something happened between them, I think, and Vaughan left town. Archer looked for him, but he couldn't find him. He was despondent for a time, but shortly before he was killed, he told us he had found another witness.'

Our arms were still tied behind us, but Caesar John's pistol was now pointed at the floor and I no longer believed we were in imminent danger.

'I discovered recently that one of the slaves on that voyage was taken back to Deptford,' I said. 'Could she be the witness he was talking about?'

'I'm certain he said it was a member of the crew. Archer grew very secretive in the days before he died. He said the less we knew the better. I could see he was afraid and he told us he was being followed. But he was excited too. I think he was nearly ready to lay his charges before a court.'

'Then the witness could be Daniel Waterman, the cabin boy,' I said, thinking about my conversation with Napier Smith and Cavill-Lawrence. 'When Archer returned to Deptford that last time, he told his sister that he was going there to collect something. I think it might have been some papers connected to *The Dark Angel*. Waterman had his leg broken just before Archer's murder, apparently because he'd helped himself to someone else's property. Perhaps he agreed to steal these documents for Archer and someone found out.' I turned to Caesar John. 'I saw you outside Archer's rooms a few nights after he died. What were you doing there?'

'Looking for him. He was supposed to represent some of our slaves in court and he didn't show. The judge wasn't happy. Neither was I. I went to his rooms to have it out with him, and thought I heard someone moving around inside. Yet when I knocked, Archer didn't answer.'

'A man employed by the ministry searched his rooms that night. He was looking for the missing papers. I think the killer is too – that's why he tortured and killed Amelia Bradstreet. The ministry and the West India lobby believe they aren't in Deptford, because the mayor, a man named Stokes, hasn't found them. I think they're wrong.'

Caesar John scowled. 'I don't give a flying fuck for any missing papers. Nor this damn ship. Am I in danger? Is Jupiter's wife? Are any of my people?'

'Not unless they had dealings with Archer over this. Did they?'

'I don't think so.'

'Then they should be safe.'

Looking at his face, I realized that I could count on little help from the Children of Liberty. Caesar John only wanted to protect his people. I could hardly blame him for that. Jupiter,

Proudlock, Amelia, her maid. The costs of Tad's inquiry were mounting.

Caesar John jammed his pistol into his belt and took a knife from his pocket. At the sight of it, Moses Graham started praying.

'Be quiet, you fat fool. I'm not going to kill you.'

He cut the ropes that bound my hands and then did the same for Graham. We flexed our fingers, blood flowing in to warm them.

'I'll have my men take you back,' Caesar John said.

We returned to the other room, where he ordered his men to ready the carriage. 'You'll be hooded again. I can't risk anyone finding out about this place.'

'I understand.' I looked at the slaves huddled on the floor, with their ragged clothes and frightened eyes, wondering what torments they'd experienced in their short lives. 'Why do you need to keep them here? Don't they have injunctions from a judge? I thought that was how it worked?'

'Oh, we have injunctions,' Caesar John said. 'The ruling of the judge is clear: their owners have no hold on them while the matter of their freedom is under consideration by the courts. It doesn't stop their masters looking for them. They pay crimping gangs to do it. Once they're on a ship bound for the Caribbean, the courts can't reach them. Nor do they try very hard.'

What a country, I thought. How we weave ourselves into knots trying to convince ourselves we are not monsters, even as we grow fat upon the profits of our monstrosity.

Caesar John placed a hood over Graham's face, but when he came to me, he paused. 'What will you do with the killer when you find him?'

'Put him on trial. See him hang.'

'You think the West India lobby will let that happen?'

I didn't answer, and he smiled. 'There's more than one kind of justice. Bring him here, if you like. Young Jupiter was popular. My men would welcome that.'

I gazed at his young, angry face with its scars. Up close I could see that the flesh had been burned, and I wondered if it was a memento of his criminal endeavours or of his time as a slave. 'I think Tad would have wanted the law to take its course.'

'The law is a cunt, that's my motto.' He placed the sack over my head. 'Remember my offer, soldier. You might change your mind.'

*

We sat hooded in the carriage, as it jolted back through London. This time our hands were left untied, and only one man kept us company. A curious calm had descended over me. Perhaps it was simply lack of sleep, or the blow to the head I had sustained.

Eventually, the carriage stopped and our hoods were removed. I blinked at the sudden brightness of the light. We were on the fringes of the Covent Garden market and barrow-men were setting out their stalls. We climbed down from the carriage, amidst the crates and spilled vegetables, the banter of the marketmen volleying around us. Moses Graham smiled at me weakly, as if amazed to discover he was still alive.

'You should go out of town, Mr Graham,' I said. 'Lie low for a while.'

'Probably I should, but I don't think so.'

'You saw what was done to poor Proudlock. If you are right, the killer will be coming for you next.'

'For all of us,' Graham said. 'Yet freedom gives one choices, does it not? I cannot accompany you to Deptford, sir. A free Londoner of my race would be of little use to you there – and

I would place myself in danger of abduction to the Caribbean. Yet there are other places I can visit, to ask around about the ship and her voyage. Black taverns. Black coffeehouses. News from Jamaica comes in all the time. And someone may have seen Proudlock in Spitalfields before the killer took him. I will go down there and see what I can find.'

I shook my head. 'This isn't wise, sir. Archer and Proudlock wouldn't have wanted you to risk your life.'

'Perhaps not – and yet I find that I must. I enjoy my food and my wine, sir, probably more than I should. I like to walk by the river, and feel the sun on my face. I like my books and my letters and my paints and my violin. I like the life I have fashioned for myself here. Yet while slavery and its practitioners prosper, I cannot stand idly by. I might also add that Mr Archer and Mr Proudlock were my friends.'

I gazed up at the pale sky, only lightly warmed by the nascent sun. 'Good luck, Mr Graham. God keep you safe.'

*

After Moses Graham and I had parted, having arranged to meet again on my return from Deptford, I walked home past maids shaking out rugs and beggars sleeping in doorways. The air was filled with the smoke of ten thousand chimneys: London brewing tea, reaching for the sugar jar.

Pomfret started with surprise when I walked into the hall. I glanced in the console mirror and saw how dishevelled I was. This was becoming a habit.

'I am perfectly fine, Pomfret. It was just a fall. Have my horse made ready, please. I'm going out.'

'Very good, sir.' I could sense Pomfret's scepticism. He probably thought I'd been out all night drinking. I went upstairs and found Caro's door was locked. She'd gone to Carlisle House last night and I wondered whom she'd seen there. Such thoughts still had the power to wound me. I walked on.

In my dressing room, I washed, and changed my coat and wig. Then I went to the nursery, where Gabriel lay sleeping. I kissed him and he stirred, murmuring something in his sleep. I fought the urge to take him in my arms and went back to my room.

I packed a bag, and cleaned my sword and pistol. Downstairs in my bookroom, I wrote a short letter to Caro, explaining that I was going back to Deptford and would be gone a few days. I wrote another to Cavill-Lawrence saying that I'd been called out of town again. I didn't expect him to believe me, but that couldn't be helped. Outside in the mews, my coachman, Sam, had Zephyrus ready. I secured my bag and pulled myself into the saddle.

I rode out into Mayfair just as the bells were tolling eight. I wondered what dangers lay ahead for me, and what would be left of my life when I returned. It made for uncomfortable thinking, and so I thought about Tad on the river. When I pictured him, his features were sharper. I carried him with me.

I rode east and then south, across the City to London Bridge. The sun on the water shimmered iridescent, like the scales of a snake.

PART FOUR

29 June to 3 July 1781

I assign the term 'bondage' to man's lack of power to control and check the emotions. For a man at the mercy of his emotions is not his own master but is subject to fortune, in whose power he so lies that he is often compelled, although he sees the better course, to pursue the worse.

IV. Of Man's Slavery or the Force of the Passions, *Ethics*, Baruch Spinoza

Chapter Thirty-Two

Mrs Grimshaw gave me a long look when I walked into the Noah's Ark. 'Frank Drake says I'm not to let you stay here anymore.'

I gave her my most gentlemanly bow. 'I'm sorry to hear that, madam. What do you say?'

She sighed. 'I say this is my inn. Who's he to give me orders? Frank Drake, who was my husband's junior officer? Besides, we need the money. Here's your key.'

I thanked her. 'Is Nathaniel at home?'

'He's gone out looking for Jago. Wretched beast has run off.'

'I'm heading up to the Broadway shortly. I'll look out for the dog.'

'If you would, sir. Perhaps you could have a word with my Nate too, if you run across him? He was upset enough as it was, what with losing his father and his apprenticeship. Now Brabazon's had to take poor Daniel Waterman's leg and Jago's gone the devil knows where. A word from you might help. He's taken quite a shine to you. Said I was to let you stay here, no matter what Drake said.'

Pleased that my alliance with the boy was bearing fruit, I said I would.

'I'm sorry to hear about Waterman. How is he?'

'He'll live, Brabazon says, but what sort of a life is a

cripple's? Nate wants us to keep him here for good, but times are hard for us too.'

I murmured my sympathy. 'I didn't realize Nathaniel had been an apprentice. I'd presumed he was always destined for slaving.'

'Oh, my Amos had grand plans for him – wanted something better for the boy. An attorney up in the Broadway took him on. We couldn't afford it anymore after Amos passed.' She brushed away a tear.

I wondered if she knew how much time and money her husband had spent in the Deptford bathhouse. It was anyone's guess. Sometimes ignorance is a godsend. Sometimes it's better to know the truth. Often we occupy an uneasy state between the two.

'I heard about you tricking your way into John Monday's house,' she said. 'You shouldn't have done that, sir. Mr Monday is a good man. After my Amos died, when he heard we were likely to lose the inn, he offered Nate an officer's place, even though the boy had never spent a day at sea. That never happens except with those who've paid for the privilege. Then there's the school he founded here in the Strand. And the surgery for the poor.'

'A living saint.'

She gave me another look. 'He does good where he sees bad. There aren't many in Deptford who do that. Have a care in these alleys, sir. Frank Drake's put the word round about you. You might come up against some of the bad yourself.'

*

It was another hot day, though the air held a faint promise of rain. I kept an eye out for Nathaniel on my walk up to the Broadway, but I didn't see him. I wondered if he'd made any progress with my silver ticket, or if he'd been too upset about Daniel Waterman's amputation. I planned to visit the cabin boy later on, and I very much hoped he'd be able to talk to me. The questions I had for him kept mounting. Was he Tad's witness? Had he stolen the missing documents? What precisely were those documents? Who had broken his leg? The closer I came to *The Dark Angel* and the crimes of her crew, I believed, the closer I'd come to Tad's murderer. If Waterman had any evidence of the insurance fraud, then I needed to hear it.

Similarly, I needed to speak to Cinnamon again. Scipio's account of her background suggested she couldn't be the female slave who had returned to Deptford on board *The Dark Angel*. Yet I wasn't sure I believed him. Scipio was anxious to preserve his position as the mayor's secretary, and the girl was his master's property. It was possible he had lied to protect his own interests. I had no desire to make trouble for him, but in this instance it couldn't be helped. If Cinnamon was the slave girl in question, then I needed to hear her story. Either way, I'd resolved to help her escape this town and her master. The upshot be damned.

I also wanted to locate *The Dark Angel*'s captain, Evan Vaughan. If he was truly losing his mind, as his landlady had implied, then he might let something slip once I put him to the question. I hadn't entirely discounted the possibility that he might be the killer, though I'd been told that he'd left Deptford some weeks ago. His addiction to opium, coupled with Tad's purchase of that same drug around the time he was killed, certainly raised interesting questions. I would have liked to return to the bathhouse, to have another stab at questioning Jamaica Mary, and to find the prostitute, Alice, whom Vaughan had allegedly assaulted. Yet the proprietor had made it plain that I was no longer welcome on his premises. Was Jamaica Mary responsible for the obeah, as Mrs Grimshaw believed? If I could prove her involvement, then I might get to the truth about Frank Drake's alibi. Mary's uneasiness when answering my questions, coupled with her false allegation against me in the bathhouse, suggested she was hiding something.

I decided to give *The Dark Angel*'s owner, John Monday, a wide berth, at least until I had spoken to his wife, Eleanor. What motive had taken her to Tad's funeral? Why hadn't she wanted to be observed there? What did she know about her husband's business and the secrets of this town? What motive too, had taken the magistrate, Peregrine Child, to London – searching the ministry's archives, as I had, for *The Dark Angel*? Given Child's ambivalence about finding Tad's killer, his purpose was a puzzle – one I was determined to solve.

First I had a more pressing piece of business. When I reached the High Street in the Broadway, I was pleased to see James Brabazon's windows standing open. A conversation with that gentleman was long overdue.

Brabazon's manservant showed me up the stairs to the surgery, where we found his master standing over a steaming kettle. The last time I'd been here, Tad had been lying on that table. It had marked the moment between before and after. I forced my eyes to Brabazon's amiable face.

'What a pleasant surprise,' he said. 'I was told you had left town.'

The Scotchman looked a little worn around the edges. Stubble darkened his chin and there were shadows beneath his mismatched eyes. Given what I knew of his duplicity, those eyes seemed now to have taken on a Janus-like aspect: one looking outward to the world, the other gazing inwards, a mirror of his secret self.

'Forgive my appearance,' he said. 'I got back from the city

late last night to find that Daniel Waterman's condition had worsened. I took his leg off above the knee in the early hours.' He smiled ruefully. 'At some point, I'll sleep. Was it my tincture for your leg you were wanting?'

'Actually, I'd like to talk to you about Mr Archer's inquiry into the massacre on board *The Dark Angel*.'

Registering my stony expression, his smile faded. 'Ah, you are upset with me. No doubt because I didn't mention it myself. Please do not read too much into it. I saw no reason to drag that unpleasant business up again.'

'Archer was branded with the mark of Monday's company. You were employed by that company, yet you never saw fit to mention it.'

'I presumed the brand had been used to implicate us. You cannot think one of us killed him? Why would we mark him with a symbol that could identify us?'

'To warn others off. Men like me.'

He gave a lopsided grin. 'That plan's not working out very well for us now, is it, Captain Corsham?'

Brabazon had sangfroid, I had to give him that. He'd evidently decided the best method to deal with my presence in Deptford was to brazen it out.

'The killer also murdered and branded two Africans in London in recent days,' I said. 'As well as Mr Archer's sister and her maid.' It had not escaped my attention that Brabazon had been in London when Proudlock had been killed there. If he only returned late last night, then he could also have been the man Moses Graham and I had encountered at Marylebone.

'Good heavens,' he said. 'Were the women branded too?'

'No, but as I disturbed the killer he may have been intending to do so.'

'Did you get a good look at him?'

'Not his face. He wore a hood.'

'I am grieved to learn of yet more tragedy.' Brabazon's expression was suitably sombre, though I watched his performance with a critic's scepticism. 'Yet I don't see that it has anything to do with *The Dark Angel*. Archer's questions were an inconvenience, nothing more.'

'You call a prosecution for fraud an inconvenience?'

'I would, yes. There was no truth in his allegations.'

Thinking about those drowned slaves, I restrained a powerful urge to beat the truth out of him. Instead, I decided to play him at his own game. 'If there is no merit in it, then you will have no objection to answering a few questions about that voyage.'

He hesitated. 'I don't like talking about it, but if it will convince you that you are wasting your time, then I suppose it is a price worth paying.' He removed the kettle from its brazier and filled a bowl with steaming water. 'You don't mind if we talk while I work? I used up my supplies of laudanum on Daniel Waterman last night.'

Brabazon took a red waxed-paper package from a drawer. More opium from the Red House. He added the contents to his bowl, and used a pestle to grind the water and opium to a paste. The story he told me as he worked was much the same version of events told to me by John Monday.

'Do not think it didn't cost us, those desperate days at sea. Playing God, deciding who should live and who should die. I tell myself that it was akin to drowning bitches in a litter. You kill the weak in order that the strongest will survive. Yet whilst the Negro is not strictly human, he is not an animal either. Animals do not cry out to their loved ones. I still hear their screams.'

'You think that? Africans are not strictly human?'

'The science is clear. The Negro is a stunted form of human

existence, more akin to an ape than you or I. Have you read Kircher? No? You should. He posits that there were once many competing species of humans. The Negro, I believe, is the last of our rivals. A few centuries from now they will doubtless die out altogether. In the meantime, I see no reason why we should not harness their labour. Yet it doesn't follow that I liked to kill them. Or that I would have done so had it not been necessary to preserve the lives of others on board.'

Somehow I found these scientific justifications for his cruelty even worse than Drake's blunt brutality and Monday's twisted religion. Yet I kept my temper in check, and asked Brabazon a few more questions about the voyage.

'Why kill the slaves in batches? Why not all at once?'

'It is hard work killing three hundred men. The crew needed to rest. If it sounds shocking, that's because it is.'

'When we last met you mentioned a sea captain who destroyed himself through opium use. Was that Evan Vaughan?'

'Yes, I tried to help him wean himself off it, but the poppy does not let go easily. It is something I'd like to research one day: the properties of addictions and how to fight them.'

'Did his habit have anything to do with the failures on that voyage?'

'Oh no, the leak could have happened to any ship under any captain. And at the time Vaughan's use of opium was purely sybaritic. It was only afterwards that it got worse, in Kingston. When we returned to Deptford, he started smoking more and more – I believe to keep the memories of that voyage at bay. I've seen it happen before, to some of the hardest men you ever saw – and God knows, Evan Vaughan is no angel. They work the Middle Passage for twenty years, and never give it a moral pause, then one day wake up weeping at all the things they've seen and done. In Vaughan's case, perhaps it is not surprising.'

'Do you know where Vaughan is? His landlord says he's left town.'

'I advised him to get out of Deptford and take some rest. He decided on Brighthelmstone, I think. Or was it Margate?'

All very vague. Perhaps deliberately so.

'How about John Monday? Does he use opium?'

'I've never observed him do so, but it's possible. A lot of seafaring gentlemen retain old habits when they retire.'

Seemingly satisfied with the consistency of his mixture, Brabazon added a clear spirit to the bowl, stirring to let it down to a liquid. Then he decanted the laudanum through a funnel into a bottle. 'This will need to steep for a while. Shall we go next door?'

Brabazon's parlour was not dissimilar to my own bookroom: a refuge of dark furniture, bound volumes and Morocco leather. A skeleton in a corner gave the only clue to his profession. There were no mementos of his slaving at all. Perhaps Brabazon, like Amos Grimshaw, preferred to forget the horrors of the Middle Passage when in port.

The manservant had brewed a pot of coffee, and Brabazon offered me a bowl. As he poured, he leaned over to close one of his desk drawers. It was one of those inconsequential gestures that seem to have no purpose, and attain every consequence and purpose as a result. I wondered if there was something in that drawer that he did not wish for me to see.

'Where were you on the night Archer was killed?'

He stirred sugar into his bowl. 'What a question. I attended a lecture that afternoon at the Naval Hospital at Greenwich. There was a dinner afterwards and I stayed almost until the end. Over thirty surgeons and physicians were in attendance. You can check.'

'I will. What time did it finish?'

'Around one, I think.'

'Did you go directly home afterwards?'

'No, I went to check on Daniel Waterman.'

'Can anyone confirm that?'

'The boy himself. He should be more lucid by tonight.'

'Those papers people say that Waterman stole. Why was everyone so convinced that it was him?' I was chancing my arm here, seeking confirmation of my suspicions.

Brabazon arched an eyebrow. 'You have been busy. Who else could it have been? I was in the warehouse myself at the time the papers went missing and I saw Waterman go up to the office. Naturally, I regret saying anything to Monday, but neither he nor I can blame ourselves. Drake was only supposed to punish the boy, not leave him a cripple. I'm afraid the other man I hold responsible is Mr Archer. He dangled an inducement in front of Waterman to tempt him into a criminal act. That's reprehensible.'

So Tad had bribed Waterman to steal the papers from the warehouse, and Monday had ordered the attack on Waterman as a reprisal, based on Brabazon's evidence. It explained Nathaniel's hostility towards them. I was not in the least surprised to learn that it was Frank Drake who'd carried out those orders.

'What are these papers?'

'They relate to *The Dark Angel*, though I'm not sure how. Monday will be able to tell you more.'

I doubted Monday would tell me anything at all. 'Did you hear about the dead bird on Monday's doorstep?'

'Another one? How tiresome. Archer spread it around town that we killed those slaves, and now the Deptford Negroes seek to punish us. To me a dead cock is just a dead cock, but this is a superstitious town. Monday's been struggling to find crew for *The Dark Angel* ever since.'

'I heard Vaughan was rather shaken up by it all.'

He smiled. 'Drake too. He denies it, but you can see that it unsettles him.'

I questioned Brabazon a little more, on these and other matters, but he seemed quite unruffled. Truly, the man was slippery as a slow worm. Yet Nathaniel had said he'd been frightened like the others. I wondered what Tad had known that I did not.

For the time being, I admitted defeat. Brabazon walked me to the door, where he laid a hand on my arm. 'A word of advice, Captain Corsham. Friend to friend, so to speak. Monday and Vaughan might not take too kindly to you repeating Archer's lies. That theory of his is slanderous after all. I'd hate to see you end up in a court of law.'

'Thank you for your concern,' I replied pleasantly, as though we were indeed good friends, 'but I don't believe you need worry on that score. I think a court of law is the last place those gentlemen would want this subject raised.'

He only smiled. He knew that I knew that he was lying. But I couldn't prove it – and to my great chagrin, he knew that too.

CHAPTER THIRTY-THREE

THE LANDLORD IN the coaching inn greeted me warmly. 'God save the King, and Yankee Doodle be damned for a dandy. What can I get for you, Captain?'

I ordered a pot of ale. 'I wondered if you'd heard anything from Captain Vaughan?'

'Not a whistle, sir, I'm afraid.'

'I'm a little anxious for him, to be honest. I wondered if I might take a look inside his room, see if there is any clue there to his whereabouts?'

His face clouded with suspicion. 'Vaughan wouldn't like that. How am I to know you're really a friend?'

'Didn't you say he owed you rent? I'd be happy to settle his bill. I'd hardly offer to do that if I wasn't a friend.'

The furrow in the man's pink forehead deepened. 'It's near two guineas.'

'As I say, I am happy to settle it.'

I could see that he liked the sound of my two guineas. He was probably wondering if he'd ever see his tenant again.

His wife emerged from the back room and deposited a tray of glasses on the counter. She gave me a nod. 'Afternoon.'

'Gentleman says he'll give us Vaughan's rent, if we let him take a look inside his room.'

She glanced at me, and then at her husband. A piece of

unspoken communication passed between them, the kind that only exists in the closest marriages. I felt a pang of envy.

'You're not to take nothing,' she said. 'I'll be watching to make sure.'

I paid the outstanding amount, and she led me upstairs to the landing, where she unlocked a door. Vaughan's room was large, furnished with mahogany pieces: a four-poster bed, an armoire, a desk and a washstand. An arrangement of chairs and a sofa stood in front of the fire. True to her word, the landlady stood watching with folded arms as I made a methodical search of the premises.

I began with the desk. The upper drawers held star charts and nautical equipment: dividers, a sextant, and a leather box containing a telescope. In a middle drawer I found a pair of account books. They revealed little except that Vaughan, like Monday, was a rich man, with over five thousand pounds in savings and investments. The lowest two drawers held correspondence, much of it business-related. I spent some time looking through it, ignoring the landlady's impatient sighs, but discovered only that Vaughan had a financial interest in a Barbados sugar plantation and an investment in a Liverpool timber yard. Nothing seemed particularly relevant, but I made a note of Vaughan's correspondents. I would write to them to see if any of them had heard from him.

On the desktop were a well-thumbed Bible, the usual writing implements, and a ceramic pot of chinoiserie design. Inside the pot was a pouch of tobacco and a small brass key.

I paused in my labours to study the painting over the desk. It depicted a colonial harbour scene, black lines of chained Africans being marched off a Guineaman. A brass plaque was screwed to the frame: *Port of Havana, Cuba.*

'That's where Vaughan was born,' the landlady said. 'His father owned a small plantation. His mother was Spanish.'

The armoire held an array of very fine clothes, and I remembered Jamaica Mary had said that Vaughan cut quite a swathe. Wherever he had gone, it didn't look as if he'd taken much with him. At the back of the armoire I found an opium pipe and a wooden box. Inside were three red waxed-paper packages. From what Brabazon had told me about the grip of the poppy drug, I was surprised that Vaughan had left his opium behind. Everything suggested that he had departed in a hurry.

I drew back the curtains from the bed and started with surprise. Lengths of string had been pinned to the canopy, and each had something tied to it: a desiccated sprig that might have been heather; brass charms like the ones the gypsies had tried to sell me the other night; a crucifix; a rabbit's foot; a number of blue glass beads painted with little white eyes. If Vaughan was trying to ward off evil, then he was leaving nothing to chance. I ran my hand across the strings and the charms tinkled softly. The landlady shook her head. 'Moon-crazed.'

In the drawer of the bedside table was a leather case containing a length of pig intestine for guarding the male member during amorous intercourse, and some mercury pills.

'Did Vaughan ever bring his women here?'

'Certainly not. I run a respectable house.'

'I apologize, madam.'

Under the bed I discovered a metal strongbox. I took it to the desk and fitted the brass key I had found earlier into the lock. Inside was a pouch containing twelve guineas, a silver caddy filled with tea leaves, a bundle of papers, and a leather-bound book.

My pulse quickened as I realized that the papers were bills of sale for slaves that Vaughan had sold for personal profit.

Monday had told me on our walk down to the dock that he allowed his captains to undertake a few such transactions on each voyage. The Governor of Jamaica had said in his letter that the surviving slave was Vaughan's personal concubine. I went through the bills until I found the one I was looking for, studying it with mounting excitement.

> *19th Day of June 1780 Captain Evan Vaughan Esq. of Deptford, England hereby contracts to sell one Negress girl of about fifteen years of age named Cinnamon to Lucius Stokes Esq. of Deptford, England for the sum of fifty guineas.*

Here was proof that Scipio had lied to me. Cinnamon hadn't been bought from a Bristol sugar merchant a year ago – and if Vaughan had kept her for a short time before selling her to Stokes, she could certainly have been on board *The Dark Angel*.

The landlady had opened the leather-bound book and was leafing through it. 'Lord have mercy. Will you look at that?'

The book's pages were covered in ink, barely an inch of paper left blank. Drawings of ships riding the waves, patterns of stars and strange fish. A skull with coins in the eye sockets. Writing ran between the drawings at odd angles, or took up whole pages, the letters large and small, hastily scrawled.

> *Last night they came again. Those long dark hours when I cannot dream, yet when I close my eyes, I hear them. Their siren song. And the children look at me. There is no respite. Ah Jesu. Your servant. Black faces. Black voices. Black like the demon in the smoke. He waits.*

Much of it was biblical verse:

For the life of the flesh is in the blood, and I have given it for you on the altar to make atonement for your souls, for it is the blood that makes atonement by the life.

Under the law almost everything is purified with blood, and without the shedding of blood there is no forgiveness of sins.

Ink spatters testified to the frenzy with which the diary had been written. I turned a page and saw a drawing of a man I took to be Vaughan. His long curly hair was thrown back from his face as he arched his spine, his mouth and eyes contorted into an expression of deepest anguish. The scar on his face had been drawn so savagely, the quill had torn the paper.

I turned another page, then another. The same words over and over again, like a child's lines for punishment. A hundred times, a thousand. I turned more pages. The landlady sucked in her breath and muttered a prayer.

For the wages of sin are death.
For the wages of sin are death.
For the wages of sin are death.
For the wages of sin are death.

Amidst all the lies I had been told, one truth stood stark: wherever he was, Evan Vaughan was not a well man.

Chapter Thirty-Four

'Toss her! crush her skull!'

'Skewer that bitch.'

'Stamp on her. Again. Give it to her.'

The bull's hide was slick with sweat. His eyes rolled back in his skull. He dipped his horns to charge the crowd, and those who'd got too close leaped back, eyes wild with excitement. The chain securing the bull snapped taut and the dogs seized their moment. One darted in and fastened her teeth deep in his flank. He bellowed and dipped his head again, spearing one of the other dogs with his horns. Sweat and blood sprayed the crowd, as he tossed her into the air. They cheered.

We were in one of the fields that banked Deptford Creek. I had heard the noise from the road, and come up here to take a look. Most of the crowd were fixated by the bait, while others were taking advantage of the action to conduct a little business. The fine clothes, groomed beards and sun-darkened complexions of one group drew my attention. Sea captains. I went over and introduced myself as a friend of Captain Vaughan. Warm with ale and the thrill of the bait, they were happy to talk to me.

'Not Brighthelmstone,' one said, in response to my queries. 'Not Margate either.' He thought for a moment, pipe-smoke wafting in the breeze. 'Bath, it was. Vaughan's gone to take the waters.'

'You cannot believe that?' another said. 'He's with one of his women – induced her to leave her husband and ran off to Spain. Vaughan has family there.'

'I heard he was dead,' said a third. 'A jealous husband put a knife in his guts and dropped him in Deptford Reach.'

'Is there any evidence for that?'

The man grinned. 'It's probably horseshit. Vaughan could cuckold the Devil himself and still talk his way out.'

I'd heard more answers to the question of Vaughan's whereabouts than I'd had hot pies. I could only conclude that he didn't want to be found. I wondered if he'd decided to get out of Deptford and lie low. As *The Dark Angel*'s captain, he would have given the primary account of the voyage to John Monday's insurers. He had more to fear from Tad's inquiry than most. Yet there was also his state of mind to consider.

I was about to return to Deptford Strand to make further inquiries, when I noticed two men standing beneath a large oak tree on the fringes of the fray. The magistrate, Peregrine Child, and *The Dark Angel*'s third officer, Frank Drake, heads bent together over the inevitable bottles in their hands. It was the first time I'd seen either of them since Drake had attacked me in the alley. I walked over to join them.

'For a man who doesn't believe in conspiracy, Mr Child, the pair of you look positively cabalistic.'

Drake scowled, and Child laid a soothing hand on his arm. 'What can I do for you, Captain Corsham?'

He listened, frowning, as I told him about Amelia and the other murders. Drake only smirked.

'Archer is dead. His sister and her maid are dead. Two London Africans are dead. Daniel Waterman is a cripple because of this man you drink with here. How many more people are going to get hurt before you act?'

Child turned to Drake, and I realized this was the first he'd heard about Waterman.

'Didn't he tell you? I'm sure it was a fair fight. That boy must have weighed at least a hundred and thirty pounds.'

Drake's bright blue eyes glittered dangerously. 'The boy was a thief. I confronted him, and he came at me with a knife. I had a right to defend myself.'

'I suppose you were defending yourself against me too, when you and Isaac attacked me in those alleys?'

He grinned. 'You said it.'

He seemed so confident that I wondered if he was paying Child off. Or if there was another aspect to their relationship I didn't understand.

'I hear you've been having trouble with dead birds, Drake. Bones, rats, dolls? Scare you, does it?'

Drake licked his lips. 'It's nothing. Nigger magic. Miserable cowards.'

'You'd know.'

His ruined drinker's face flushed scarlet. 'You know why I had it out with Waterman? Because Mr Monday told me to. You know why I drowned those slaves? Because Captain Vaughan ordered it. You know why I didn't kill your friend, though Christ knows he had it coming? Because Mr Monday ordered that he not be harmed.'

This was new. 'When was this?'

Drake hesitated, but Child gave him a nod to continue. I wondered if he wanted to hear Drake's answer as much as I.

'The morning before they found his body. Monday had heard that Archer was back in town. He summoned me and Brabazon to his house, and said no one was to touch him. So there we are.'

'You don't strike me as a man who does what he's told.'

'Shows what you know. My family have sailed the Middle

Passage since the days of the Virgin Queen. There have been Frank Drakes here in town ever since the first Drake set out to find black gold on the Guinea coast and knocked up a Deptford doxy on his way through town. I was twelve years old on my first voyage. I saw a Negro put a spike through my best friend's skull because he hadn't followed orders. On a slave ship the captain's word is God, and it's good discipline that keeps a crew alive.'

'You weren't on a slave ship when Archer was killed.'

'If I ever hoped to be again, then I had to do what Monday said. A man gets blacklisted, he's finished in this town.'

'That's true,' Child said. 'And I believe Jamaica Mary told you she was with Drake in the bathhouse all night.' So he had heard about my visit there. No prizes for guessing who'd told him. 'It seems to me that Mr Drake is in the clear. As I believe I told you myself some days ago.'

'Where is Captain Vaughan?' I asked Drake.

'How the hell should I know? In some cat-house probably.'

'You spend a lot of time in brothels?'

'What do you think?'

I took the silver ticket from my pocket and showed it to him. 'You ever see one like this before? In any of your brothels?'

'No.'

'How about you?'

I thought I caught a trace of unease on Child's face, but he shook his head. 'You could buy half the whores in Deptford for the price of that ticket.'

I returned it to my pocket, and took out my notebook and pencil. 'Would you write your name down for me, please, Mr Drake?'

'What the devil for?'

'A letter was left for me at the Noah's Ark a few nights ago.

Its author threatened my life. He used some choice phrases that reminded me of you.'

'I don't have to listen to this.' Drake threw his bottle over his shoulder into the field. 'Fuck your questions. Fuck your friend. Fuck you.'

He strode over to join the bait, and I raised my eyebrows at Child. 'For an innocent man, he seems very upset.'

'He can't read or write. It is common with seafaring men. Perhaps if you tried harder not to upset people, then you wouldn't receive such letters.'

The bait was growing louder, nearing its climax. I raised my voice over the bellowing of the bull. 'Mrs Grimshaw says you were fixing a window in the inn on the day the letter was delivered. Did you see anyone who could have left it there?'

'I'm afraid not.'

Child had been in London when Proudlock was killed. He had looked into *The Dark Angel* while he was there. Should I treat him as a suspect? I couldn't see a motive. And surely he was too short to be the man I'd encountered last night at Marylebone? Yet I couldn't quite put my finger on Peregrine Child.

'On my last visit here, I asked you about *The Dark Angel*. You pretended you'd never heard of her. How was your trip to Whitehall? Did you find anything interesting in the ministry's archives?'

If he was surprised that I knew his movements, he didn't show it. Like Brabazon, he had sangfroid. 'Just keeping myself informed.'

'I confess I hadn't associated you with such diligence.'

'*Ad altiora tendo*. We all strive to better ourselves.'

His flippancy angered me. 'Do you ever think about the dead slaves? I do. They fought, I have heard, but their limbs were wasted. They threw women and children to their deaths too. Did you know that? The infants screamed for their mothers, but their mothers couldn't help them. They must have sunk like stones when they hit the water. What would you have done? Stood by and watched?'

My words sparked a greater reaction than I had anticipated. Child moved so fast, he caught me by surprise. He grabbed me by the collar and slammed me up against the trunk of the oak tree. He put his face up to mine, so I could make out the network of broken veins around his nose.

'I don't care how many Yankee soldiers you've killed. Or whose arse you kiss at the War Office. Talk to me like that again, and I'll break your nose.'

CHAPTER THIRTY-FIVE

I WAS BAFFLED by Child's assault on me, not least because it was the first time I'd seen him animated about anything. He had always struck me as lazy and self-interested, but, fleetingly, I had seen a fury in his bloodshot eyes that had frightened me.

A little unnerved, I rejoined the High Street, which was busy with people returning from the bull bait. I noticed *The Dark Angel*'s owner, John Monday, walking on the opposite side of the road, but I didn't approach him. I wanted to find out more about his stolen papers first. I planned to talk to Daniel Waterman tonight.

Walking beside Monday was the young mulatto boy whom I had seen at his house. Several passers-by turned to stare as they walked past. I felt a stab of compassion for the boy, an object of spectacle in this pitiless town. He reminded me a little of Ben, who'd been about the same age when we'd been parted.

I walked back along the road to Deptford Strand, deep in thought. Evan Vaughan. Opium. Monday in the Red House. The timings of Tad's visits to Deptford. I was still trying to make sense of it all, when a handsome turquoise-and-silver carriage swept past me, then clattered to a halt a few yards further on. Two black footmen were clinging to the back, and with a sinking heart, I recognized the protruding eyes and squashed nose of Abraham, the mayor's footman. As I drew level with the vehicle, the window was lowered, and Lucius Stokes's head emerged. Behind him I could see Cinnamon in the carriage.

'Captain Corsham,' Stokes said. 'You have returned.'

I smiled as cheerfully as I could. 'As you see.'

I tried to catch Cinnamon's eye, but she was staring at the floor. Her scarlet dress was cut low in the bodice, as all her gowns seemed to be. Red silk roses adorned her piled hair. How was I ever going to get a chance to talk to her alone?

'I confess I am a little surprised,' Stokes said. 'I had been told that you now understood how unwise it was for you to be here.'

'Whoever told you that must have been mistaken.'

He smiled. 'I fear it is you who has made the mistake, sir.'

He rapped on the roof with his gold-topped cane, and the coach moved off again. Abraham turned to eye me sullenly, though whether on his own or his master's account, I couldn't know. I'd hoped to have longer in Deptford before Stokes learned of my return, but perhaps that had been wishful thinking. No doubt letters would soon be winging their way to Napier Smith and Nicholas Cavill-Lawrence. I'd been trying not to think about Smith's threats and ongoing inquiries, but with this untimely reminder, how could I not?

*

I decided to wait until after dark before trying to talk to Daniel Waterman, in the hope that I could do so unobserved. In the meantime, I walked down to the dock. An idea was taking shape in my mind, and I wanted to test it.

Mindful of Mrs Grimshaw's warning, I avoided the Blackamoor's Head and the other slaving taverns, opting instead to walk along the quays. Little groups of sailors and stevedores sat around in the evening sun, playing cards or dice, drinking and smoking. The cheaper sort of whores paraded their dubious wares, and grunts of copulation drifted from the alleys.

As a gentleman, it wasn't hard to make friends down here. I went from group to group, playing games of 'Find the Lady', buying an overpriced scrimshaw carving, paying to hear a sea shanty, asking questions. I discovered that Captain Vaughan was in London, as well as Margate, as well as Bath, that he was dead, that he was in gaol, that he was anywhere in the world save for Deptford.

'Do you remember who told you?' I asked one meaty bull of a fellow, who was convinced I could find Vaughan in Lyme Regis.

He shrugged. 'A sailor.'

'Do you remember which ship he crewed?'

'*The Phoenix*,' he said, after a moment's thought.

I nodded, unsurprised. One of Monday's men.

A little further along the quay, I noticed the old seadog I'd talked to in the Blackamoor's Head, playing cards with some other sailors over a barrel. The game looked as if it was going badly for him, probably due to his evident inebriation.

I bought a bottle of rum from one of the hole-in-the-wall ventures selling liquor, went over and showed it to him. 'Care to take a walk with me?'

He eyed the bottle longingly. 'You're not that redcoat Drake's been on at everyone to watch out for, are you?'

'Drake?' I said. 'Who's he?'

The man grinned and took the proffered bottle.

We wandered along the harbourside, passing the bottle back and forth. He drank most of it, giving me the occasional side-long glance to see if I'd noticed. He'd heard nothing more about Vaughan since the last time we'd talked.

'Tell me, how do things stand between Vaughan and John Monday?' I asked. 'I heard they were close.'

'Go back years,' the man said. 'Vaughan was Monday's first officer when he captained for Lucius Stokes. Went with him when Monday set up on his own.'

'There's loyalty there then?'

'Plenty of it. They say Vaughan saved Monday's life once. He was knocked off deck by a block and tackle during a storm, out cold in the water. Vaughan risked his own neck to jump in after him. They're different stripes of men, one of those friendships that's hard to fathom, but I'd warrant Monday would run into fire for Evan Vaughan.'

The wharves were busy. A fleet of barges were ferrying the cargo of a merchantman moored in the dock. On the quayside, stevedores swarmed around the unloaded shipping crates, fastening them to ropes attached to thirty-foot cranes, hoisting them into a row of adjoining warehouses.

'Tell me about the lad in Monday's household, the one with African blood.'

'The blueskin boy? What about him?'

'Is he Monday's child? I confess I find it hard to imagine him taking a black mistress.'

The man grinned, showing me his bright ivory teeth, pipe-smoke shrouding his grizzled chin and bloodshot eyes.

'Depends if by "Monday" you mean the husband or the wife. This was a taste for black cock, not black cunny.' He cackled, enjoying my evident astonishment. 'She weren't Eleanor Monday back then, but Eleanor Forrester. Owen Forrester was her first husband, one of Monday's captains. Owen was delighted, they say, when his wife got with child. Less delighted when the baby came out brown. Now Eleanor tried to claim the child was a throwback. That happens on the plantations. A planter gets a by-blow on one of his Negresses, the child comes out white, and he raises it as his own. All well and good, until a few generations down, when out pops a tar-baby. Well, no one in Owen, nor Eleanor's families had ever set foot on a plantation. The story was horseshit and everyone knew it.

'Some in town said a Negro had molested her, and she didn't want to admit it for the shame. That's what Owen chose to think too. He blamed his house-slave, a boy named George. Owen and two of his friends took young George out to marshes yonder.' He pointed over the water to the Isle of Dogs. 'They say his screams carried all the way to Bromley. What he told them, nobody knows, but we can guess. The next day Owen up and left his wife.'

'He thought she went with George willingly?'

'Would you want a wife who liked black cock?' His leer subsided into a frown. 'Not everyone believed it, mind. Some in town thought she'd been badly done by. Old Monday tried to change Forrester's mind, to no avail. He moved away to Liverpool and his ship went down a summer later with all hands. Then Monday went and married her – raised the tar-baby as his own.' He shook his head. 'Too much God. Sentimental old fool.'

For my part, I thought the story reflected well on Monday. 'The child seems unhappy.' I remembered how his half-sister had tormented him.

'Mixing the blood weakens it. Everyone knows that. Probably touched in the head.'

Such prejudiced nonsense aside, it was a sad story – though one I doubted bore any relevance to my inquiry. 'Are Vaughan's relations with his officers—'

'Beware below!'

The shout went up. I heard a faint whistling, the spin of a frictionless wheel. Glancing up, I grabbed the seadog and dived to the right, just as a net of shipping crates slammed into the quayside where we'd been standing. A snake of rope followed it down, the crash echoing around the wharves. I stared at it, shaking.

'Are you hurt?' I helped the seadog to his feet.

Stevedores hurried over to inspect the splintered crates and their contents. They seemed remarkably unperturbed about the near-fatal incident, more concerned with the question of how to get their sacks of sugar into the warehouse. As they pulled apart the netting, I stooped to examine the rope. The end was smooth, as though it had been severed with a knife.

Chapter Thirty-Six

FORTIFIED BY ONE of Mrs Grimshaw's anchovy suppers, I sat in a secluded corner of the taproom in the Noah's Ark, still shaken by the near miss on the quayside. It was the first time I had stopped in two days, and I only now realized how exhausted I was. I found myself thinking about Peregrine Child. His visit to the ministry's archive showed he was more interested in Tad's murder than I'd first supposed. Did he want the killer caught after all? I thought I'd seen a glimmer of humanity beneath the ambivalence that day at the dock. He had intervened with Drake in those alleys to save my life. Yet I also remembered the murderous look on his face when he'd slammed me up against that tree – and his friendship with Frank Drake suggested darker motives. I dwelled on the inconsistencies until my head hurt. Then I gave up, pushing all thought of them aside.

Long hot evenings are made for drinking and the taproom was crowded. I looked around for Nathaniel, but he wasn't there. Perhaps he was still out looking for his dog, or making inquiries about Tad's silver ticket. If I didn't see him tonight, then I'd seek him out tomorrow.

A fiddler was playing a jig, trying to get people to dance and give him money. I stared through him. I had these moments with increasing frequency now, when grief gnawed at me like a canker. Tad would come so near I could almost touch him. I'd started to live for them.

I can't find him, Tad. It's too much of a thicket. I can't see my way through all the tangles.

Of course you can. You only need patience.

You're a fine one to talk. When did you ever have patience?

I waited years for you, Hal. You never came.

I'm here now, aren't I?

Then stop asking me for help. This is your penance, not mine.

It isn't penance, Tad.

What is it then?

A debt. A journey. Your last days. My life in yours.

That won't bring me back.

You're here now, aren't you?

And then, just to spite me, he wasn't.

I sat there drinking more than I should, until I decided he wasn't going to return tonight, no matter how inebriated I became. The drinking songs were in full sway, and it was dark outside. With luck Daniel Waterman would be alone, awake and lucid. I went out through the door onto the High Street, then doubled round through the carriage arch into the stable-yard. I walked up the stairs to the living loft and tried the door. It wasn't locked.

Candlelight cast a soft glow over Waterman's sickbed. Cinnamon stood beside it, holding a copper basin. The sheets were drawn back, and Eleanor Monday was sponging Waterman down. The women were talking, but fell silent as I entered.

Such irony! How badly I wanted to speak to all three of them. Yet not together like this. What was Cinnamon doing here, after all she'd told me about Waterman drowning the infant slaves?

The boy moaned and writhed under the sponge. I winced at the sight of his stump, swathed in bandages. How easily that could have been my fate. 'Close the door, please, sir,' Mrs Monday said. 'Or he'll catch a chill.'

She was wearing a dark cloak with the hood tipped back, her black hair worn in severe style, barely piled at all. A silver crucifix glittered at her throat. She resembled an abbess from Thomas Malory, attending to a fallen knight. A picture of virtue – had she really bedded her house-slave? It was hard to imagine.

'I came to see how he was.'

The boy groaned again and Mrs Monday stroked his forehead. 'He won't be able to talk to you about *The Dark Angel*, sir. Not tonight. Isn't that why you've come?'

Her directness took me by surprise. 'Yes, it is.'

I glanced at Cinnamon, trying to convey with my eyes that I was willing to help her. She looked away.

'Even if he could talk,' Mrs Monday said, 'what makes you think he would tell you the truth?'

'He probably wouldn't. I am used to lies in Deptford.'

She nodded. 'People lie for all sorts of reasons. Out of fear, or to protect the ones they love. Sometimes they lie to themselves. Those are the hardest to detect.'

Her words and her stare were unsettling. She appeared outwardly composed, yet her calmness struck a false note. Her hands twitched, and I sensed her emotions lay near to the surface.

Waterman moaned. 'Mama.'

'Hush, child. Your mama is gone. Yet I am here, Daniel. Mrs Monday.'

His voice rose. 'The nigger has the knife, Mama. It burns.'

A sudden crash startled us all. Cinnamon had dropped her basin. The metal vibrated, water soaking the wooden floor.

'Careless girl,' Mrs Monday admonished her.

'Forgive me, madam. I will go fetch some more.'

'Quickly now. You know Mr Stokes doesn't like you wandering off alone. And don't go getting any ideas. It is a long way to London, and they will find you if you run.'

On her way to the door, Cinnamon's eyes slid to meet mine. I knew she wanted me to follow, but it would be too obvious if I did so right away.

The door closed behind her, and I addressed Mrs Monday: 'I saw you at Archer's funeral.'

'You are mistaken, sir.'

'No, I'm not.'

She dabbed Waterman's forehead with her sponge.

'I think you don't like what's been going on here in Deptford. First Waterman's leg. Then Archer's murder. Now two women and two Africans in London, brutally slain. Few here seem to give a damn, except I think you do. You went to Archer's funeral. Now you tend to this boy.'

'I attend to Daniel because he crewed one of my husband's ships. His men are as family to us, sir.'

'I'm glad I'm not a relative of yours. Your husband ordered this done.'

She flushed. 'The boy was a thief. It wasn't John's fault that Frank Drake went too far in the matter.'

'How does your husband feel about you attending Archer's funeral? Perhaps I'll ask him.'

Now she looked at me. 'I would prefer it if you did not.'

So Monday hadn't known she'd gone. Good. 'I am happy to keep it between ourselves, provided you answer my questions.'

She frowned. 'Blackmail is a sin, sir.'

'I do what I have to do.'

'As do we all.' She smoothed a few loose strands of hair back from her face. 'Very well, sir. Ask your questions, if you will.'

I didn't have long. Cinnamon was waiting for me. Yet I couldn't let this opportunity pass me by. 'When did your husband first learn about the insurance fraud?'

'From Mr Archer, the first time he came to town.' Her voice rose. 'But there is no proof that it happened as Archer said it did. My husband does not believe it. He says Captain Vaughan would never have countenanced such a thing.'

'What do you believe?'

She lowered her eyes. 'I believe as my husband does, sir.'

'Do you know where Vaughan is?'

'No, sir. I do not.'

'There is a silver box in your husband's study. It has compartments for three knives, but it only holds two. Do you know what happened to the third?'

'It was stolen. John thinks one of the servants took it.'

'When did it go missing?'

'About two weeks ago.' She stopped, and I could see she was thinking the same thing as I. 'Everyone in Deptford has a knife. Why would the killer steal ours?'

'I don't know. But Brabazon thinks a long knife was used, and yours is missing.'

Waterman stirred again. 'The knife, Mama. It burns.'

'Hush, Daniel.' She tucked the blanket around him. When she next spoke, her voice was resolute: 'If you believe that knife was used to kill Archer, then you must discount Captain Vaughan from your inquiry. My husband too.'

'Why is that?'

'Evan Vaughan hasn't been to our house in several weeks. And my husband would hardly have used his own knife and not put it back.'

'The knife might have been damaged or lost.'

She held my gaze. 'The night your friend died, my husband

was at home with his family. He didn't want Archer harmed. He ordered his officers not to touch him.'

'Was that the same day the knife disappeared? The day before they found Archer dead?'

She said nothing, but I could see the answer on her face. 'Did anyone else other than Drake and Brabazon come to the house that day?'

She thought for a moment. 'Our mayor, Mr Stokes, brought Cinnamon to the house. Then she and I came down here to tend to Daniel. I believe our magistrate, Mr Child, accompanied Mr Stokes. They stayed to talk to my husband.'

Could Stokes have taken the knife? It was hard to imagine him torturing someone to death. Then again, he didn't strike me as the stripe of man who'd dirty his own hands. I studied Daniel Waterman. *The nigger has the knife.* Was it possible that Waterman knew something about the murder? Could someone have confided in him, or could he have overheard something discussed by his bedside visitors? Could Stokes have ordered one of his black servants to commit the murders?

'Did Scipio accompany Stokes to your house that night?'

She turned away slightly. 'Who?'

'His secretary, Scipio.'

Scipio, who had been in Marylebone on the night the killer almost caught Moses Graham and I.

Her hand fluttered to her crucifix. 'Not his secretary, no. He was accompanied by his footmen.'

'Could either of them have taken the knife?'

'I don't think so. They waited outside.'

It was a foolish idea in any event. I had seen the hand of Amelia's killer, and he was white. It was possible that Stokes had taken the knife himself, and then passed it on to some unnamed assassin, but I couldn't see a motive – Archer's murder had caused as many problems for the West India lobby as it had solved. The same went for Child – which took me back to Monday and his officers.

Waterman stirred again. 'She has the knife.'

I leaned forward. 'Who has the knife, Daniel?'

His cracked lips parted. I strained to hear his whisper: 'Brabazon.'

'He must be talking about last night when Brabazon took his leg.' Mrs Monday stroked his hand. 'Hush, child.'

She had a faint bruise on her cheek the same colour as her eyes, and I remembered the way she'd flinched from her husband. 'I beg you to tell me anything that will help me in this matter, madam. If you are frightened of your husband, I can protect you.'

Her gaze was steady, her eyes perfectly clear. 'I am not afraid of my husband, sir. I am afraid of you.'

*

I looked for Cinnamon downstairs in the stable-yard. Singing from the taproom mingled with the clatter of cutlery in the dining room. One of the horses in the stables stamped and whickered.

A hand took my arm and drew me into the shadows by the stable door. I could hardly see her face in the darkness, but I could smell her rose perfume and hear the rustle of silk each time she moved.

'You were on *The Dark Angel*,' I said. 'You survived and were brought back here to Deptford.'

'I saw it all,' she said. 'Mr Archer called it fate.'

'Why do you tend to Waterman like this? After what you told me he did to those children?'

'I have no choice. Some people in town don't like that

Mr Stokes keeps me the way he does, so he has me undertake good works with Mrs Monday.' She gripped my arm, her fingers digging into my flesh. 'I have to get away from here. Will you buy me from Mr Stokes?'

'No, but I will take you to London and keep you safe. I'll arrange for a lawyer to win your freedom.' What consequences would follow for me and mine? I didn't know, but they wouldn't be good. Yet I needed to hear her story, and I wanted to help her too. 'You can trust me, I promise. Now, will you tell me about the voyage?'

She stepped away from me. 'No, I'll not make that mistake again.'

'What do you mean?' I drew her back, remembering the way she'd spoken about Tad at the dock. 'Did Archer fail you in some fashion?'

'He lied to me. Tricked me into telling him what I knew. He promised to take me to London, but he betrayed me.'

'When was this?'

'The last time he came to Deptford. I was to meet him by the creek, and we would ride to London together. It was hard to get away from Scipio and Mr Stokes, but I was able to eventually. I waited there all afternoon, but he never came. In the end, I went to the Strand to look for him. I found him by the boatyards. I could see from his face that he'd forgotten all about me. He was full of excuses, but I'd had my fill of his lies. He promised to take me with him when he left town, but that was too late.'

'Too late for what?'

'For everything. The next day they found him dead.'

I wondered again what was so vital that Tad had changed his plans, and stayed another night in Deptford at the last minute. And why would he have abandoned Cinnamon like that, a living witness?

'You can ride?' I asked.

'A little. Enough.'

'I will need to hire another horse, but I could do that tomorrow.'

'Tomorrow is no good. Mr Stokes is entertaining guests at the villa. The following day he goes to play whist in Charlton, and always stays late. Scipio has business out of town too. I could get out once the servants are asleep.'

I arranged to meet her outside the villa at half past midnight. All being well, we would be in London before anyone realized she was gone. Cinnamon turned to go back upstairs, but again I drew her back. 'The obeah, the dead birds. Do you know anything about it?'

'Obeah is the religion of the Igbo, my mother's tribe.'

'What do the dead birds mean?'

'That the duppies see those men. They don't forget.'

'What are duppies?'

'Demons, bad spirits.'

'Then it is a curse?'

'Those men are already cursed. Each day is another step along the path of bones.'

'What is the path of bones?'

'Eternal torment.'

'Do you know who is behind it? Is it you?'

We had moved a little further into the light, and I could see Cinnamon's face more clearly. Her smile was knowing. 'I will speak when I am safe, not before.'

A shadow fell across us. I turned and saw Scipio standing there. 'What are you doing out here, girl? Where is Mrs Monday?'

'I dropped some water.' She spoke breathlessly, lifting her bowl to show him.

He examined our faces, evidently suspicious. How much of our conversation had he heard? I wasn't sure.

The door to the stable-loft opened, throwing light into the yard. Mrs Monday came to the top of the stairs and stared down at us. 'What is keeping you, child? Where is that water?'

Cinnamon hurried up the stairs, and Mrs Monday gave me a nod. 'Goodnight, Captain Corsham.' She didn't acknowledge Scipio at all.

I waited until the door had closed. 'Were you looking for me? I am sorry I left you so abruptly in the Yorkshire Stingo.'

Scipio didn't answer at first. He was still gazing after the women. I repeated my apology, and he turned. 'Mr Child told Mr Stokes that there have been more murders. Two Africans slain in London. Is this true?'

'Yes, it is.' I summarized the mutilations, while he closed his eyes and breathed deeply. I could see the news had a profound effect on him.

'Captain Corsham, I ask that you come with me.'

I studied him sceptically, mindful of danger. 'It is late to be going anywhere tonight.'

'Don't you understand?' His face contorted with frustration. 'I'm trying to help you. Now let us go.'

Chapter Thirty-Seven

✳

Scipio and I walked swiftly through the darkened streets of Deptford.

'Aren't you worried about people seeing us together?' I asked.

'If they do, and Mr Stokes gets to hear of it, I'll say I pretended to befriend you in order to learn more about your inquiry.'

It had crossed my mind that this was precisely what he was doing. He seemed to read my thoughts. 'I want to help you catch this animal,' he said. 'Brabazon came to see my master earlier. He told him about your visit. You are right about the insurance fraud. The officers of the ship have always denied it, but Stokes and the West India lobby know they are lying. Monday too, I think.'

We had reached the fringes of the alleys that led down to the dock. I held back. 'Where are you taking me?'

'Frank Drake is your principal suspect, but in Jamaica Mary he has an alibi. You need to speak to her again.'

'I had some trouble the last time I was at the bathhouse. I'm not sure they'll let me in.'

'They will if you're with me. Stokes owns the place, though it is not the stripe of business with which he likes to associate publicly. Everything goes through me. They do what I tell them.'

It seemed Scipio had influence in Deptford. He'd built a life for himself here, but where did his loyalties really lie? Could I trust him? He had lied to me once before, about Cinnamon.

'I have one stipulation,' Scipio said. 'I ask again that you leave Miss Cinnamon alone. She had dealings with Mr Archer, as I'm sure you're aware by now. When Stokes found out, he punished her severely. I tell you this not just for the girl's sake, but also for my own. I am Mr Stokes's steward, as well as his secretary, and his property is entrusted to my care. That includes his slaves. He threatened me with dismissal last time for not keeping a better eye on her. If I am to help you, then you must promise to stay away from her.'

I hesitated, knowing it was a promise I would not keep. 'You have my word.'

*

For a woman who earned her living pleasing men, Jamaica Mary needed to work on her welcome. She scowled at Scipio and I, as the proprietor of the bathhouse showed us into his anteroom. The room had been cleared of customers, and we sat at one of the tables, a single candle flickering between us.

'Now, Mary,' Scipio said. 'Tell Captain Corsham what you told me.'

She was wearing a grubby shift and stays, much stained by the seed of her customers. Her yellow cat-like eyes flicked from Scipio to me, and her scowl deepened. It was plain whom she held responsible for her predicament.

'Mary lied to you before,' she said. 'Frank Drake was with her until ten. Then he left.'

I smiled. 'Why did you lie?'

'Drake paid Mary ten shillings. She was nervous about taking it, what with the murder and all. But Drake told her she wouldn't get in no trouble with Perry Child.'

'Did he say why not?'

She shrugged. 'They family.'

'I believe Child's late wife was Mr Drake's sister,' Scipio said.

So Child and Drake were related by marriage. That explained a lot.

I recalled that Mary had also been evasive on the topic of Captain Vaughan. 'Did you ever hear of any trouble between Evan Vaughan and the dead man, Archer?'

'Mary told you, she heard nothing. You want to know who killed him, you talk to that Scottish sawbones.'

'Brabazon?'

She nodded. 'Mary saw them arguing down Greenwich way.'

Nathaniel had said he'd seen Tad heading in that direction. 'When was this?'

'The day before they found him at the dock.'

'Where in Greenwich did you see them?'

'A tavern, the Artichoke. Mary was upstairs, taking leave of a customer, when she saw them coming out of one of the private rooms.'

'Did you hear what they were saying?'

'No, but they weren't friends.'

I recalled that Mary hadn't seemed to like Brabazon very much. It was possible she'd manufactured the incident. On the other hand, Brabazon had told me he'd been in Greenwich that day, attending a lecture at the Naval Hospital.

I wanted to ask her about the obeah, but not with Scipio sitting there. There was little chance she would admit to it if she thought the mayor might hear of it.

Scipio regarded her sternly. 'You won't tell Drake that we were here, now will you, Mary? I'd take that sorely, and you like working here. The same goes for Mr Child.'

'Yes, sir. Mary's a good girl.'

'See that you are.' He passed her a coin. 'We're done here.'

Her shadow slid up the wall as she rose. At the door, she hissed: 'Master's nigger.'

Scipio's face remained impassive, though I knew he must have heard.

'I'd like to talk to another of the whores,' I said. 'A girl named Alice.'

Scipio called the proprietor back, and conveyed this request. The man gave me a dirty look, plainly annoyed by my presence here, but he didn't argue.

The girl he brought in to us a few minutes later wore a threadbare green dress over her skinny frame. She had greasy yellow hair, and looked about seventeen years old. 'I'm not doing it with no Negro,' she said, when she saw Scipio.

'We only want to talk to you,' I said.

'Tell them whatever they want to know, Alice.' The proprietor withdrew.

She rolled her eyes. 'Well?'

'A few weeks ago you had an altercation with a customer named Evan Vaughan.'

'An altercation? That fuckster tried to kill me.'

'Why did he do that?'

She shook her head. 'It's daft.'

'I'd still like to hear it.'

She huffed. 'I wouldn't tell him I forgave him, that's why.'

'Forgave him for what?'

'He got rough with me a different time, about two years ago. Knocked out three of my teeth. I never did find out why. Sometimes they take something you said the wrong way. Or they imagine a look you gave them. I knew a girl who was beaten half to death for smiling. Customer thought she was laughing at him.'

'Vaughan wanted your forgiveness for assaulting you two years ago? Why now?'

'How should I know? He got down on his knees as if he was praying. Kept talking about penance and asking my forgiveness.' She tapped her skull. 'Belongs in bloody Bedlam, if you ask me.'

'And when you refused he tried to strangle you?'

'Wrapped his hands so tight around my neck, I saw the stars. He kept demanding I forgive him, but I wouldn't. I couldn't scream, but I managed to knock over a jug of water. Mister Fred came to see what the racket was about, and pulled him off me.' She touched her neck. 'He would have killed me, I'm sure of it. He kept saying I was a bloody hells-bitch in league with the black demon.'

'Why didn't you do what he wanted? When you realized he meant to kill you?'

Her eyes narrowed. 'They get to fuck me. They get to beat me. They get to call me names. They don't get to make me tell them I don't mind.'

I gave Alice sixpence, and Scipio and I walked out of the bathhouse together. His skin shone in the light of the burning torches, a dark bronze glow. He gave me an odd look. 'The black demon?'

'Archer liked to wear black. He went to visit Vaughan at his rooms at around the same time he attacked Alice.' I told him about the book I'd found there. 'Vaughan was already in a precarious state of mind. Brabazon attests that he was smoking a lot of opium. I think Archer confronted him about the dead slaves, and it precipitated a personal crisis.'

'And now he seeks forgiveness for his crimes?'

'Only in words. Archer would have demanded a higher price, I think. His testimony in court, perhaps.'

'I cannot imagine Vaughan would have agreed readily to

that. He might have ended up on a hangman's rope. Yet if the whore's experience is anything to go by, Archer's refusal to forgive easily would have angered him. Do you think in Drake we have the wrong man?'

'I don't know.' I gazed up at the narrow strip of stars above the alley. 'But I think we need to find Evan Vaughan.'

*

We parted at the end of the alleys, and I walked back to the Noah's Ark, thinking about Vaughan. It was possible that he really had gone away to recuperate. It was even possible that he was dead – killed, not by a jealous husband but by one of his officers to stop him talking to Tad. But I didn't think so.

The seadog had said that Monday would run into fire for Vaughan. He'd saved Monday's life. Perhaps murder was a solution Monday couldn't countenance. Perhaps instead Vaughan had been concealed somewhere to keep him away from Tad. I had seen Monday buying opium in the Red House, and whatever Brabazon said, he didn't strike me as the stripe of man likely to use it. Perhaps Evan Vaughan had never left Deptford at all.

I tried to develop this strand of thought, but exhaustion overwhelmed me. When I reached the Noah's Ark, I went upstairs to my room. There on the floor, inside the door, I discovered a letter. I broke the black seal, studying the handwriting with little surprise, the familiar clutch of fear's cold hand upon the back of my neck.

> *ILE CUT OWT YUR EYES, NEGRO LUVVER,*
> *AND FEED THEM TO THE DEPTFORD*
> *DOGS. GET OWT OF TOWN. I WONT BE*
> *TELLIN YOU AGIN.*

CHAPTER THIRTY-EIGHT

THE SCREAM STARTLED me awake. My heart thudding, I leaped from the bed. I heard it again, a woman's cry. I hurried to the window and pulled aside the curtain, blinking in the sudden flood of daylight. Brabazon was running up the stairs to the stable-loft. I dressed swiftly and went to find out what was going on.

I found Mrs Grimshaw inside the stable-loft door, her breathing coming in heaving gulps. I presumed it had been her cries I'd heard. Nathaniel sat on the rocking chair, his head in his hands. Brabazon was bending over Daniel Waterman on the bed. Waterman's eyes were open, but they held a deathly stillness.

The surgeon gave me a nod. 'A sad day, sir. The strain of the amputation must have been too much. His heart gave out over-night.'

I stood by his side, gazing down at the boy with despair. There had been so much I'd hoped that he could tell me. 'You're sure it was his heart?'

'I've seen it happen before, usually in older patients.' Brabazon shook his head. 'I had such high hopes for his recovery.'

I didn't believe it. It was too convenient. 'Perhaps someone didn't want him to recover.'

Nathaniel's face was white, his eyes red-rimmed. 'What are

you saying, sir? That someone killed him? Why would they do that?'

The door opened, and Peregrine Child walked in. Behind him I glimpsed Mrs Grimshaw's stable boy, who had evidently been dispatched to fetch him here. The lad lingered, probably hoping for a penny from the magistrate. Child approached the bed, grim-faced.

'What has happened here, Mr Brabazon? I asked to be appraised of this boy's condition.'

He must have given that order yesterday, after I'd told him about Drake's assault on Waterman. I wondered again if a conscience lurked somewhere beneath Child's ambivalent exterior.

Brabazon repeated his explanation about Waterman's heart.

'I knew his father,' the magistrate said. 'He was practically a child himself. God damn it.'

I looked around the room for anything to support my suspicions. It all seemed much as it had last night.

'Have you even examined him properly?' I said to Brabazon. 'Look, there's blood on that pillow. Is that usual when a heart gives out?'

Mrs Grimshaw stopped crying long enough to peer at the pillow. Nathaniel looked away.

'Maybe someone thought Waterman would be upset about losing his leg and his livelihood,' I went on. 'Maybe they feared he'd talk to me, and made sure he wouldn't.'

'You never stop, do you, sir?' Brabazon said. 'There was nothing the boy could have told you, or anyone else, because your conjectures are entirely fanciful.'

Child picked up the blood-stained pillow and examined it. 'Well, Brabazon? Is it normal?'

'Whether it is normal or not is beside the point. This boy had just undergone an amputation – the trauma to the body . . .'

'That wasn't what I asked,' Child said.

'You could always send for a physician from London to examine him,' I said. 'I'd gladly pay.'

'Let's not get ahead of ourselves.' Brabazon made dampening gestures. 'If it is Mr Child's wish, I will examine him further.'

I watched over his shoulder, not trusting him at all. Waterman's face was bluish white, the skin dotted with faint red marks. The whites of his eyes were also covered in little red spots. Brabazon prised the boy's jaw open, and with the aid of a stick from his bag, drew out the tongue. It was swollen and lacerated and in one place it looked as if Waterman had almost bitten right through it.

'My father died from his heart,' Mrs Grimshaw said. 'I don't remember his eyes looking like that. And what in the name of God did he do to his tongue?'

Brabazon frowned. 'On closer examination, I believe Captain Corsham is right. The signs are consistent with suffocation. I think someone held that pillow over his face.'

'Mercy.' Mrs Grimshaw started weeping again. Nathaniel stared hard at the floor.

Brabazon glanced from me to Child. 'I think someone should inform Mr Stokes.'

I felt a grim sense of satisfaction. I'd had to drag Brabazon's diagnosis out of him and I knew he wouldn't have confirmed foul play at all, had he not known that I would have consulted other physicians about those symptoms. Brabazon was not an easy man to pin down, but for once I had.

I took a last look at Daniel Waterman, and felt a twinge of pity. He had drowned those infant Africans, but he had killed because poverty and slavery had forced his hand. I left the stable-loft vowing retribution.

*

Three hours later we were assembled in the mayor's private study. Stokes, Cinnamon and Scipio – with the footman, Abraham, in attendance. Mrs Grimshaw and Nathaniel. Peregrine Child and Brabazon. John Monday and his wife. The only people missing were Frank Drake and the elusive Captain Vaughan.

The study was painted a vibrant shade of Tuscan red, the walls hung with pictures of Pompeii and the Coliseum in Rome. On a table between the long windows was a model of Stokes's proposed dock, complete with miniature Guineamen and tiny shipping crates the size of dice. I could see that it would be many times larger than the current dock. If Stokes's plans ever came to fruition, they'd transform Deptford.

Monday's gaze fell on me. 'Why is he here?'

He had a nasty-looking scratch down one cheek, and I thought immediately of Tad's sister, Amelia, fighting for her life. As a West India merchant, Monday would presumably have been in London for the lobby's meeting the night Moses Graham and I had been followed at Marylebone.

'Captain Corsham saw Daniel Waterman late last night,' Child said.

'Yes, my wife told me. Nevertheless, this is surely a Deptford matter?'

'He has a point,' Stokes said. 'Mr Child?'

To my surprise, Child stood his ground. 'I want to hear from everyone who was with the boy. Who found the body?'

'I did.' Nathaniel's voice was tight with emotion. 'I came back from my shift at the warehouses about a quarter after six this morning. I didn't look too closely and just lay down beside him. I only realized he was dead when I awoke a few hours later. He wasn't breathing. Then I saw his face.'

'Who was the last person to see him alive?'

'I believe that must have been Miss Cinnamon,' Mrs Monday said.

Cinnamon flushed under our scrutiny. 'As we were leaving last night, Mrs Monday went to talk to Mrs Grimshaw about Mr Waterman's condition. I tidied up, and then met her downstairs in the yard. Abraham escorted us back to the Broadway.'

'My footman,' Stokes said. Abraham bowed.

'Did you see anything suspicious?' I asked Abraham.

'No, sir,' he said sullenly.

'Was the door to the loft locked overnight?' Child asked.

'We haven't locked it since Danny came to stay with us,' Nathaniel said. 'Mr Brabazon needed to come and go, as well as those who came to sit with him.'

'So anyone could have walked in,' Stokes said. 'It seems plain to me that burglary is the most likely explanation. Waterman probably woke up and the villain panicked.'

'This is hogwash,' I said, appealing to Child. 'Waterman was the only member of *The Dark Angel*'s crew still in Deptford who wasn't implicated in the insurance fraud. He was just following orders and made no personal profit. That made him a threat to these men here. He'd talked to Thaddeus Archer before, and someone wanted to stop him from talking to me.'

Monday brought his fist down on the arm of his chair. 'There was no fraud. This boy's death is a tragedy, as were the deaths of the slaves on board that ship, not to mention that of Mr Archer himself. But only a man intent on mischief would link them together.'

Brabazon seemed to have recovered his self-assurance now

he was under Stokes's roof. 'I have told Captain Corsham this, but like Mr Archer before him, he refuses to listen.'

Child held up a hand for silence. 'Did Waterman say anything at all last night? Upon this topic or any other?'

'He talked a lot about knives,' Mrs Monday said, with a little shiver. 'Mr Brabazon's name was mentioned.'

'He was delirious,' Brabazon said, 'consumed with nightmares about the operation to remove his leg.'

'What nonsense is this?' Mrs Grimshaw said suddenly. 'All this talk of dead slaves. Why won't anyone speak the truth? We all know who killed him, the same man who attacked him before. That filthy louse Frank Drake.'

'Now hold on, Marilyn, there is no evidence of that,' Child said.

'Hold on nothing, Perry Child. You know what he's like better than anyone. A blustering bully, who thought nothing of breaking a young man's leg. Now he's come back to finish the job he started. He was probably scared Waterman would tell you who attacked him and he'd end up in gaol.'

From what I'd seen, Drake would have had to murder the royal princes in front of the Horseguards before Child would act against him. Yet Drake was certainly a suspect in my eyes.

'Drake may be innocent, he may be guilty,' I said. 'Why not bring him here and question him? Then we can find out.'

'Well, Child?' Stokes said. 'Is that what you want? You are the magistrate of this town. You have a free hand.'

The insinuation in his tone suggested quite the contrary.

Child stared hard at the model of the dock. 'No,' he said at last. 'A burglary seems the most likely explanation. I'll issue a reward and see if anyone comes to claim it.'

For a brief moment I'd thought he might do the right thing. I saw little point in arguing further, and Mrs Grimshaw evidently felt the same, muttering darkly beneath her breath. Child's verdict pronounced, the meeting soon broke up.

As we were filing out of the room, everyone gave me a wide berth, save for Scipio. He didn't speak to me, but he slipped a note into my hand.

I waited until I was out on the drive to read it. *I am making inquiries about Frank Drake. I'll come to your room at the Noah's Ark after nine. S.*

I couldn't deny that Scipio's help was bearing fruit, and I chastised myself for my earlier suspicions about his motives. That was the trouble with this place. Distrust was contagious.

Child had stayed behind to talk to the mayor, and I waited for him on the drive. The footman, Abraham, stood on the steps, watching me, until the magistrate emerged.

'Do you think your friend, Waterman's late father, would believe that justice was served here today?' I asked him. 'Drake's alibi is a lie, by the way, but I think you know that.'

His voice was weary. 'Drake didn't do this. Nor did he kill Archer.'

'Because he's innocent? Or because he's your brother-in-law?'

He lifted a finger. 'Careful, sir.'

I contemplated his pink, be-veined face. 'I can't work you out, Mr Child. You don't want me dead, but what do you want? Sometimes I think you want me gone. Sometimes I think you want me to do your job for you. The only thing I know for certain is that you want to protect Frank Drake.'

He looked beyond me to the gate. Bees buzzed in the lavender beds. 'Right now,' he said, 'I want a drink.'

CHAPTER THIRTY-NINE

WE MADE AN odd procession walking back along the wooded lane from Stokes's villa to Deptford Broadway. I wanted to talk to Nathaniel, but he had marched off ahead, plainly deeply affected by his friend's death. I decided I'd look for him at the warehouse later tonight.

Mrs Grimshaw and Peregrine Child walked abreast, perhaps settling their differences over Frank Drake. Mr and Mrs Monday walked behind, together, but with distance between them. Once he took her arm when she stumbled, and I noticed how swiftly she took it back. Theirs was not a happy marriage. I knew the signs.

My bad leg pulling, I caught up with Brabazon, who walked alone.

'I hope you are done with your diagnoses, Captain,' he greeted me. 'Or I will be out of a job.' His smile looked as if it was starting to strain his mouth.

'Daniel Waterman said something curious last night,' I said. 'He mentioned a nigger with a knife. I wondered if you'd heard him say anything like that before?'

'Yes, several times. There is no great mystery there, I think. On Waterman's first voyage, the one we have heard so much about lately, one of the female slaves put a curse upon Frank Drake. It was all perfectly harmless, of course, but the Negroes believe in the obeah themselves and it can be rather intimidating when they are in full sway. Drake is a superstitious creature and it distracted him. The Negress grabbed his knife and tried to kill him. It was Waterman who saved his life. Yet he was rather shaken by the incident. Life on board a slave ship takes some getting used to.'

'Was the woman who attacked him one of the slaves you later drowned?'

He pursed his lips. 'No, she was already dead by then. Drake crucified her from the mizzen-mast. He said it was the correct way to kill a witch. I tried to put a stop to it. It was barbaric and it unsettled the slaves. But Vaughan can be superstitious too.'

I stared at him in disbelief, appalled both by the act and by the casual manner in which such matters were discussed in this town. We had reached the top of the High Street. Ahead of us the Mondays had parted company; Mr Monday continuing on towards Deptford Strand, Mrs Monday heading in the direction of their home.

'An interesting woman,' Brabazon said. 'Looks like she wouldn't say boo to a goose, but she insisted on staying when I took off Waterman's leg. She held the boy's hand throughout. Many women couldn't have done it – many men too – but I honestly believe that if circumstances had demanded it, she would have taken up the saw herself.'

'Mr Monday ordered you and Drake not to touch Archer,' I said. 'Did he make a similar proscription regarding Evan Vaughan? You must have been worried. Vaughan losing his mind, gaining a conscience.'

Brabazon's smile faded. 'We had nothing to be worried about. As for Vaughan, Monday would never have needed to make such a proscription. Everyone knows how Monday would react if Vaughan were threatened or harmed in any way.'

'Torture a man? Cut his throat?'

'I didn't say that.' He bowed stiffly. 'Good day to you, Captain Corsham.'

I walked on towards the Strand. Ahead of me on the road, John Monday was striding with singular purpose. When we were about halfway to the river, he turned off the main track into the grounds of the bright white church I'd noticed on my previous visit to the Broadway. I went after him.

St Paul's was one of the finest parish churches I had ever seen: a pretty, Baroque confection of soaring pilasters, Venetian windows and a cylindrical steeple. I could hear raised voices in the churchyard, and I followed the sound, looking for Monday. Instead, to my surprise, I found Nathaniel, talking to a tall, pasty-faced gentleman in a red silk coat. It took me a moment to realize where I'd seen him before. He was the same gentleman I'd seen with Nathaniel outside the warehouse, on my last visit to Deptford. I wondered if Nathaniel had walked here so quickly because he needed to get to this meeting.

The gentleman pushed Nathaniel in the chest, and he fell back against the church wall. 'Damnable wretch.'

Nathaniel stood his ground, though he looked a little scared. He said something to the gentleman I didn't catch. The man pushed him again, his face blotched pink and white.

'What's going on?' I said. 'Nathaniel, are you hurt?'

They turned as one, faces contorted with alarm. The man pulled his hat low, and walked swiftly past me, back towards the street. Nathaniel was breathing heavily. I went to his side.

'What was that all about? If you are in trouble, I might be able to help.'

'It's nothing, sir,' he muttered. 'Just a passing stranger. I asked him if he'd seen Jago, and he turned nasty.'

It was obviously a lie. I presumed the argument must have something to do with whatever it was I'd witnessed between them at the dock. 'Well, if he or anyone else turns nasty again, you come to me.'

He nodded without much conviction, and sank down on a tombstone. 'Ah, Danny.' He gazed up at the sky.

My voice softened. 'I'm sorry. I know what it's like to lose a friend. I want to find the person who did this to him.'

'You really think it was the same man who killed Archer?'

'As I said at Mr Stokes's, there are good reasons why the killer might have wanted Daniel dead. Will you tell me about Drake's attack on him? I need to know about the documents Daniel stole from Monday's warehouse.'

Nathaniel shook his head. 'Danny didn't steal nothing. Who told you that? Let me guess. Brabazon.'

'It isn't true?'

His tone was bitter. 'Danny came to me not long before your friend was killed. He said some papers had gone missing from the warehouse and everyone was convinced he'd taken them. He was frightened, worried someone was going to hurt him. He said the real thief put the blame on him to conceal what he'd done. Our good surgeon.'

'Danny thought Brabazon was the thief?'

'He said no one else went up to the warehouse office that night, apart from Monday and his wife. It wouldn't have been either of them, so it must have been Brabazon.'

It didn't make any sense. 'But Archer's inquiry was potentially to Brabazon's detriment. He could even have hung for his crimes. Why would he have helped? Not for the money. He's a wealthy man.'

'I'm only telling you what Danny said. Archer did try to talk

to him about those dead slaves, but Danny wouldn't tell him
nothing. He was like that – loyal. Drake took him to an abandoned warehouse and tried to make Danny tell him where the
papers were. Danny didn't know, but Drake didn't believe him.
He put Danny's leg between two shipping crates, and hit it with
a stevedore's hammer.'

'Did Danny say where this warehouse was?'

'Just that it was somewhere near the dock.'

'You never thought to involve Mr Child?'

'What good would that do? Drake and Child are family. Ma
says since Child's wife died, it's as if Drake has some sort of
hold on him.'

'How did Mrs Child die?'

'Drowned in Deptford Reach. She took their son swimming
in the creek, and they got caught in a rogue current.'

'Child's son died too?'

'Yes, sir. He was not yet six years old.'

I felt a rush of pity for the man, and a pang of irrational fear
for Gabriel. Now I understood why Child had turned on me so
violently at the bull bait. I'd asked him if he ever thought about
drowned children.

'The night before you found Archer dead, Scipio said he saw
you in the stable-yard. The obeah doll was left there that same
evening. Miss Cinnamon came to tend to Waterman that night,
didn't she?'

'Yes, sir. She came with Mrs Monday.'

'Could she have put the doll there?'

'Perhaps, but it was two men I saw running away the other
time.'

'You're sure?'

He frowned. 'Why would I lie?'

'I only meant you might have been mistaken.'

He shook his head. 'I wasn't. Two muscular blacks who looked like footmen. That's who I saw.'

I thought of the mayor's footman, Abraham, who had been at the Mondays' house the day the dead rooster was left on the doorstep. And yet Mrs Monday had told her husband that it couldn't have been him.

'I asked around about your ticket, sir, in all the brothels and the gaming dens. No one's seen anything like it. Are you sure it's from Deptford?'

'Not sure, no.' Perhaps it had nothing to do with this business after all. 'Thank you for trying.' I gave him half a crown.

He looked disappointed. Perhaps he'd hoped for more. 'I'd better get on, sir. The undertaker's coming for Danny.'

As we parted, I realized that I'd been trying to ignore an uncomfortable truth. Nathaniel's father had been an officer on *The Dark Angel*, and had played an active part in the drowning of those slaves. He'd also received a portion of the voyage's profit. If the fraud could be proven in court, then Amos Grimshaw's family, already struggling, would have to repay money they'd likely already spent. That would mean bankruptcy. The horror of a debtors' prison. It gave me pause.

I liked and pitied Nathaniel. I found him an intelligent, sensitive boy. It was hard to imagine him hurting anyone, let alone torturing one of his mother's customers to death. Yet I had to be dispassionate, had to consider all possibilities, however unlikely. Against every instinct, I must treat Nathaniel as a suspect.

*

The interior of the church was Romish and theatrical, full of dark oak pews and galleries, and Corinthian columns. Everything gleamed, and I recalled Stokes saying the Deptford slave merchants gave a lot of money to the church. Perhaps, given the nature of their trade, they felt St Peter would strike a hard bargain at the gates of heaven.

John Monday was on his knees before the sanctuary. I couldn't see anyone else around. His eyes were closed and his lips moved in prayer.

'Do you pray for Daniel Waterman?' I asked. 'Or for Mr Archer? Or for three hundred dead Africans? That would take a lot of prayers.'

He opened his eyes, but otherwise didn't move. 'I pray for them all.'

'How does insurance fraud sit with God? Where do the apostles stand on men murdered to line your pockets?'

'It isn't true,' he said, eyes fixed ahead. 'Evan Vaughan and Brabazon swore to me upon the Bible that it did not happen.'

'Some part of you must have doubted them. Did you care? Or did you tell yourself that what was done was done? Nothing you did would erase the crime, so better to keep the money and pray?'

The scratch on his cheek stood stark in the light flooding through the Venetian window. A weathered crusader, kneeling before his God.

'Or perhaps you took a more active part? Drake went too far with Waterman, and you decided you could no longer trust your own men to carry out your orders. Did you take up the sword yourself? Is it murder that sits so heavily upon your soul?'

'No. Why would I? Even if what you say is true – that a fraud was committed – I had nothing to fear from Archer. The loss of my share of the profit, I could easily sustain. I had no cause to kill him. Nor these others.'

'Are you sure? I've been thinking about those papers Waterman stole. They can't have contained proof of the fraud, because why would you have kept that? Yet Archer wanted them enough to risk his life for them. Napier Smith mentioned legal documents, contracts. I'm guessing they were your contracts with the syndicate that financed *The Dark Angel*.'

He made no reaction, but I knew I was right. 'There aren't many men in the kingdom who can afford to invest in a slaving voyage. Prominent, wealthy gentlemen with reputations to protect. Drag their names into a courtroom, throw murder into the mix, and you have the makings of a modern scandal. I ask myself how your other investors would welcome that. Not well, I suspect. *Atlantic Trading and Partners* would do little trading, and have no partners. The consequences for you and your family would be catastrophic.'

All this time, while I'd been talking, he'd knelt there, gazing at the altar. Only when I'd finished, did he turn. His eyes held a strange glint, or perhaps it was just the light. His hand shook, as he touched the scratch on his cheek.

'You think you understand the consequences of Archer's visit here? You haven't the first idea. Now leave me in peace, Captain Corsham. Let me pray.'

Chapter Forty

I spent the rest of the day wandering the streets in and around the Public Dock. First I returned to the hook where Tad's body had been found, and walked from there to the warehouses where Nathaniel kept watch. It was about two hundred yards, I judged, turning back to gauge the distance. A long way to come for a smoke at that time of night.

Unlike the Private Dock, many of the warehouses down here were in a sorry state of repair. Some looked to have been abandoned altogether. As Child had said, there were many quiet places where Tad might have been tortured and killed. I managed to get inside a couple of them, through holes in the rotting wood or crumbling masonry, but found only flocks of pigeons, empty shipping crates, and a musty stench of dust and decay. In one I found a beggarly family sitting around a fire. At least a dozen dirty children blinked at me through the smoke. Their mother stumbled towards me, eyes mazy with drink. 'Thruppence for a fuck?' I beat a hasty retreat.

If you were going to hide Captain Vaughan in Deptford, I thought, it would be somewhere like this. When Monday had disappeared after buying opium that night, it had been near here. And Tad had been looking for Vaughan, just as I was. He'd bought opium on his first visit to Deptford, when he'd spoken to Vaughan initially, perhaps to grease the wheels of their interaction. Then on his final visit, he'd bought opium again.

I went through it all chronologically, plotting each step. Tad had come to town that last time to collect the contracts stolen by Daniel Waterman – or Brabazon if you believed Nathaniel Grimshaw. He'd been intending to head directly back to London, taking Cinnamon with him. Yet something had changed his mind, something important enough to risk his life for. Looking around at the mouldering warehouses, the peeling paint, the empty windows, I wondered if he'd found Evan Vaughan.

*

Scipio came to my room just after nine as we'd arranged. 'Did anyone see you?' I asked.

'I don't think so.'

I had bought a bottle of wine, and we drank it sitting on the floor, away from the windows.

'I didn't find out much,' he said. 'Frank Drake likes to throw his weight around. Most in town give him a wide berth. He likes the usual things: women, beer, dice. Splashes a lot of gold around too. He has a house down here on the Green in Deptford Strand. A nice place for a third officer.'

'Where's he getting his money?'

'No place legal, I would think. I'm told he goes fairly often to the city. He's fond of the playhouse apparently. Comedies. He was in London the night that second African was killed.'

'So were the rest of them. Did anyone say anything about a place Drake owns near the river? A shed or a warehouse? Another house?'

'No. Why do you ask?'

'The killer would have needed somewhere near the dock for the torture. I took a look down there today – there's a lot of likely places, but it would take days to check them all. Wherever it is, I think Captain Vaughan might be there too. I think someone concealed him there – or he concealed himself – to keep him away from Archer. John Monday knows where, I think. I saw him buying opium in the Red House, and I don't think it was for himself. The others might know too. I think Archer found out where Vaughan was, and when he went there, someone killed him. Perhaps none of them know which one of them it was – except the killer. It could even be Vaughan himself.'

'Do you really think Monday could have killed him? The Bible has firm opinions about murder, as I recall.'

I remembered Monday whip in hand. 'Perhaps he saw it not as murder, but as just punishment.'

'And himself as judge and executioner?' Scipio frowned. 'The torture I understand, but why use the brand? It led you to the ship and its officers.'

I sighed, for I had pondered this myself. 'Perhaps we are looking for rationality where there is none. Or rather, the motive may be rational, but the killing he enjoys. He may have wanted to leave his mark. Slaving seems to do dark things to men's souls.' I remembered Vaughan's book, that silent, anguished scream.

He looked interested. 'You think our killer is mad?'

'I think he may not be entirely sane. To do what he does, how can he be?'

He was silent a moment. 'When I first arrived in Dominica, I wanted more than anything to escape my new existence. I saw how men who disobeyed were punished, and those who did not were rewarded. I chose the latter course – a master's nigger, as Jamaica Mary put it so eloquently last night. When I turned sixteen, I was made an overseer. I wielded the whip, I tied men to posts, I tortured them.'

I studied his tense, lined face. 'You escaped slavery the only way you could. No one can blame you for that.'

'Those men I flogged and tortured – they blamed me. But that is beside the point, I mean only to say that an act can be both appalling and rational.'

'If there is any rationality in branding a man before you cut his throat,' I said, 'I struggle to find it. Have you ever read Spinoza?'

'Let us presume not,' Scipio said.

'He believed emotion to be the enemy of the rational mind. Most people rarely pause to consider the effect of their emotions upon their decisions. They think they act rationally, but they do not. At the extremes, emotion may master a man entirely. His reasoning not only becomes irrational, but dangerous. I met men in America like that, scarred from battle on the inside. They'd found a taste for killing, lost touch with that part of themselves that corrects the basest desires. They looked quite sane, but I fear they were perfectly mad.'

Scipio frowned. 'Can't emotions lead us to better ways of thinking? What of love, for instance? Or honour?'

'Spinoza didn't think so. He never married, never had children. He placed intellectual love before all else.'

'It seems a bleak existence.'

'I concur.'

Something about the way I said this seemed to give him pause. 'You are married, Captain Corsham?'

'For nearly four years.'

'Children?'

'A boy, Gabriel. He's not quite two.'

A faraway look had entered his eyes. 'Childhood was my happiest time. I belonged to a tribe of fishermen, deep in the

African interior. We liked to dance. I remember my brother spinning and spinning. A lot of laughter.'

'Do you ever think about going back?'

'Where would I go? My village was destroyed. My family are dead. I would be as much an oddity in Africa now as I am here.'

'Your brother died too?'

'Yes, we were captured together. I was eight and he was nine. We were taken to the slave fort at Whydah, where from the windows of our cell we could see the Guineamen anchored out at sea. Adebayo thought they were giant fish, waiting to swallow us up. He dashed his brains out on the wall, rather than face his terror.'

'I'm sorry.'

His face creased with pain. 'It gets harder to remember the time before. Sometimes I wonder if my memories are real, or if I have written them myself. When I have children of my own, perhaps I will remember it better.'

'A fine ambition.' I raised my glass. 'First you need to find the right woman.'

'So I do.' He stared into his wine. 'A hearth, a home. The warmth of a woman. Heaven indeed.'

'To some heaven. To some hell.' I was thinking of the Mondays' marriage. Perhaps my own.

'Not if it is God's plan.' He gave me a bleak, empty smile. 'As for hell I've been there, and it's called the Middle Passage.'

We had become distracted from what Scipio had learned about Frank Drake, and I was about to turn our conversation back to him, when a frenzied shout rang out below. 'Fire in the stables! Fire in the yard!'

I ran to the window, and saw the yard was filled with flames and thick black smoke. Zephyrus. In two strides I was at the door.

Downstairs, the place was in chaos. No one wanted to be caught in a tavern blaze. I forced my way through a press of men fighting to get to the door. When I emerged into the yard, I was brought up short by the sight that greeted me there.

A large circle had been made from logs, saturated in whale oil – the air thick with its rancid, fishy odour. The logs blazed merrily away, and the horses, smelling the smoke, were kicking and whinnying in their stalls. Less merry was the thing in the centre of the circle. I shielded my face from the blaze and the smoke, trying to confirm what I knew I'd seen. The severed head of Jago, Nathaniel Grimshaw's dog.

Nathaniel dashed into the yard and gave a hoarse cry. He ran towards the fire, and fearing he would harm himself, I caught him. He writhed in my arms, and I wrestled against his strength. His face was yellow in the flames, and he was sobbing. 'Bloody bastards. I'll kill them all.' He noticed Scipio, who had followed me out. 'Was it you, blackbird? I'll cut your balls off, shitten fuckster.'

Scipio was staring at the flames in horror. He turned at Nathaniel's words. 'What are you talking about? I had nothing to do with this.'

I wanted to speak up for him. He hadn't left my side in the last half hour, but I couldn't do so without revealing our association.

'Liar,' Nathaniel said. 'I'll find you, blackbird. One day when you least expect it. By the end you'll be praying for the hang-man's rope.'

With a great wrench, he broke free from my grip, sinking to his knees. The groan he gave was one of utmost despair.

CHAPTER FORTY-ONE

IF DEPTFORD WAS a drunken doxy, ungainly sprawled on the banks of the Thames, then her neighbouring port of Greenwich was a dowager duchess, occupying her place upon the river with stately splendour. Elegant villas in pretty parks dotted the banks around the Naval Hospital, the town laid out in squares with fountains and pagodas.

I had come here inquiring after James Brabazon's alibi on the night of Tad's murder. Later I intended to visit the tavern where Jamaica Mary claimed to have seen him arguing with Tad. Nathaniel's belief that Brabazon had stolen the contracts had lent these tasks a new urgency. I considered Frank Drake and John Monday more likely suspects for Tad's murder, but I didn't rule the surgeon out. Behind those smiles, I sensed a man close to the edge of his own denials.

After we'd put the fire out last night, I'd realized that Nathaniel hadn't stayed to help. I'd gone down to the dock and looked for him at the warehouses, but I didn't find him. I'd looked for him again at the stable-loft this morning, but my knocks went unanswered. The boy's unhappiness concerned me – I suppose I saw parallels with my own troubled state after my father's death.

The other matter preying on my mind was my appointment to meet Cinnamon later tonight. Earlier I had hired a horse from the coaching inn for her to ride. Anxiety made me twitchy.

If I was caught, reprisals would surely follow. The law was ambiguous as to Cinnamon's status as property, but in Deptford I knew they'd call it theft. I doubted I'd be able to count on Peregrine Child's protection in the face of Stokes's wrath. Even if we got safely to London, if my part in her escape was discovered, my conduct would invite public scandal. Another unravelling of the fraying ties that bound me to Caro. I tried not to dwell on it.

The Royal Naval Hospital was built on a terrace abutting the bank of the river, an enormous quadrant with four pretty palaces, one in each corner. I strolled the grounds in the company of Jeremiah Robertson, the Physician-in-Charge, who presumed I was here on official War Office business. I made no effort to correct this misconception on his part, and indeed it is possible that I had been responsible for placing it there in the first place. Such crosses my conscience would have to bear.

'Certainly there was a dinner that night,' Robertson said. 'It followed the afternoon's lecture. I presented a paper on the use of Peruvian bark to treat tropical fevers.' He was a small, wiry gentleman with a high domed forehead, a beaky nose and darting black eyes. I could imagine him counting coins into coffered chests by the light of a candle, or spinning some unfortunate maiden's hair into gold.

'There were about forty-five of us in attendance. Mostly members of the Company of Surgeons, though a few physicians with an interest in naval medicine usually join us. Several papers were presented, and as always there was a demonstration. That afternoon it was the *ardor urinae*. Mr Greaves showed us how to insert a catheter – a silver tube pushed into the penis to aid urination.'

I winced. We were walking down a wide avenue that stretched between the two riverfront wings of the Hospital. The avenue led to the great park, the dome of the Royal Observatory peeking above the treetops.

'Do you remember if a Deptford surgeon named James Brabazon was present?'

'Oh yes, Mr Brabazon was there. He comes to many of our lectures and dinners.'

'Can you remember what time he left?'

'I believe he had to go back to Deptford to treat a patient after the lecture, but he returned later for the dinner. He stayed almost until the end. Left around one, I believe.'

'You are certain?'

'Not to the precise time, but there was an incident involving Brabazon towards the end of the night. That's why I remember.'

'An incident?'

He hesitated. 'Do you mind if I ask what all these questions are about? I don't like to gossip.'

My tone was severe. 'Mr Brabazon lives in close proximity to the Navy Yard, sir. The allegiance of a Scot to the English crown can never be taken for granted.'

'Yes, of course,' Robertson said. 'You will find no greater patriot than I, sir.'

'Then tell me about this incident, if you will.'

He frowned. 'It was rather an odd matter. One of the visiting physicians that night was a fellow countryman of Brabazon's, a Glasgow man. He seemed to recognize Brabazon, only he didn't call him by that name, he called him Price.'

Whatever suspicions I had been harbouring about Brabazon, this wasn't one of them. 'What did Brabazon do?'

'He went very pale, and told the physician he had made a mistake. As a gentleman, the physician accepted the explanation, though he did not look convinced. Afterwards I heard him say: "I could have sworn that gentleman was Richard Price." Brabazon didn't stay long after that.'

'What did you make of it all?'

'I presumed he'd changed his name when he moved south. He wouldn't be the first gentleman to have done so. He might have had a rupture with his family, and not wished to be reminded of his past. There are many innocent explanations.'

And many not so innocent. I estimated that even if Brabazon had left at one, it would still just about have been possible for him to have returned to Deptford, then waylaid, tortured and murdered Tad. Just about.

We returned to Robertson's office, where I took down the name of the Glasgow physician, a Dr Calum Blair.

'I don't envy you staying in Deptford,' Robertson said. 'I had lunch with the Commissioner of the Navy Yard the other day. How he stands it, I don't know. Our dealings with the town here in Greenwich are fair for the most part, but in Deptford they learn villainy in the cradle. The authorities are no use either. The magistrate used to be a carpenter, they say.' He gave a wry smile. 'Do you think he fashioned his own bench?'

'I understand he and the Commissioner have had their share of disagreement?' Brabazon had told me as much when we'd dined together.

'Every week something goes missing from the Navy Yard. Carts, horses, gunpowder. It's plainly thieves from the town, but the magistrate doesn't do a thing about it. The Commissioner complained to the Lord Chancellor and tried to have Mr Child removed from his post, but the mayor got the West India lobby involved, and who wants to cross them? Only a fool.'

'Who indeed?' I said, with a heavy heart.

Chapter Forty-Two

I ASKED AROUND near the parish church for the Artichoke Tavern, the place where Jamaica Mary claimed to have seen Brabazon arguing with Tad. The directions I was given took me to that part of Greenwich which forms the armpit between the Thames and Deptford Creek. This was the rougher end of town, though unlike in Deptford, I did not fear for my safety here. Yet there were similarities. Taverns, brothels, gaming houses. Sailors and their whores. Drunks.

The Artichoke was a large timbered tavern built around a squalid yard. I waited while the landlord finished serving a pair of customers, and then inquired about his upstairs rooms, giving him descriptions of both Tad and Brabazon.

The man had a thin sharp face, and a sparse growth of beard. 'Aye, I remember them.'

'Which one of them rented the room?' I slid two shillings across his bar.

'My memory's a mite hazy to be honest.' He stared pointedly at the coins, until I added a third. 'Ah, I recall it now. It was the short skinny one who rented the room. The big one asked for him at the bar. I sent him upstairs.'

'I heard they argued. Did you hear anything like that?'

'It gets busy at lunchtime. I wouldn't have heard nothing unless they was screaming bloody murder. I do recall one thing, though—' He stopped. 'No, it's gone again.'

Wearily, I added a fourth coin to the pile on the bar. The man grinned and put on another show of recollection.

'The first time they was here, the tall one looked upset as they was leaving.'

'They came here twice?'

'That's right. The first time would have been about five weeks ago.'

Which would have coincided with Tad's second visit to Deptford. I wondered why he'd chosen to meet Brabazon here. Presumably so they wouldn't be seen together. I gave much more credence now to the claim that it was Brabazon, rather than Daniel Waterman, who was Tad's informant. The first time they'd met, Tad could have given him instructions to steal the contracts. The second meeting, the day before Tad died, was presumably when Brabazon handed them over. Which meant they must still be in Deptford.

Why would Brabazon help Tad? Not for the money. Brabazon's unhappiness suggested he was coerced. I wondered if Tad's hold on him had something to do with Brabazon's past. I sat in the tavern and wrote a long letter to Dr Calum Blair, care of the Faculty of Physicians and Surgeons in Glasgow.

*

I walked back into Greenwich, deep in thought. So deep in thought, I was almost run over by a passing brewer's dray. The driver had been going much too fast, though that did not preclude a barrage of expletives from his lips.

Had it not been for this distraction, which restored my attention to the world around me, I might have missed it. I stopped and stared, ignoring the driver's volley of curses. A tall, muscular man was walking on the opposite side of the road. He wore a dove-grey coat and gloves, his hat pulled low over his face. From a distance, you might not have realized he was black.

Scipio. Not so surprising, except that before we'd parted company last night, he'd told me that Stokes's business was taking him to London today. He'd said he would be leaving at six this morning and wouldn't be back until tomorrow. We'd made plans to reconvene tomorrow afternoon. His arrangements could have changed, and yet something about the way he was walking, his swift stride, his lowered head, suggested that he did not want to be observed. Intrigued, I decided to follow him.

He crossed the road by the church, heading towards the Navy Hospital. I walked about twenty paces behind him. We came to a small parade of shops, and he ducked into a coffee-house. The establishment was small, and I couldn't follow him inside without being seen.

I loitered outside, watching through the window. Scipio greeted someone and sat down, another gentleman. I couldn't make out the man's face in the gloomy interior. They spoke for perhaps five minutes, and then Scipio rose and left. I drew back behind the stall of a man selling writing ink. Scipio walked off in the direction of the river, and I was caught on the horns of a dilemma. To follow, or to wait and see whom he'd been meeting? I opted for the latter course.

The gentleman finished his coffee, and then he too left. He crossed the road to a large black carriage waiting there. I watched it drive off, heading for the toll bridge and the road to London, my mind a roiling stew of doubt and confusion. Try as I might, I could conceive of no benign reason why Scipio should be meeting so covertly with my patron, Under-Secretary Cavill-Lawrence.

Chapter Forty-Three

Scipio and Nicholas Cavill-Lawrence. I pondered it that night as I sat in the taproom of the coaching inn at Deptford Broadway. Was Scipio, to use a phrase employed by the thief-takers, 'double-crossing' his master with Cavill-Lawrence? I had always suspected that Cavill-Lawrence had an agenda distinct to the West India lobby's. Or was Scipio 'double-crossing' me, encouraging me to enmesh myself deeper in this business, then reporting my activities back to Cavill-Lawrence? I couldn't see why he would, but I resolved to share no more confidences with him.

I waited in the taproom until midnight. Then I went to the stables, where I collected Zephyrus and the spirited bay mare I had hired for Cinnamon to ride. I led the horses through the darkened streets of Deptford Broadway, past the church, and up the wooded lane that led to Stokes's villa.

The mare kept whinnying and tossing her head. I soothed her, my nerves taut, my body tense. At Stokes's gate, the porter's lodge was in darkness. Leading the horses into the trees, I tethered them there. I took out my pocketwatch. It was nearly half past twelve, the time Cinnamon had said she would meet me.

I waited, increasingly anxious, as the minutes slid by. To steel my resolve, I kept reminding myself why I was doing this. Cinnamon's testimony was surely significant – and once I unlocked the chains of secrecy that encircled *The Dark Angel*, there would be few places left where Tad's murderer could hide. It was also the right thing to do. I had seen how Stokes mistreated her. What virtue in principles if a man didn't act on them too?

Little moonlight penetrated the trees, and I started every time I heard a rustle in the undergrowth. The air was rich with vegetal scents, the horses' breath coming in steaming clouds. It was nearly one o'clock. Where was she? Had she been caught? I kept expecting to hear shouts, to see lanterns coming at me through the trees.

I crept back through the woods, until I had a good view of the gate. All was quiet. I fretted about what to do. Continue to wait, though Stokes might be home at any minute, or go back to the Strand alone and abandon Cinnamon to her fate?

I was still pondering this question when I glimpsed a flash of white in the darkness. Cinnamon, in her ivory gown, running down the drive. We stared at one another across the road, through the bars of the gate. I had been wondering how she intended to get out of the villa grounds with their high walls. Now I saw she meant to climb the gate. The ironwork was wrought into elaborate curlicues and flourishes. There were many points of purchase for her feet. Still I marvelled that she was able to do it. Desperation could make athletes of the weakest men – it seemed women too.

She neared the top of the gates, easing one leg over. Then froze as the door to the porter's lodge flew open. The elderly African shuffled out, humming to himself. He hobbled to the verge, where he urinated noisily. I started forward, but she gestured me back. When the porter turned, he would surely see her. He took a long time to finish, and then hobbled back, fumbling with his breeches, plainly in his cups. The task occupied his attention all the way back to the lodge. The door closed.

Cinnamon descended the gate swiftly, jumping the last few

feet. She ran across the road to meet me and I led her through the trees. It was less than an hour's ride to London, but a lot depended on how well Cinnamon rode. If Stokes realized she was gone when he got home, he might send men after us. There were other dangers too: a lame horse, or thieves on the road. I breathed to still the beating of my heart.

We were nearing the place where I'd left the horses. I could only see Zephyrus, and I looked around for the bay mare. Cinnamon cried out, and my hand flew to my pistol. Scipio was standing amidst the trees, holding the bay by the reins.

'Judas,' he said. 'You made me a promise.' He let go of the horse, and grabbed Cinnamon by the arm. 'I told myself that my suspicions were unfounded, even as I knew that they were not.'

'Please,' Cinnamon said to him. 'I cannot endure it any longer. Let me go.'

Scipio's voice was cold. 'You care nothing for those you'd leave behind? The consequences I'd endure?'

'If you lose your place, I give you my word that I'll help you find a post in London,' I said. 'You of all people cannot reproach her for wanting her freedom. All you need do is turn a blind eye.'

'You don't understand.' A new wildness had entered his voice. 'Everything I have is here in Deptford. I will not let you take it from me.'

We didn't have time to argue. I drew my pistol. 'In all good conscience, I cannot let you do this.'

'In all good conscience? I suppose your motive for helping her has nothing to do with *The Dark Angel*? Has she told you what she knows yet? It will be a short conversation.'

'No,' she cried. 'Scipio, please don't.'

'What do you imagine she knows?' Scipio went on. 'Evidence of the insurance fraud? Do you really think the crew would have had such discussions in front of the slaves? She saw slaves being drowned, as she told you, but she saw and heard nothing else. Stokes has already questioned her. I have too. Do you think they would let her stay here in Deptford if she could harm them?'

I could see from Cinnamon's face that it was true.

'She told Archer she knew nothing, and he abandoned her. You would be best to do so too. If you let us go now, I can get her back to the house before anyone realizes she is missing.' He started dragging her towards the road, though she fought him all the way.

I hesitated. Helping Cinnamon wouldn't aid my cause, and would bring further troubles down upon my head – my part in her escape couldn't be concealed now Scipio knew. She had also lied to me – I presumed because she feared that, like Tad, I wouldn't help her. Except Tad would have helped her, I knew he would. He only got distracted, and then never had the chance. I couldn't abandon her now, just to serve myself.

I caught up with them on the road. Cinnamon was still pleading with Scipio, but his expression was resolute.

'I will take her to London anyway,' I called after them. 'Let her have this chance.'

He kept moving. 'Then you'll have to shoot me.'

'How can you do this?' Cinnamon cried to Scipio, as we reached the road. 'After everything you told me?'

The door to the lodge flew open again, and the porter emerged, holding a musket. 'What's happening? Mr Scipio? What's the girl doing here?'

Cinnamon moaned, a low guttural sound.

Scipio's voice was authoritative. 'I am escorting her back to the house. You saw nothing, understand? Open these gates.'

Even before he'd finished his sentence, we heard the clatter of an approaching carriage. The porter started forward with his keys, but it was too late. Lamplight swept the road, and then Stokes's turquoise-and-silver carriage rattled around the bend. The coachman gave a shout, and pulled on the reins. The vehicle halted, and the door opened. Lucius Stokes stepped out. Abraham and the other black footman jumped down from the back of the carriage to flank him.

The mayor's gaze travelled over our group. 'What have we here?'

Scipio stepped forward. 'I was returning from the city, when I heard a noise in the woods. Captain Corsham had Miss Cinnamon up against a tree.'

I saw what he was doing. The punishment for a tryst in the woods would surely be less than that for escape.

Stokes eyed me. 'Did he now?'

'The girl was willing enough,' I said. 'I promised her a half-guinea.'

'I don't care if she was willing. She is my property.' Stokes glanced at the girl. 'He is handsome, I'll give you that. What would you buy with a half-guinea, I wonder? Don't I give you everything you need?'

Cinnamon's face was deathly pale. 'Yes, sir.'

Off in the trees, the bay mare whinnied. I held my breath, hoping that Zephyrus wouldn't join in. If Stokes discovered there were two horses, then Scipio's story would not hold water.

'Abraham, take her inside. Search her thoroughly. I'll be in to deal with her in a moment.'

The porter had unlocked the gate, and Abraham pulled her, unresisting, up the drive towards the house. Anger surged in my breast. We'd be on our way to London by now if Scipio hadn't stopped us. Our eyes met, and his gaze mirrored mine. He blamed me for this, just as I blamed him.

Stokes turned to me. 'Do you know what they do to thieves on the plantations? They cut off their hands.' His gaze dropped to my pistol, took in the tenseness of my body, and he smiled. 'It's a good job we are not savages, like the planters. Yet I confess I am disappointed, Captain Corsham. If a gentleman wants to borrow something from a friend, it is customary to ask. Who knows, I might have said yes. I have before.'

'We are not friends, Mr Stokes.'

His smile broadened. 'Then I believe you owe me a sovereign, do you not? After all, the girl had no right to hire herself out. The fee is mine.'

My voice was flat. 'You are in such dire need of a half-guinea?'

'There is a principle at stake, sir. An important one.'

Stokes held out his hand for the coin, and in the end I gave it to him, fearing that things would go worse for Cinnamon if I did not. He offered me a sardonic bow, and walked back towards the gate, followed by Scipio and his footman. Scipio did not look at me, and I presumed our association was at an end. After the night's events, I could not say I was sorry. Off in the trees, the bay mare whinnied again. This time Zephyrus joined in. Stokes paused, just for a moment, and continued on up the drive. I didn't know if he had heard – and there was little I could do about it if he had. All told, the night had been an abject disaster.

I collected the horses, and led them back to Deptford Broadway, where I returned the bay mare to the coaching inn. I rode Zephyrus back to the Strand, dispirited, worried about Cinnamon. She had looked so broken, so afraid. I wondered what she endured behind closed doors, and the thought turned my anger against Scipio and Stokes into rage against myself. I had failed her.

In the Noah's Ark they were singing again, the taproom heaving. I went upstairs to my room and unlocked the door, half expecting to see another letter waiting for me there. Instead I froze. Slung over one of the ceiling beams was a noose. Two hooded figures stood either side of it. I reached for my pistol, just as a third man came up behind me in the hall. He put a pistol against my head. 'Don't move, fuckster.' I didn't recognize his coarse Deptford accent. He pushed me inside.

The door closed, and one of the men took my pistol and sword. I could see the whites of their eyes through their hoods. One of them hit me hard in the stomach.

I was no match for three men. Every time I went down, they hauled me up and hit me again. I shouted for Mrs Grimshaw and Nathaniel, but no one came. I covered my face with my hands, but they pulled them aside and stamped on my fingers. No one said a word. The silence was unnerving.

At some point, they tied my hands behind me. I tried to speak, but my mouth was too full of blood. They pulled me to my feet, and I began struggling as I realized what they meant to do. The noose was placed over my head, the rope tightened around my throat. My legs went from under me as I was hoisted into the air.

The rope bit. I couldn't breathe. Panic took hold. It was the scene from my worst nightmares. The fear inside me. I kicked out, finding nothing. Distantly, I heard laughter. My vision filled with constellations. My eyes bulged.

I was tugged on a black wave towards unconsciousness, and found I craved it. Anything to stop the burning in my lungs, the pain in my skull. My feet kicked again, this time involuntarily.

Suddenly the world dropped back into focus, and I hit the

floor like a sack of sugar. The rope was still around my neck, but I found that I could breathe. Someone thrust a knife in front of my face, and I guessed it was the one they'd used to sever the rope.

'Next time, Negro-lover, we let you choke.'

CHAPTER FORTY-FOUR

I LAY THERE for a very long time. Agony had transported me to a place where I knew my body more intimately than I ever had before, yet I was also detached from it, each bone in its own private hell. The pinnacle of the pain lay just above my consciousness, so that each time I approached it, I was swallowed again by the black depths.

When I resurfaced, I felt unimaginably hot. Sweat coated my face, the salt burning my skin. I craved air and I crawled to the window, struggling to open the casement. The air outside was no cooler. It smelled of the slaughterhouse. Lights moved out on the water, travelling along the deck of one of the Guineamen. 'I see you,' I said.

At some point in the night I must have crawled into bed. I dreamed of Caro – the kinder Caro, when we were courting. At times she became Amelia, at times Cinnamon, at times Tad. He was running up a hill ahead of me, the sun behind its crest. His shadow had elongated legs and arms, a chalk man carved into grass. I ran to catch him, but he ran faster. I awoke weeping.

I dreamed I was looking down at myself on the bed. I lay very still, and I wondered if I was dead. The room filled with white light. I wasn't alone. Someone was looking through the chest of drawers, going through my things. I shouted a mangled protest, and Nathaniel stared up at me.

I awoke much later, curled on my bed, burning up. Daylight

made me wince. Outside I could hear the familiar sounds of Deptford. I sat up and the room turned. The pain had receded a little, and by resting my weight upon the bedframe, I managed to stand. I could hardly bend my bad leg and the good one wasn't much better. It took me a very long time to walk downstairs.

Mrs Grimshaw was clearing tables in the dining room, and I realized they had been laid for lunch, rather than breakfast. She gave me a troubled look. 'Lord have mercy, Captain Corsham. What happened to you?'

'I was attacked in my room last night. You didn't hear anything?'

'No, sir. The singing . . .'

She was as bad a liar as her son. I didn't believe my cries had gone unheard, and I wondered about my assailants. Frank Drake and his friends? Or men hired by Stokes and the West India lobby? Why hadn't they killed me?

'I need to talk to you, sir,' Mrs Grimshaw said. 'Those things you said the other day at Mr Stokes's – about an insurance fraud. Mr Child says you think my Amos was a party to it.'

I was too befuddled to make a sensible decision about how to answer. 'Yes, I think he was.'

'Then your inquiry could be to my family's detriment?'

'That was never my objective,' I said. 'Yet if the killer is caught, and the fraud comes to light, I imagine the underwriter would want his money back.'

Her fingers tugged at her apron strings. 'Then I must ask you to leave, sir. We have worked so hard to keep this roof over our heads. Nathaniel has sacrificed so much. I would be a fool to let you stay here under those circumstances.'

She had a point. I staggered back upstairs and packed, every task a torment. In the stables I collected Zephyrus, but couldn't bring myself to mount him. I walked him up the road to

Deptford Broadway, where I took a room at the coaching inn at exorbitant cost. Rosy, the landlady, clucked over my injuries. 'You need to see a physician, sir,' she said.

I decided a surgeon would suffice.

*

Brabazon surveyed me with a trace of amusement. 'Found yourself another war, Captain Corsham?'

'That tincture you offered to make me. I need it now.'

'It looks to me, sir, like you need rest and a lot of it.'

'The tincture, Mr Brabazon, if you please.'

I stood watching over him while he mixed it at the table in his surgery. I didn't think he'd poison me, but I was leaving nothing to chance. He poured Rhenish wine into a jug, and added a measure of the laudanum he'd made the other day.

'What a shocking thing to happen,' he said. 'You didn't see your assailants?'

'No, they were hooded.'

'As was Mrs Bradstreet's killer, I think you said.'

'I don't think this was him. There were three of them for a start. He kills those he stalks, whereas this was meant as a warning.'

'One you don't intend to heed? I can't help thinking that is a mistake.'

'I'm sure you do.'

The room was spinning again. Brabazon was adding other ingredients to the tincture: cinnamon bark, saffron, powdered wormwood. I tried to read all the labels, but my vision blurred.

'There was one other thing I wished to ask you about.' My voice sounded strange to my ears. 'Why did you never mention that you had seen Archer in Greenwich the day before he died?'

My senses were oddly heightened, aware of details I wouldn't normally see. I watched a bead of sweat form on his upper lip, before he wiped it away. His mismatched eyes seemed very bright. 'There are no secrets in Deptford any longer, I see. As you say, I encountered Archer there. I was in Greenwich for my lecture, and I was walking past a tavern – the Artichoke, I think it was called. I saw Archer inside, I put my head in and we talked. Not for long. I was late for my lecture.'

'You argued, isn't that right?'

'Yes, we did,' he said slowly, as if trying to guess how much I already knew. 'I was angry with Archer, as I told you, because of what happened to young Daniel Waterman. Something had happened the night before to make me angrier. I had some business down at the dock, and as I was walking past the Garraway warehouse, I saw Archer talking to Nathaniel Grimshaw. I believe I saw money changing hands.'

He waited for a reaction. 'Don't you see? I was worried about the same thing happening again. Archer tempting young lads with money, inciting them to betray their friends. I didn't want anyone else to get hurt because of one man's misguided crusade.'

Had he really seen Nathaniel and Tad together? Nathaniel hadn't mentioned it, but if Tad had given him money for information, I could see why he wouldn't. The image of him searching my bags last night had stayed with me. I'd checked my possessions, and nothing seemed to be missing. Had it been a dream? I wasn't sure.

Even if Brabazon was telling the truth, he was certainly lying about his visit to Greenwich. I didn't believe it was a chance encounter. He'd met with Tad there twice in a private room. Twice they had parted on bad terms. I believed he was Tad's informant and not a willing one at that. Yet unless I could discover the hold Tad had over him, he'd never admit it.

Brabazon stoppered the vial and wrote out a label. We went through to his parlour, where he sat at his desk to pen a receipt.

'Could I also trouble you for some liniment for these bruises?'

'Certainly, just a moment.'

He returned to the surgery, and I moved as fast as my aching body would permit. Luckily it didn't take much effort to slide open the drawer Brabazon had closed the last time I'd been here. I barely had time to register the contents, before I heard him coming back. I closed the drawer and retook my seat as he walked in, bottle in hand.

'That will be eight shillings, ten pence,' he said.

I paid him, exhilaration sending life through my fragile veins. There in the drawer, amidst balls of sealing wax and other clutter, was a silver ticket about the size of a large snuffbox. The number seven in Roman numerals was stamped into the metal, surrounded by engraved flowers that might have been lilies.

CHAPTER FORTY-FIVE

THE TINCTURE MADE me feel lighter in body. The pain dulled, yet my blood coursed like a millrace. My mouth was dry, and water didn't seem to refresh it.

I kept thinking about the silver ticket, sitting there in Brabazon's drawer. I still didn't understand its significance, but my initial suspicions had been correct: the near-identical ticket I'd found in Tad's rooms must be connected to his inquiry into *The Dark Angel*. Was the ticket somehow part of Tad's hold over Brabazon? Or did it have some other relevance? My discovery had led to more questions than answers, and yet I burned with the excitement of a huntsman drawing in on his quarry.

I tried to eat at the coaching inn, but found I had no appetite. I slept for a couple of hours, then took another draught of the tincture. An hour later, and my leg was moving much more easily. I cleaned my weapons, and then limped down to Deptford Strand. The light was fading in the fields, and the tincture gave the world an unreal quality: the clouds defined and purple, the people blurred and indistinct. I was as Orpheus, passing through the underworld.

In the dockside quarter, men were finishing for the day. I made a few purchases at the wholesalers, and then walked down to the river. Boatyards lined the mudflats, and from one such venture I hired a small wherry overnight.

'Taking a young lady out for a moonlit row?' the boatman leered.

Between us we carried the wherry down to the water, where I tied her up. I put my purchases in the bottom of the boat, and returned to the harbourside. Exhausted, I sat on the wall, waiting for nightfall. I could see *The Dark Angel* from here, the winged woman gazing out at the darkening water. What had Moses Graham called her? A vessel of lost souls.

I'd been sitting there a little while, when the sounds of a quarrel reached me, the usual chamber music to Deptford life. I turned and saw two figures struggling on the quayside. The man was wearing a woollen sailor's smock. The woman I recognized. Jamaica Mary – presumably with one of her customers. She tried to run, but the man grabbed her wrist and pulled her back. He struck her in the face with his fist, then dragged her to the wall, where he hoisted her skirts, fumbling with his breeches.

He was so intent upon copulation, that he didn't hear me cross the quay. I drew my sword and placed the tip at his throat. 'Stand away.'

He did so, confused. 'Who the fuck are you?' I plainly did not look like a thief to him.

'Nobody you know.'

'Then what quarrel do we have?'

'This woman does not seem willing.'

Mary was holding her face, glaring at us both. She pulled her grubby skirts down over her cunny and spat blood on the ground.

The man laughed. 'You'd kill me for a penny-fuck whore? Have you lost your mind?'

I pricked his Adam's apple. 'Apologize.'

'Steady on.' He raised his hands. 'I'm sorry.'

'Not to me. To her.'

'I'm sorry.'

'Sorry don't cut it,' she said. 'He promised Mary two shillings.'

'That's a lie, we said a shilling.'

'It was a shilling before you hit her,' I said. 'Make it three.'

He fumbled for his purse, and gave her the coins. I let him go, and he ran off down the quay. Mary walked over to the harbour wall, where she sat, holding her face. Already tiring, I went and sat beside her.

'What do you want? A free fuck?'

I almost laughed. 'I told you, I'm married.'

'So you did.' She gave me a long look. 'What happened to you?'

'I fell off a horse.'

'Have big fists did he, this horse?'

I smiled. 'How long have you lived in Deptford, Mary?'

'Near twenty years.'

'Did you come here as a slave?'

'You think Mary would come to this hell-hole willingly?'

'How did you get your freedom?'

She shrugged. 'Made an old man happy, a Deptford merchant. He freed Mary in his will.'

'And you stayed in Deptford?'

'Tried London, didn't like it. Came back here.'

'How well do you know Peregrine Child?'

'Well enough.'

'Do you remember when his wife and child died? The accident?'

She snorted. 'That weren't no accident.'

'I heard they drowned in Deptford Reach. It isn't true?'

She wrapped her arms around herself. The last glow of the

sun was fading. 'Ten years ago it was. The child was born simple. Mary used to see them around town, the little boy holding his mother's hand.' She pulled a slack, stupid face. 'Some say it drove the mother mad, as sure as it drove Perry Child to drink. She took the little boy down to the creek one day and filled their pockets with stones. Then they paddled along the creek until they reached the river.' She sniffed. 'Bad waters these. The Devil's Reach.'

I felt another rush of pity for Peregrine Child. 'Why does he feel so beholden to Frank Drake?'

'Perry thinks it was his fault. Damn, it probably was. And Drake, being his dead wife's brother.' She shrugged again. 'Drake knows how to play people. Always did.'

There must be more to it than that, I thought, especially so long after the event. We sat there for a time in silence, each lost in private contemplation. The moon was fat, the colour of old candles. It was windier tonight, the air humid again. The rain was less a promise, more a threat.

'I heard another story too, about a slave who ended up in the Reach. People said he fathered Mrs Monday's eldest child. Her first husband and his friends took him out to the marshes over there.' I pointed to the far bank.

She nodded. 'Gentle George. There's not a Negro in Deptford believes he made nasty with that woman.'

'You think they got the wrong man?'

'Must have done. If these mudflats could talk, they'd have a host of tales to tell.'

'There was never any gossip among the slaves?'

'None would admit to it. And she wasn't saying nothing. Mary heard George knew, though. He'd seen them together, and it wasn't rape he saw neither.'

'Who told you that?'

'Mary forgets. It was years ago.' She grinned. 'You wouldn't think it to look at her, would you?'

My mind was wandering again. I thought of Caro, the one from my dream. The young viscount, my wife's lover. I thought of Scipio gazing after the women in the stable-yard. Spinoza's dangerous passions. Tad's letters blackening in the flames. His bleak face. I touched my own face, and found I was crying again.

'It true what they say?' she asked. 'Vaughan. Brabazon. Drake. They drowned three hundred slaves at sea? Children too?'

'Yes, it is.'

'Will they hang for it?'

'I doubt it.'

She nodded, unsurprised. 'Pity.'

'Someone seeks to punish them, though. You remember the obeah? Those dead birds drove Vaughan half out of his mind.'

Her face flickered; a trace of amusement?

'Mrs Grimshaw saw you at the Noah's Ark the day an obeah doll was nailed to the stable door. Was it you who put it there?'

Her smile was similar to the one Cinnamon had given when I'd asked her about the obeah: suggestive, a little sly. 'No, sir.'

'Do you know who is behind it?' I persisted.

I suspected she did. I believed Deptford's Africans knew full well who was behind it. Perhaps they all were. Whatever the truth, Mary wasn't saying.

She turned again to look out at the river. The moon was reflected in the water, a drop of wax in a puddle of ink. 'They'll probably pull Mary out of here one day. They say drowning doesn't hurt.'

I thought of Amelia, the slaves on *The Dark Angel*. 'They're lying.'

'Ah well, Mary will probably go in dead anyway. It might have been tonight, if you hadn't come along.' She held her hand up to the moon, and closed her fingers around it, making a fist. 'Then it would all be over. The blink of an eye.'

Chapter Forty-Six

Rowing proved torturous work. I pulled against the tide, my tormented body protesting each heave. I'd taken another draught of Brabazon's tincture before I'd set off, though he'd explicitly warned me against it. Fog drifted along the surface of the water. The ships creaked, over the splash of my oars.

Guineamen loomed over me, a school of Jonah's whales. I picked out their names with the bull lantern I'd bought earlier. *The George*, *The Black Prince*, *The Phoenix*. Their stench was ripe. All the flavours of death: vomit and corruption, blood and disease, excrement, piss and human suffering.

I forced my muscles to work harder to counter the swell. The sternpost hurt my back, where I braced myself against it. She was above me now, a deeper black against the night sky. A siren, or a fury, heralding death. I put out my hand and touched the rough grain of her timbers.

I'd bought a rope and grappling hook, but I saw with relief I wouldn't need them. A rope ladder dangled from the ship's northern side. Several small boats and barges were secured to the anchor chain, and I tied mine up alongside them.

Climbing the ladder wasn't easy. My sword proved too cumbersome, so I unbuckled it and left it in the boat. The rope grazed my palms, and my limbs burned. Dizziness kept overcoming me, and I thought I was going to be sick. The movement of the water made it harder, and I almost slipped several times.

I forced myself to look up, to the point where timber met sky, willing myself on. At last, I hauled myself over the side, and collapsed on deck, sucking in the putrid air.

Once I had recovered my breath, I staggered to my feet. The ship rolled beneath me, and I almost fell over again. I'd had to leave the lantern in the wherry, but the light of the moon was strong. Three masts towered above me, the edges of their furled sails snapping in the breeze. I identified the dark mass of the forecastle, and caught the odour of old food. I guessed this was where the kitchens were housed. I edged my way along the deck, rounding an enormous wooden tub. The smell hit me hard, and I recoiled. I remembered Tad, long ago, telling me about the necessary tubs, where slaves were forced to squat amidst the faeces of their fellows. Sometimes they slipped and fell in, and had to be hauled out. Sometimes they were given a dunking as a punishment.

A large metal grating in the deck led down to the slave holds below. I stiffened as I heard a noise, a voice or a moan. Human or timber? I couldn't tell.

The quarterdeck lay to the stern and I crossed to it swiftly, filled with an overwhelming desire to get off this ship. I tried the door and discovered it was unlocked. A lantern hung on a peg next to the jamb, and I lit it with my tinder. A short corridor stretched in front of me, with several cabins opening off it. This must be where the ship's officers slept. The men would sleep out on deck, as they had on my American crossings. I drew my pistol.

The first cabin had a pair of hammocks slung from the ceiling. Two seamen's chests took up most of the floor. I tried the chests, and found both were unlocked and empty. Through the porthole, I could see the lights of Deptford.

The next cabin was similar to the first, though slightly larger.

Again the seamen's chests were unlocked and empty. Again I found nothing of any consequence. The crew had probably cleared the vessel of any personal belongings when the ship had docked.

The third cabin was plainly occupied by the captain. It held a carved oak bed, a map chest, and a table for studying charts. No sign of occupancy. No linen on the bed. A gust of wind rocked the ship, travelling through the old timbers. My stomach turned.

The final cabin was the largest. In the centre of the room was a chair, fixed with metal bolts to the floor. Against one wall was a stove, next to a stand of branding irons. Other implements hung on the walls, many of which I recognized from the ironmonger's shop. Metal masks. Fetters. The speculum oris.

A dresser held bottles and jars, bowls, a pestle and mortar. I opened a drawer and saw surgeon's knives and other tools. My eye fell upon a small metal device. Even before I picked it up, I knew what it was. A thumbscrew. It was heavy in my hand. Under the screw were metal teeth, and I slipped one of my fingers between them, turning the screw until I felt pressure bearing down. I stared at the chair, suddenly knowing with a fierce certainty that this place, part sanatorium, part torture chamber, was where Tad had been killed.

Why had he come here? Because like me he'd come to believe that Evan Vaughan had never left Deptford. Because like me he'd concluded that this was where Vaughan was being kept. Cinnamon was no good as a witness. Brabazon was unwilling. Perhaps Tad hadn't trusted him to stand up in court and implicate his friends and himself. Yet he'd believed Vaughan was near to breaking. A prize worth having.

The prospect of the next part of my search filled me with horror. I returned to the deck, taking the lantern with me.

I wrestled with the bolts on the hatch that led down to the slave decks. When I raised the hatch and lowered it, an even viler stench rose up to meet me. The tomb and the plague pit and the charnel house. A ladder stretched down into the darkness.

I had to holster my pistol to descend. The ship seemed to sink beneath my feet, and my stomach swam again. Every part of me recoiled, but I pressed on until I reached the bottom. My lantern illuminated only a small circle around me, with a vast, black space beyond. The ceiling was low, about six inches above my head. The creaking of the ship was much louder down here. I heard the moan again, like a voice heard underwater, or the crying of a child in a dream. Again, I drew my pistol.

Set into the floor ahead of me was another hatch, this one leading down to the lower slave deck. Something flashed as it caught the lamplight, something shiny. I drew closer, and saw that a large padlock secured the hatch, dazzling in its newness against the older metal.

I rattled it. 'Captain Vaughan? Are you down there?'

Nothing. I shivered, though it was infernally hot. I called again, and again was met by silence.

If Vaughan was down there, he was not a willing prisoner. I remembered the opium Monday had bought. Were they keeping him stupefied, malleable? I wondered which of them Tad had encountered here that night. Brabazon or Drake or Monday? Or had he met Vaughan himself, down here in the dark? Had the captain struck down the black demon who so tormented him?

I could not hope to break the padlock open with my bare hands, but there might be something down here, or back in the surgeon's cabin, that I could use to spring the lock. I walked further into the hold, occasionally stumbling over lengths of chain or coils of rope. I made out the wooden racks to hold the slaves that Monday had described in his warehouse. Cannons at the gun ports were secured with heavy blocks and tackle. Every time the ship rocked, Deptford air travelled through the holes in the ship's side. It was the sweetest odour I had ever smelled.

Something moved in the shadows and I raised my pistol. 'Captain Vaughan? My name is Captain Henry Corsham. I'd like to talk to you.'

Another flicker of movement, this time off to my left. I could see something there. A dark shape. A man? Cautiously, I walked towards him. Then I stopped.

A length of rope was fixed to a hook in the ceiling. A man hung by the neck from a noose, just as I had last night, his toes nearly touching the floor. His face was livid and bloated. His bright blue eyes bulged unnaturally. Frank Drake.

Was it the movement of the rope that had stirred the shadows as he swayed? Or was someone else down here? I peered into the darkness, but saw no one.

At Drake's feet was a large leather bag. Keeping one eye on the shadows, I bent swiftly to retrieve it. I shook it open, and a bundle of clothes tumbled out. I stirred them with my toe, keeping my pistol high. A black coat and breeches. A pair of silk stockings. Boots. A white shirt, stiffened with blood. I searched the coat's lining until I found the tailor's label. It was embroidered with the owner's name: TG Archer.

I stared up at Drake. He had a livid bruise on his temple. I felt in his pockets, and removed the things I found there. A purse of gold. Dice. A pack of cards. A crumpled playbill from one of the London theatres. I turned it over, and saw that someone had drawn a map on the reverse. It looked like London. I put it in my pocket to study later.

Something small and square and white caught my attention in the shadows. Cautiously, I walked over to inspect it. A piece of paper was secured to the side of the ship with a knife. A long knife, with a finely worked silver handle. Flakes of brown clung to the blade like rust. There was writing on the paper, and I stared at it, until a noise made me turn. Light was filling the hold. I heard footsteps on the ladder. Someone was coming.

Chapter Forty-Seven

I waited, pistol in hand, as the lamp drew nearer. A stocky, dark figure at the centre of the blaze. When he was a few feet away, he stopped. Peregrine Child also had a pistol in his hand.

He looked at Frank Drake's corpse. His expression didn't change. 'When did you find him?'

'Just now.' I eyed his pistol, reminding myself that he couldn't be the killer. Child was too short.

The magistrate's lips were set, his bloodshot eyes unreadable. 'Someone saw lights on the ship. They were concerned it might be thieves.'

I didn't believe him. Since when was Child so diligent in his duties? I pointed to the clothes on the floor. 'Those belonged to my friend. And over there, pinned to the wall, you'll find Drake's confession. It says he killed Archer in revenge for the fight they had at the dock. It makes no mention of *The Dark Angel* or the massacre. Drake says he cannot live with the guilt. Does that sound like him to you?'

Child was still staring at Drake's corpse. 'Maybe I didn't know him as well as I thought.'

'You told me he couldn't read or write.'

'Perhaps he learned.'

'I thought you were convinced of his innocence. Now, after all this, you'll accept his guilt?'

'If he says he's guilty, he probably is. Ockham's Razor.'

'Or perhaps it is a convenient outcome that everyone will accept. No need for a trial. No talk of *The Dark Angel*.'

'Have you considered that might be best for everyone concerned, including you? Have you seen your face lately?'

'I think a man stands for something or he doesn't.'

'It's that simple?'

'If you like.'

Child shook his head. 'This is the scene of a crime. It's also private property. Leave now, before I'm forced to arrest you.'

'Not before I see what's down on the lower slave deck. We could search it together? This deck too. I think someone else might be down here. Perhaps Captain Vaughan.'

Child raised his pistol. 'I said I want you to leave. You have ten seconds before I arrest you. If you resist, I'll shoot you dead.'

He had a look in his eyes I hadn't seen before. Not the hot fury at the bull bait, but a cold, resigned glaze. I wondered if he meant it, and decided I wasn't prepared to take the risk.

'I hold you in part responsible for Archer's murder,' I said. 'Whoever did this believed they could get away with it because they knew Stokes and the West India lobby would conceal the crime, and you would be their willing lapdog.'

'Has it ever occurred to you,' he said, 'that you don't know half as much as you think you do?'

'I know you're an embarrassment to the bench.' I walked back towards the ladder, casting a long glance at the slave hatch with its padlock as I passed. 'You should have stuck to carpentry, Mr Child.'

*

On my way back down the rope ladder, it took enormous effort to focus on the boats in the roiling waters below. I took another pull on Brabazon's tincture before I cast off. Rowing took even more effort than before. An age to reach the Deptford bank, then another age to drag the wherry up to the boatyard. My muscles were a furnace, sweat soaked my clothes. I wasn't sure that I could make it back to the Broadway unassisted.

I didn't fancy a walk through the alleys in such a condition, so I decided to take the long route along the quays, then cut up past the gates of the Private Dock. It was possible the guards there would assist me. Yet the darker stretches of the dock weren't devoid of danger either. I kept a hand on my sword, knowing I presented a vulnerable target.

The dock was nearly deserted. Sometimes people called out to me: whores or beggars or thieves. I ignored them, and kept moving, dragging my leg behind me. The walls of the Private Dock were still a quarter of a mile away. I needed to rest, and I sat down in the doorway of a shipping office, massaging my leg. The world was muting at the edges, attaining a softness I found comforting. Even the bricks felt soft when I laid my head against them. I closed my eyes, everything spiralling inside my skull.

Tad, are you there?

Always. Wake up.

I wasn't asleep.

A smile. *Liar.*

I opened my eyes and saw the sky held a brilliance I had never known before. A dazzling firmament soared above me, the stars playing silver music against the violet heavens. Someone was standing over me, and I couldn't see if it was Tad or God. His hands soothed me, lifting my arms, unbuttoning my coat. I allowed him to do it, until I felt a hand on my purse. With a cry, I pushed him away, then thrust at him with my sword. He fell backwards.

It was a ragged boy of about twelve and I'd almost killed

him. Seeing my confusion, he scrambled to his feet and ran away.

I forced myself up, and continued along the quay, holding myself against walls when I threatened to fall down. The Private Dock still seemed very far away. One foot. Then the other. I repeated it, like a psalm, until a burly figure stepped out to block my path. He said something indistinct, and again I lunged forward with my sword.

'Captain Corsham,' he cried. 'It's me, Nathaniel.'

His smiling, dimpled face swam with the lights. My good leg buckled, and he caught me as I fell. 'Lean on me. That's it, sir. Come inside.'

I realized we were in the same spot where I'd seen him with the stranger from the churchyard. He led me inside the warehouse, supporting me each time I stumbled. The building had an abandoned, disused feel, like the warehouses I'd visited the other day. Light emanated from an office at the top of a flight of stairs, like the one in Monday's warehouse. A foul, sweet smell, like carrion, pervaded the place. It reminded me of the slave ship.

'It's just a dead pigeon, sir,' Nathaniel said, seeing my discomfort.

My thoughts came sluggishly. 'Why are you guarding this place? It's empty.'

'The owner's seen a downturn in his business. He pays me to keep an eye on it, stop the gypsies and the Irish moving in while he's trying to sell it.'

He helped me upstairs to the office. A lamp and an open book lay on a table, and I guessed this was where Nathaniel passed the time between his rounds. A trestle bed stood against one wall, made up with blankets and pillows. It confused me.

Nathaniel didn't strike me as the stripe of boy who'd shirk his duties.

'I need to talk to you,' I said. 'Did you see Mr Archer here, the night before he was killed? I need to know what dealings you had with him. The truth this time.'

He hushed me as if I was a child. 'We can talk about that later, sir. You're not right. You need to rest.'

The softness of his tone made me want to weep. He guided me to the bed, and at his urging, I lay down, unable to resist any longer. I tried to ask him something else, but the words came out backwards, and I wondered if I was already dreaming. The black waters closed over my head, and I drifted on the currents.

Chapter Forty-Eight

Something was wrong. My nakedness for a start. The warm, naked woman lying next to me in the bed. It wasn't Caro. I was in Deptford. What the devil?

Things swam into focus around me. It was dark, but the window cast soft moonlight. I was in the warehouse office. Alarmed, I turned to the figure lying next to me. I made out the musculature of the shoulders, the horsehair wig on the floor. Nathaniel Grimshaw.

I drew back in horror, and a jolt of pain ran through my body. Nausea assailed me, all the old agonies returning. As quietly as I could, I crept from the bed. I found my breeches on the floor, and put them on, still gazing, appalled, at the naked boy. I groped around for my stockings, and knocked something over in the dark. Nathaniel rolled over. He smiled at me sleepily. 'Captain Corsham, it's still dark. Come back to bed.'

'No,' I muttered. 'I have to go.'

'There's still an hour until my four o'clock round. We could make good use of it.' There was a coyness to his voice that made me recoil. 'Archer told me about you, sir. We talked a lot, he and I. He said there'd once been a man he'd loved with a passion that'd make Ganymede blush. I knew as soon as I saw you. I can always tell.'

'No, you have this wrong. I'm not like him at all.'

'It seems to me, sir – and after tonight, I should know – that you're just like him.'

'Don't be ridiculous.' It was a lie. I knew it was.

Nathaniel rose from the bed and came towards me. Conscious of his nakedness, I averted my eyes. He held out a hand. 'Come, sir, let's get you back to bed.'

I knocked his hand away, as a new realization hit me. 'Did you come here with him? With Archer? Were you looking for him that night you found his body?'

'Aye, he came here several times. Archer had a lot of scruples, sir, not like you. I wanted him, but he said I was too young. But he talked to me – gave me counsel. It's a lonely path we tread, dangerous too.'

'This has nothing to do with me. Do you hear?'

Fumbling, going too fast, I buttoned my shirt. Nathaniel walked to the table, still naked, and lit the lamp. 'You're leaving? That's a shame. Just one thing before you go. Last night you promised me money. I wouldn't ask, but times are hard.'

I didn't believe him, but I reached for my purse, scattering some coins on the table to be rid of him.

He examined them doubtfully. 'That's not quite what I meant, sir. I don't want to go slaving, see. Nobody does, not really, but don't underestimate the measure of my distaste for it. I need two hundred pounds to get the inn out from under, and then another hundred to get my apprenticeship back.'

Blackmail. Tad had told me about it long ago. The predators who enticed their fellow mollies into acts of depravation, then threatened to go to the authorities unless they paid up. Nathaniel had made no threats yet, but I knew they'd follow if I refused. I remembered the merchant in the churchyard. Nathaniel hadn't been the victim of that piece, as I'd presumed.

'Think on it as a scholarship,' Nathaniel said. 'The Corsham Endowment.'

'You're lying. Nothing happened between us.'

Yet I couldn't prove it – and if Nathaniel made a complaint, I didn't imagine Deptford justice would be kind to me. Nor would Cavill-Lawrence lift another finger to protect me.

Nathaniel's smile vanished. 'I remember it differently, sir. I think I know who the mayor and the magistrate will believe.'

I gazed at him helplessly. 'I don't have three hundred pounds.'

'I know you don't, sir. Not here anyway.'

I remembered that half-dream, him going through my bags. He had planned this.

'I've asked around, sir. You're a wealthy man, I hear. Your wife's father owned a bank. How would she take the news of our little night here?'

Tell him anything. Just get out of here. 'I'll get your money, but I need to return to London first.' I pulled on my coat and boots, buckled my sword.

Nathaniel nodded. 'I know you will, sir. I'll be waiting. Not too long, mind, else I'll have to come and find you.'

I opened the office door, and that foul, carrion smell hit me once again. I turned back. 'Did you extort money from him too? From Archer?'

His face was watchful, a new hardness to his soft green eyes. 'Archer gave me a little blunt because he pitied me going slaving, but his pockets weren't deep like yours. Not worth the trouble. It was him who put this idea into my head, as it happens. He warned me to be careful of –' he paused, and smiled – 'I suppose he warned me to be careful of men like me.'

*

My heart raced, and my skin crawled. As I walked up to Deptford Broadway, I thought of the boy undressing me, touching me. Pausing by the roadside, I retched up the little I'd eaten. I needed a clear head to think, and I threw Brabazon's tincture into the fields.

Even in my panicked state, the questions still gnawed at me. Not Frank Drake. Not Peregrine Child. Then who? By the time I reached the Broadway, I was no nearer any answers.

A few dedicated patrons were still drinking in the taproom of the coaching inn. One of them rose to meet me. Scipio. His eyes travelled over my bruises, and his hands twisted the brim of his hat.

'Mr Stokes is sending Cinnamon to his plantations in Bermuda. She needs your help.'

I sat down before I fell down, regarding him coldly. As far as I was concerned, this was on him.

'He got the truth out of Cinnamon last night,' Scipio said. 'I couldn't prevent it, though I tried. He says he can no longer trust her. She will die there. I know she will. I cannot have that on my conscience too.'

'Had you let her go when you had the chance, she would be free and in London.'

'I know.' He rubbed his eyes. 'Please help her, Captain Corsham. I would go myself, only I don't believe the magistrate will give me an injunction.'

'I doubt Child will give me one either.'

'She's in Woolwich, not Deptford. That's under the jurisdiction of the Greenwich magistrate. No Guineamen were sailing to Bermuda from Deptford until next week, and Stokes wanted her gone. He's like that when he makes a decision. The ship is called *The Princess Charlotte*. She weighs anchor at six this morning. That's less than two hours.'

If I did this, there would be no hiding my involvement. It would be done in the public gaze, with all the attendant scandal. Alternatively, it could be a trap. 'I saw you in Greenwich,' I said. 'You were talking to Nicholas Cavill-Lawrence.'

His voice rose with urgency. 'What has that to do with anything?'

'I'd like to know what you discussed.'

'Just business. Stokes's plans for the new West India dock.'

'You expect me to believe that Stokes would send his secretary to such a meeting?'

Scipio pressed his fingers to his temples. 'It was not a meeting Stokes wished to attend himself. Little discussion took place, certain assurances were given. Mr Cavill-Lawrence went away a happy man.'

He meant a bribe. The more I thought about it, the more it made sense. As Under-Secretary of State for War, charged with protection of the Caribbean colonies, Cavill-Lawrence would doubtless be involved in the key discussions over the siting of the new dock. Corruption was rife across Whitehall, even within the Cabinet. It didn't come as any great surprise that Cavill-Lawrence was lining his pockets.

'So Stokes will get his dock?'

'Perhaps. I imagine the Wapping men have also been busy.'

I closed my eyes to stop the room from spinning. Scipio gave a grunt of impatience. 'You haven't much time.'

I could sense his desperation. In how many directions he'd been pulled. His desire to build a normal life for himself here in Deptford. Forced to act as gaoler to Cinnamon, Abraham, and Stokes's other slaves. His affinity to his brother Africans that he'd tried so hard to suppress. Now something in him seemed to have broken. Part of me pitied him. Part of me was determined to use his torment to my advantage.

'Why did you and Peregrine Child search Archer's room the morning his body was found? Were you looking for the syndicate's contracts that were stolen from John Monday?'

He made a sweeping gesture. 'We can talk about this later.'

'I'm not going anywhere until you've answered my questions, so you'd better be quick.'

'Yes, Mr Stokes ordered us to go there.'

'It needed two of you?'

'One to watch the other. Those contracts were important to Stokes. I don't know why.'

'Did you find them?'

He hesitated. 'Yes. Archer had concealed them behind the washstand. It was Child who found them. He gave them to Mr Stokes.'

So the mayor had had the contracts all along. Yet he hadn't returned them to John Monday, nor given them to Napier Smith and the West India lobby. A lot of things were falling into place. I remembered my assailants last night, my bafflement that they hadn't killed me. Only one explanation made sense.

'The help you gave me – with Jamaica Mary, asking around about Drake, talking things through. You were doing it on Stokes's orders, weren't you?'

His hands bunched into fists, and he stared at them. I didn't care about his shame, I wanted to know.

'Well?'

'Stokes thought the murders were a threat to his dock, to Deptford's reputation. He wanted the killer caught, but he needed to do so covertly, without the West India lobby finding out. That's why he told me to help you. I'm sorry I couldn't tell you.'

That might have been what Stokes had told Scipio, but I believed his motives to be somewhat more complicated. 'As it happens, I don't think that's true, but let's not worry about that now. Why did Stokes go to John Monday's house the night Archer was killed?'

'I don't know. I swear it. I didn't go with him. Please, Captain Corsham, I have answered your questions. Will you help her?'

Of course I was going to help her. It would probably be the last nail in the coffin of my political ambitions. Caro would think I'd lost my mind. Yet I was going to get Cinnamon off that boat, or die trying. There was one other thing I wanted to ask Scipio, but it could wait. As he said, I didn't have much time.

PART FIVE

3–7 JULY 1781

The human mind cannot be absolutely destroyed along with the body, but something of it remains, which is eternal.

V. Of Man's Freedom or The Power of the Understanding,
Ethics, Baruch Spinoza

Chapter Forty-Nine

THE RIDE TO Greenwich felt as though I was taking a beating all over again. The pain acted as a spur to drive me on. I couldn't save Tad or Proudlock or the drowned slaves or Amelia, but I could save Cinnamon. In that moment, everything else had ceased to matter.

Greenwich turned from grey to pink to gold as the sun rose higher in the sky. It slid over me, then onwards towards London. We rode at a gallop. Zephyrus's flanks were already soaked in sweat. I urged him on.

I tied Zephyrus up at the Navy Hospital, where I'd walked with Jeremiah Robertson only two days ago. Few people were about at that hour, but eventually I found someone who could give me directions to the magistrate's house. He lived in a street of new townhouses bordering the park. I hammered on his door for several minutes before a manservant appeared. He took one look at my face. 'If you're here to report an assault, sir, come to the courthouse after ten.'

He made to close the door, but I jammed my foot in the gap. Speaking in a tone that brooked no refusal, I told him to send for his master.

It took half an hour for the magistrate to receive me.

His face and hands were covered in liver spots, and his ginger eyebrows drew together, as I related my request. 'You got me out of bed for a Negress slave?'

'The ship sails in an hour.' My watch was in my hand. 'Less.'

'And you're quite sure the girl doesn't want to go?'

'She told me so herself several times.'

Sighing deeply, he took a sheet of parchment from his desk and drew up his inkwell. He sat scribbling, while I paced the room. He asked me a few particulars, and then I had to endure another wait while he sent for his clerk to witness the document. By the time I left, clutching the injunction, I had less than twenty minutes before the ship sailed.

We took the road east at a gallop, each stride sending a stabbing spasm through my innards. It was high tide and the river broadened as we rode. By the time we clattered into Woolwich, ten minutes later, the north bank was nearly a mile distant.

Woolwich was a similar river port to Deptford, though its royal connections lent it an air of respectability the latter lacked. I asked a passing collier for the harbour master's residence, and was directed to a row of little houses near the clockhouse. The harbour bristled with masts, the river reflecting the sky and the gathering clouds. Seagulls soared above, and I tasted salt. The harbour master was awake, though no more pleased to see me than the magistrate. A small plump man with round owlish eyes, he read my injunction impatiently on his doorstep.

'You're too late,' he said, handing it back. '*The Princess Charlotte* has already sailed. You missed her by nearly an hour.'

Despair and confusion assailed me. 'But I still have five minutes.'

'The ship due to sail at five wasn't ready. *The Charlotte* took her place in the queue.'

I knew how congested the river could get – how ships queued and captains bribed their way to better sailing times. 'How far will she have got by now?'

The harbour master held a finger to the breeze. 'Halfway to Thurrock, I would think. If you're lucky she'll be held up at Erith Reach.' He peered at me. 'You know that's one of Napier Smith's ships? I wouldn't cross the Chairman of the West India lobby for all the sugar in Jamaica.'

Scipio had neglected to tell me that. Perhaps he'd thought I wouldn't go after her if I knew. Yet it caused me only a moment's hesitation. A woman's freedom, perhaps her very life, hung in the balance.

The river road grew rougher the further I rode from London. Through Charlton and Plumstead, across the Plumstead Marshes. Zephyrus was starting to tire, and I knew if I didn't catch *The Princess Charlotte* at Erith, he could never maintain this pace all the way to Tilbury. Beyond there the estuary widened dramatically, and I'd never catch her.

The river swept south again, cutting through the marshes. I felt a surge of exhilaration, as I glimpsed a queue of ships lying at anchor in Erith Reach. A merchantman was navigating the bend in the river, her sails plump as pillows, pennants fluttering.

Erith was a two-street town, perched between water and marsh. Fat river flies and mosquitos swarmed around us. The harbour was barely worthy of the name: a few boatyards scattered over a gravelly patch of shore. A man was scrubbing down a painted sailing boat, and as I dismounted, I called out to him. 'Have you seen *The Princess Charlotte* go past?'

He didn't look up. 'Can't say I have.'

I scanned the ships on the river: Guineamen and Indiamen, a few brigs and pinnaces, looking like toys in the wake of the larger vessels. I couldn't read their names at this distance, and I thrust a handful of coin in the man's face. 'Can you take me out to them? I need to intercept one of the Guineamen.'

He raised his head to study me, then examined my money with a scholar's solemnity. 'I can do that.'

We sailed against the wind, tacking north, then south. It took us about fifteen minutes to draw alongside the nearest merchantman. *Nassau* was her name. In size she outstripped even the Guineamen I'd seen in Deptford dock. Crew swarmed over her rigging, and I called up to them.

'*The Princess Charlotte.*' The wind snatched my words away, and I repeated them several times. Eventually one of the men understood. 'She's four ships down, I think.'

Relief overwhelmed me. A cry went up on deck: 'Raise anchor.'

'Better get out of the way,' the sailor shouted down. 'Or you'll be swamped.'

The swell rocked us violently. My boatman swore, but he kept us righted. As we tacked north again, I shaded my eyes. I could see her now. A Guineaman with a figurehead of a fair-haired woman wearing a crown. A more pleasing omen than *The Dark Angel*, yet her purpose was the same, and as we pulled nearer, I caught the familiar stench of corruption.

We drew alongside her, and again I called up to the sailors climbing the rigging. 'I have a document for your captain, an order from a magistrate. Fetch him, please!'

A man, an officer from the look of his attire, appeared at the side, frowning down at me. 'Who the devil are you?'

'My name is Captain Henry Corsham. This ship carries disputed property. Fetch your captain now, sir. I need to board you.'

The face disappeared, only to return a minute later together with a man wearing a black naval coat and a gold-trimmed bicorne. 'I am Captain Blake. What do you want?'

Our craft lurched up on an eddy, turning my stomach to

soup. I shouted over the wind and the waves. 'The slave girl you have on board. You are to surrender her to my care. I have an injunction to that effect signed by the Greenwich magistrate.'

'You are mistaken, sir. I spoke to the girl's owner myself.'

'When the courts uphold her claim to freedom, she'll have no owner. While her status is under dispute, she is not to be removed from English soil. If you refuse to let me have her, you'll be in contempt of court. This man here is my witness.'

My riverman, pleased to be the centre of attention, grinned gummily.

I could see the captain calculating. His pride versus a world of trouble for himself. In the end, convenience got the better part of valour. He made a signal with his hand, and a rope ladder dropped down. I instructed the boatman to wait, and steadying myself against the swell, began to climb it. When I reached the top, I ignored the hostile faces I found there.

'Where is she?'

The captain studied my injunction, and then nodded to one of his men. 'Take us down.'

The hatch in the deck was much like the one on board *The Dark Angel*. We descended the ladder, and the crewman paused to light a lantern. The hold was packed with shipping crates, a long aisle running between them. Guns, beads and liquor, I presumed, remembering Monday's lecture in the warehouse.

'When we reach Tilbury, I intend to send a message to Napier Smith,' the captain informed me. 'He'll know of this by tonight, I assure you.'

'Just take me to her.'

We were nearing the end of the hold. The sailor turned to shine his light upon a gap in the stacks of crates. Cinnamon lay there, naked, chained like an animal. She put up her hands to shield her face, and I saw bruises on her wrists, breasts and thighs.

I knelt on the boards beside her. 'It is I, Captain Corsham. You'll soon be free. I'm taking you to London.'

I had to repeat this twice before she seemed to understand. She put out a hand to touch my face, staring at me as if I was an apparition.

The captain ordered her chains unlocked, and I took off my coat to cover her. I lifted her and carried her bodily from that place. She didn't say a word, even when we were safely ensconced in the sailing boat. She only clung to me like flotsam in a storm.

CHAPTER FIFTY

WE CROSSED THE Thames on the Woolwich ferry, after I'd purchased a shift and a shawl for Cinnamon. Even once she was dressed, an army officer and a beautiful mulatto girl, riding two to a horse, attracted much attention on the Ratcliffe Highway. For this reason, I avoided the city, taking the lanes cutting north of London, eventually joining the New Road linking the outlying villages of Islington, Somer's Town and Tottenham Court. Zephyrus was exhausted after his gallop, struggling under the weight of two. I slowed him to a walk, and it was ten o'clock by the time we reached Marylebone.

We rode into the Yorkshire Stingo's yard, and I lifted Cinnamon down. A young black boy was kicking a cabbage around, and I paid him a penny to watch Zephyrus. In the taproom a few of last night's drinkers still jabbered incoherently. The same hostile African tapwoman was behind the bar. Her eyes were bleary, her apron stained, and I guessed she'd been up all night. She came alive as her eyes fastened on Cinnamon, seeming to understand the situation without being told.

She helped Cinnamon to a chair, and called to her potboy to fetch warm ale. A blanket was procured. Cinnamon wouldn't stop shivering.

'I need to see Caesar John,' I said. 'This woman needs help.'

The tapwoman nodded, and disappeared through the curtain. When she returned, she beckoned us through, to a wood-panelled room furnished with a large dining table and chairs. Caesar John and three of his men sat around it drinking and smoking. I recognized the huge African built like a boxer and the elderly coachman. I guessed their night's work had just come to an end.

Cinnamon stared at them. I wondered if she'd ever seen free blacks like this before. Empty plates littered the table, and the air was rich with the smell of bacon. Caesar John pointed at Cinnamon with his toothpick. 'Who the fuck is she?'

'A slave girl owned by the mayor of Deptford. He was trying to send her to his plantations. I took her off a Guineaman.'

'She have anything to do with that other business? With Archer's ship? Those drowned slaves?'

'Yes, she was on the ship when they drowned them.'

'Is that why they were sending her away?'

'I don't think so. She doesn't know anything.' I looked at Cinnamon. 'Do you?'

She seemed close to collapse, her skin ashen, eyes unfocused. 'I heard no discussions between the sailors,' she said softly. 'I wish I had, but it was just as Scipio told you. I'm sorry I lied.'

Another black man walked in through the curtain, coated with dust from the road. Caesar John rose to meet him, and they conferred in hushed tones. The man seemed to be giving him bad news. Caesar John looked over at me, glaring.

'I want the girl gone. Take her somewhere else. I can't help her.'

'There's nowhere I can take her where she'll be safe. Her master is a vindictive man. He'll be looking for her.'

'That's not my problem.'

The tapwoman laid both palms flat on the table. 'Did I hear that right? You going to send this girl away?'

'Quiet, woman! You don't know what you're talking about.'

'I know she's a child. I know she looks sick. You scared, John? I thought I knew a man, not a mewling boy.'

In another time and another place, I might have enjoyed the spectacle of Caesar John being flayed by his woman. As it was, my stomach was too curdled with anxiety and dread.

'Listen, Bronze,' Caesar John said. 'I'm thinking of you, of all of us. You don't know what these fucksters can do.'

'Oh, I know, John. I seen it my whole life. That's why you have to help her. Look at her, man. Where else is she supposed to go?'

Caesar John made a fist on the table. 'One week,' he said at last. 'No more. You find somewhere else by then, or I'm putting her out on the street.'

Bronze kissed him and he shook her off. 'Jezebel.' He nodded to the coachman. 'We take her to the sponging house. Ready the carriage.'

He beckoned me to him. 'There's something you need to know.' He nodded at the man with the dusty clothes. 'Tell him.'

*

London was bathed in a weak wash of afternoon sunlight, filtered through a brooding, pewter sky. One minute the whores and pigeons preened in it, the next they plumped resentful feathers. The curved shop windows of the Strand flashed black and gold with the movement of the clouds.

Between the street and the river stood a large, derelict hospital, its ancient brick halls open to the elements, gutted by fire two years earlier. Mendicants and Irish had moved in, and as I walked across the site, I saw men huddled around campfires, and women pegging washing strung between the ruined buildings.

I needed to rest. I needed to think. But I needed to see this first.

Following the directions Caesar John's man had given me, I walked down towards the river. Ahead was a large roofless hall, its blackened beams rising from the brickwork like a skeleton's ribcage. Outside it two men stood next to an oxcart, their staffs and greatcoats marking them out from the mendicants.

They challenged me as I approached. 'You can't go in there, sir. Orders of the Bow Street magistrate.'

'War Office business.' I waved my letters of credential. 'Show me, please.'

The interior of the hall was filled with rubble. I presumed this was why even the beggars had given it a wide berth. The remnants of a large fire smouldered in a spot that had been partially cleared of debris. More Bow Street Runners stood around it, gazing towards the roof. A man was hanging from one of the beams, over the fire.

Many of his injuries were familiar to me. His back laid open by the whip. His swollen, tortured hands tied behind him. John Monday's slave brand seared into his chest. His throat slashed.

The flames had reached halfway up the dead man's pendulous thighs, just below the point where they met the heavy rolls of his stomach. The skin of his legs was blackened, horrifically burned. I imagined him writhing and rolling on the rope, trying to raise his body above the flames. Moses Graham had died badly. I stared at his rictus mouth and bulging eyes, gripping my hands into fists to stop them trembling.

The Runners were trying to work out how to get him down, neither man inclined to climb up to the beam to cut the rope.

'When was he found?' I asked.

'This morning. A vagrant stumbled across him.' The man sounded uninterested, almost bored. 'From the smell of him, I'd say he's been up there a couple of days.'

'There were no witnesses? He can't have died quietly.'

'We asked around the camps. No one remembers seeing him. I suppose you wouldn't spot him in the dark. Probably a dispute between villains. A fight got out of hand.'

'This man was not a villain. He was a gentleman, an artist.'

He shrugged. 'Put a wig on them, it don't change their true nature. Violence is in their blood. Negroes are the descendants of Cain, you know. God stained his skin dark to punish him for the killing of his brother, Abel. Read your Bible, sir, it's all in there.'

I spoke quietly in an attempt to rein in my rage. 'He was one of the gentlest men I ever met.'

CHAPTER FIFTY-ONE

THE LOURING SKY matched my mood, as I rode home through the hot dusty streets. The gathering wind felt portentous, though I struggled to see how things could get worse. Every time I thought about that fire burning under Moses Graham, something stabbed inside me. I thought it likely my ribs were broken. Sweat rolled off me.

Outside my door, a large black-and-gold coach-and-six was drawn up. Beggarly children crowded around it, impressed by the footmen and the glossy black horses. The coachman flicked them with his whip when they strayed too close.

Pomfret met me in the hall. He had evidently grown tired of being surprised by my appearance, for he merely bowed. 'Mr Napier Smith is waiting for you in the drawing room, sir.'

Of course he was.

*

Napier Smith was standing, studying Caro's portrait. He appraised me fleetingly with his cold blue eyes. His youthful face was flushed with anger, and I remembered the Woolwich harbour master's words: *I wouldn't cross the Chairman of the West India lobby for all the sugar in Jamaica.*

I was too weary for niceties. 'What is it you want, Mr Smith?'

'Lucius Stokes tells me that you've been back to Deptford.

I've written to Nicholas Cavill-Lawrence to let him know. Disregarding your patron's orders – now that's a bold step. Taking that slave girl off my ship – I'd call that bold too.' He smiled coldly. 'You know, I've been trying to work out why you would do all this. Risk a glittering future for a man such as Archer. Finally, I think I understand.'

Blood pulsed behind my ears, a primal sense of warning.

Smith turned back to the portrait. 'A beautiful woman. If she were mine, I wouldn't leave her at home to go delving after dead men in Deptford. But perhaps you do not place as high a premium upon her worth as another man might.'

'I don't grasp your meaning, sir,' I said, though I feared I did.

'Don't you? We've been looking for a molly whom Archer trusted, someone from his past. I think that person was right under our noses all along.'

I like to think that I kept my nerve, that my voice didn't shake. I'm not sure I did. 'If you mean to imply what I think you do, then I will not dignify such an allegation with a response. Except to say that if you repeat it publicly, I will sue.'

Smith smacked his gloves against his hand, a duellist's slap. 'If proof exists then I will find it. And if it doesn't – well, perhaps I'll find it anyway.' He turned a circle, looking around the room as he did so. 'This house isn't yours, they tell me. Everything's in trust for your wife. Old Craven didn't have much faith in you as a son-in-law, eh? Good guess.' His eyes flicked back to me. 'You will cease your hunt for Archer's killer, or I'll take everything you have left. Your name. Your reputation. Your family's happiness. Oh, and I want the slave girl too. And a letter of apology for the temerity of your theft.'

It was one of those moments on which a man's future turns. On one side certain ruin. On the other a woman's life, a dead man's memory, and a gentleman's ability to live with himself. When put like that, my reply came readily enough.

'You asked me before if I supported abolition, Mr Smith. I lied. I support it entirely – with every sinew in my body, every rational thought I've given to the subject, every decent, human impulse I've ever had. Your trade disgusts me, sir. You and your friends disgust me. Now leave my house, before I have my footmen throw you out.'

*

I was still sitting there, several hours later, when Caro came home.

She stared at me. 'Oh, Harry. What have they done to your face?' She walked over and touched my cheek, the first time she'd done so in many months. 'You are a bonfire. I will send for Doctor Everett.'

'Please, won't you sit down? I must tell you something.'

Perhaps hearing some hint of my inner turmoil, she did as I asked.

'It's about Tad,' I said. 'He and I.'

She was holding herself tightly, and now she looked away. 'Do we really need to talk about Thaddeus now?'

'I'm afraid we do. Napier Smith came to the house earlier. He is unhappy about some of the things I've been doing in Deptford.' I stopped, drew a breath. 'He has made certain allegations about Tad, and now he threatens to draw me into them too. There is no truth to them, but I am not sure that will matter. I tell you this because I want you to consult a lawyer. Someone who can guide you on how best to shield yourself and Gabriel from any unpleasantness that will follow. I'll not take Gabriel from you. It is important that you know that.'

I readied myself for a salvo of questions, but her eyes were distant as oceans. Just when I was starting to wonder if she'd even heard, she spoke again: 'Did Thaddeus ever tell you that he came to my father's house to see me?'

I shook my head, confused. 'Came to see you when?'

'Not long before we were married. He was drunk and rather upset. I had to bribe the servants to ensure Father never heard of it. He'd come to tell me you didn't love me. That you loved somebody else and always had.'

I stared at her. 'That isn't true. I did love you. I do.'

I felt as if I was falling with no idea what was beneath me. The buzzing in my ears had stopped. I heard her very clearly, perhaps more clearly than I had ever done before.

'That's what I told him. He went away disappointed. I think he hoped I'd manufacture some reason to break off our engagement.'

For once I could read the hurt in her eyes, understood it. 'But you believed him.'

She stared intently at the portrait over the fire, the happier Caro.

'So why didn't you?' I said hoarsely. 'Break off our engagement, I mean.'

'Because I'd fought so hard to have you. I'd used up all my capital with Father, and I didn't want to have to marry the manner of man he'd have chosen for me. Sometimes all our choices wear cruel faces. This was one such time. Nor would I give Thaddeus the satisfaction.'

I wasn't falling, but sinking. The shadow of *The Dark Angel* above. The depths below full of shipwrecks, so many ghosts. Many things suddenly made sense to me, and I wondered that I hadn't seen it before. Her distance before the wedding, which I'd put down to nerves. The spectre that had always lain between us in the marital bed.

'I regret that he caused you pain – more than you can know. He had no right to do that.'

She was silent a long moment. 'Does Napier Smith have any proof of his suspicions?'

'There is no proof. I told you. It isn't true. But he implied he would falsify proof if necessary.' *And if he talked to Nathaniel . . .* The thought made me recoil.

She rose from the sofa and took a turn about the room, something she did when she wanted to think more clearly. She stopped in front of the window, a black silhouette against the glare. I couldn't read her expression.

'I don't want a divorce or a separation, Harry. Nor do I want a scandal. I want Gabriel to grow up proud to be your son. If Smith means to destroy you, then we must make the consequences unpalatable to him. He is a man of business. Let him see the debit side.'

Something about that 'we' touched me inexpressibly. My voice thickened. 'Hurt a man like Smith? I'm not sure we can.'

'Will you tell me about it – Deptford? Thaddeus's murder?'

We talked for several hours, long after the light had faded and she called for candles. Caro had always been a good listener, and she saved her questions until the end. I left out only Nathaniel. Everything else we discussed and sifted. The strangeness of it all did not escape me. We were like two allied generals advancing towards a common enemy, with only ancient treaties to define us. Gradually a strategy took shape and gathered form.

Our plan was not without risk, but we both agreed that it might work. From the theory, came the means, came the method. At one point she paused to pour more wine, and I felt compelled to speak. Not out of expectation, nor even hope, but because I needed to hear her say it.

'This ship on which we sail – is there truly no way of righting her?'

I saw from her expression that she understood we were no longer talking about Smith and his threats – but about Carlisle House, about young viscounts, and separate rooms.

Her smile contained worlds: intimacy and distance, anger and absolution, defiance and regret. 'It is the curse of the Cravens to want it all. If we don't have it, we feel compelled to go out and find it. Nothing's perfect, Harry. I understand that now. We simply have to make the best of the cards we've drawn.'

Chapter Fifty-Two

WE MET IN St James's Park. Ladies and gentlemen were strolling the lime walks. Soldiers drilled on the grass. An old woman was selling milk, still warm from her red cow. Idling apprentices made eyes at whores they couldn't afford. My patron, Nicholas Cavill-Lawrence, Under-Secretary of State for War, gazed inscrutably at one of the girls.

'I cannot imagine what you think we have to say to one another. I only agreed to this meeting for Caro's sake. Did you ever stop to think of her? She valued our friendship. I did too.'

Caro had said he would start like this – ramble on about loyalty first – she said he liked to believe he was the stripe of man who cared about such things. I waited for him to talk himself out.

'The ministry's borough-mongers have withdrawn your funding for the by-election. I hear the West India lobby are planning to stand a candidate against you. If I were you, I'd withdraw now. Save yourself the embarrassment. I'd like you to clear your desk at the War Office by the end of the week.'

I heard the news distantly, as if it had happened to someone else. Someone with whom I was acquainted, but didn't like very much.

'I understand, sir. I won't seek to change your mind. Yet I must ask for your help with one small matter. Not for my sake,

350

for Caro's. Napier Smith plans to slander my reputation with lies that would hurt her and Gabriel.'

'What did you expect?' His expression didn't soften. 'You're hardly helping yourself. Smith says that even after all of this, you intend to return to Deptford.'

'I do.'

'Have you identified the killer yet?'

'No, but I will.'

'And the missing papers? Any trace of those?'

'They are in Deptford, I'm sure of it. Archer took possession of them the day before he died.'

My answer, whilst equivocal, was not nearly so interesting as the question. Napier Smith hadn't asked about the contracts when he'd come to my house yesterday, but then perhaps they were only of secondary importance to him. Not, I felt, to Cavill-Lawrence.

He took a silk handkerchief from his pocket, and mopped the sweat from his grey, lined brow. 'I cannot help you. It is unfortunate for Caro that she married a man so hell-bent upon his family's unhappiness. Yet she has made her bed. It isn't my place to ameliorate the cost of her decisions. Nor the cost of yours.'

Caro had said that this would be his answer. I almost smiled.

I watched him walk off down one of the paths that bordered the canal, heading in the direction of St. James's. As he passed the old woman and her cow, a short muscular African in a red hat detached himself from the group queuing for milk. He turned fleetingly, and our eyes met, though we made no acknowledgement. The scars on his face caught the light, as he fell into step behind Cavill-Lawrence.

*

The roads east of Southwark High Street, beyond Thomas Guy's hospital, were narrow and airless. Most of the houses were half-timbered survivors of an earlier London, home to workers on the cotton and wine wharves that lined this stretch of the Thames. I wasn't due to reconvene with Caesar John until later that evening, and so I'd walked down here, breathing in the rich odours of the river and its industries.

Tooley Street was thronged with workers from the tanneries and foundries, calling out to one another in their salty, riverside tongue. They weren't heading home to their wives, but to the many bear gardens, theatres, bagnios and gaming houses that drew visitors south of the river.

Outside the Southwark Commedia a sign advertised a production of *The Tempest*. A pair of gaudily painted women, rouged nipples peeking over the tops of their stays, were sharing a pipe, watched over by a surly doorman. They tried to entice me inside, and I retreated a short distance to study the playbill I'd found in Frank Drake's pocket on the ship.

The hand-drawn map on the reverse contained no street names, nor any writing at all. I took it as further proof of Drake's illiteracy. It was clearly supposed to depict London – I could tell by the sweep of the river, the position of the bridge, and the dome of St Paul's. The playbill advertised a production of Sheridan, held last month at this same theatre, which was marked on the map with an X. A second location nearby was also marked with an X, and I wanted to find out what it was.

Following the route on the map, I walked down a couple of side streets, heading away from the river. Eventually, I came to the road on which the X was marked. The street was lined with shops selling dusty vegetables, old furniture and clothes, as well as a tavern. On the map, these buildings were depicted by little squares. Two of the squares were annotated with symbols: a fish and three balls. The building marked with the X lay between them.

I walked along the street until I came to a pawnbroker's. Two properties down was a fish market, and between them a masonry yard. The sign above the yard read: *JM Law, Quarried stone, slate and marble.* I stood back to allow a covered wagon to enter the gates, then followed it through.

A mason was squaring off blocks of stone in the yard with a rock-hammer. Other men ran to unload the wagon. To the side of the yard, outside a low building, two gentlemen stood talking. A large brown dog was chained up outside the building, and it barked as I approached.

'Mr Law?'

'Who wants to know?'

The man who had spoken was slovenly in dress, his wig and stockings yellowed. Masonry dust covered his shoulders like dandruff. His skin had a pink, hard-boiled shine, little piggy eyes peering at me over a receding upper lip. He aimed a kick at the dog. 'God's blood, Caligula, be quiet.'

'Captain Henry Corsham.' I bowed.

'Jacob Law. You want stone or a mason?'

'Neither. I'm making inquiries about a man named Frank Drake, a Deptford sailor. I think you may have had some dealings with him here?'

Law spat a lump of phlegm into the dust. 'Don't know the name.'

'Let me describe him.' As I did so, I saw his bearing stiffen.

'Send you here, did he?' His eyes had narrowed to a squint.

'I'm afraid he's dead.' I held up a silver crown. 'Can you tell me about the business you had together?'

He knocked the coin from my hand with his fist, eliciting a fresh round of barking from Caligula. 'I said I don't know him, you stupid, deaf cunny. Now get out of here before I set my dog on you.'

I thought about the significance of this encounter for many hours afterwards. When the answer finally came to me, I thought of Peregrine Child. For the first time, I believed, I properly understood the part he'd played in Tad's murder and the events that followed. I felt anger, but also satisfaction.

Chapter Fifty-Three

THE DRUM OF Zephyrus's hooves upon the highway echoed inside my skull. Each vibration sent fresh agonies through my body. Caro had sent for the physician last night and he had strapped up my ribs, yet they still skewered my insides every time I moved or coughed, as I seemed to be doing with increasing frequency. My fever hadn't abated. I was hot as Lucifer.

Caro had begged me to wait before returning to Deptford. Yet, conscious that *The Dark Angel* would be sailing any day now, I had insisted. She and I had parted on distant terms. Perhaps, like me, she'd thought she should say more, but hadn't been able to find the words. Gabriel had waved to me from the window. When I come back, I thought, I'm never leaving you again.

I'd returned to the Yorkshire Stingo late last night. One of Caesar John's men had driven me across town, blindfolded once more, to the sponging house. There I'd found Cinnamon and Caesar John.

Cinnamon was sitting on the floor, wrapped in a blanket, a little way apart from the other runaways. She didn't look up, or otherwise acknowledge me, seemingly lost within herself. Bronze, the tapwoman from the Stingo, was making soup for the slaves. Caesar John took me into one of the other rooms.

'Well,' I said. 'Where did he go?'

'Piccadilly. At first I thought he was heading to one of the gentlemen's clubs, but he was paying a house call.'

Caesar John described a large, elegant mansion on the park-side of Piccadilly. I knew it well. Everyone did. I had once met the duke who owned it at Carlisle House.

'Mr Cavill-Lawrence seemed to be known there,' Caesar John went on. 'He was inside nearly three hours. After about an hour, a number of other visitors arrived in fine carriages.'

'Did you see who was inside them?'

'No, but I bribed one of the footmen for the names.' He handed me a list. The names were all, without exception, famil-iar to me. One Member of Parliament, one judge of the King's Bench, two peers of the realm, one not-so-distant relative of the King of England.

'I think you just met *The Dark Angel*'s syndicate,' I said.

***

Before I left the sponging house, I sat with Cinnamon. Hollow-cheeked and hollow-eyed, she pressed a finger against the bruises on her wrists while we talked.

'I return to Deptford tomorrow morning,' I said. 'Before I go, I need to ask you about the obeah. Were you the one behind it?'

She gave that strange smile again. 'It wasn't I.'

'Do you know who it was?'

'I only know who it was not.'

'I don't understand.'

'It isn't real.'

I remembered Jago's head in the flames. 'It looked real enough to me.'

'That is because you know nothing of obeah.' She licked her cracked lips. 'Neither does the person doing this. Maybe they've read or heard a few things. Birds and bones, yes. But rats, cats, dogs … It isn't real.'

*

'I say, sir, are you all right?' The ferryman's voice cut through my thoughts. 'You look rather pale.'

'I am perfectly fine.' The Rotherhithe horseferry had docked on the south bank of the river. Clouds black as Cinnamon's bruises scudded across the sallow sky. I mounted Zephyrus, still thinking about what she had told me.

The Africans had known, I thought, remembering Jamaica Mary's smile – but they'd kept silent, enjoying the terror of the slave ship sailors. Someone had wanted to put the fear of God into them. Someone white.

*

My farewells in the sponging house had varied in length, but were consistent in theme.

Bronze gave me a look that said 'damn fool'.

Cinnamon offered me only a little more. She clutched my arm. 'Don't go back. It is dangerous in that place.'

'I need to find the man who killed my friend, Mr Archer.'

She nodded, biting her lip. 'Please, tell no one where I am.'

'Even Scipio?' I told her how I'd never have got her off the ship without his help. 'I know he feels very badly about what happened that night at the villa.'

'No.' She said it forcefully. 'I want nobody from Deptford to know where I am. Promise me, please, say you won't.'

I could hardly blame her for mistrusting him. 'Then I will tell no one.'

I gave Caesar John ten guineas. 'This is for the girl. If I don't come back, see that you find her a good lawyer. You should be careful too. Moses Graham will have told the killer everything. He'll know that you know about *The Dark Angel*.'

'I can look after myself.' Caesar John cocked his head, examining my bruises. 'Sure you can?'

'I have so far.'

He smiled, unconvinced. 'Sit down a moment.'

'What is it?'

'I want to tell you a story about a slave I once knew.'

Caesar John didn't strike me as a man for stories. Nor was I inclined to hear one right now. Yet I was dependent on his goodwill for Cinnamon's welfare.

'This slave was born here in London,' he said, once we'd taken seats by the fire. 'His mother was a slave to a West India planter. He was taken from her when he was just five years old, and sold to a new master, who made a present of the boy to his lady wife. The lad was fine-looking and the lady made a pet of him. She dressed him up in a velvet suit and educated him alongside her own children. Sometimes she sat him on her lap, and fed him sweetmeats. In time he forgot his mother. The love of his mistress was all that mattered.'

I thought of Ben, my childhood companion. A little boy, plucked from his home. He'd found happiness of a sort with us, until it was torn from him once again.

'As the boy grew older and less pretty, the lady's manner towards him changed. She called him stupid and clumsy and sometimes she would strike him. When he was thirteen years old, he tried to run away, but he was caught.'

Caesar John played with his toothpick as he talked, turning it round in his fingers. 'He expected his mistress to be angry, but the fact that he no longer wished to live with her seemed to chasten her. She told him she was sorry, and much of her old affection returned. When he cried with relief, she stroked his hair. She asked her footmen to bring a brazier, so they might roast sugared cobnuts together as they'd used to. They laughed and ate the nuts, and his resentment receded. Then she clapped her hands, and announced that he had yet to be punished. He saw a look in her eyes that frightened him, and he tried again to run. Her footmen caught him, and dragged him back. The lady herself pushed his face down onto the brazier.' Caesar John's fingers worked the raised ridges of his cheek.

'Some months later, another black servant, seeing how he was mistreated, whispered to him the name of Thaddeus Archer. The boy managed to get a message to his chambers, and Archer came to the house that same day. He was armed with an injunction from a court, and he took the boy under his protection.' His shrewd brown eyes met mine. 'I know what it is to owe Thaddeus Archer.'

I smiled. 'Do I take it there's a lesson here somewhere?'

'Stay alive, that's the lesson.' Caesar John stabbed the air with his toothpick. 'Archer was brave and principled. He is also dead.'

*

I rode on towards Deptford, my mind a whirl of disconnected thoughts, trying to see the patterns that emerged. The obeah. The threatening letters. Monday's slave brand. The silver ticket. Amelia's murder. Stokes and the missing contracts.

I was running up that hill again, Tad the chalk man at its zenith. My leg moved as freely as it had before Saratoga. I put on a burst of speed and crested the rise, the sun brighter than a thousand stars. I spun him around laughing, but his countenance was sombre.

Don't you ever heed anyone's advice? Go home.

Follow your own path, I thought that was your motto?

Mine, not yours. You're the one who always cared what people thought.

I wish I'd cared less, Tad. I really do.

A ghost of a smile. *If wishes were wine, Hal, I'd never be sober.*

I'm getting close to him now. I know I am. I can feel him, but I can't quite see him.

He can see you. He's watched you from the first. And he'll come for you, just like he came for me.

CHAPTER FIFTY-FOUR

※

THE PORTER AT Lucius Stokes's gate refused to admit me at first. His pinched face twitched with agitation.

'I don't care what you were told,' I said, twisting Zephyrus's reins around my fist. 'Tell your master I have made an important discovery in my search for Archer's killer. He'll see me.'

I was counting upon Stokes's curiosity. Only lately had I begun to understand how important my inquiry was to Deptford's mayor.

When the porter returned, he had Abraham with him. He unlocked the gate, and the footman escorted me up to the house.

Stokes was in his study, standing over his model of the dock, adjusting some part of it that was not to his liking. 'He returns. A thief in the night,' he said. 'That girl was my property, sir. Give me one good reason why I shouldn't summon Child to lock you up.'

'It would be unlawful imprisonment for a start. I had an injunction from a magistrate.'

His face darkened. 'You owe me fifty guineas, sir.'

Examining his countenance, I decided his anger was genuine. It was about the only thing that was, aside from his love of his dock. Everything for Lucius Stokes began and ended there.

'Frank Drake didn't kill Thaddeus Archer,' I said.

'We have a suicide note that says differently.'

'It is forged. Drake couldn't have killed him. I'll soon be able to prove it.'

Stokes waved a hand. 'Child is to convene a coroner's court to discuss Drake's suicide and the murders. You are welcome to say your piece there, if you dispute his culpability.'

'I expect you're counting upon me to do just that.'

He frowned, straightening his cuffs. I caught a waft of his civet scent. 'What is this nonsense, sir? I don't have all day. You said you had made an important discovery relating to the murders?'

'Yes, I have learned the whereabouts of the contracts Mr Archer had stolen from Mr Monday.'

'Oh, where are they?'

'Right here in this study, I should think. Sometimes the simplest explanations are also the most likely. Ockham's Razor. Peregrine Child told me that. You had Archer's room at the Noah's Ark searched the morning after his murder. That was where Child and Scipio found the contracts and they brought them here to you.'

He laughed. 'Had I found those contracts, I'd have given them to Napier Smith.'

'I have a theory about why you decided to keep them. Perhaps you'd like to hear it?'

'It would be a waste of both our time, so I think not.'

'Perhaps I'll try my theory out on Napier Smith? I think he would be interested to hear it. Or perhaps you'd like to listen after all?'

He didn't respond, and I took it as an invitation to continue.

'It's quite simple really. You wanted the West India lobby's support for your dock, but you were starting to fear you wouldn't get it. When Archer was murdered, you sensed an opportunity: those missing contracts.'

'Preposterous,' Stokes said, but his voice lacked his earlier conviction.

'You needed *The Dark Angel*'s massacre to become a public scandal, because otherwise those contracts would be no use to you. Had I not returned to Deptford, doubtless you'd have found some other way. Yet you didn't need to, for I was intent upon doing it for you.'

I was seeing a lot of puzzling events in a new light. 'You couldn't be seen to be working against the West India lobby, but that's precisely what you were doing. I thought you were my enemy, yet all along you were my secret ally. You were hostile in public and private. You had Monday throw me out of his house. You sent those men to my room to beat me, and I imagine you told the West India lobby what you'd done, posing as their faithful servant. Yet you ordered Child to keep an eye on me, and make sure I wasn't killed. You delayed telling Monday my real identity, so I could make progress, and you twice delayed telling Napier Smith that I was in Deptford. You also instructed Scipio to help me. He did, you'll be pleased to know.'

Stokes reached out a hand to right a fallen model of a Guineaman, placing it gently at anchor on his plaster waves.

'You see, if I found the murderer and prosecuted him, the investors behind that voyage, men of wealth and influence, would be desperate to keep their names out of it. The sole means to do so would lie within your hands. What price would you demand for the return of those contracts?' My eye fell upon the model of his dock. 'It isn't hard to guess. If I explain all this to Napier Smith, I think he'll appreciate the reasoning behind it.'

The room was silent except for the ticking of a clock.

'Or we could continue to be secret allies. You give me those contracts, in exchange for my silence. It makes a lot of sense, when you think about it. You were prepared to gamble the future of your trade against the future of your town. Your private interest against that of your brother merchants. Mr Smith is unforgiving when he's crossed, I have discovered that myself. This way we both get to protect ourselves.'

Risk and reward. That's what it came down to in the end. Stokes displayed no emotion. He ran a hand through his thick powdered hair. Then he crossed to a mahogany bureau between the windows, and unlocked it with a key from his pocket. He returned with a sheaf of papers in his hand.

I leafed through them. Seven contracts, each signed by Monday and one of the syndicate. The Duke, the five visitors to his Piccadilly mansion, and the seventh: Nicholas Cavill-Lawrence.

'They are wrong,' Stokes said. 'The West India lobby are a bunch of old women, and they always were. There will be a scandal, but it will be short-lived. People will forget. They won't waste their pity upon a boatload of Negroes halfway across the world. Pounds, shillings and pence, that's what will count at the end of the day. The price of tobacco, the price of sugar. Nothing more.'

I tucked the contracts inside my coat, giving him a last considered glance. 'No,' I said. 'They are right, and you are wrong.'

*

I stabled Zephyrus at the coaching inn on Deptford Broadway, then walked down to the Strand. I stood for a time on the dock, watching black clouds roll in off the water. The air was heavy, and I felt the first pricks of rain. *The Dark Angel* lay out on the Reach, the winged woman's austere gaze cast over Deptford. I would go to her again later, after dark.

I hired another boat from the same yard I'd visited before.

Then I walked along the quay, turning my collar up against the rain. The sky trembled with a distant rumble of thunder.

The wharves were quieter because of the rain, only the stevedores out in force. Heads down, loading and unloading. I reached the warehouse where Nathaniel had taken me the other night, trying not to recall his nakedness, his lies.

I rattled the warehouse doors, and found them secure. From what Nathaniel had told me, I knew no one would be in there during the day. A passing stevedore shot me a suspicious glance, and I decided against going in the front. I walked round the side, looking for another way in.

In an alley round the back I found another door, also locked. I knelt in front of it, taking a slim leather roll from my pocket. It had been lent to me by Caesar John, and his men had spent the better part of an hour schooling me in the use of the tools inside.

Picking a lock, with guidance, in the warmth and safety of the sponging house, proved a different proposition to doing so here, out in the open. The lock was old and rusting, but I still made hard work of it. The rain ran down my face and froze my fingers. After about fifteen minutes, during which time I tried different sizes of pick, I felt something spring, and when I tried the door, it opened.

Immediately, I was hit by the foul stench inside. It was much stronger than it had been three days ago. I walked further into the warehouse, trying to ascertain where it was coming from. The smell was strongest at a point beneath the office stairs. A pile of old pallets and crates were stacked there, and flies swarmed around them. I swatted them from my face. A large tarpaulin lay on the floor behind the crates, covering something large and soft and heavy.

Steeling myself, I drew my sword, and used it to flick the

tarpaulin back. A thick cloud of flies rose up, and I stepped back, covering my mouth. Filled with revulsion, I stared down at the body lying there.

He had plainly been dead some time, the flesh rotten, writhing with maggots. The cause of death was decapitation, flies feasting thickly upon the blood. The corpse of Jago, Nathaniel Grimshaw's dog.

CHAPTER FIFTY-FIVE

THE RAIN WAS coming down harder now, the light eerie, a tobacco sky. I sheltered in the archway leading to the stable-yard of the Noah's Ark, until I caught sight of the stable boy. I whistled, and he came to meet me, looking wary.

'Mistress said I wasn't to talk to you no more.'

I held up a penny. 'Can you give this note to Master Grimshaw?'

Greed worked its magic as it so often did in Deptford. My note asked Nathaniel to meet me at the coaching inn up in the Broadway. No doubt his own greed would bring him running.

By the time I reached the Broadway, the rain was coming down in sheets. The High Street was a torrent, people running for cover. I noticed Mr and Mrs Monday hurrying by on the other side. They were followed by the mulatto boy, the little girl, and a black footman with an umbrella. Mrs Monday spotted me, and put her hand on her husband's arm. The boy saw me too, and gave me a frank, curious stare. They hurried on.

I glanced up at Brabazon's rain-washed window and saw a blurred figure behind the glass. He drew back, but I'd seen him, just as he'd seen me.

I heard someone calling my name and looked around. It was Scipio, running across the road to meet me. He raised his voice over the rain.

'Abraham told me you were back. You saved her. Was she hurt?'

I remembered Cinnamon's bruises, that silent stare. 'Only a little. She is safe now.'

'Thank the Lord.' He wiped the moisture from his face, the rain pouring from his hat. 'Stokes has dismissed me. He guessed I told you about Cinnamon.'

'I'm sorry.' I meant it. None of this was his fault – not really.

'I don't regret it. I couldn't have her upon my conscience too.'

'What will you do now?'

'Try to find another post in Deptford, though I don't expect it will be easy. Mr Stokes is dedication itself when it comes to a grudge. If I can't, I'll go to London. Try to find a post there. Hope I don't end up like those drunks in the Yorkshire Stingo.' He smiled sadly. 'Perhaps I will look up Miss Cinnamon. Do you know where I can find her?'

I felt awkward. 'I'm sorry. She doesn't want anyone to know where she is.'

His smile faded. 'I need to make my peace with her.'

'That is her choice, don't you think? You can't blame her for mistrusting you.'

He didn't answer and I could sense his pain. I spoke more gently: 'You were your own man when it mattered. I'll make sure she knows it. Perhaps in time she might change her mind.'

He stared into the rain, looking tired, suddenly older. 'There's something else I came to tell you. You asked me last time we met what Mr Stokes discussed at John Monday's house the night Archer was killed. Abraham accompanied our master there, and overheard his argument with Peregrine Child afterwards. It seems it was Eleanor Monday who summoned them there, not her husband. She told them Captain Vaughan was being kept on board *The Dark Angel* and that Archer knew this.'

'That was my suspicion too.' I frowned. 'John Monday wasn't there?'

'Apparently he'd left the house earlier with Mr Brabazon.'

Then Eleanor had been lying about his alibi. 'Do you know why she told them this?'

'She was worried someone would get hurt. Abraham said Child wanted to go to *The Dark Angel*, but Stokes wouldn't let him.'

'Why didn't Stokes tell you this before, so you could tell me?'

'He would have been implicating himself. He and Child knew a murder was likely to take place, and did nothing to prevent it.'

It made sense, and yet Scipio might have other motives for wanting me to suspect John Monday. I thought of the mulatto boy; Scipio gazing after Mrs Monday in the stable-yard.

'When did you first come to Deptford, Scipio?'

He looked surprised by the question. 'In the winter of '74. Why do you ask?'

Then he couldn't be the father. The child was at least nine, if not older. 'Nothing. Just a foolish idea I had.' Reassured as to his motives, I held out my card. 'Call on me if you come to London. I may be able to help you find a new position.'

He didn't take it at first, and I wondered if he was moved by the gesture. Perhaps he simply doubted that I'd make it back to London alive. Then he pocketed the card, and we shook hands.

He walked off down the High Street, and I watched until he was swallowed by the mist and the rain. A man who lived each day beneath the shadow of the slave ship's mast.

*

In the taproom of the coaching inn, I took a seat near to the fire, where I sat steaming. The place was packed with merchants using the excuse of the rain to get drunk. I noticed Peregrine Child sitting alone, a bottle of wine in front of him. He studiously avoided looking in my direction.

Nathaniel Grimshaw arrived half an hour later. He was out of breath, his face flushed, his eyes bright. He plainly thought it was all within his grasp: the reprieve from slavery for which he'd debased himself and others.

'Well, Captain Corsham,' he said, seating himself opposite me. 'Do you have it?'

'No, Nathaniel. I have not brought you any money.'

It was almost cruel to watch the destruction of his hopes. His head jerked, and his breathing quickened. That hard, flinty look came into those soft green eyes. 'I notice Mr Child sitting over there. Why don't we see what he has to say about that night we spent together at the warehouse? I'll tell him how you held me down. Made me touch you.'

'Yes,' I said wearily. 'Why don't we? While we're about it, we could take him down to the warehouse, and show him what's underneath that tarpaulin of yours.'

Rarely had a face undergone so much metamorphosis in such a short time. His mouth went slack, and he made an odd noise in his throat. 'What tarpaulin?'

Nathaniel might have been adept at concealing his true motives, but when taken by surprise, he was still the world's worst liar.

'It was well thought out, I'll give you that. You might have made a fine attorney with a mind that devious. I'm guessing it went like this. You knew something about obeah – from your father, I suppose – and so you decided to fashion a little play: the slaves' revenge. You left the dead birds and those other offerings at the houses of the *The Dark Angel*'s sailors. It was probably you who spread the rumour the ship was cursed. You left offerings at your own house, so you wouldn't be suspected. I think that's what you were doing that night your mother saw Scipio, and you turned on him in the stable-yard. You also told Child you'd seen two African footmen running away to cast the blame elsewhere. Your plan worked, when the ship's crew refused to serve on her. Vaughan went mad, and you were granted a temporary reprieve from slavery. You took advantage of the delay to extort money from frightened men, so that you could pay off your mother's debts, and be spared slaving altogether. I'm afraid that's the part I can't forgive.'

Nathaniel narrowed his eyes, his defiance not quite spent. 'You think I killed my own dog? You're touched in the head.'

'Yes, I do. I imagine all my questions about the obeah scared you, and you were determined to put me off the scent. You were probably saving the dog's carcass for a repeat performance.'

I could almost hear the cogitations of his mind as he rethought his strategy. 'I'd have had to get rid of Jago anyway, if I'd gone slaving.' He licked his lips. 'But who's going to listen to you? Especially when I tell them how much you wanted my soft white arse. The mayor doesn't like you, and Child does what he's told. They'll both want to believe me.'

'I'm afraid the mayor and I have reached an accommodation. If Child does do what he's told, then it won't be to your benefit. Should you proceed with your allegations, I will tell everyone in Deptford about the obeah. I'll also sue you for defamation and buy the judge. If that doesn't ruin you, I will buy up your mother's debts and foreclose. You need to understand what you're dealing with, Nathaniel. The only person who risks ruin here is you.'

I willed him to accept it. My tone softened a little. 'You didn't want to end up like your father and Frank Drake, I understand that. But there has to be another way. Not this.'

His words came out in an angry, choking sob: 'If there was another way, don't you think that I'd have found it?'

He rose from the table, and I watched anxiously to see if he'd go over to Child. Yet he only stormed from the tavern, banging the door behind him.

CHAPTER FIFTY-SIX

NOTHING NOW STOOD between the killer and I, except my own ability to see the truth. I bought an ale, and then walked over to join Peregrine Child.

'May I?'

'I'm too drunk to stop you.'

I saw the truth of it in his glassy gaze, his flat, mottled face.

'You came back,' he said. 'Death or glory. I salute you.'

'Did you think I wouldn't?'

He ran his tongue over his wine-stained teeth. 'Hoping is different to thinking.'

'I know you've been taking Stokes's orders from the start. First he made you stand by while Archer was murdered. Then he made you protect me so I could solve the crime. Your head must have been spinning.'

He shrugged. 'I like my job. I wanted to keep it.'

'Why did you keep telling me to leave town? That wasn't what Stokes wanted.'

'You didn't know what you were mixed up in, did you?' He screwed up his eyes as the landlord lit the lamps against the gathering gloom. 'If my days in Deptford have taught me any-thing, it's that when a rich old bastard like Lucius Stokes gets clever, the rest of us had better run for cover. If I dance upon his strings, at least I choose to do so. You had no idea.'

'Is that why you went to the archive? Were you trying to work out Stokes's game?'

'It made no sense to me. Usually it does. I didn't like it.'

'Then there's Frank Drake. For a long time, I thought you were protecting a guilty man.'

'I wasn't. I did try to tell you.'

'Yes, you were. He just wasn't guilty of the crime I thought he was. Drake had dealings with a masonry and quarrying yard down in Southwark. I went there yesterday. The owner claimed never to have heard of him, but he was lying. I couldn't think what business they might have had together, until I remembered the theft of gunpowder from the Navy Yard. It was the same night Archer was killed. I think you knew he was innocent of the murder, because you knew what he was really doing. How much did Drake pay you to turn a blind eye?'

Child called to the serving girl to bring another bottle. Very slowly and deliberately, he filled his glass, and drank it off in two gulps. 'I imagine you look at Deptford, and see a midden of crime and corruption, but you don't know what it was like here before my watch. I keep the thieves out of the warehouses, I stop the dockside feuds from spiralling, and if a woman's husband gets too free with his fists, she knows she can come to me. Laws are just ink on a piece of paper. You can enforce the letter, not the spirit. Or you can do it the other way around. I take a fraction of the bribes of my predecessors, and I never lock up men I know to be innocent. I don't say it's perfect. I don't deal in absolutes.'

'And Drake?'

He was silent a moment. 'Drake was different.'

'Because he was your dead wife's brother?'

He filled his glass, drank it down. For another long moment he said nothing, and I thought he was going to close up on me again, but then he spoke: 'Drake got to me at a bad time – just after Liz and our child died. I'd not been magistrate very long, only a year. I let Drake off a crime I shouldn't have – a woman died, he said it was an accident. Perhaps I felt I couldn't judge, I don't know. Anyway, it tied us together. I couldn't ever send him down for anything after that, because if he was facing a hanging, he had nothing to lose by peaching on me.'

I felt as if he was telling me this because he wanted me to understand him, because he didn't want me to lump him in with Stokes and Drake and all the rest.

'That night Mrs Monday summoned you to her house,' I said. 'She thought either her husband or Brabazon was going to kill Archer. Which one of them was it?'

'I don't know. I don't want to know.'

Brabazon must have gone straight to his dinner in Greenwich after he'd left Monday's house, but he could have gone to the ship afterwards. I only had his word that he'd called in on Daniel Waterman – and Waterman was dead. But Monday had no alibi either. One or the other – or both together? Captain Vaughan would know – assuming he was still alive. So many of the answers lay on that ship.

'I liked Archer, you know,' Child said. 'He had spirit. Funny too. And he didn't give a fuck who told him no. I respected that.'

I took the silver ticket from my pocket and put it on the table between us. 'When I showed you this ticket before, I think you recognized it.'

He made no move to touch it. Nor would he look at me. He just stared at the ticket, and seemed to supress a shudder. 'There is a house near Greenwich, on the outskirts of Lee, outside my jurisdiction. The owner pays off the magistrate, so they never have trouble. You take that ticket there, you'll see what I mean.' He described the house and gave me directions to it.

'Why didn't you tell me this before? Stokes wanted you to help me.'

'I didn't see what it could have to do with any of this. And I wanted nothing to do with that place – I never did.'

'Is it a brothel?' His squeamishness was as uncharacteristic as his reticence.

'I wouldn't call it that. Look, go there, if you must, but just know this: I didn't let them set up shop in Deptford. They offered me a lot of money, but I didn't take it. Believe me on that, Captain Corsham, if nothing else.'

Glancing at my watch, I calculated that I could make it to Lee in less than half an hour. Assuming my inquiries there didn't take too long, I could be back in Deptford to go to *The Dark Angel* later tonight.

'I heard you took Stokes's Negress off that ship,' Child said. 'I am glad of it. Will you tell her I'm sorry I couldn't help her?'

I frowned. 'She came to you?'

'Not this time. The last time. The day before Archer was killed. She came to the watchhouse, crying, saying Stokes was going to send her to his Caribbean plantations. She wanted an injunction. Archer had explained the law to her.'

I stared at him. 'Stokes was going to send her away before?'

'Aye, like I said.'

That was what Cinnamon had meant, I realized, when she'd said that it would have been too late for Archer to take her to London. Another day, and she'd have been aboard a Guineaman.

'Why was Stokes sending her away? Why did he change his mind?'

'She was on that ship when the slaves were drowned. The West India lobby didn't want her in England. They were worried she might tell Archer what she knew. After Archer was killed, Stokes convinced them to let her stay.'

I saw the logic in what he was saying. Now my inquiry must have unnerved the lobby again, and the order to send her away had been reinstated.

'But she doesn't know anything.' I closed my eyes, correcting myself. 'She doesn't think she knows anything.'

Child didn't seem to be listening. 'I told her I couldn't help her. It might be the law, but this was Deptford. The look she gave me . . . Will you tell her? That I'm sorry, I mean.'

I glanced at him distractedly. 'Yes, of course.'

Child poured himself another glass, and raised it to an absent host. *'Feci quod potui, faciant meliora potentes.'*

I have done what I could, let those who can do better.

CHAPTER FIFTY-SEVEN

I RODE SOUTH, skirting Greenwich, towards Lee. Blackheath was notorious for highwaymen, and I kept one hand on my pistol. The rain drove harder, the wind stripping leaves and twigs from the trees, hurling them against my face. The road was a bog, and I was forced to check Zephyrus's stride several times. Often, I could hardly see the road ahead of me. As I rode into Lee, thunder seemed to cleave the sky.

Dark brick houses behind ivied walls were shuttered against the elements. Following Child's directions, I rode through the village and out the other side, emerging into open countryside once more. Forks of lightning lit up the fields for miles around. I glimpsed cottages and barns, manor houses and windmills. Then everything was plunged into darkness again, and little was visible through the rain. Another flash, and in the distance I saw the house Child had described. A mock castle in the Gothic style, a crenellation of battlements and turrets against the thin blue sky.

I reined in Zephyrus at the gate and dismounted. Tipping my hat to pour off the rain, I rang the bell. A servant, bundled up in a greatcoat, carrying a lantern on a pole, came out of the lodge and stuck his hand through the bars of the gate. I passed him a coin, but he frowned, shaking his wrist. I took it back, confused, before I realized what he wanted. Then I placed Tad's silver ticket in his hand. He peered at it, smiled, and unlocked the gate.

In the courtyard, he took Zephyrus from me, handing me over to a burly footman, who had emerged from the house. 'Come inside, sir,' the footman said, with a wink. 'We'll soon warm you up.'

I walked up the steps to the front door, which was flanked by stone griffins. In the hall, I stood dripping on a Persian carpet, while the footman fetched towels. The air was impregnated with scents of orange, clove and cinnamon. A door opened, and a tall woman in a grey silk dress came forward to greet me. She was perhaps fifty years old, in the autumn of her beauty, with streaks of silver in her black piled hair.

'Good evening, sir.' She held out her hand for me to kiss. 'Welcome to the House of Lilies.'

I started to introduce myself, but she cut me off. 'No names, sir.' Her smile was coquettish. 'Only the fairest blooms you've ever seen.'

Once I had dried off, I followed the woman into a large parlour. I was offered a seat by the fire, and furnished with a glass of champagne. A few other gentlemen sat around singly or in pairs.

'Your timing is exquisite, sir,' our hostess said. 'I was just about to call the girls.' She crossed to a mahogany sideboard, and rang a bell.

I heard a patter of light footsteps on a staircase, and then a procession of girls filed into the room. Each wore a gown of satin or silk, trimmed with lace and bright ribbons. The fashions were Parisian and expensive. Their hair was coiled in glossy ringlets, and they smiled with invitation in their eyes. Our hostess commanded them to lift their skirts, so we might admire their stockings. They were, in other words, much like any other whores in any other exclusive brothel. Except that not one of them was over ten years old.

*

I feigned an attack of dropsy to get out of that place. Then I rode back to Deptford, buffeted by the winds and the rain. At least it served to cool the anger that ignited my soul. I understood Tad's hold over Brabazon now, how the surgeon had been forced to become his creature. I wondered if Brabazon had been the sailor Tad had paid Caesar John's man, Jupiter, to follow, and I supposed I'd never know. Yet somehow Tad had found his way here to the House of Lilies, and learned Brabazon's foul secret.

I rode on, my thoughts spiralling, linking cause to cause like a chain. The first link the massacre, the last this point I'd come to now. Stokes and the contracts. My conversations with Scipio and Child. Monday's lack of alibi. Vaughan's insanity. Brabazon's secrets. My conviction that Cinnamon knew something that could implicate the officers. Then suddenly I saw it.

I reined in Zephyrus on a rise, my heart pounding. I could see the killer's face. I understood how it had happened. If I'd thought the knowledge would bring me peace, I was wrong. In the distance I could see the river. *The Dark Angel* was waiting for me there. So too was Captain Vaughan, locked down in the lower slave hold, hidden from those who would use his tortured conscience to further the cause of abolition. I understood the dangers. I could guess what else awaited me there. One way or another, this would end tonight aboard that ship.

*

In Deptford Broadway, I stabled Zephyrus at the coaching inn. When I was certain I was unobserved, I concealed the syndicate's contracts inside his saddle. Then I walked down to the

Strand and the dockside again, where I stood, rain lashing at my face. The wind had whipped the water to a heaving swell, even the largest ships tugging at their chains like tethered Leviathans. Each time the lightning flashed, I met *The Dark Angel*'s gaze, her wings unfurled, as if coasting the currents of the storm.

I imagined the river as a claw, cleaving the chalk of the Kent countryside, gouging the shores of Iberia, snatching up human plunder on the Guinea coast to deposit in the Caribbean – then shrinking back into this robber baron's lair we called England. It corrupted everyone it touched, reducing each man to his price. Cavill-Lawrence and his friends in the ministry. Nathaniel Grimshaw and Daniel Waterman, boys chewed up and spat out. Frank Drake, who hadn't been born a monster. Scipio, who blamed himself for the crimes of his masters. Each caught by the creature that was man's avarice. The Devil's Reach.

CHAPTER FIFTY-EIGHT

THE RIVER'S CURRENT was fierce. The storm whirled around me. Rain beat against the rowing boat and my frozen face and hands. I kept getting caught in treacherous eddies, spun around, sucked downstream. A spear of lightning split the sky, turning the ships blue, iridescent. I heaved on the oars, my ribs stabbing my innards.

I had been wracked several times by shivering fits during the ride back from Lee, and I was gripped by another one now. Lightning flashed again, and I glimpsed the winged woman above me. The ladder still dangled from the ship's northern side. I tied up my boat, and unbuckled my sword, before beginning the arduous climb to the deck. The heaving of the ship on the waves made it harder going than before. I gripped the ropes, buffeted by the wind and the spray. When I reached the top, I suffered the worst shivering fit yet.

The deck rose with each heave of the waves, the creaking of her timbers very loud. Drawing my pistol, I headed for the quarterdeck, and lit the lantern hanging inside the door. I stuck my head inside each cabin, but nothing seemed amiss. In the surgeon's cabin, a couple of bottles had been dislodged by the rolling of the waves, and lay smashed on the floor. Otherwise everything was as it had been on my last visit.

Returning to the deck, I contemplated the hatch leading down to the slave decks. Steeling myself, I heaved it open, and descended the ladder. Lightning flashed, enough light penetrating the hatch and the air holes to bathe the entire vast space in a blue, ethereal glow. Chains, slave racks, cannons. Then everything was plunged into darkness once more, save for the small yellow circle around my lantern. The storm was nearly overhead now. Thunder rolled around the belly of the ship.

I put the lantern on the floor by the hatch to the lower slave deck. Kneeling to examine the padlock, I took out my roll of lockpicks. The lock proved much harder to pick than the one at the warehouse, and the light was worse. Eventually I found a pick that slid smoothly into the lock's interior. I worked it around, keeping one eye constantly on the shadows, making my task harder.

I was acutely aware of how vulnerable I was. I had to use both hands to work the pick, my pistol jammed in my belt, the pool of light at my feet, the darkness beyond impenetrable. Finally, my pick found a new part of the lock to excavate. Very swiftly came a click, and the shackle fell open. I removed it and put both the shackle and the pick in my pocket, to preclude anyone locking me in.

I raised the hatch, and descended further into the bowels of the slave ship. Less light from the moon and the lightning reached down here. The air was fouler, the temperature hotter. Rain drummed against the sides of the ship, a constant ticking, like beetles. I held the lantern up. 'Captain Vaughan?'

Silence. I inhaled the ripe stench, trying to detect the sweet aroma of opium beneath the flavours of death and corruption. A spike of bile rose in my throat, and I spat it out, shivering again. Once it had passed, I walked further into the hold. All I could hear was the creaking of timber and the rain and the thunder.

I moved like a tacking ship, from one side of the hold to the other, my circle of light travelling with me, my pistol drawn. I found more slave racks, more chains, more blocks and tackle to haul the cargo. But I found no trace of Evan Vaughan.

Only at the far end of the hold, where the shadows were thickest, did I find something interesting. A stack of shipping crates, about fifty of them, each stamped: PROPERTY OF HIS MAJESTY'S ROYAL NAVY. Drake's gunpowder, I presumed, and much else besides. He'd probably been robbing the Navy Yard for years – whenever he was in port. He must have stored his spoils here until he'd accumulated enough to make a trip to London worthwhile. I wondered if it had been his lantern I'd seen out here, traversing back and forth. Then where was Vaughan?

Not down here, was the inescapable conclusion to which I came. I wondered if he could be somewhere else on board. I hadn't yet checked the kitchens and ancillary offices in the forecastle.

Anxious to leave these oppressive confines, if a little troubled by the absence of Vaughan, I walked back to the hatch. I put my pistol in my belt, and holding the lantern in one hand, climbed awkwardly up the ladder again.

As I neared the top, and my head emerged into the upper slave deck, a dark mass detached itself from the blacker shadows around it, and came towards me fast. I reached for my pistol, forced to drop the lantern, but the man – for I knew it was a man now – kicked me in the face. I dropped back through the hatch, hitting the floor, striking my head.

The lantern had shattered and I'd dropped my pistol. I grappled around for it in the dark, staring in the direction of the hatch. I heard a thud as the man jumped down into the hold.

Lightning turned everything a dull grey. The man was striding towards me. I was on all fours, still scrabbling around. My fingers closed on the pistol. I rolled onto my back, and swivelled it round. I fired, the hammer dropped, and nothing happened. Everything went black. I fired again. Again the hammer clicked, and I realized, with a sinking, awful feeling of despair, that the powder must have got wet during my voyage out here. The man was nearly upon me. I scrambled to my feet. My escape to the ladder was cut off. I could see nothing in the dark. A primal instinct overtook me. Run.

I didn't get far in the dark. My bad leg caught on one of the slave racks, and I went down a second time. Again the lightning flashed. I turned to see my pursuer bearing down on me. He had a length of chain in his hand, swinging it like a flail. Darkness again. I heard the whistle of the chain through the air. Then a crack and a loud rumble of God's own thunder.

CHAPTER FIFTY-NINE

COLD METAL AGAINST my skin. Blood on my face. Terror in my soul.

I knew right away where I was. In the surgeon's cabin. Secured by fetters to that chair, my ankles chained. Hands manacled behind me.

A lamp flickered. On the wall opposite, I could see slave brands, thumbscrews, the speculum oris, like the tools of a medieval dungeoner. He had removed my coat and shirt. I could see them on the floor. On the dresser lay my pistol and the roll of lockpicks. Sweat glistened on my skin. The stove had been lit. My eye rested on its squat, black shape. I shivered.

I heard footsteps in the corridor. The doorway filled, and Scipio walked into the room. He went to the stove and raised the lid.

'I guessed it was you,' I said. 'For a long time I was distracted by the trail of misdirection you laid.'

And by my glimpse of Amelia Bradstreet's killer. That pink hand gripping the bannister pole. I remembered Scipio's shock when I'd told him of Amelia's murder in the Yorkshire Stingo.

'Archer broke under torture,' I said. 'He told his killer everything. If the murderer had wanted the missing contracts, he could have gone to Archer's room and retrieved them. There was no need to torture Amelia and her maid, no need to kill them. Once I knew the contracts had been found here in Deptford, I should have realized that those two poor women were killed by someone else.' Remembering Amelia, anger flooded through me. Scipio might not have killed her, but she was dead because he'd set out upon this path. I thought of Moses Graham and Ephraim Proudlock. Their faces contorted in agony. Caesar John's man, Jupiter, whom I'd never met. Most of all I thought of Tad and my voice thickened with fury.

'To you those contracts meant nothing. You didn't care about the syndicate. Nor *The Dark Angel*. Nor the massacre. Not really. I only guessed the truth when I learned Stokes had been planning to send Cinnamon away before.'

'If you knew, then you should not have come back.' Scipio blew softly on the coals in the stove. They glowed orange, scattering sparks. He turned to me. 'No part of me wants to be here. Not for you. Not for Archer. All I wanted was to be left alone, to build a new life for myself here – but you could not even let me have that. You and Archer brought this upon yourselves, and by God, I wish you had not.'

'You told me Vaughan was on the ship to lure me out here, just as you lured me to the Yorkshire Stingo, that night you hoped to kill me. Did you lure Archer here too?'

Scipio was pulling on a pair of thick leather gloves. 'No, that was Brabazon – he hoped John Monday would kill him here, I think. I waited at the dock first to see if Monday would come. But he didn't have the stomach for it. I cannot say I was surprised. Monday is too much in thrall to his religion to kill a white man, whereas Brabazon is the stripe of man who can only order others to kill. So I came out here and dealt with Archer myself.'

'And Vaughan? Did you kill him too?'

'That was my intention, but Vaughan wasn't here. I'm not sure he ever was.'

He seemed satisfied now by the heat of the stove. I watched, my mouth dry, as he took a long iron rod down from the wall, and thrust it into the coals. I twisted my hands in the fetters, trying to work them loose, but it was hopeless.

'It was clever,' I said, aware that I was talking very fast. 'Marking Archer with Monday's brand, hanging him up at the dock, choosing slaving punishments for your torture, using Monday's knife. Everyone presumed one of *The Dark Angel*'s officers killed him, and the town closed ranks, protecting its own.'

His patrician countenance was perfectly calm, but his eyes burned with anger. 'Until you came.'

'I presumed a Deptford motive, and that was a mistake.' I eyed the iron in the fire, sweat trickling from my fettered hands. *Keep him talking.* 'I presumed money was the guiding principle: the insurance fraud and its consequences. At root they were, I suppose, but only because they threatened the one thing you wanted.'

I pictured that chain again: each link a cause, followed by another link, another cause. I'd presumed the massacre to be the first link in that chain, but it stretched much further back than that. To a day when an eight-year-old boy had been taken from his village of dancers and fishermen and locked in irons ...

I had seen Scipio's darkness for myself, when we'd drunk at my room in the Noah's Ark. That long glance after the women in the stable-yard. His longing for a wife, for children. A woman as God's plan. A way of making sense of a world so cruel it defied understanding.

It had all been there in plain sight, and I marvelled that it had taken me so long to see it. Every time we'd met, he'd warned me to stay away from Cinnamon. His anger at the way she was treated, coupled with his determination to keep her here in Deptford. Her anguished cry in the face of his fury that night at

Stokes's villa: *How can you do this after everything you told me?* Scipio's curse was not to love a white woman, as I'd first presumed, but to love his master's mistress.

'What does Cinnamon know about the massacre?' I asked. 'The West India lobby ordered Stokes to send her away before, and you had to kill Archer to get her back. Now they've tried to send her away again. What is it she knows that she doesn't think she knows?'

He took the rod from the flames. The ship lurched, and bottles slid along the shelves. Scipio grabbed hold of the doorframe to steady himself. He held the iron before my face. The tip was hot and white.

'You are going to tell me where she is, and then I will bring her back to Deptford. Stokes will give me my old position back by way of reward. Drake will be blamed for the murders, and once the West India lobby discover that you are dead, they will let her stay, as they did before.' He moved the rod closer, so I could now feel its pulsing heat against my face. I flinched from it. 'If you tell me now, it will be quick. I told Archer much the same, but he didn't listen. He lasted nearly two hours, but he broke in the end.'

I struggled wildly, the cuffs cutting into my wrists. Again I remembered Tad's death-rictus leer, his silent scream. Again I thought of Proudlock's mutilated body. Moses Graham's bulging eyes. Gabriel growing up without a father.

'I'll pay you. Enough to buy Cinnamon. More.'

'There is a point through which a man journeys from which there is no path to return. Much like the Middle Passage. We are past that now.'

'They will know when they find my body. They'll know Drake wasn't the killer. My wife will demand answers. They'll come searching for you.'

'No, they will expect you to be burned.'

I shrank from him, but there was nowhere left to go. He pressed the iron against my chest. I heard hissing, smelled my flesh burning. Then a pain so pure, so white, there was nothing else in the world. I heard myself screaming. I bucked against my chains. Scipio repeated his question calmly, and when I did not respond, he pressed the rod against my upper arm. I screamed again.

'There are other places we can try. The pit of the arm, the testicles. It is an art, knowing how much pain a man will take. On the plantations, the first time they made me torture a brother African, I killed him without meaning to. I lit a fire under him, as I did to Moses Graham. Only I burned him too much, and his heart gave out. I was flogged for destroying my master's property. After that, I learned fast.'

I heard these words distantly. Every part of me was fixed upon the task of not telling him where Cinnamon was. Even if I couldn't save my own life, I could deny him what he wanted. I forced my mind to Tad. Conversations we'd had, songs we'd sung. I sang them again now, shouting them in my mind, to drown out his questions, to drown out the pain.

'Very well,' Scipio said eventually, returning the iron to the coals. 'We begin again.'

Agony scrambled my thoughts. But my anger was pure too, and it brought me back to myself. 'You could have helped Cinnamon escape at any time. You could have left Stokes's employ and lived together in London. You could have let me take her there, and then joined her yourself. Why didn't you?'

I knew the answer, but Scipio chose to maintain the fiction he'd written for himself.

'Stokes is a vindictive man. He'd have blackened my reputation, so I could never find another post. We would have been just another pair of poor, unhappy Negroes, tilling London's soil for scraps. In another year, I'll have enough money to buy her. I already have a small house in Deptford. We will raise our children there.'

'You would condemn her to another year of Lucius Stokes?'

A spasm contorted his features. 'She only needs discipline, patience. What is a year, compared to a lifetime? If I could endure it, then so can she.'

'And when you've bought her? Will you free her then?'

I saw the answer written on his face. Perhaps if I angered him enough, he would lose control and kill me before he made me talk.

'You don't think she'll stay with you willingly, given the choice. What's more, I think you're right. That's why she doesn't want you to know where she is. She doesn't love you, whatever lies she might have told you in the past. Every chance she got, she tried to get away from you.'

Every blow I landed felt like a small victory. 'You would be as much her keeper as is Stokes. That isn't love, it is possession. Your embrace is a slave collar, your kisses a brand.'

He snatched the rod from the coals and thrust the iron against my shoulder. I screamed again. He stroked the tip against my stomach, a caress of agony so intense I shouted mangled words of profanity that made no sense. I don't know how long I lasted. It might have been a minute or an hour. But at some point the words bubbled out of me, and I found myself telling him about the contracts in Zephyrus's saddle, about Caesar John and the Children of Liberty, about the sponging house and Southwark and the tannery I'd smelled nearby, about the run-away slaves and the stolen goods and Bronze and the African coachman and anything else I could think of, only stop the blessed pain. Make it stop.

Chapter Sixty

I WAS ALONE. Head slumped against my chest, chains biting into my wrists. My burns singing with agony. My body exuding heat, a pulsing pain. My ribs were an afterthought now. A sharp pain in my left thigh barely registered at all. The only thing more powerful than the pain was my sense of shame. The one task left to me had been to protect Cinnamon from this madman, the next in her line of masters. Yet I had failed.

I raised my head with difficulty, wondering where Scipio had gone. My eye fell on my pistol, over on the dresser, before I remembered that it was useless. Yet if I could reach the lockpicks ...

I moved a little, trying to see what slack there was in my chains. Very little. I hadn't a hope of reaching the lockpicks. The stabbing in my thigh intensified with each movement. Something was digging into my leg, something in my breeches pocket. Suddenly I remembered the pick I'd used to unlock the padlock on the hatch to the lower slave hold. I swung my thigh round to meet my hands, trying desperately to reach it. Sweat ran into the scalded flesh, bringing fresh agonies.

Eventually I managed to wedge the tip of my middle finger into my breeches pocket. I moved my thigh up and down, hoping to manoeuvre the pick upwards, trying to work another finger in so I could pull it out. A fraction at a time, until I could pinch it. Carefully, so carefully – convinced that at any moment it would fall from my fingers – I slid it into my palm.

The manacles around my wrists each had a standard barrel lock. Manoeuvring the pick between my fingers, I managed to push it into one of the keyholes, trying to ignore the rocking of the ship and the pain from my burns. I slid the pick this way and that, trying to find the point of ingress as Caesar John's men had shown me. How much harder it was without being able to see what I was doing. My hands were slippery, and I was terrified I would drop it.

I could smell burning. Smoke was drifting into the cabin. What had Scipio said? *They will expect you to be burned.* Sweet Jesu, he was setting fire to the ship. I jiggled the pick furiously, inhaling smoke, coughing. I had to force myself to slow down, to keep a cool head. Yet how could I? Thinking of the gunpowder in the hold, I jabbed again and again with the pick.

When it happened, I was entirely unprepared for it. The cuff slipped suddenly from my wrist, and I tried to catch it, only succeeding in dropping the lockpick. Yet I had one hand free, and though the other was still attached to the manacles, it meant I could unthread my hands from the back of the chair. My feet were still shackled to it. I couldn't go anywhere. Yet I had greater movement now, and I tried leaning backwards to find the lockpick.

I was still groping about in this way when I heard footsteps in the corridor again. I pulled myself upright, resisting the urge to cry out, thrusting my hands behind me, dropping my head to my chest, a broken man. I prayed he wouldn't notice the manacle dangling freely to the floor.

Scipio smelled powerfully of lamp-oil. The cabin was filling up with smoke. He lifted my chin, and I kept my eyes closed. Through narrowed lids, I watched him take my cravat from the dresser. He wrapped the ends around his hands to make a ligature.

I moved faster than I ever had before. Rising from the chair, I jerked my arm around his throat, taking him by surprise. I pulled sharply backwards, swinging my manacled hand towards him, catching the chain with my other hand, pulling it taut.

The chain bit into his neck. I pulled and pulled. He tried to use his strength and weight to throw me, but here my shackles were my friend. Fettered to the chair, which was secured to the floor by iron bolts, I had nowhere to go. His arms flailed, trying to reach me, but the angle was all wrong for him. His fingers sought my face, then clawed at the chain sunk into his neck. My burns were hell's torment. My muscles corded, my strength weakening. Still I pulled.

What felt like several lifetimes later, his legs suddenly went from under him. His weight jerked me forward, and I pulled him back. His heels drummed against the floor. Then he lay still.

I was choking on the smoke, my eyes streaming. Dizziness overcame me. I was too weary to move, but I must. I hauled Scipio's body towards me, and searched his pockets. The smoke was very much thicker, and I struggled to see. Eventually, I found a ring of keys, and – oh, Jesu, yes! – one of them unlocked the fetters around my ankles, another the manacle around my wrist. I staggered into the corridor, so dense with smoke now that I couldn't see my hands in front of me. Disoriented, I spun, hit a wall, and then edged my way along it.

My vision was coming and going in jagged waves. I saw someone ahead of me, a figure in the smoke. I called out to him.

'Tad. Wait!'

I collided with a door. My senses were slipping. My lungs burning. I looked around for Tad, but I couldn't see him. My fingers found the handle and it turned. The door didn't open.

I hit it with my burned shoulder – crying out, as I fell forward into the rain.

I drew long breaths, down on my knees, out there on deck. Smoke belched from the forecastle, as well as from the quarter-deck. The rain was coming down hard, but it wasn't going to put the fire out. I needed to get off this ship.

I crawled across the deck, eventually reaching the point where I'd climbed aboard. I eased my legs over the side, onto the rope ladder, gazing down at my boat, tossing and turning on the waves below. It seemed unimaginably far. Too far. The smoke and the river blurred. I turned back towards Deptford. Lights spilled out of the dockside taverns.

I looked down at the water again, preparing myself for the jump, thinking of the drowning slaves, the crying children, the obeah-woman's curse. I tensed my knees, sprang forward, felt a rush of cold air against my face.

Then the world turned to fire around me.

Chapter Sixty-One

I was standing on the banks of the Cherwell, lifting the sack of sugar. Beside me Tad clapped his hands, shouting encouragement. I tipped the sack and Tad danced upon the grass. White grains rippled the surface of the water.

I was lying beneath the water, watching slave sugar sink towards me. I could see Tad on the bank, a watery blur. He kept dissolving in pools of coloured light. I kicked out, trying to swim back to him, but the pain fractured the pool of light into a thousand splinters of glass. The pull of the water was too strong. It tugged me down. Then I realized he was swimming there beside me.

He somersaulted, a fish, swimming down into the black depths. Towards a place I could never reach him, unless I followed. My chest was bursting, everything fading in and out. I swam after him.

Then I was jerked upwards, violently. I struggled, and took in lungfuls of brackish water. My head broke the surface and I vomited. Rain assailed the river, and I was lifted on the swell. Slave sugar drifted towards me. It tasted of ash. On the surface of the river were ten thousand pieces of wood and rigging and sail. I could no longer see *The Dark Angel* amidst the serried ranks of Guineamen. Lights flashed on the Deptford bank. A bell was ringing.

I went under again, and again I was yanked back. Something

dug into my spine, pulling at me. My head struck something hard, and I cried out. Hands gripped my body, and I struggled to free myself. Someone hit me on the side of the skull. 'Try, damn you,' a familiar voice said.

My senses returning, I endeavoured to cooperate. With a lot of heaving and pulling, I managed to get one leg over the side of the small wherry riding the waves beside me. Another heave and I collapsed into it, rocking it alarmingly. I lay there shivering, looking up at the rolling black sky.

Jamaica Mary's face filled my vision. 'Damn near blew up Deptford. Mary had a customer on the quay – he thought the French had come.'

She rowed us to the shore, to the point where Deptford Creek flowed into the Thames. I helped her haul the boat up beyond the gravelly beach. My burns hurt more in the air than the water, and she grew irritated by my stumbling clumsiness. I left her to it, my attention caught by something down on the beach.

A dark shape. A body. I turned it over, and saw that it was Scipio. Part of his skull was missing and he had lost an arm and part of his leg in the explosion. Rain pounded his blood into the mud and the gravel.

Jamaica Mary appeared at my elbow. 'That Negro dead.'

She asked no questions about the conjunction of events that had brought us here, but led me across the bank, through a copse of trees. We were on the outskirts of Deptford Strand, where run-down cottages and makeshift shacks sprouted on the mud like mushrooms.

Mary's shack was a one-room affair, with no glass in the windows and a roof plugged with rags. Buckets and chamberpots were positioned to catch the worst of the leaks. The trickling of water distracted me a little from the pain. She sat me on a stool, and then knelt to build a fire from a few meagre sticks of kindling. I was shivering furiously. She frowned at my burns. 'Want Mary to fetch a sawbones?'

Pain washed over me in waves. I could hardly find the words. 'I just need some dry clothes. Can you get me some? I'll pay you.'

She nodded and went out, leaving me to steam by the fire. The heat was unbearable against my burns, already stinging from the salt of the creek. I wanted to move away, but I was so cold.

I thought about Scipio, remembering those men I'd known in America, whose minds had been so eaten by the darkness they were no longer capable of seeing the light. Their reasoning had been destroyed by war, just as Scipio's had been destroyed by slavery. Perhaps he'd known it. Perhaps he'd thought his love for Cinnamon could heal him. Only it had dragged him down still further, into a hell he could not escape.

*

The lamp was sputtering, and I walked over to lower the flame. A number of letters were stacked on the shelf behind it. Surprised that Mary should be literate, I picked one up and stared at the address. Then, fearing I might fall down, I replaced it and went again to sit by the fire. I was still sitting there, thinking, when Mary returned.

She'd brought a baggy brown suit for me to wear and some linen for bandages. The suit smelled of must, and I wondered if it had come from the bathhouse. She sat scowling at me as I bound my burns as best I could. It did nothing to ease the pain, but at least it stopped my burns chafing against the coarse cloth.

'I lost my purse in the river,' I said, once I was dressed. 'But I'll send you money to cover the cost. If you write it down, I'll sign a promissory note.' I nodded at the inkwell on the shelf. 'Who taught you to write?'

Her eyes followed my gaze. 'Mary's old master.'

I spoke gently, because she'd helped me, and I did not wish to frighten her. I didn't want her punished, I wanted only to understand. 'That night Mrs Grimshaw caught you at the Noah's Ark. She thought you were skulking around, acting suspiciously. I put it down to prejudice, but she wasn't altogether wrong. She thought you were there for the obeah, but it wasn't that, was it?'

Her eyes slid to the door. I smiled to reassure her.

'I received two letters whilst I was staying there. Mr Archer received three from the same author. I think you wrote them.'

Her nostrils flared. 'Mary wanted you to leave Deptford, didn't she?'

'Why? What did you have to fear from me?'

She scratched her arm, scuffing the floor with her dirty pink slipper. 'You and your friend were the same. Always asking questions. Trying to get people into trouble.' She glared at me. 'People here always looking for someone to blame.'

'To blame for what? I'll tell no one that you told me, I swear.'

Despite my efforts not to scare her, her pupils were little black tunnels of fear. Her voice dropped to a whisper: 'Evan Vaughan.'

Chapter Sixty-Two

It was a little after five in the morning. My burns throbbed, my brow glistened with fever. The streets of Deptford Broadway were quiet, but in John Monday's house they had already been up for some time. I could tell by the sleepless eyes of the maid-servant who came to the door, and the general air of disturbance that pervaded the house.

The maidservant was uncertain about letting me in at that hour, and I was in too much pain to press the point forcefully. Yet Monday must have heard our conversation on the doorstep, for he barked an order to let me come inside. The mulatto boy was playing with a spinning top in the hall, and he watched me as I limped into his father's study.

Monday looked up from his papers. '*The Dark Angel* burned in the dock last night. I was just attending to my insurance docu-ments.' His eyes travelled over my old suit of clothes, my wigless state, my bandaged hand. 'But perhaps you already know this?'

'Mr Stokes's secretary, Scipio, destroyed the vessel deliber-ately,' I told him. 'He tried to kill me, just as he killed Archer and Moses Graham and the two other Africans in London, Jupiter and Proudlock.'

'Then it wasn't Frank Drake?'

'No, Scipio killed Drake too.'

The door opened, and Mrs Monday walked into the room. She looked pale and drawn. 'Is there any news, John? Oh—'

I guessed I looked as terrible as I felt.

'Madam.' I was hurting too much to bow, but under the circumstances, civility be damned. 'I was just telling your husband that the murderer is dead.' I repeated my explanation about Scipio. 'Perhaps this will ease the burden of your conscience. Your husband was not involved in Archer's murder.'

Monday turned to her. 'You thought that, Eleanor?'

She flushed. 'I didn't know. After Mr Brabazon came and you went out ...'

'Who was it you were trying to protect when you summoned the mayor and the magistrate here that night?' I asked. 'Archer? Your husband? Or someone else?'

She didn't answer.

Monday looked grave. 'How could you have believed that, Eleanor? I made it plain to Mr Brabazon. Nobody was to touch Archer. There had been too much killing, too much disregard for God's laws.'

I was unsteady on my feet, my head spinning, still so cold. Yet I pressed on. 'That wasn't the only reason, though, was it?' I said. 'After all, Brabazon was wrong. He thought Vaughan was on the ship, and he thought if you knew Archer was heading there, you'd kill him to prevent their meeting. Perhaps you would have done so in other circumstances. Only you knew Vaughan wasn't on that ship. He never was.'

Monday looked away.

'I don't understand,' Mrs Monday said. 'What does he mean?'

I had little sympathy for her distress, nor her confusion. 'Tell me, madam, do you ever pray for George, your old house-slave? He didn't get a funeral, did he? He ended up in Deptford Reach, a scapegoat. Does he trouble your conscience? Or don't Africans count before your God?'

She frowned at my words and my tone. 'What does George have to do with this?'

'I only wonder why you did nothing to prevent his murder? When one word from you could have saved him.'

Her lip quivered. 'I told them the truth. I never went with any Negro. They didn't believe me.'

'You only needed to mention your lover's name. You said the child was a throwback, and so he was. But you let people believe you meant your throwback, or your husband's, whereas the African blood was on your lover's side.'

It had been right in front of me all along, but I had missed it. Vaughan's curly black hair, his swarthy skin, his birth on a plantation, all those rumours he spread about his Spanish blood.

'Brabazon guessed,' I said. 'He told me he wasn't surprised that Vaughan lost his mind. I didn't see what he meant at the time, but I do now. People say mixing the blood weakens it. It's balderdash, of course, but Brabazon believes it.'

Her eyes met mine, and I was surprised to see defiance there, rather than shame. It angered me. 'George must have seen you together, and under torture, he told your first husband. That's why Owen Forrester wanted nothing more to do with you after that. But it was too late for George. If it doesn't trouble your conscience, then it should.'

Monday passed a hand across his weathered face. 'It is an old sin. There is no need to rake over it now.'

Mrs Monday's hands were crossed in front of her. She tugged at the elbows of her dress. 'What did he mean, John, when he said Vaughan wasn't on that ship? Brabazon said he was.'

'That's what Brabazon believed,' I said. 'Your husband told his officers that he'd moved Vaughan to a safe place in order to prevent him from speaking to Archer. He even went so far as buying opium to maintain the pretence. I think Brabazon saw lights on *The Dark Angel*, put two and two together, and came up with five. Just as I did.'

'Then where is Evan?' she said.

Monday pursed his lips. I remembered him down on his knees in the church. *You think you understand the consequences of Archer's visit here? You haven't the first idea.*

'Evan Vaughan was already sick when Archer first came to town,' I said, 'but Archer's visit turned his conscience inside out. Archer refused to give him absolution for the drowned slaves, and so Vaughan sought forgiveness for his other crimes elsewhere. Then he disappeared. Before he did, he and your husband went for a drink together down in Deptford Strand.'

Mary had been out on the quayside that night. She'd just finished with a customer, and was taking a rest in one of the alleys. Vaughan and Monday had come walking along the dock, arm in arm, a friendship forged in the crucible of the Middle Passage. Vaughan was drunk, Mary said, his voice loud and ragged, doing most of the talking. Monday had listened, and then suddenly stepped away. Vaughan spoke more urgently, and Monday turned his back. Vaughan ran after him, and angry words were exchanged.

In the fight that followed, no knives were drawn, but neither man gave any quarter. The blow that finished it was glancing, but Vaughan fell badly and hit his head. Monday had stared down at him, Vaughan groaning, asking for help. Then Monday had rolled him to the edge of the quay, and pushed him over.

Mary, in the shadows, had heard the splash. She'd watched Monday walk away, and then crept onto the quayside. There she'd found Vaughan's purse, fallen from his pocket during the struggle. It held six guineas and some banknotes, and so she decided to ignore the noises she heard from the water, considering it a night well done. She'd sold the banknotes in Greenwich for a fraction of their worth, and afterwards regretted it. The notes had been signed over to Vaughan by their previous owner. They could be traced to him, and thence to Mary. For weeks she'd waited nervously for the magistrate's knock. A rich gentleman had been murdered, she'd stolen his money. Who'd believe her story?

Yet the magistrate never came, and she'd started to breathe more easily. Then Tad had come to see her, asking all his questions about Evan Vaughan. The letters were only supposed to frighten him, just as they were later supposed to frighten me. She'd left me the first letter the night I'd interrogated her about Vaughan at the bathhouse, slipping it under my door when the inn was busy, while I'd been at the opium house. She'd sent the second after she'd heard I was back in town. I couldn't hold it against her, especially after she'd saved me from the river. In the great scheme of things, her crimes amounted to little.

'Where is Evan?' Mrs Monday asked again.

Her husband raised his head. 'He told me you still looked at him as you used to, tempting him with Eve's promise. That he tried to resist, out of deference to our friendship, but he was a man and hot-blooded. He wanted my absolution, but I wouldn't give it. It wasn't like that, was it, Eleanor? He forced you, was that it?'

She was still looking at me. 'Where is Evan, sir? It is important that you tell me.'

'Evan Vaughan is dead, madam.'

She groaned and sank onto a chair. Monday rose and knelt before her, gripping her hands. 'He didn't love you, Eleanor. He never did. Did he stand by you when you got with child and were shamed by your husband? If he made dalliance with you consequently, it was because it was there to take. You opened your legs for him like a whore – with Evan Vaughan who had lain with half the women in Deptford.'

To my shock, she flew at him, clawing and scratching, her features contorted, mewling an animal sound. Monday raised a hand and hit her across the face. 'We signed a contract, properly witnessed, there was no duress. I will not tolerate thievery, madam, I never did.'

I left them to their bitter marriage and their troubled consciences. In the hall, the mulatto boy was still spinning his top, and as I reached the front door, he spoke to me. 'Please, sir,' he said, staring at my olive skin. 'Are you my father?'

'No,' I said, my voice thick with compassion and pain and fatigue. 'I'm sorry. I am not.'

He held my gaze a moment longer, as if to ascertain the veracity of my answer. Then he turned back to his top, spinning it down the hall.

I walked out of that strange, unhappy house, thinking of Evan Vaughan. I had never met him, and yet the damage he had wrought by his various crimes had confronted me everywhere in Deptford. That poor boy was another victim. I never did learn his name. Perhaps I could have done more for him. I wish I had.

I found Zephyrus at the coaching inn, checked his saddle, and was relieved to see that Monday's contracts were still there. We took the Kent Road out of Deptford, and I didn't look back. The storm had blown itself out overnight, the sun high, the air fresh. In the distance I could see London, a city of gold.

Chapter Sixty-Three

A DAY LATER, I stood in Nicholas Cavill-Lawrence's wood-panelled office overlooking the Horseguards' parade ground. My burns had been properly dressed, though I still moved gingerly. Deptford had left me with many scars, not all of which would heal.

Cavill-Lawrence pressed his manicured thumbs together. A portrait of King George the Third gazed down upon his loyal servant.

'I met with Lucius Stokes and the Deptford magistrate this morning,' he said. 'We are all in agreement. Thaddeus Archer was murdered by a slave ship officer named Frank Drake, a villain engaged in thievery from the Navy Yard. During his stay in Deptford, Mr Archer uncovered his crimes, and so Drake killed him. He also murdered his accessory, a cabin boy named Daniel Waterman. The magistrate was on the verge of arresting Drake, but he hung himself before he could be apprehended. The explosion on *The Dark Angel* was an unfortunate accident, in which the mayor's secretary also sadly died. Mrs Bradstreet and her maid were murdered by an intruder, entirely unconnected to these other matters.'

'And the dead Africans in London? Moses Graham and Proudlock?' I decided not to mention Jupiter, judging that it was best to keep Caesar John's name out of this.

Cavill-Lawrence regarded me haughtily. 'Nobody cares

about dead Negroes. An inquest will be held into Drake's suicide, which you are under no circumstances to attend. I'm told this magistrate, Child, is a good man. He'll do what he's told.'

'I'm sure he will,' I murmured.

'There is one thing Stokes wanted me to ask you. A surgeon named James Brabazon – he's gone missing apparently. Nobody's seen him since the night of the explosion. Stokes thought you might know something about it?'

My gaze didn't falter. 'I'm afraid not.'

Cavill-Lawrence nodded, not caring. 'Which brings us back to business. I have spoken to Napier Smith, and explained that due to your war record, your reputation is of paramount importance to the crown.' He glanced up at the portrait. 'His Majesty likes his heroes – and Lord knows, we have few enough of them in this war. I have made it plain to Smith that any attempt to blacken your reputation would be looked upon most unfavourably by the ministry. It took him a little while to understand, but he does now. Your post here remains open, should you wish to resume it until the by-election. Your opponent has withdrawn his name from consideration, I am told.'

I was thinking about Amelia, her cold damp face in my lap. I was remembering the man I'd seen at Tad's rooms: Cavill-Lawrence's agent. Had that same man killed Amelia and her maid? Had it been his pink hand I'd seen, grabbing the bannister? Cavill-Lawrence had certainly been determined to find those contracts. Murder seemed excessive, but maybe it hadn't been a question of orders. Maybe Amelia had simply returned home unexpectedly. Or maybe the assassin had been sent by someone else, another member of the syndicate, one of those fine, upstanding gentlemen, desperate to protect his good name and reputation?

Perhaps a better man than I, given these suspicions, would have refused Cavill-Lawrence's offer of patronage. Yet I had a duty to the living, as well as to the dead. I owed it to Caro and Gabriel.

I took the contracts from my coat, and placed them on the desk in front of Cavill-Lawrence. He picked them up and walked to the fire, where he raised a flame by jabbing the coals with a poker. It made me think of that night at Tad's rooms, when I'd burned his letters. *Now I'm just a ghost in a story you once told of yourself.*

I had few illusions about Cavill-Lawrence. With the contracts burned, I'd lost my hold on him. Ostensibly we had a deal, but there would come a time in the future when Cavill-Lawrence needed the West India lobby more than he needed my goodwill. Caro put the odds that he'd renege at a shilling to a guinea.

Whilst I'd been in Deptford, she'd gone to see her brothers, the bankers. The Cravens were a tight clan, and they stuck together. She had explained a tiny fragment of the situation in which we found ourselves, and thereby procured copies of Cavill-Lawrence's banking records.

It was all there in his accounts. Cavill-Lawrence had been busy. Several large deposits coincided with the granting of army contracts. Several more came from gentlemen who had subsequently been awarded high offices in prestigious regiments. Cavill-Lawrence had chosen to invest these monies in the slave trade, and was growing richer by the day.

Ministerial corruption was a little like adultery, Caro had said, without a trace of irony. Keep it out of the drawing room, and nobody cared. Put it on the front page of a newspaper, and it was a different story.

Perhaps I wouldn't need it. I hoped that I would not. Call it an insurance policy, if you will.

*

Cinnamon was sitting in the same place I'd left her, near to the fire in the sponging house's parlour. She looked a little healthier, but she still sat apart from the other slaves. She held my gaze with that strange intensity, then turned away.

Caesar John drew me aside. 'They've had men looking for her all over London. Crimping gangs, thief-takers, slavers. Bronze says informants have been to the Stingo. The girl's bounty is set at two hundred guineas. That's far more than she's worth. What the devil is going on?'

'I'm not sure. We need to talk to her, but we must do so gently.'

One of his men made a fire for us in the storeroom. We sat on a damask sofa, the room lit by silver candlesticks upon black-and-gilt torchères.

'Scipio is dead,' I told her.

She went very still.

'He was the murderer, but I think you already know that. It's why you tried to stop me returning to Deptford. Was that for his sake or for mine?'

'I thought he would kill you.'

'Did you ever love him? He believed that you did.'

'I let him think it, because I thought he'd help me escape from Mr Stokes. My mother said men never find it hard to believe that a woman loves them.'

Her plan had worked better than she'd ever hoped. Instead of becoming her saviour, Scipio had become another gaoler.

'Whose idea was it to kill Archer? Yours or Scipio's?'

'Scipio discovered that Stokes was planning to send me away.

He said it was because I'd spoken to Archer. The West India lobby were nervous that I would lie in court – that I'd say I overheard the sailors plotting to kill the slaves. I tried again to convince Scipio to help me escape, but he wouldn't do it. He said killing Archer was the only way to keep me in England.' She turned, one half of her face in candlelight, the other in shadow. 'I hoped Archer would take me to London – then he wouldn't have to die. But he betrayed me. After that, I stopped trying to change Scipio's mind.'

'Did you know about the others? The Africans in London?'

'Scipio said they were Archer's friends, and unless he killed them too, they might come to Deptford, as Archer had. I couldn't be safe unless *The Dark Angel*'s officers were also safe.'

'Then why did you tell me about her, that first day I was in Deptford?'

'Because I wanted to be free – of all of them. All I needed was to get to London. If you thought I knew something, I hoped you'd take me there.'

'Tell me about the knife,' I said. 'Scipio didn't go to the Mondays' house the day it disappeared, but you were there.'

She stared into the fire. 'I went into the study while Mrs Monday was meeting with Mr Stokes and Mr Child. I knew the knives were there. They were a gift from an African prince. Captain Vaughan had shown them to me on our voyage back to Deptford. He told me if I ever ran away from him, then he'd cut my pretty throat.' She wrapped her hands around her neck. 'We needed it to look as if Monday or one of his officers killed Archer. Then they wouldn't hunt for the killer. I hid the knife in the stable-loft when Mrs Monday and I were attending to Daniel Waterman. Scipio went there later to retrieve it.'

Where he'd encountered Mrs Grimshaw, and then Nathaniel. 'Did Daniel Waterman see you with the knife in the stable-loft, or was it Scipio he saw?'

'I don't know. Perhaps neither. Mr Brabazon thought he was talking about something that happened on board the ship. There was a woman slave—' She broke off.

'But you couldn't risk it, so you killed him anyway. Held a pillow over his face while Mrs Monday was talking to Mrs Grimshaw in the yard.'

She met my gaze, the candles making bonfires of her eyes. 'Do you want me to say that I am sorry? He dropped children into the sea. While they screamed for their mothers.'

I felt desperately sad. I knew what Tad would have wanted me to do. He would have said it wasn't her fault, it was slavery's. I wished I could hear him say it, to give me the strength to go on, but since the destruction of *The Dark Angel*, our conversations had fallen silent.

'He came to Deptford to help you,' I said, 'to help Africans everywhere.'

'You say it as though I had a choice. This was my life, my hope of freedom. That's all there is.'

My eyes were pricking, a burr constricted my throat. 'I don't think they were sending you away because they thought you'd lie in court. I think they were afraid you'd tell the truth – that you know something about that voyage that could have helped Archer. Will you tell me about it? Everything, from the beginning?'

For a moment she said nothing, her gaze fixed on some unspeakable place inside herself. Then she leaned towards me, and the shadows crowded in. 'The slavers came the day my father died,' she said.

CHAPTER SIXTY-FOUR

SHE TOLD IT softly, looking at the flames, her voice devoid of emotion. Perhaps there was no other way to tell it.

'The fort at Cape Coast was large and white. It gleamed in the sun like bleached coral. We had an apartment there. It was the only home I'd ever known. Papa looked very handsome in his uniform, and Mama wore dresses sent from London. She used to laugh, imagining the faces of the mantua-makers, if they ever knew their fine gowns were worn against African skin. For twelve years I was happy. Then Papa fell sick.

'For weeks our rooms were filled with death and decay. The fort doctor came, but he told Mama he could do nothing. When the doctor had gone, Mama worked obeah spells, but Papa's ancestors were calling him, she said. I kissed Papa, and sat with him. Sometimes Mama cried. Once Papa woke and murmured my name. Then he closed his eyes, and did not open them again.' She blinked, her shadow dark against a square of firelight on the wall. 'That afternoon, the slavers came for Mama and I.'

She had been reading in her room, but she ran in when she heard her mother scream. Captain Jackson – her father's friend – was standing in their parlour. He had hold of Mama, which confused her. Two strangers were with him. One big and broad, with a pock-marked face and a bald head. The other had long flaxen hair like one of her dolls. The flaxen man walked up to Mama, and gripped her by the jaw. He told her to open her mouth, and when she refused, he hit her.

She knew what it meant. She'd lived all her life in a slave fort. Captain Jackson was trying to sell them to these men. She tried to run and get help – from where? from whom? – but the bald man caught her. Her mother asked them to take her, only please, leave the girl, but they ignored her. The bald one's fingers were rough. He touched Cinnamon's skull and her teeth, put his fingers inside her ears, felt her arms, her legs, her breasts, her secret part.

After that they sat and talked, negotiating. At the end, they shook hands, and the flaxen one said: 'We'll try them here.'

Cinnamon's voice was a perfect facsimile of Frank Drake's Deptford twang. It made me wince.

'Can't you do that on the boat?' A clipped voice, haughty, not unlike my own. Captain Jackson.

'The young one's personal for Evan Vaughan. He don't like to share. Join us if you like?'

'God, no.'

She cried out to the captain to come back, not to leave her alone with these men. He had dined at their table, and Papa had promoted him. He looked at her oddly, not with hatred or dislike, but as though she had ceased to hold any significance for him at all.

Cinnamon's voice grew halting at this point, as if her memories were scattered and blurred. 'Flaxen hair forced Mama to her knees. I was in the bed where Papa had died. I was naked, and so was the bald man, who told me to call him Mr Grimshaw. I stared out of the window at a fragment of sky. The men swapped round. Mr Grimshaw wanted me to like him, but the Flaxen Devil was rougher.'

Later, still bleeding, they had been hustled out of the

apartment, into the sunshine, forced across the yard, under the eyes of the men who had served under her father's command. The soldiers watched without much interest, slapping the flies from their sunburned necks.

'Grimshaw and the Flaxen Devil pushed us into a canoe. The Flaxen Devil rowed. Grimshaw whistled a tune. I gazed back at the shore. The fort was dazzling, ochre and white. A line of village children ran along the beach. Then I looked up, and saw her.' She shivered. 'The winged woman staring down at me. She was the most terrifying thing I had ever seen. We were hoisted up on deck, where a long-faced man told me to take off my clothes again. I tried to jump off the ship, but they pulled me back. The long-faced man had a stove on deck, with many slave brands heating there. He pressed one into my skin. It took me a long time to stop screaming after that.'

She pulled down her shift, so I could see the crown and crescent moon seared into her shoulder. Then she described the conditions on board the slave ship. The dark, fetid decks, hot as an oven when it was calm. The shit, the blood, the filth. The shackles chafing the skin. The sweltering, sleepless nights, the hold echoing with moans and sobs and the clanking of fetters, the unforgiving wood against her naked skin.

'When at last we put to sea, I desired nothing but to die. The ship bucked and rolled in storms and tropical tempests. We slid along the decks, pulled back and forth by our chains, lubricated by the filth and vomit of other slaves. Some died, and their corpses were thrown overboard. Sometimes I was cleaned and taken to the captain's quarters, to be used for his pleasure. He didn't speak, except to tell me he would kill me if I disobeyed him. He said he owned me now. He enjoyed saying that.

'Once a day we were brought up on deck. We were washed, and our chains were inspected. The food was served in tubs.

Beans and yams, a little meat. Water we lived for. I held it in my hands, and it sparkled like crystal. Sometimes we were made to dance. The crew liked that part. The Flaxen Devil carried a whip, and he liked to use it on the women if they didn't dance fast enough.'

She trailed off, staring into the hell of her past, before beginning again.

'At night, Mama and I clung to one another, and she would whisper of the vengeance the obeah gods had planned for these men. One day, when the Flaxen Devil was down in the hold, Mama cursed him. She called down the wrath of our ancestors, the priests who walked the path of bones. She asked them to punish this man who had raped her daughter. Then she made a grab for the Flaxen Devil's knife. She would have killed him, I think, had the cabin boy not grabbed her wrist.

'All the slaves were taken up on deck to watch. The crew were twitchy, cruel with their whips if anyone moved too slow, or gave them a look they didn't like. The captain sat apart from it all. He smoked a pipe, watching, as they tied ropes around Mama, and hoisted her into the air. I tried to reach her, but the chains made me stumble, and I was whipped. I screamed and screamed, so I wouldn't hear Mama screaming, as the Flaxen Devil drove the nails into her hands. She lasted nearly two days up there, under the burning sun, her arms splayed like a dying bird or the dark angel to the fore. Her cries for water grew fainter, until they ceased altogether. Then they cut her down and tossed her over the side.'

Caesar John met my eye. Even he looked troubled.

Cinnamon spoke very softly: 'The following day was when the thirst began.'

On the first day the slaves were brought up on deck as normal, fed, but not washed. The food was the same, but the water tubs were only half full. They asked for more, and they were beaten. On the second day, the water was reduced by half again.

By the sixth day, slaves were dying below decks. Cinnamon felt dizzy and sick. People were hallucinating. They pissed brown water, or not at all. Some fell on the ground, and shook with convulsions until they died. The crew threw their bodies overboard.

'On the eighth day, when we were taken up on deck, the long-faced man patrolled the ranks of slaves. He selected the sickest. I thought they were going to be given more water, and I wished I had pretended to be sicker than I was. Then they pulled the first man towards the side of the ship. When he realized their intention, he fought them. They had to crack his fingers with a club before he would let go. I remember his scream as he fell. He disappeared when he hit the water, but I saw him come up again. He swam after the ship for nearly six hours. They killed thirty-two men, sixteen women and two children that day. Two days later, they killed seventy more.'

I didn't want Cinnamon to go on. Neither, from the look of him, did Caesar John. He was staring at a spot on the wall. Cinnamon was still gazing at the fire. Then she resumed her story.

'By the twelfth day, my stomach was swollen, and I had stopped passing water. I dreamed often of Mama, and sometimes when I opened my eyes, I saw her face. I knew it was impossible, because I'd watched them kill Mama. I began to suspect then that I was dying. When we were next taken up on deck, the long-faced man picked me out. They killed fifteen slaves before they came to me. I wanted to fight, but I had no strength left. My legs went from under me, and one of the men picked me up. The air burned my lungs and seemed to shimmer. I saw creatures on the deck with horns and tusks and golden eyes. Looking down at the slaves in the water below, I saw sea monsters and mermaids. A dolphin leaped, silver in the sun.

'In my mind, I was already dead. Then I heard the captain's voice: "Not this one. She's one of mine. She should have been getting extra rations. I won't be bilked, Brabazon."

'"Aren't we all in this together? The weakest slaves was what we agreed."

'"Nobody said anything about my slaves. Take her below and put her with my others. Give her water. She'll be worth fifty guineas to the right buyer." They exchanged a glare. "You can write your own rules when you captain your own ship."'

I was listening out for anything that might implicate the crew. This couldn't be it. Vaughan wanting to protect his property at the expense of the officers' share wouldn't make a difference in court. It wasn't evidence of fraud.

'Go on,' I said gently.

'On the thirteenth day, when we were taken up on deck, I was kept apart from the others, together with five slaves who also belonged to the captain. Over half the slaves were gone now. The extra water hadn't been enough to stop the hallucinations. In the food tubs, I saw tiny Africans drowning in a sea of mashed beans. I looked up at the sky, and it wasn't blue anymore. It was black, as if the duppies were angry. In the clouds, I saw the faces of Mama and my ancestors. I looked down at the deck, and a coin formed in front of my eyes. Another coin formed nearby, then another and another. If I gathered all the coins together, I thought, I might have enough to purchase my freedom. I tried to pick one up, but it dissolved beneath my fingers. Then I realized the coins were falling from the sky.'

My body tensed, realizing what she'd just said. Dear God, there it was. 'Are you saying that on the thirteenth day it rained?' My tone was urgent. 'How long for?'

'A day and a night. We could hear it below decks. Our ancestors were weeping. I wanted to weep too, but I had no tears left.'

Caesar John had seen the change come over me, but he didn't seem to understand. 'The water tanks would have been filled by the rain,' I said. 'But they killed the last two batches of slaves anyway. Any ship in the vicinity will have a record of the storm in her journal. It will verify her story.'

I turned to Cinnamon. 'Do you want others to hear this? To know what they did? Can you bear to tell it again? It must be your choice.'

She looked at me for a long moment, and then nodded.

I had promised Caro that I wouldn't involve myself in this business again. It was also a condition of my deal with Cavill-Lawrence. But Caesar John had made no one any promises.

'I need you to go to Lloyds coffeehouse, Pope's Head Alley,' I said to him. 'Find a gentleman there named Hector Sebright. Bring him here to hear her story.'

He frowned, evidently still shaken by what he'd heard. 'You think a gentleman's going to go off with some Negro he's never met?'

I glanced at Cinnamon. She still seemed to be on that ship. Her eyes were almost luminescent in the firelight.

'Tell him it concerns a vessel he once insured, by name *The Dark Angel*. He'll remember. Tell him you have one of the slaves who survived that crossing. Tell him you act as her negotiator. Tell him her story stands to make him very rich.'

CHAPTER SIXTY-FIVE

IF THIS WERE a different, better world, then the murder of Thaddeus Archer might have changed history. Hector Sebright would have won his claim against *Atlantic Trading and Partners*, heralding a public outcry over the drowning of the African slaves. All Napier Smith's fears would have been realized: petitions and pamphlets, people disavowing West Indian sugar. The death knell for slavery would have been sounded.

Yet as Caro likes to say, this is the world we live in. Few people other than those who now read this manuscript have ever heard of *The Dark Angel*. Still less give any thought to the three hundred and six African men, women and children who were murdered aboard her over the course of seven abhorrent days in December 1778.

Hector Sebright did come to the sponging house to hear Cinnamon's story, and he was greatly interested in what he heard. His claim against *Atlantic Trading and Partners* was lodged before the court of the King's Bench only a week later. In response, the West India lobby did what they have always done when their interests have been threatened: they paid a lot of money to make the problem disappear.

To Sebright's credit, he played a good hand well. Sensing the lobby's desperation, he held out until the eve of his day in court, when he accepted a sum of twenty-five thousand pounds, nearly four times the amount he'd paid out on the claim. *The*

Dark Angel sailed quietly into the annals of the nation's secret history, a vessel of lost souls, a ship of ghosts.

In only one small respect was justice done. The West India lobby, aggrieved by the cost of the claim, took their resentment out upon John Monday. His lines of credit dried up, and he found few investors for his slaving voyages, declaring bankruptcy in the spring of 1782. He ended his days in a debtors' prison. Mrs Monday and her children were thrown upon the mercy of the workhouse.

Monday's last slaving voyage before the banks foreclosed, was made by *The Phoenix* in the autumn of 1781. She sailed without incident to the Bight of Bonny, where over four hundred African slaves were purchased, then sold in the Caribbean. On her return passage to Deptford, the ship encountered heavy weather in the north Atlantic, and went down with all hands. Among the list of the dead was the ship's third officer, Nathaniel Grimshaw.

*

Cinnamon lives quietly now, in a little cottage west of Hampstead. Under the terms of the agreement negotiated for her by Caesar John, she received a five per cent share of the payment made to Hector Sebright. Lucius Stokes was forced to renounce all claim on her. Her freedom was confirmed by the courts. She wants for nothing, save the ability to forget.

For my part, I have sat now in Parliament for nearly a quarter century. Though high office has eluded me – due in part to the enmity of the West India lobby – some years ago I was appointed Parliamentary Secretary to the Board of Trade. One of my first tasks in this role was to chair the standing committee formed to consider the siting of the new West India dock.

The passage of years had not been kind to Deptford's claim, and my committee considered the merits of only two rival propositions: the first, to enlarge the existing port of Wapping; the second, an audacious plan to cut a channel through the marshland on the Isle of Dogs. I guided the committee, and later the House of Commons, towards this latter scheme, which received royal assent in 1799. Though it played little part in my reasoning, I will own to a small measure of satisfaction that Lucius Stokes, now in his dotage, is forced to gaze upon these works every time he visits the dock at Deptford.

Finally, there is the matter of James Brabazon's disappearance, an event at first accounted a mystery in Deptford, then later – after certain letters from Scotland were received by the mayor and the magistrate – regarded as a distasteful matter the town preferred to forget. Those who did give it any thought presumed that Brabazon had taken his own life, when he realized certain events from his past were likely to catch up with him. The truth, as is so often the case in Deptford, was rather different.

My final visit to James Brabazon's surgery took place a few hours after the explosion of *The Dark Angel*, not long before my call upon Mr and Mrs Monday. I found Brabazon, like the Mondays, already awake. A large travelling trunk stood in the centre of his parlour, partially filled with clothes and other possessions.

'Are you going away, Mr Brabazon?' I asked.

He flashed a quick, nervous smile. 'Just a short visit to an aunt in Weybridge.'

Professing himself appalled by my injuries, and despite the hour, he graciously consented to treat my burns. While he applied ointment and bandages, I told him about Scipio's confession and his death.

'That such savage acts were committed by a Negro scarcely surprises me,' he said. 'Those who account the black race equal to the European can have little understanding of the base nature of the African brain.'

'He didn't kill because he was African,' I said. 'He killed because slavery had destroyed his mind.' Afraid I would lose control, and beat him to a pulp, I drew a breath and adopted a more measured tone. 'I have been to the House of Lilies,' I said.

A shadow seemed to pass across his face, as it had that day I'd asked him about going to Greenwich to meet Tad.

'I will have that place closed down, even if I have to burn it to the ground myself. I cannot prove you went there, but I know you were Archer's informant. You stole the contracts for him, and then cast the blame on Daniel Waterman. You tried to convince John Monday to have Archer killed, so he wouldn't force you to testify in court. Monday refused, but fortune smiled on you when Scipio intervened. Not anymore.'

He started to protest his innocence.

'Don't.' The force of my tone shocked him into silence. 'The silver ticket in itself wouldn't have been enough, I don't think. Archer must have had more. Perhaps the ticket gave him the clue, and he subsequently made inquiries about Richard Price in Glasgow – as I have done. Was there another girl in Scotland? As young as those in Lee? Or was there more than one? Soon I'll know, so you might as well tell me.'

Brabazon's Adam's apple bobbed. 'It isn't how you think. I loved her and she loved me. You need to know that our laws are based upon a flawed understanding of science. In many parts of the world, girls are wed at seven and eight. If they are mature for their age, there is no medical case against it.'

Listening to his justifications, my curiosity swiftly evaporated. 'Just tell me one thing: was it your idea to drown the slaves? I ask because from everything I have heard about Vaughan and his state of mind, I cannot imagine it originating with him. It would need a clever, scientific brain to conceive of something quite so wicked.'

He just sat there, looking at me, and in the end, I lost patience.

'Well, perhaps by the time you return from Weybridge, I will have heard back from my Scottish correspondents. Maybe then you will be more forthcoming with your answers.'

In the years afterwards, I often wondered if I did the right thing. Many will say that Brabazon should have been tried for his crimes in a court of law – both against the little girls and the drowned slaves. Yet at that point, I had no evidence to have him arrested on either count, and I feared that Brabazon would simply disappear as he had disappeared before, emerging in some new town under a new name.

Even if I had later caught up with him, and laid charges against him, I had my doubts. Juries are capricious creatures, and I had experienced Brabazon's persuasive mendacity for myself. I could well imagine him talking a courtroom round to his way of thinking. Or as Caesar John might put it, the law can be a cunt.

The High Street outside Brabazon's rooms was bathed in the pale half-light of pre-dawn. A few yards further on, I turned into an alley with a good view of his front door. Jamaica Mary was waiting there, a bedraggled, black crow in her cloak and hood. Behind her loomed two muscular figures: Abraham and another black footman I didn't recognize.

'He's going to run,' I said.

Mary nodded sagely, gazing up at Brabazon's window. Shadows were moving around in the room behind the drapes.

Her yellow eyes narrowed. Her smile held a lover's promise. 'He won't get far.'

*

Two years after the events described in this account, I received a visit from the abolitionists Granville Sharp and Olaudah Equiano. Old acquaintances of Tad's, they had heard certain rumours regarding my inquiry into his murder, and wished to know more. At Sharp's prompting, I gave them an edited version of this account, whereupon Equiano told me that another massacre aboard another Guineaman had occurred. That vessel was named *The Zong*, and like *The Dark Angel* before her, she'd run out of water during the course of the Middle Passage. Satisfied that their purchase costs were covered under the ship's insurance policy, the crew had thrown one hundred and thirty-three African slaves overboard to drown.

Sharp expressed little surprise that such an atrocity could have happened twice. Indeed, he was of the view that many such massacres had likely occurred in the centuries since white men had discovered black gold on the Guinea coast, and had the ingenuity to insure their human prisoners as cargo. *The Zong*'s case differed from the *The Dark Angel*'s in one significant respect: the insurer refused to pay out on the claim, and the owner sued. The West India lobby, having failed to dissuade the slave merchant in question, brought all its influence to bear upon the ministry. The Cabinet conferred, and the Solicitor-General himself advocated in court on the slave merchant's behalf.

Despite these efforts, the accounts of the massacre given in court made for uncomfortable reading in polite London society. *The Zong* became a symbol of the worst excesses of the slave trade, and when the judge found for the insurers upon a technical point of law, the claim was abandoned. Granville Sharp, unable to prove that an insurance fraud lay behind the massacre, tried and failed to have the crew of *The Zong* prosecuted for murder.

The Solicitor-General's response to these efforts was brusque and to the point: '*What is this claim that human people have been thrown overboard? This is a case of chattels or goods. Blacks are goods and property; it is madness to accuse these well-serving honourable men of murder . . . The case is the same as if wood had been thrown overboard.*'

Yet people remembered. And from small acorns grow mighty oaks.

I began writing this account on the 23rd day of February 1807, the day the Bill for the Abolition of the Slave Trade was passed in the House of Commons by a count of 283 votes to 16. I walked through the lobby in the wake of the Bill's architect, William Wilberforce, and Thaddeus Archer was walking there beside me.

I still catch sight of him sometimes, when I turn a corner too quickly, or glimpse his reflection in a mirror behind my own. I need no letters to remember. I remember him every day. The bank of the Cherwell. Sugar flowing through his fingers. The sun on the water. The curve of his cheek as he laughs.

Eram quod es, eris quod sum. I was what you are, you will be what I am.

CAPTAIN HENRY ROBERT CORSHAM
London, 12 March 1807

Historical Note

By 1781, Deptford had been a slaving port for more than two centuries. In *Blood & Sugar*, I have focused on that aspect of the town's economy, and less on those that stand up rather better to modern eyes. Ship-building, the spice trade, pottery and market-gardening were among those industries important to Deptford's prosperity and growth, though slave-trading was always strongly associated with the town. In my portrayal of Deptford, I have taken two liberties with the historical record. The town was governed in the eighteenth century by a vestry, or parish council, on which the leading local merchants would have played an important role. For the sake of simplicity, I gave my fictional merchant, Lucius Stokes, an ill-deserved promotion to mayor. As for Peregrine Child, it is likely that Deptford would have fallen under the jurisdiction of the Greenwich magistrate, with law enforcement provided by a small number of watch constables, alongside private security guards, such as Nathaniel Grimshaw.

The dramatic expansion of the slave and sugar trades during the eighteenth century, along with the growing size of the Atlantic-going Guineamen, placed the existing Thameside ports under considerable pressure. A purpose-built West India dock was the obvious solution. Plans for the new dock were not formalized until some years after the events of *Blood & Sugar*, and Lucius Stokes's campaign to locate it in Deptford is an invention. However, given that many potential sites along the Thames were considered and rejected over the latter years of the eighteenth century, it is far from implausible. Work to build the new West India Docks on the Isle of Dogs commenced in 1800, and it remained one of London's principal ports until its closure in 1980. The gleaming towers of Canary Wharf occupy that site today, along with the Museum of London Docklands, which has a disturbing and fascinating exhibition on London's role in the sugar and slave trades.

The legal status of slaves in Britain during the period of *Blood & Sugar* was mired in ambiguity. The 1772 case brought by the slave James Somerset against his master, Charles Stewart, ended in victory for Somerset and those who opposed the African trade. It was widely believed that the judgement granted freedom to all black slaves in Britain, and many immediately left their masters or demanded wages. However, under a strict legal interpretation, the case upheld only Somerset's right not to be forcibly deported to his master's Virginian colonies. The leading abolitionist, Granville Sharp, though cheered by the decision, was unconvinced that the ruling had legally ended slavery in Britain. His opinion was shared by many slave owners.

For years after 1772, black slaves continued to be offered for sale in British newspaper advertisements, alongside rewards for the return of runaways. The threat of forcible deportation to slave-holding colonies had in theory been lifted, but it was no easy matter for black slaves to avail themselves of the courts, and covert abductions continued in the decades to come. Yet the Somerset case was one of the first real blows against the might of the West India lobby, and boosted the morale of Britain's fledgling abolitionist movement.

Most free black Londoners continued to work as servants for their former masters, eking out a meagre wage in circum-

Historical Note

stances not greatly changed. Others became soldiers, sailors, actors and musicians. A few educated Africans, like my fictional former slaves, Scipio and Moses Graham, became well-known figures in London society. Yet life for most black men and women in Britain, whether free or not, remained extremely hard, and poverty drove some to lives of crime, beggary and prostitution. David Olusoga's *Black and British* (Macmillan, 2016) and Gretchen Gerzina's *Black England: Life Before Emancipation* (John Murray, 1995) give compelling accounts of these different experiences.

The massacre on board *The Dark Angel* is a work of fiction, but the *Zong* massacre was an all-too-horrific reality. Though Granville Sharp and his allies were unable to prove that an insurance fraud underpinned the massacre, the stark and brutal facts of the case, the logical and horrific consequences of treating human beings as cargo, brought the cruelty of the slave trade home to a much wider audience. For those interested in reading more about the massacre, the court cases that followed, and their impact on the cause of abolition, I recommend James Walvin's excellent book *The Zong* (Yale University Press, 2011), as well as his *Black Ivory* (Wiley-Blackwell, 2001) for a wider perspective on the horrors of the Atlantic slave trade. The sexual exploitation of female slaves is commonplace throughout the historical record, with some slave merchants and plantation owners recounting their abuse in their diaries with appalling frankness. The sufferings endured by my fictional slave, Cinnamon, were in no way extraordinary.

Granville Sharp, Olaudah Equiano and the other early heroes of abolition sowed the seeds of a great political movement that culminated in the petitions and boycotts of the late eighteenth and early nineteenth centuries. Despite these efforts, the power of the West India lobby and their supporters in

429

Parliament meant the slave trade was not outlawed until 1807. It took another twenty-six years – sixty-one years after the Somerset ruling – for slavery to be abolished throughout the British Empire. Under the Slavery Abolition Act 1833, slave owners were compensated for the loss of their 'business assets' to the value of £20 million. This comprised forty per cent of the entire annual Treasury budget, and amounts in today's terms (calculated as wage values) to approximately £16.5 billion.

Acknowledgements

Blood & Sugar's voyage to publication took several years, and many people offered me their advice and support along the way. Thank you firstly to my wonderful agent, Antony Topping, and everyone at Greene & Heaton, especially Kate Rizzo. Antony guided me through the most exciting few days of my life with calmness, wisdom and appropriate levity. His enthusiasm for this book and my writing was clear from our very first meeting, and his advice is always thoughtful and considered.

An equally big thank you goes to my amazing editor, Maria Rejt, whose editorial insights and experience have been invaluable. Her excitement for *Blood & Sugar* was clear from our very first meeting, and her passion for good books and great writing is inspiring. Between her and Antony, I couldn't be in better hands.

I am also incredibly grateful for the hard work of the team at Mantle and Pan Macmillan – especially Josie Humber, Kate Tolley and Rosie Wilson. And a big heart-eyes to Ami Smithson for giving *Blood & Sugar* such a fabulous and evocative cover.

I am also grateful to all those who read this book along the way, and gave me so many ideas and comments in the early stages. In particular: Claire McGowan and all those at City University; Hellie Ogden; and most of all, Roger Morris, who was there at the beginning and the end. Thanks also to the members of the greatest writers' group in the world: David

Young, Steph Broadribb, Rod Reynolds, Seun Thomas, Robert Hogg and Jamie Holt. And to my early readers: Luke Shepherd-Robinson, Steve Page, Martin O'Donovan, Helena Braun, Paul Heneker, Helen Sims, David Black, Julia Bye and Rishi Dastidar. And not forgetting Mark Hill, winner of the Facebook 'Name the Eighteenth-Century Dog' competition.

A big shout-out to my squad: the brilliant, talented, ever-supportive Ladykillers: Steph Broadribb, Nicci Cloke, Elle Croft, Fiona Cummins, Rachel Edwards, Emily Elgar, Caz Frear, Karen Hamilton, Jo Jakeman, Olivia Kiernan, Laura Marshall, Jenny Quintana, Amanda Reynolds, Laura Smy and Caz Tudor. Here's to many more lunches at Zedel's.

A very special thank you goes to Jeremy Duns, a brilliant author who gave an unpublished writer he barely knew hours of his time, along with his advice and encouragement when she needed it most. He says he did nothing. He did everything.

The support of my family when I decided to try to write a book touched me more than I can say. In particular, thanks to my dad, who first taught me about writing and whose bedtime stories have never left me. His love, patience and knowledge are a constant source of inspiration. My mum loved books and reading until her last days, and was so excited when I first told her that I planned to write a novel. My only regret is that I didn't write it fast enough, as I know she would have really loved to read it.

Most of all, my thanks go to my husband, Adrian, who gives me so much love and support every day. His belief in me never wavered, and kept me going through the toughest times. If love is measured by the heart, then mine's lost count.

Book Group Questions

1. How well do you feel the book portrayed life in eighteenth-century Britain and the ever-expanding London? Did you get a sense of Britain's place in the world, and how the British viewed themselves as a nation?

2. How did the book make you feel about Britain's role in the slave trade? Did the author manage to convey the horrors of the Middle Passage, despite illustrating these through character accounts rather than directly?

3. Did you get a sense of the tension between Britain's reliance on slavery and the values of the Enlightenment? Are there any modern-day phenomena that this reminded you of?

4. Freedom is a theme of the book, not just in terms of slavery but also the freedom to live one's life as one chooses. Which characters does the author use to illustrate this theme? How do the Spinoza quotes at the beginning of each part of the book reflect it?

5. What do you think was the nature of the relationship between Harry and Tad? Did that relationship make Harry a more or less sympathetic character in your eyes? How much do you think Harry's wife, Caro, knew about the extent of their friendship?

6. Several unhappy marriages are depicted in the book. How did they make you feel about the choices available

to women at this time? Did the lack of options open to women make you sympathize more with Caro and Mrs Monday?

7. How did you feel about the author's decision to use one first-person narrator? Would the book have benefited from other points of view? Or did you like the sense of being on a journey with Harry, knowing only what he knows when he knows it? How reliable was Harry as a narrator?

8. Which characters did you like, and which did you dislike? Did you change your mind about any of them? For better or worse?

9. What were the similarities between Harry, Scipio and Tad? What were the differences?

10. How did you feel about the end of the book? Did you have a view on Harry's choices and compromises? What would Tad have done differently?